'A great contemporary story and a powerful drama that reminds me of David Mamet's *Glengarry Glen Ross*. Will Volley has a real sense of atmosphere and manages to conjure great suspense and intensity out of the mundane'

Jake Arnott

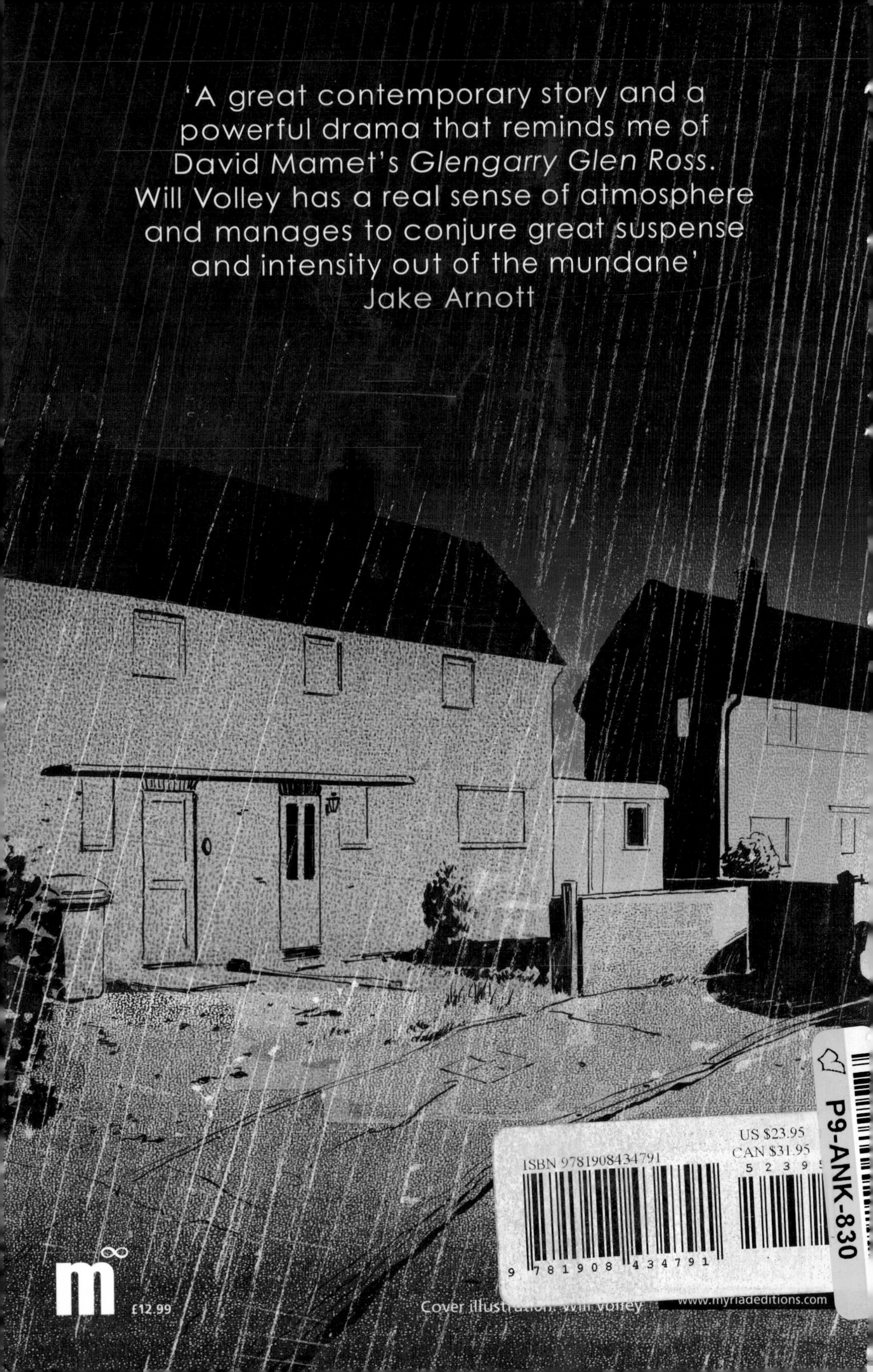

Cover illustration: Will Volley

£12.99

www.myriadeditions.com

ISBN 9781908434791

US $23.95
CAN $31.95
52395

9 781908 434791

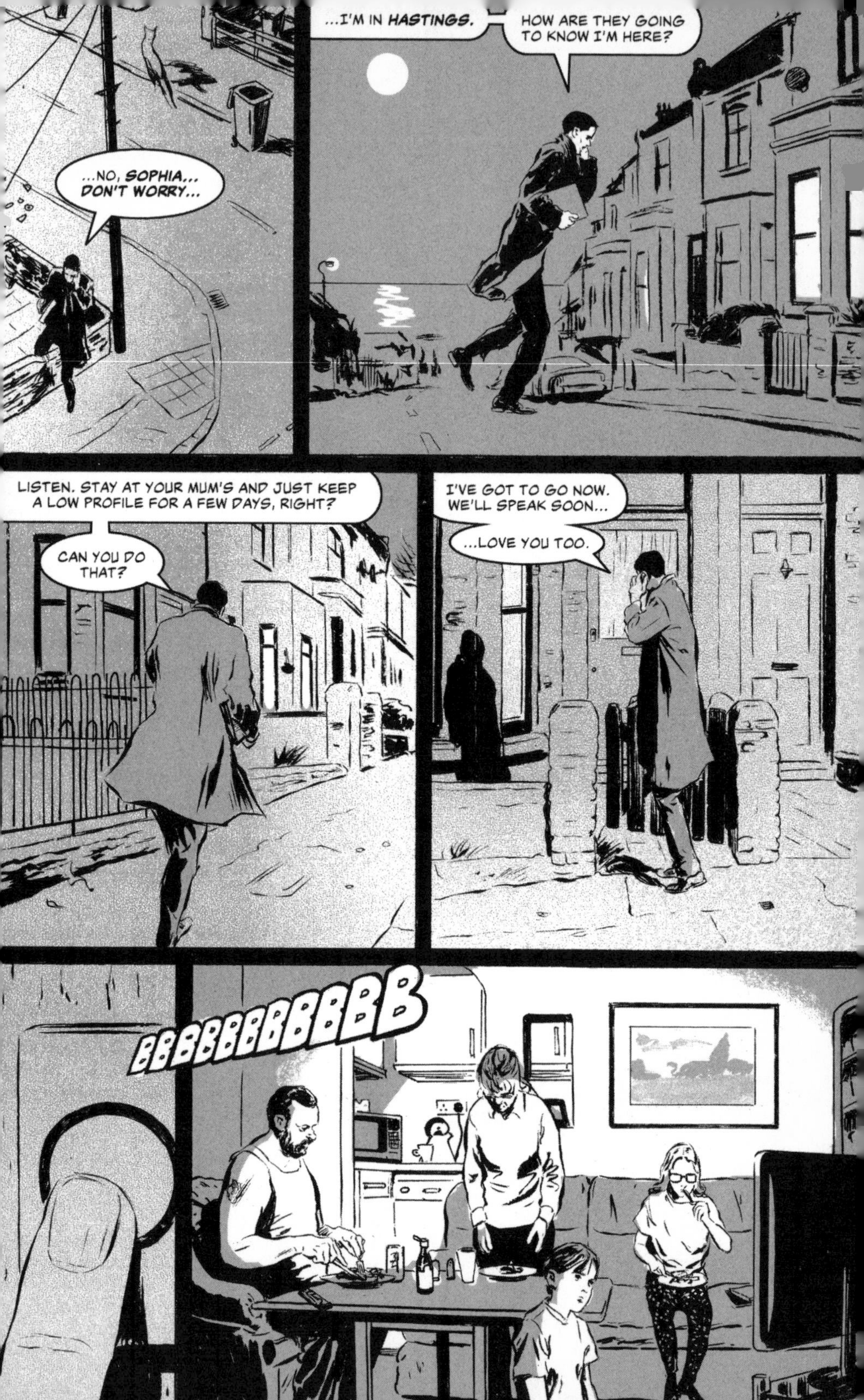
...NO, SOPHIA... DON'T WORRY...
...I'M IN HASTINGS.
HOW ARE THEY GOING TO KNOW I'M HERE?
LISTEN. STAY AT YOUR MUM'S AND JUST KEEP A LOW PROFILE FOR A FEW DAYS, RIGHT?
CAN YOU DO THAT?
I'VE GOT TO GO NOW. WE'LL SPEAK SOON...
...LOVE YOU TOO.
BBBBBBBBBBBB

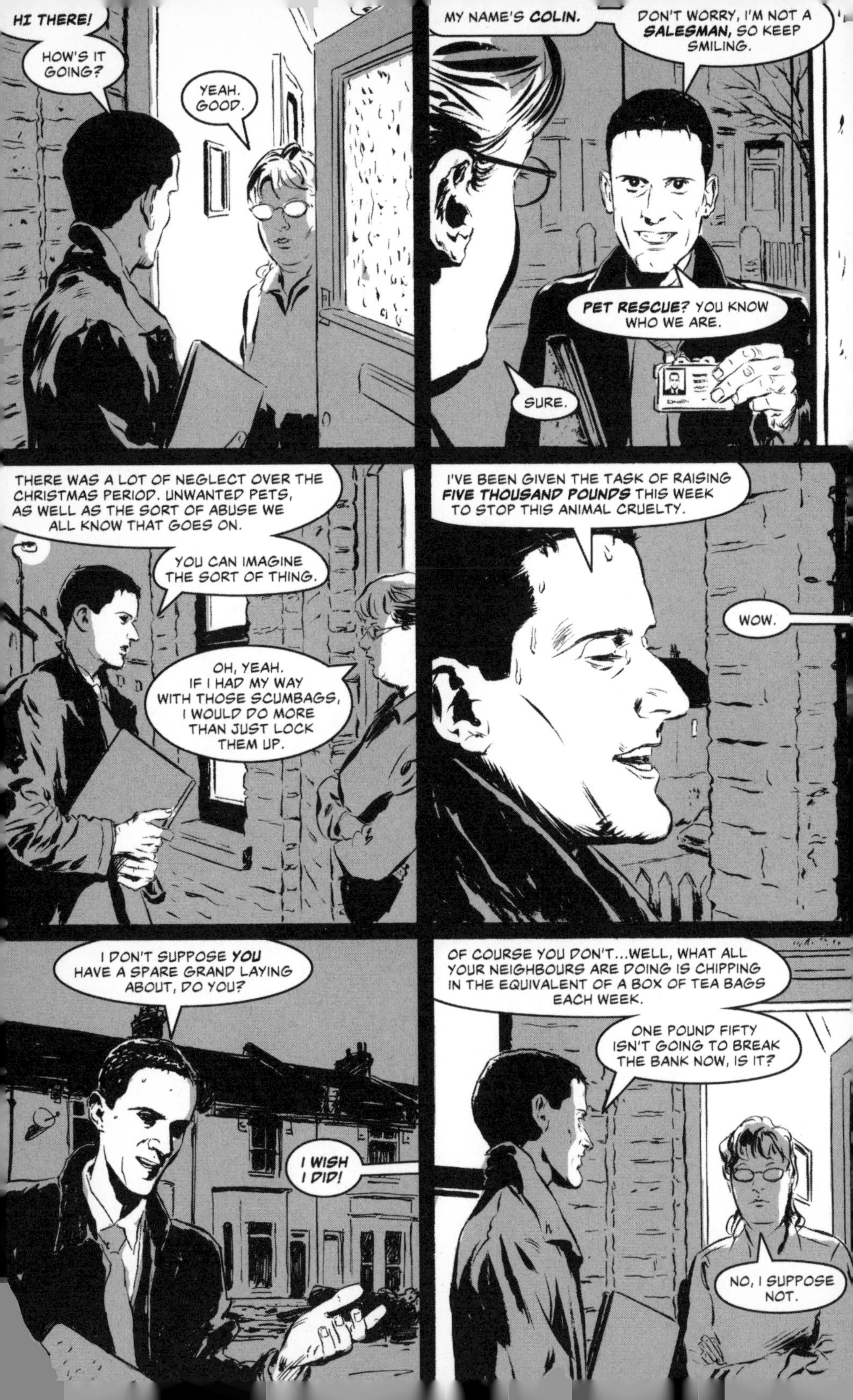
HI THERE!
HOW'S IT GOING?
YEAH. GOOD.
MY NAME'S COLIN.
DON'T WORRY, I'M NOT A SALESMAN, SO KEEP SMILING.
PET RESCUE? YOU KNOW WHO WE ARE.
SURE.
THERE WAS A LOT OF NEGLECT OVER THE CHRISTMAS PERIOD. UNWANTED PETS, AS WELL AS THE SORT OF ABUSE WE ALL KNOW THAT GOES ON.
YOU CAN IMAGINE THE SORT OF THING.
OH, YEAH. IF I HAD MY WAY WITH THOSE SCUMBAGS, I WOULD DO MORE THAN JUST LOCK THEM UP.
I'VE BEEN GIVEN THE TASK OF RAISING FIVE THOUSAND POUNDS THIS WEEK TO STOP THIS ANIMAL CRUELTY.
WOW.
I DON'T SUPPOSE YOU HAVE A SPARE GRAND LAYING ABOUT, DO YOU?
I WISH I DID!
OF COURSE YOU DON'T...WELL, WHAT ALL YOUR NEIGHBOURS ARE DOING IS CHIPPING IN THE EQUIVALENT OF A BOX OF TEA BAGS EACH WEEK.
ONE POUND FIFTY ISN'T GOING TO BREAK THE BANK NOW, IS IT?
NO, I SUPPOSE NOT.

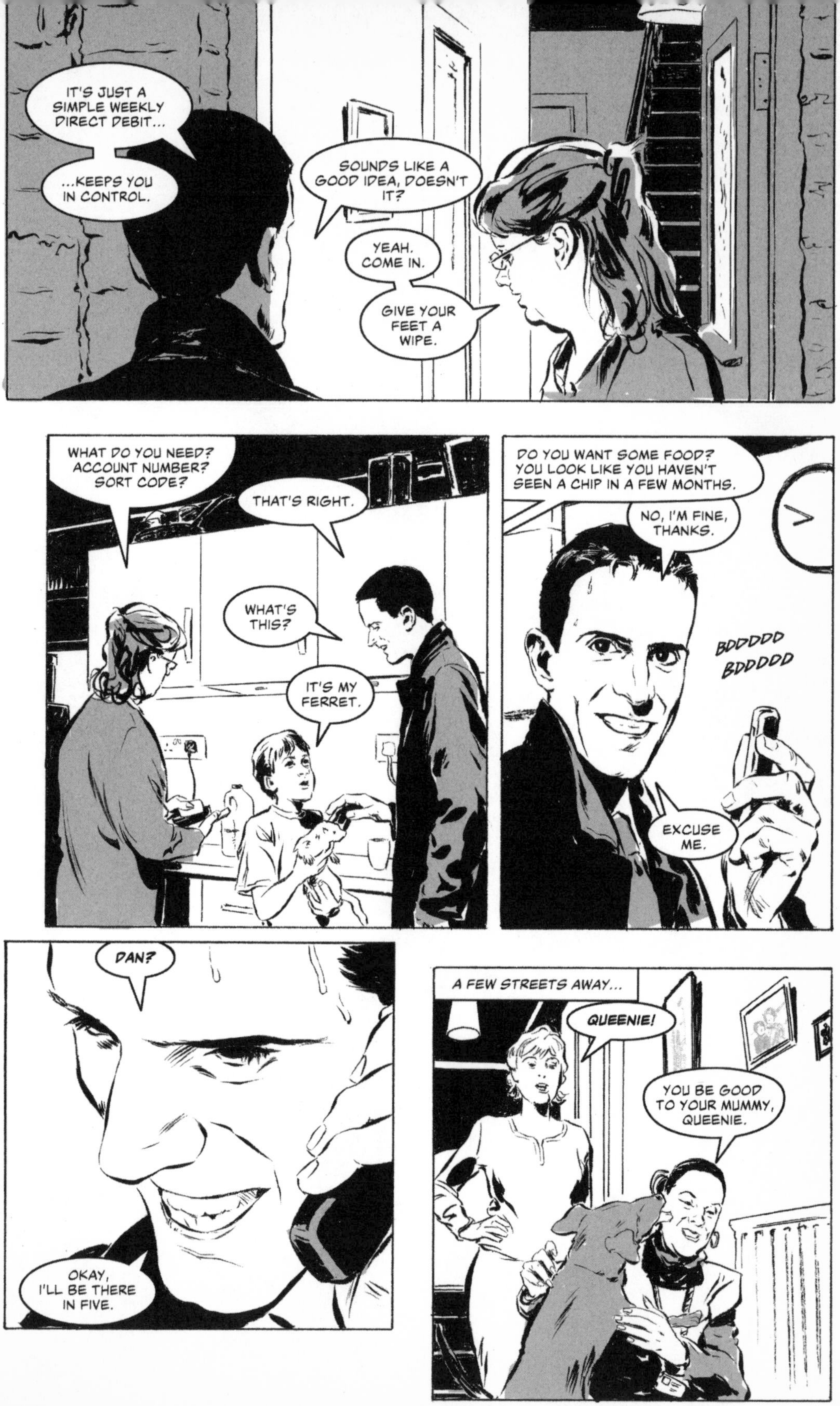
IT'S JUST A SIMPLE WEEKLY DIRECT DEBIT...
...KEEPS YOU IN CONTROL.
SOUNDS LIKE A GOOD IDEA, DOESN'T IT?
YEAH. COME IN.
GIVE YOUR FEET A WIPE.
WHAT DO YOU NEED? ACCOUNT NUMBER? SORT CODE?
THAT'S RIGHT.
WHAT'S THIS?
IT'S MY FERRET.
DO YOU WANT SOME FOOD? YOU LOOK LIKE YOU HAVEN'T SEEN A CHIP IN A FEW MONTHS.
NO, I'M FINE, THANKS.
BDDDDD BDDDDD
EXCUSE ME.
DAN?
OKAY, I'LL BE THERE IN FIVE.
A FEW STREETS AWAY...
QUEENIE!
YOU BE GOOD TO YOUR MUMMY, QUEENIE.

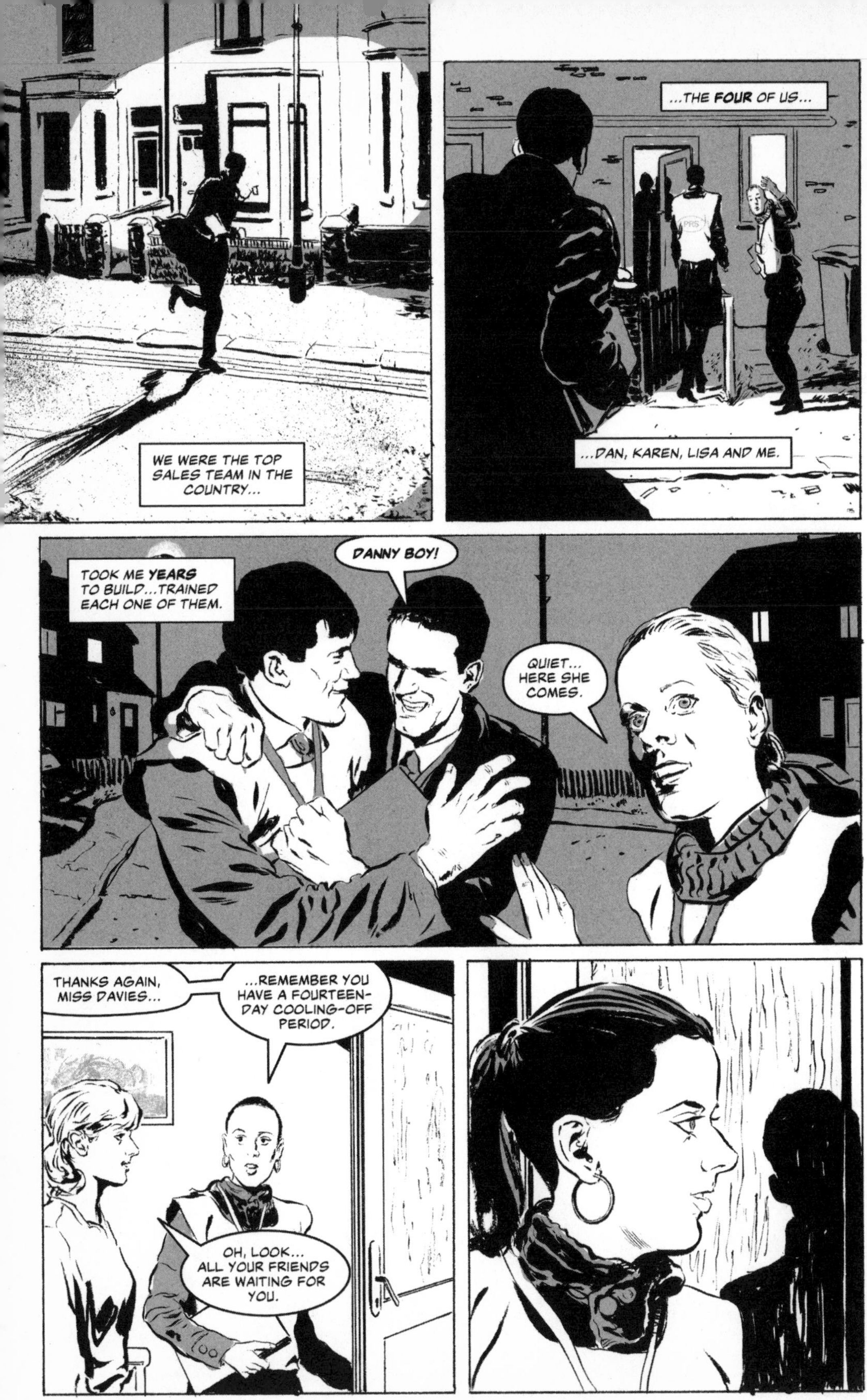
WE WERE THE TOP SALES TEAM IN THE COUNTRY...
...THE FOUR OF US...
...DAN, KAREN, LISA AND ME.
TOOK ME YEARS TO BUILD...TRAINED EACH ONE OF THEM.
DANNY BOY!
QUIET... HERE SHE COMES.
THANKS AGAIN, MISS DAVIES...
...REMEMBER YOU HAVE A FOURTEEN-DAY COOLING-OFF PERIOD.
OH, LOOK... ALL YOUR FRIENDS ARE WAITING FOR YOU.

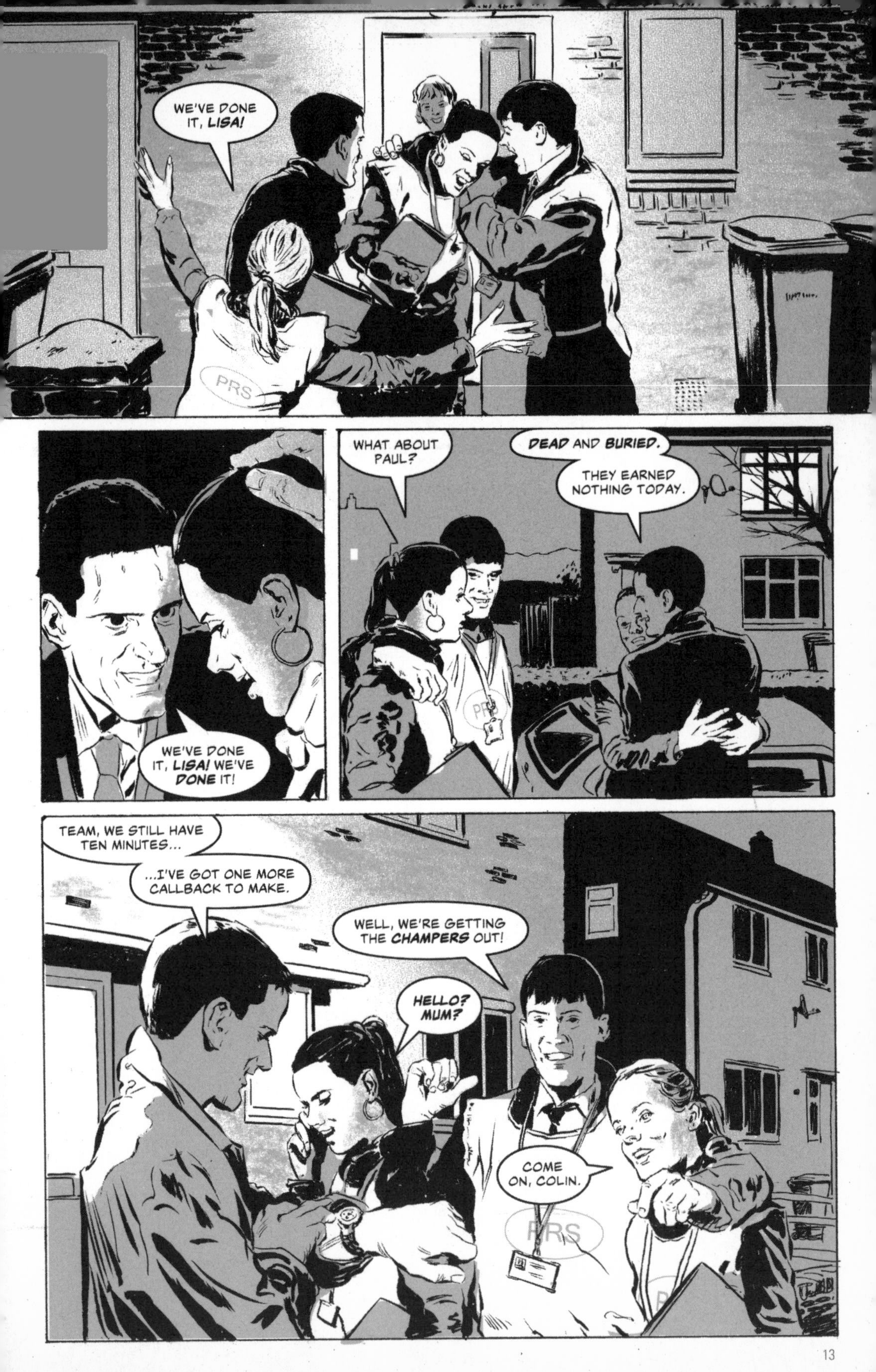
WE'VE DONE IT, LISA!
PRS
WE'VE DONE IT, LISA! WE'VE DONE IT!
WHAT ABOUT PAUL?
DEAD AND BURIED.
THEY EARNED NOTHING TODAY.
PRS
TEAM, WE STILL HAVE TEN MINUTES...
...I'VE GOT ONE MORE CALLBACK TO MAKE.
WELL, WE'RE GETTING THE CHAMPERS OUT!
HELLO? MUM?
COME ON, COLIN.
PRS

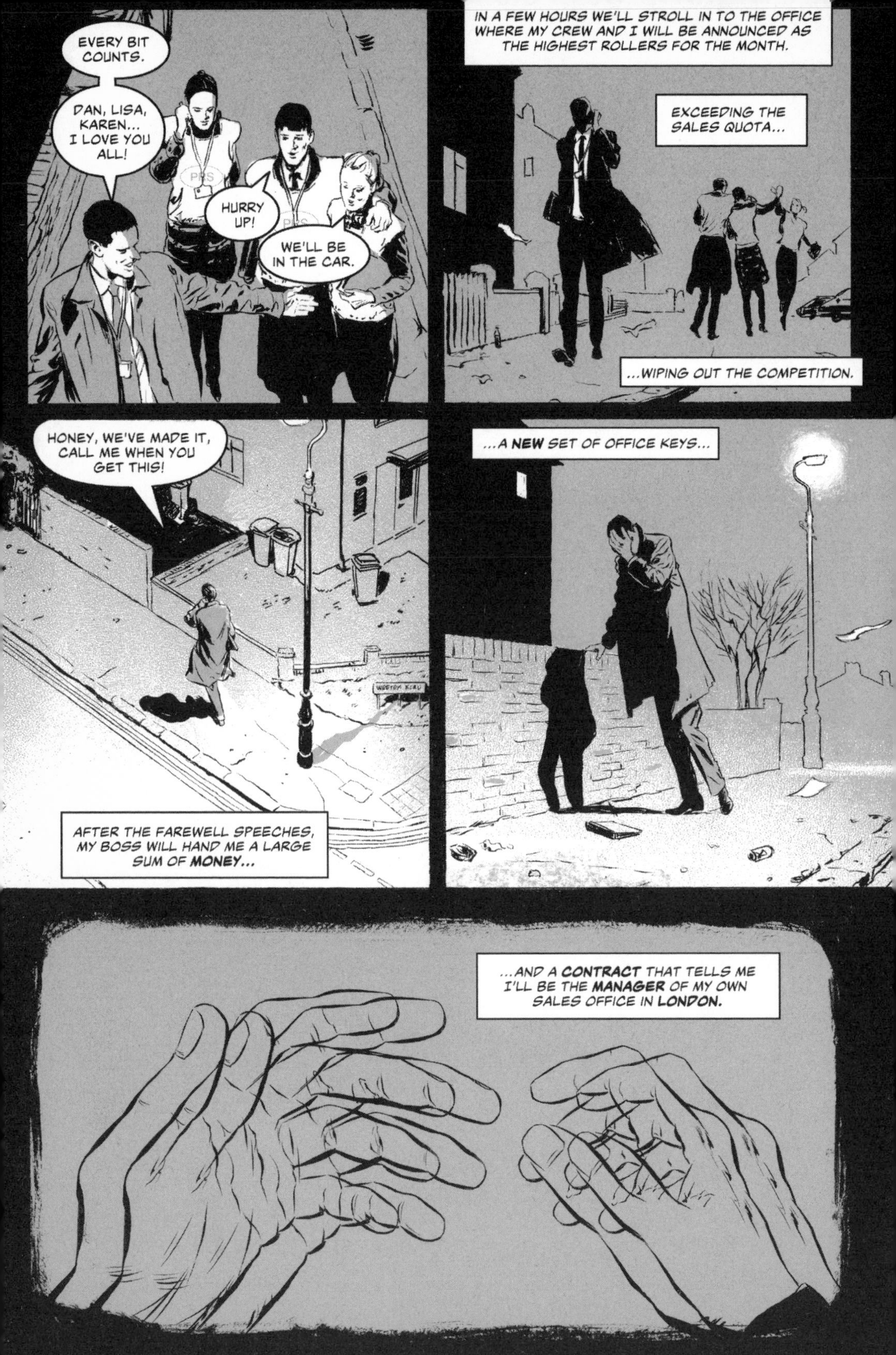
EVERY BIT COUNTS.
DAN, LISA, KAREN... I LOVE YOU ALL!
HURRY UP!
WE'LL BE IN THE CAR.
IN A FEW HOURS WE'LL STROLL IN TO THE OFFICE WHERE MY CREW AND I WILL BE ANNOUNCED AS THE HIGHEST ROLLERS FOR THE MONTH.
EXCEEDING THE SALES QUOTA...
...WIPING OUT THE COMPETITION.
HONEY, WE'VE MADE IT, CALL ME WHEN YOU GET THIS!
AFTER THE FAREWELL SPEECHES, MY BOSS WILL HAND ME A LARGE SUM OF **MONEY...**
...A **NEW** SET OF OFFICE KEYS...
...AND A **CONTRACT** THAT TELLS ME I'LL BE THE **MANAGER** OF MY OWN SALES OFFICE IN **LONDON.**

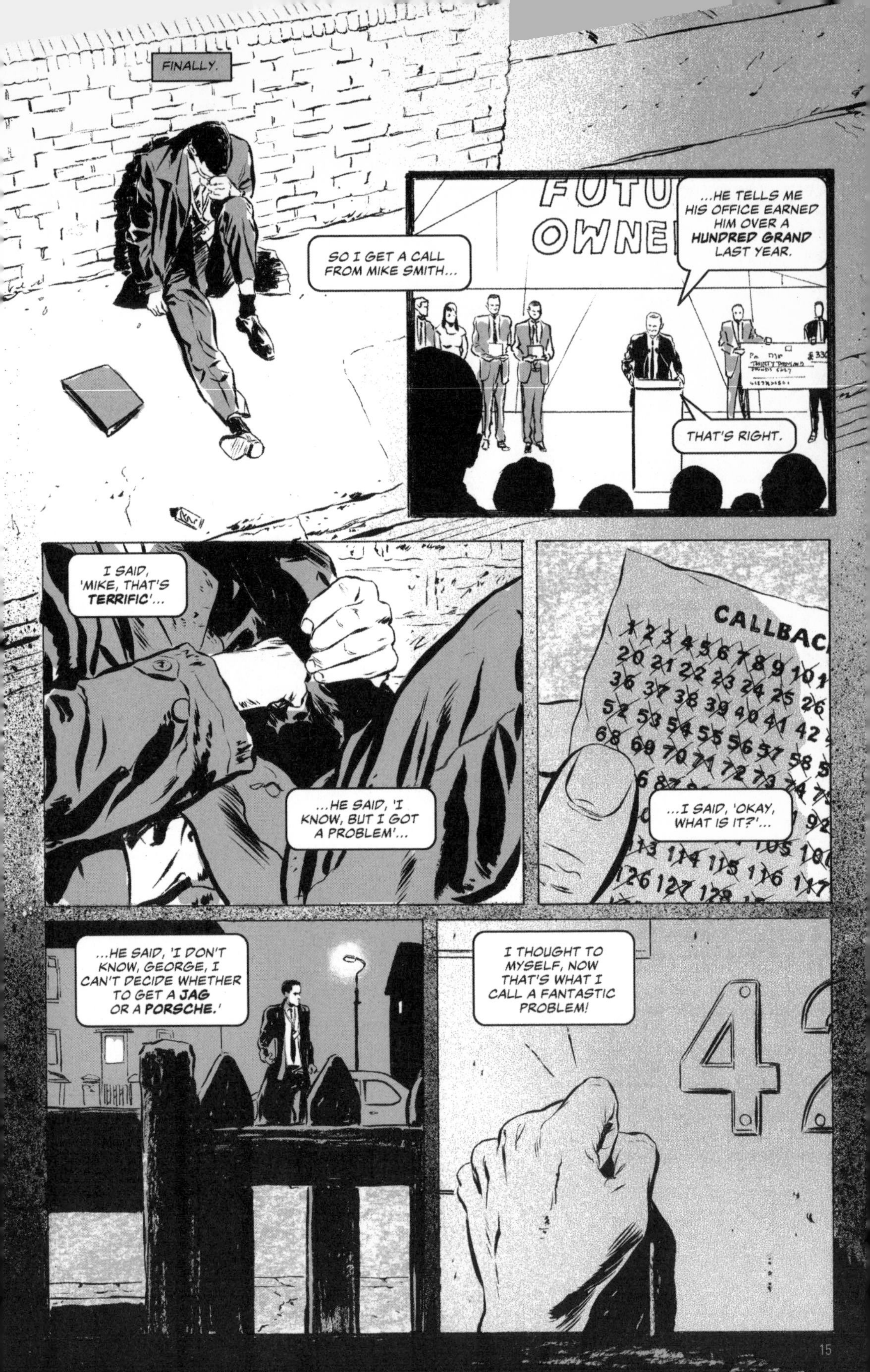
FINALLY.
SO I GET A CALL FROM MIKE SMITH...
FUTU
OWNE
...HE TELLS ME HIS OFFICE EARNED HIM OVER A **HUNDRED GRAND** LAST YEAR.
THAT'S RIGHT.
I SAID, 'MIKE, THAT'S **TERRIFIC**'...
...HE SAID, 'I KNOW, BUT I GOT A PROBLEM'...
CALLBAC
...I SAID, 'OKAY, WHAT IS IT?'...
...HE SAID, 'I DON'T KNOW, GEORGE, I CAN'T DECIDE WHETHER TO GET A **JAG** OR A **PORSCHE**.'
I THOUGHT TO MYSELF, NOW THAT'S WHAT I CALL A FANTASTIC PROBLEM!

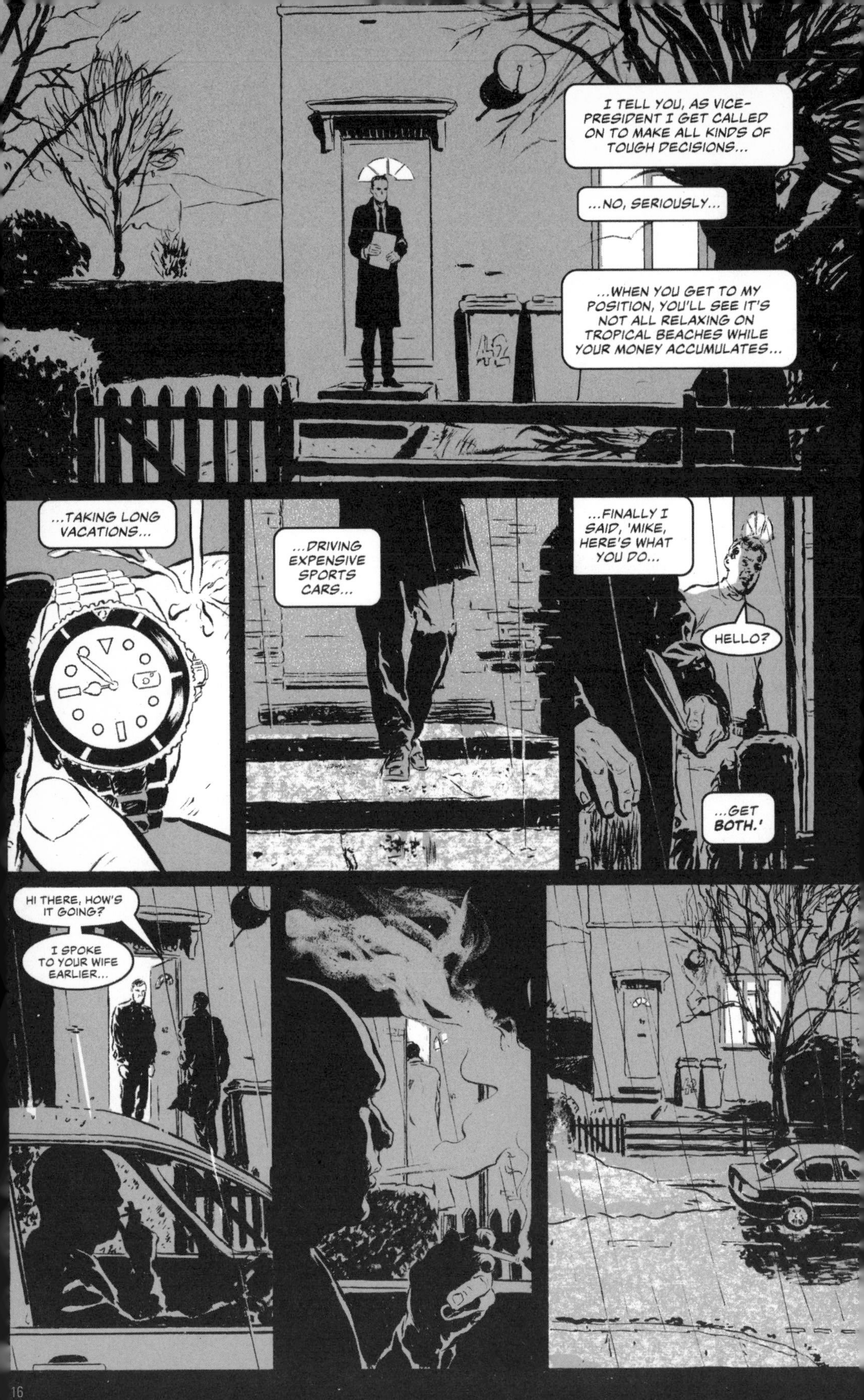
I TELL YOU, AS VICE-PRESIDENT I GET CALLED ON TO MAKE ALL KINDS OF TOUGH DECISIONS...
...NO, SERIOUSLY...
...WHEN YOU GET TO MY POSITION, YOU'LL SEE IT'S NOT ALL RELAXING ON TROPICAL BEACHES WHILE YOUR MONEY ACCUMULATES...
...TAKING LONG VACATIONS...
...DRIVING EXPENSIVE SPORTS CARS...
...FINALLY I SAID, 'MIKE, HERE'S WHAT YOU DO...
HELLO?
...GET BOTH.'
HI THERE, HOW'S IT GOING?
I SPOKE TO YOUR WIFE EARLIER...

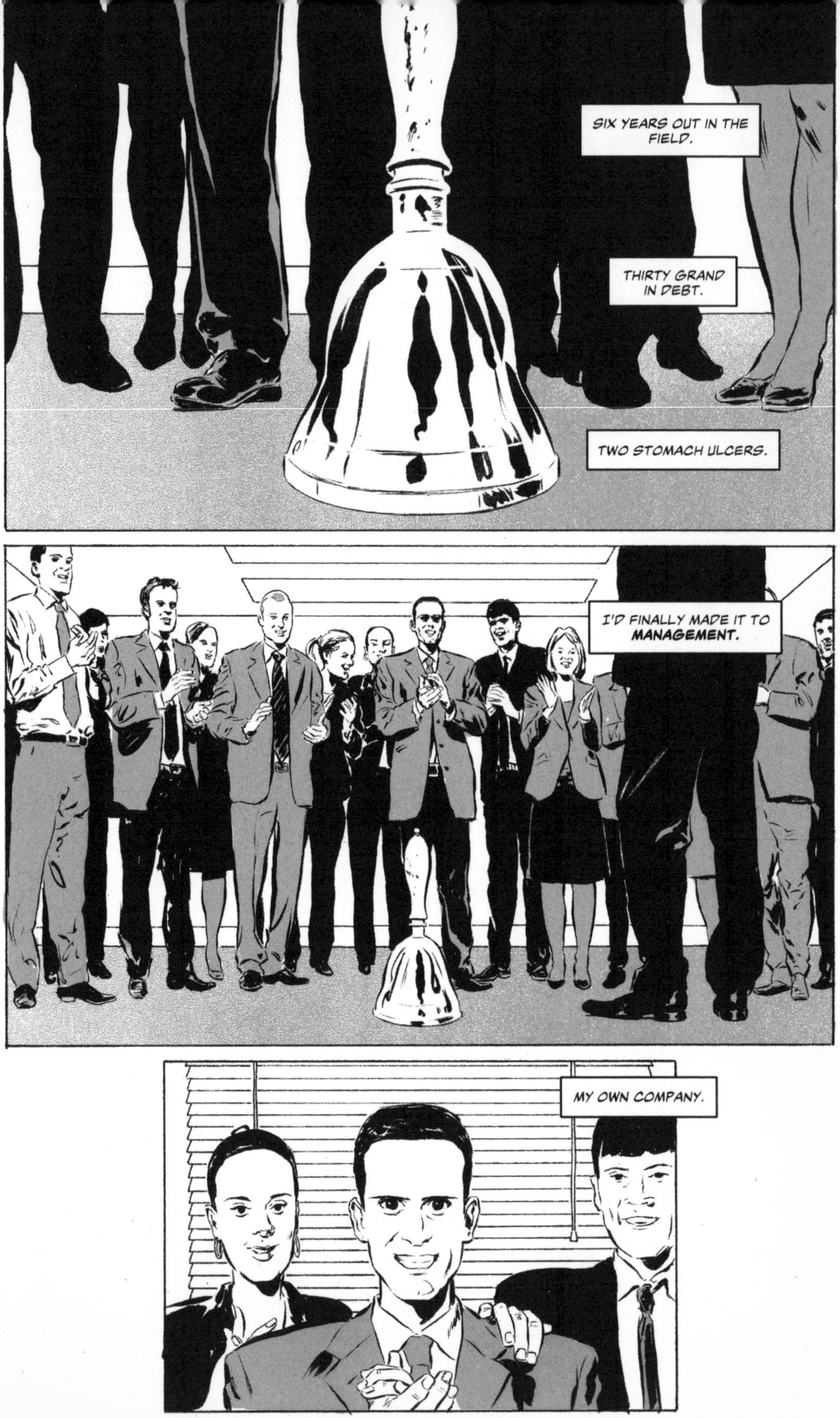
SIX YEARS OUT IN THE FIELD.
THIRTY GRAND IN DEBT.
TWO STOMACH ULCERS.
I'D FINALLY MADE IT TO **MANAGEMENT.**
MY OWN COMPANY.

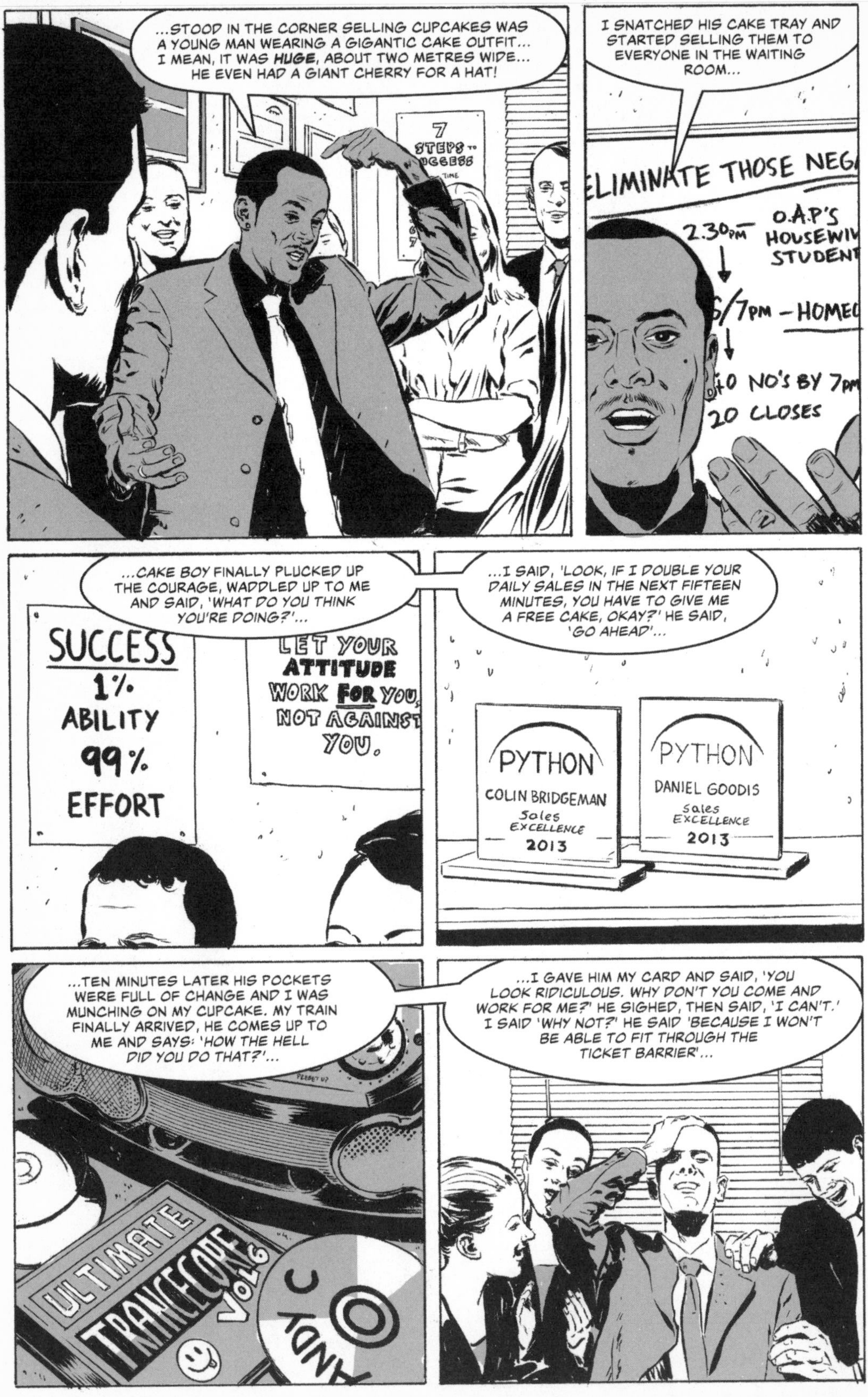
...STOOD IN THE CORNER SELLING CUPCAKES WAS A YOUNG MAN WEARING A GIGANTIC CAKE OUTFIT... I MEAN, IT WAS HUGE, ABOUT TWO METRES WIDE... HE EVEN HAD A GIANT CHERRY FOR A HAT!
7 STEPS TO SUCCESS
I SNATCHED HIS CAKE TRAY AND STARTED SELLING THEM TO EVERYONE IN THE WAITING ROOM...
ELIMINATE THOSE NEG
2.30PM O.A.P'S HOUSEWIV STUDENT
6/7PM - HOMEC
40 NO'S BY 7PM
20 CLOSES
...CAKE BOY FINALLY PLUCKED UP THE COURAGE, WADDLED UP TO ME AND SAID, 'WHAT DO YOU THINK YOU'RE DOING?'...
SUCCESS 1% ABILITY 99% EFFORT
LET YOUR ATTITUDE WORK FOR YOU, NOT AGAINST YOU.
...I SAID, 'LOOK, IF I DOUBLE YOUR DAILY SALES IN THE NEXT FIFTEEN MINUTES, YOU HAVE TO GIVE ME A FREE CAKE, OKAY?' HE SAID, 'GO AHEAD'...
PYTHON COLIN BRIDGEMAN Sales EXCELLENCE 2013
PYTHON DANIEL GOODIS Sales EXCELLENCE 2013
...TEN MINUTES LATER HIS POCKETS WERE FULL OF CHANGE AND I WAS MUNCHING ON MY CUPCAKE. MY TRAIN FINALLY ARRIVED, HE COMES UP TO ME AND SAYS: 'HOW THE HELL DID YOU DO THAT?'...
ULTIMATE TRANCECORE VOL 6
ANDY C
...I GAVE HIM MY CARD AND SAID, 'YOU LOOK RIDICULOUS. WHY DON'T YOU COME AND WORK FOR ME?' HE SIGHED, THEN SAID, 'I CAN'T.' I SAID 'WHY NOT?' HE SAID 'BECAUSE I WON'T BE ABLE TO FIT THROUGH THE TICKET BARRIER'...

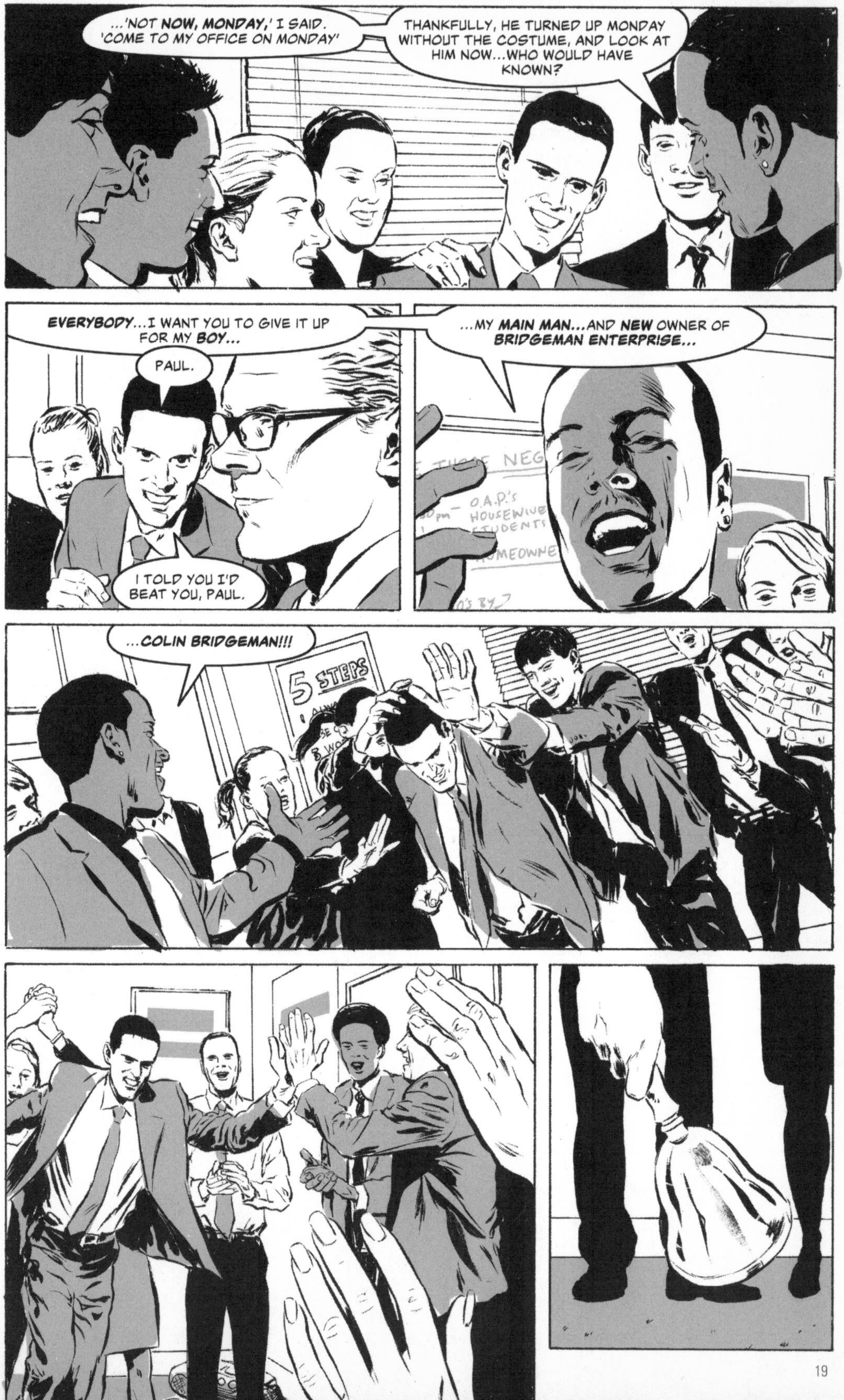
...'NOT NOW, MONDAY,' I SAID. 'COME TO MY OFFICE ON MONDAY'
THANKFULLY, HE TURNED UP MONDAY WITHOUT THE COSTUME, AND LOOK AT HIM NOW...WHO WOULD HAVE KNOWN?
EVERYBODY...I WANT YOU TO GIVE IT UP FOR MY BOY...
PAUL.
I TOLD YOU I'D BEAT YOU, PAUL.
...MY MAIN MAN...AND NEW OWNER OF BRIDGEMAN ENTERPRISE...
O.A.P.'s
HOUSEWIVE
STUDENTS
HOMEOWNE
...COLIN BRIDGEMAN!!!
5 STEPS

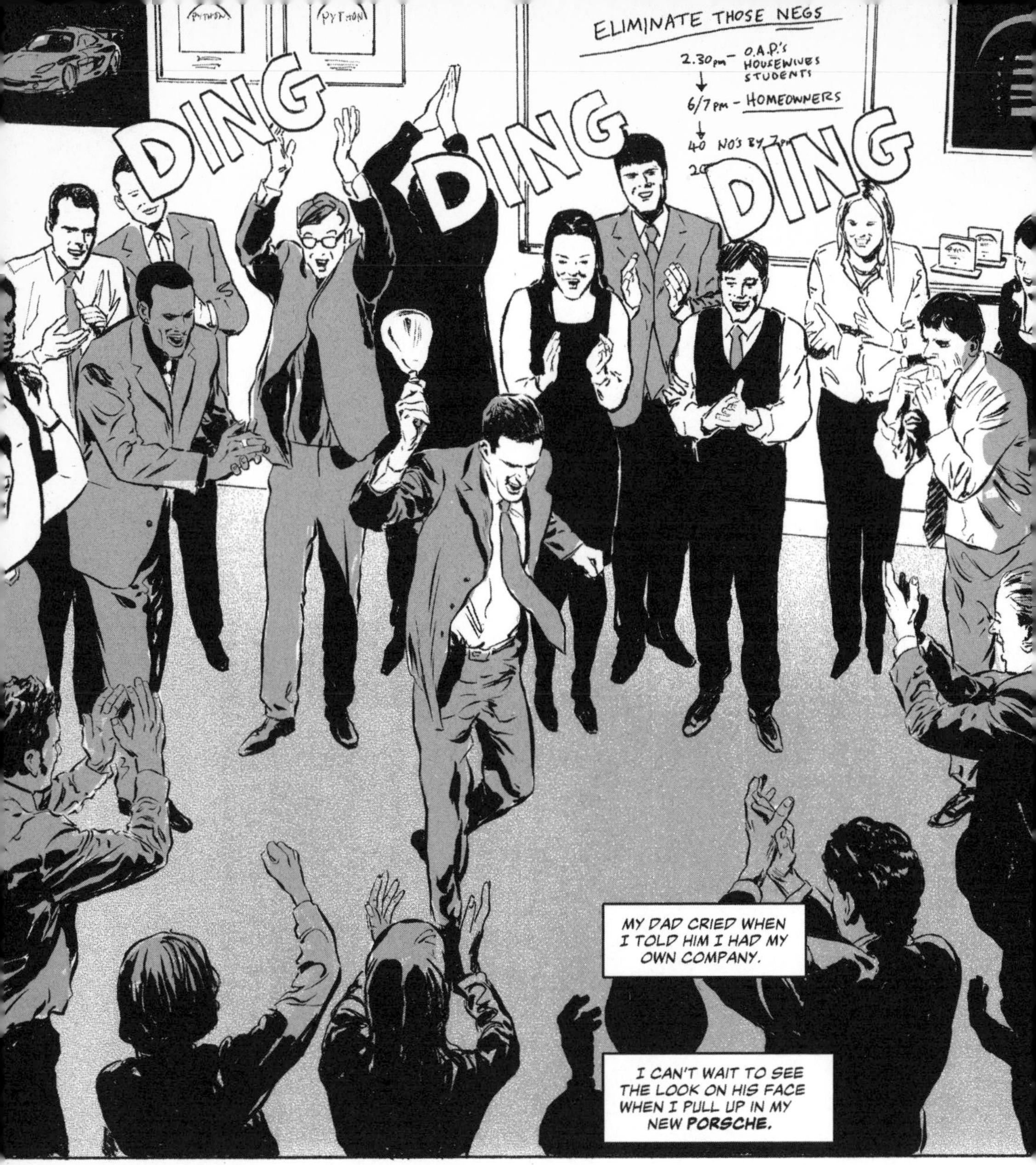
PYTHON
PYTHON
ELIMINATE THOSE NEGS
2.30pm - O.A.P.'s HOUSEWIVES STUDENTS
6/7pm - HOMEOWNERS
DING
DING
DING
MY DAD CRIED WHEN I TOLD HIM I HAD MY OWN COMPANY.
I CAN'T WAIT TO SEE THE LOOK ON HIS FACE WHEN I PULL UP IN MY NEW **PORSCHE.**

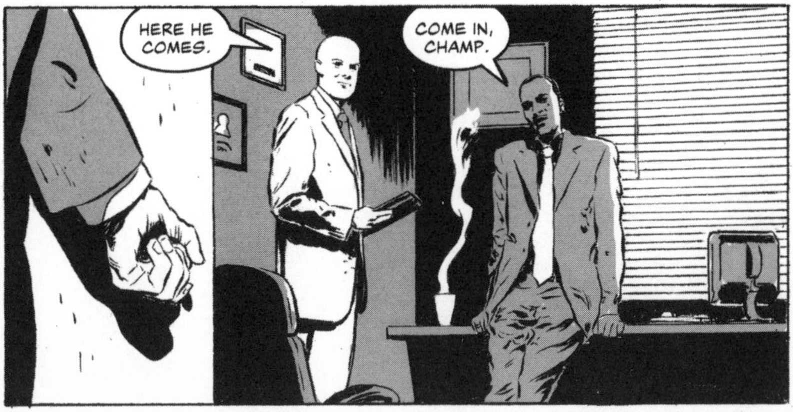
HERE HE COMES.
COME IN, CHAMP.

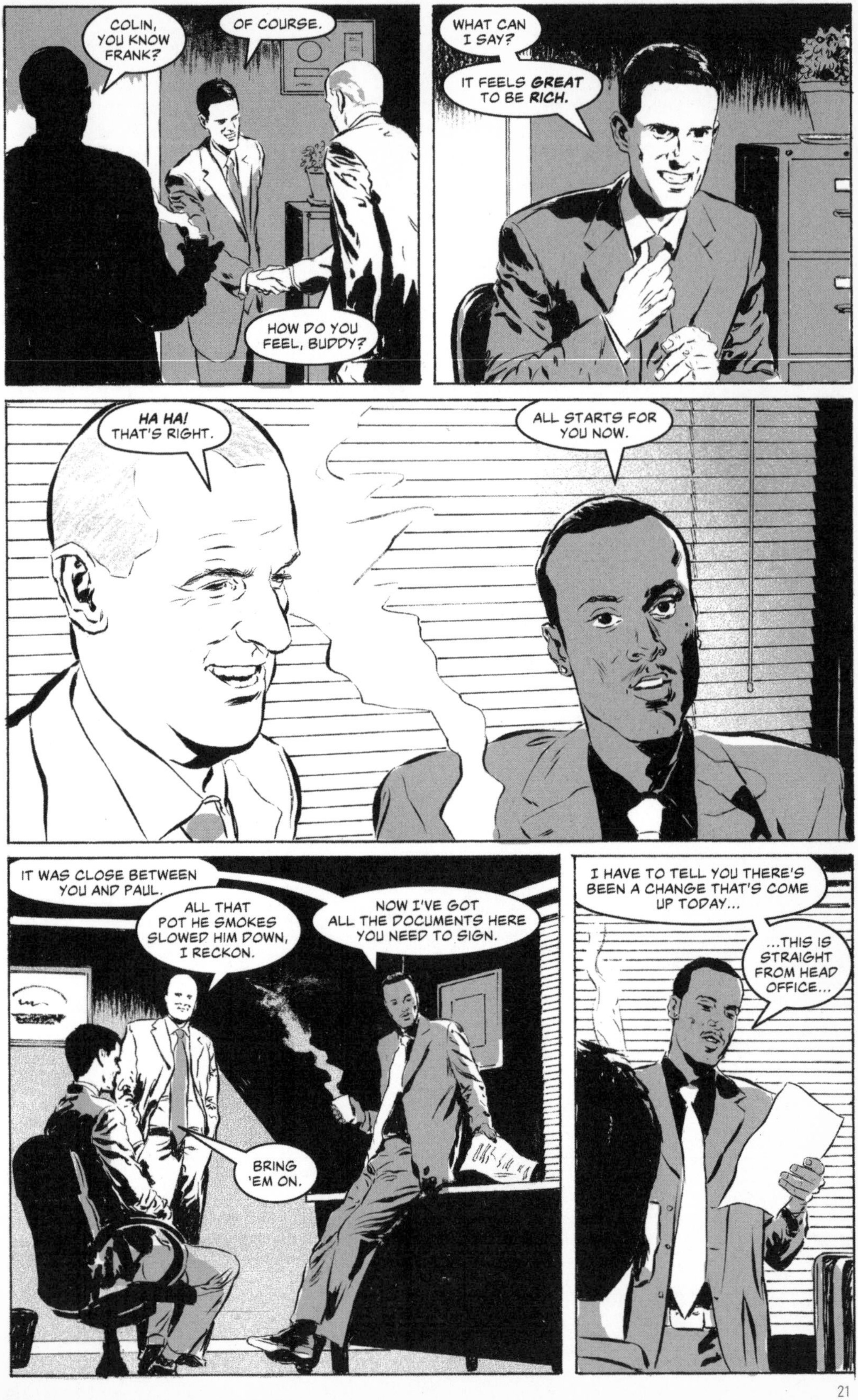
COLIN, YOU KNOW FRANK?
OF COURSE.
HOW DO YOU FEEL, BUDDY?
WHAT CAN I SAY?
IT FEELS **GREAT** TO BE **RICH.**
**HA HA!** THAT'S RIGHT.
ALL STARTS FOR YOU NOW.
IT WAS CLOSE BETWEEN YOU AND PAUL.
ALL THAT POT HE SMOKES SLOWED HIM DOWN, I RECKON.
NOW I'VE GOT ALL THE DOCUMENTS HERE YOU NEED TO SIGN.
BRING 'EM ON.
I HAVE TO TELL YOU THERE'S BEEN A CHANGE THAT'S COME UP TODAY...
...THIS IS STRAIGHT FROM HEAD OFFICE...

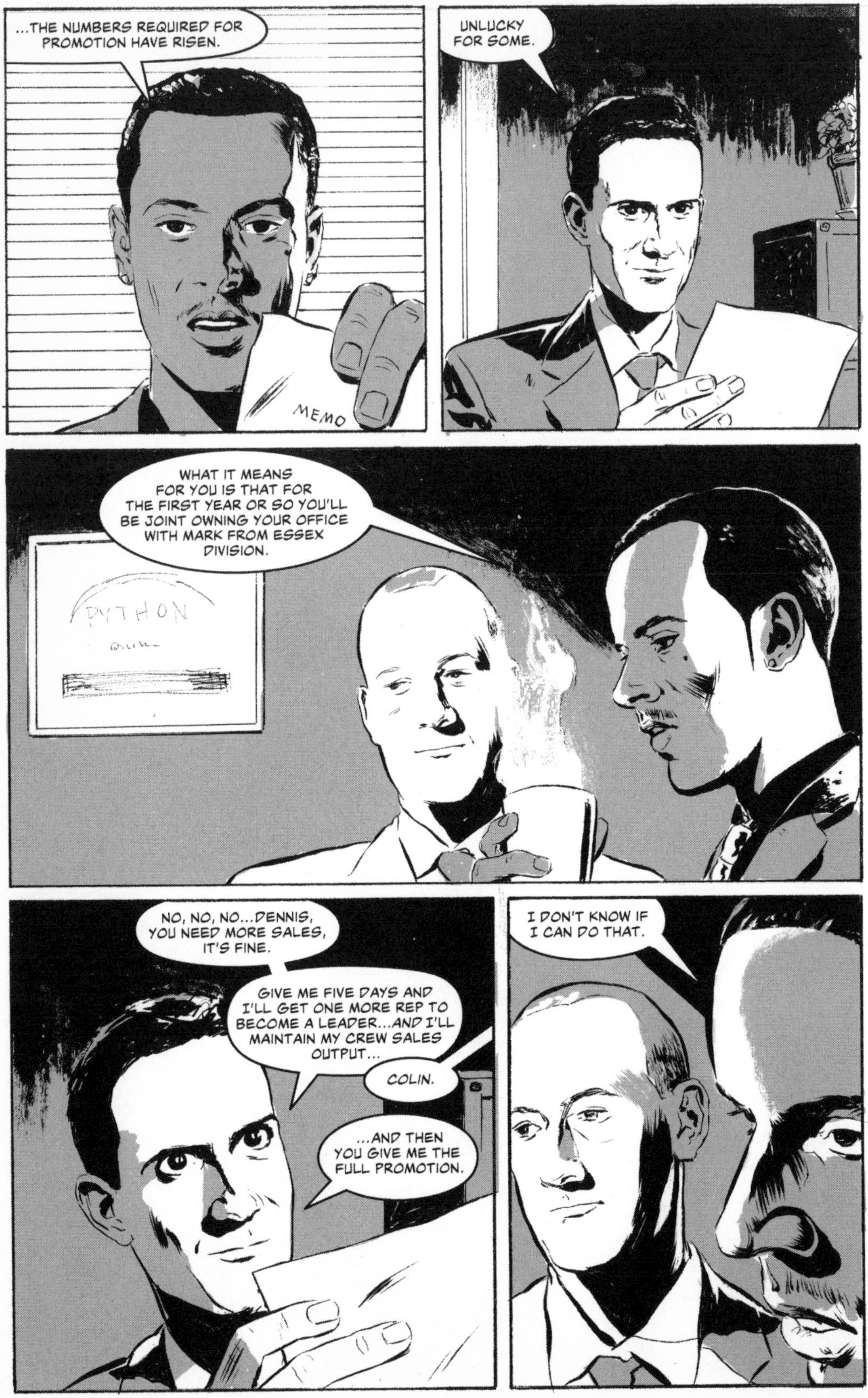
...THE NUMBERS REQUIRED FOR PROMOTION HAVE RISEN.
MEMO
UNLUCKY FOR SOME.
WHAT IT MEANS FOR YOU IS THAT FOR THE FIRST YEAR OR SO YOU'LL BE JOINT OWNING YOUR OFFICE WITH MARK FROM ESSEX DIVISION.
PYTHON
NO, NO, NO...DENNIS, YOU NEED MORE SALES, IT'S FINE.
GIVE ME FIVE DAYS AND I'LL GET ONE MORE REP TO BECOME A LEADER...AND I'LL MAINTAIN MY CREW SALES OUTPUT...
COLIN.
...AND THEN YOU GIVE ME THE FULL PROMOTION.
I DON'T KNOW IF I CAN DO THAT.

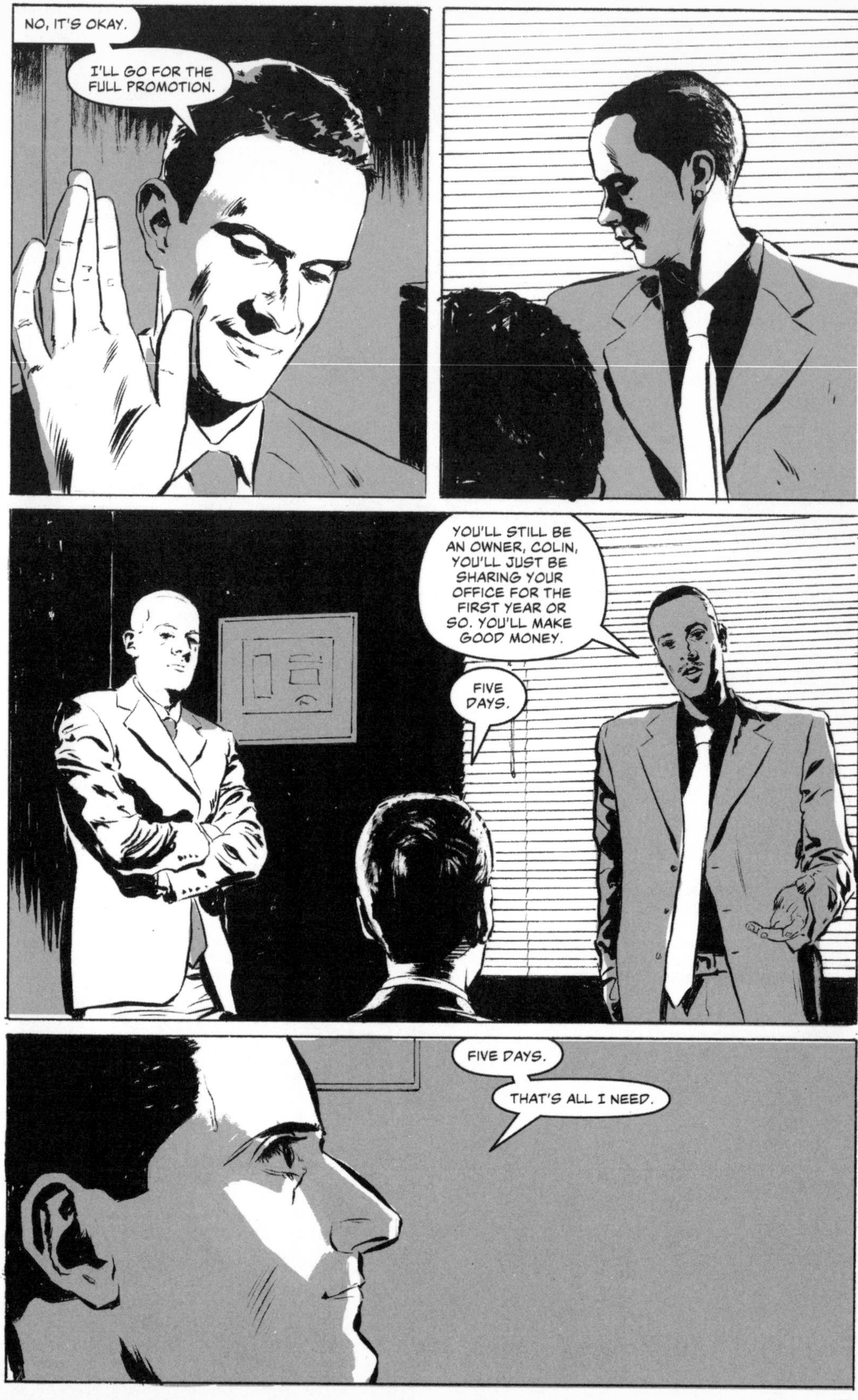
NO, IT'S OKAY.
I'LL GO FOR THE FULL PROMOTION.
YOU'LL STILL BE AN OWNER, COLIN, YOU'LL JUST BE SHARING YOUR OFFICE FOR THE FIRST YEAR OR SO. YOU'LL MAKE GOOD MONEY.
FIVE DAYS.
FIVE DAYS.
THAT'S ALL I NEED.

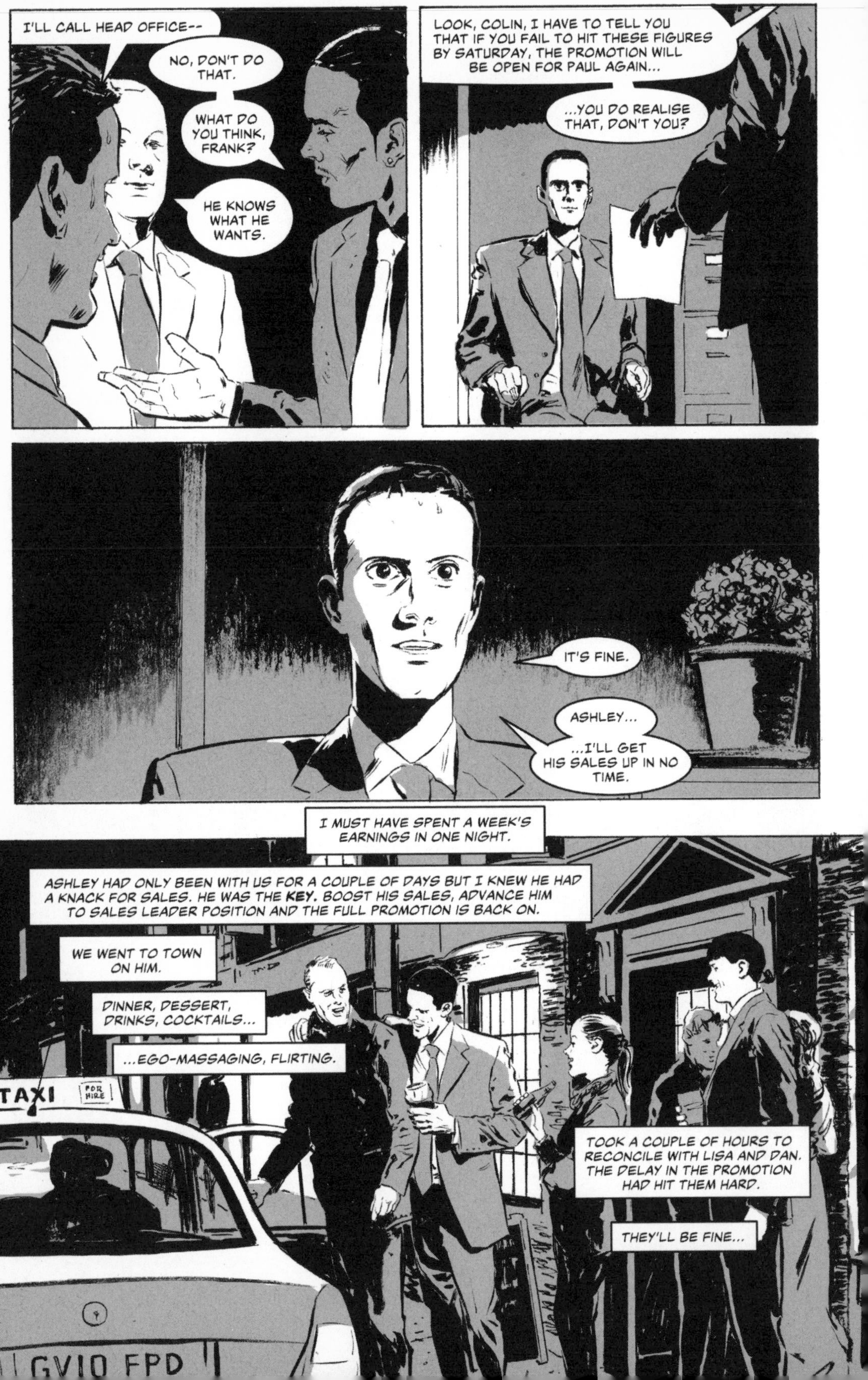
I'LL CALL HEAD OFFICE--
NO, DON'T DO THAT.
WHAT DO YOU THINK, FRANK?
HE KNOWS WHAT HE WANTS.
LOOK, COLIN, I HAVE TO TELL YOU THAT IF YOU FAIL TO HIT THESE FIGURES BY SATURDAY, THE PROMOTION WILL BE OPEN FOR PAUL AGAIN...
...YOU DO REALISE THAT, DON'T YOU?
IT'S FINE.
ASHLEY...
...I'LL GET HIS SALES UP IN NO TIME.
I MUST HAVE SPENT A WEEK'S EARNINGS IN ONE NIGHT.
ASHLEY HAD ONLY BEEN WITH US FOR A COUPLE OF DAYS BUT I KNEW HE HAD A KNACK FOR SALES. HE WAS THE **KEY.** BOOST HIS SALES, ADVANCE HIM TO SALES LEADER POSITION AND THE FULL PROMOTION IS BACK ON.
WE WENT TO TOWN ON HIM.
DINNER, DESSERT, DRINKS, COCKTAILS...
...EGO-MASSAGING, FLIRTING.
TAXI
FOR HIRE
TOOK A COUPLE OF HOURS TO RECONCILE WITH LISA AND DAN. THE DELAY IN THE PROMOTION HAD HIT THEM HARD.
THEY'LL BE FINE...
GV10 FPD

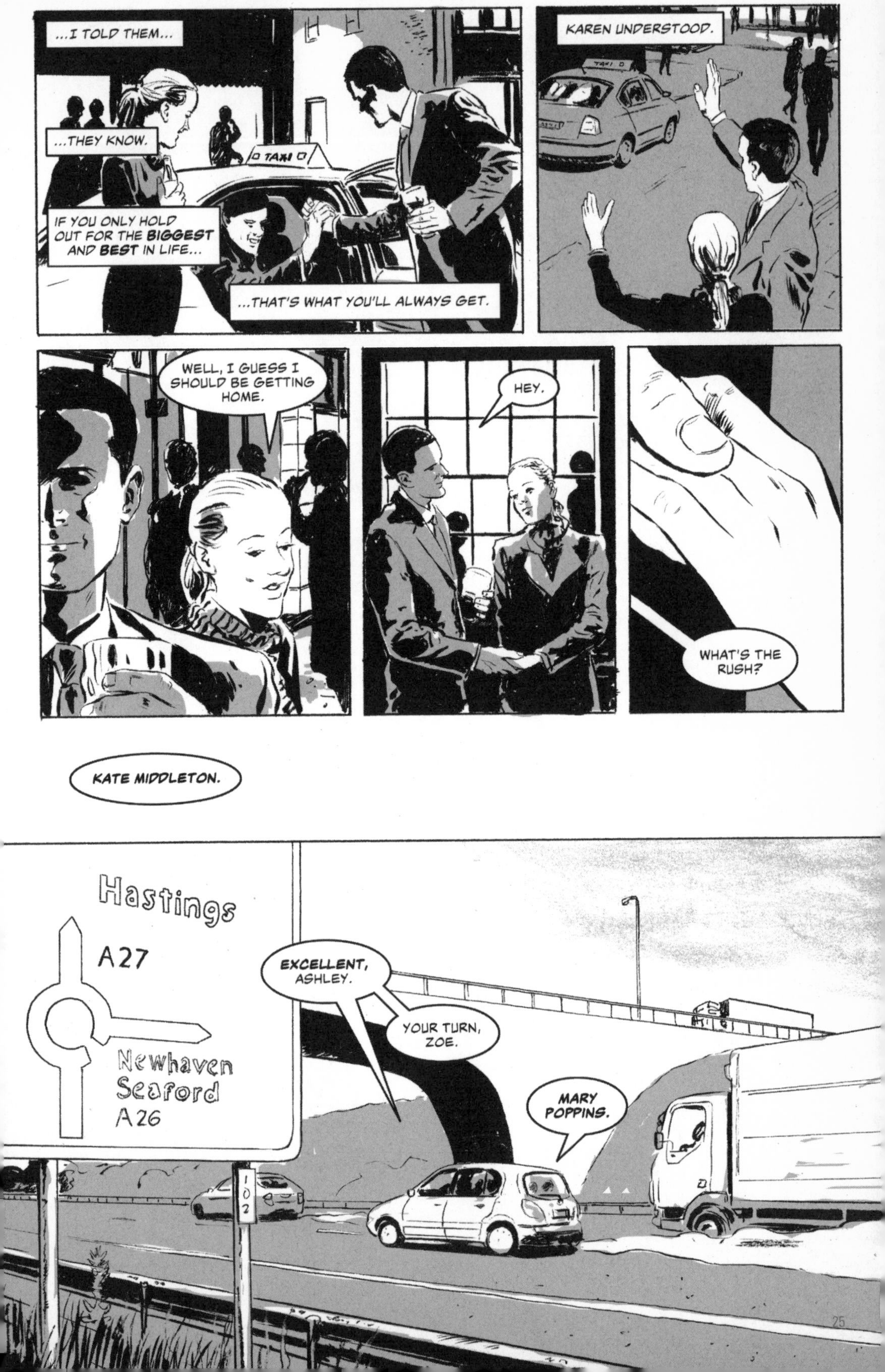

...I TOLD THEM...
...THEY KNOW.
IF YOU ONLY HOLD OUT FOR THE BIGGEST AND BEST IN LIFE...
...THAT'S WHAT YOU'LL ALWAYS GET.
TAXI
KAREN UNDERSTOOD.
WELL, I GUESS I SHOULD BE GETTING HOME.
HEY.
WHAT'S THE RUSH?
KATE MIDDLETON.
Hastings
A27
Newhaven
Seaford
A26
EXCELLENT, ASHLEY.
YOUR TURN, ZOE.
MARY POPPINS.

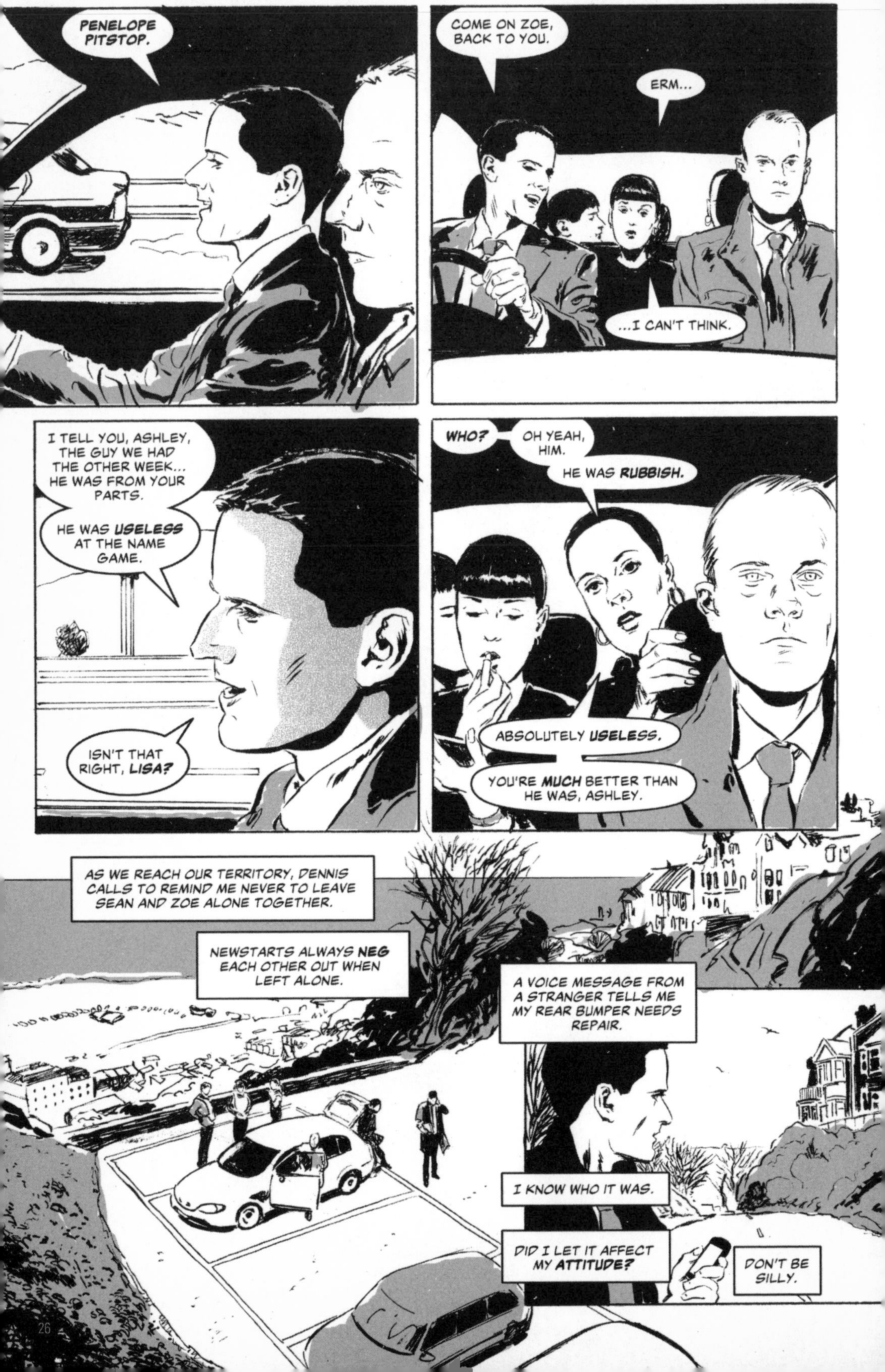
PENELOPE PITSTOP.
COME ON ZOE, BACK TO YOU.
ERM...
...I CAN'T THINK.
I TELL YOU, ASHLEY, THE GUY WE HAD THE OTHER WEEK... HE WAS FROM YOUR PARTS.
HE WAS USELESS AT THE NAME GAME.
ISN'T THAT RIGHT, LISA?
WHO?
OH YEAH, HIM.
HE WAS RUBBISH.
ABSOLUTELY USELESS.
YOU'RE MUCH BETTER THAN HE WAS, ASHLEY.
AS WE REACH OUR TERRITORY, DENNIS CALLS TO REMIND ME NEVER TO LEAVE SEAN AND ZOE ALONE TOGETHER.
NEWSTARTS ALWAYS NEG EACH OTHER OUT WHEN LEFT ALONE.
A VOICE MESSAGE FROM A STRANGER TELLS ME MY REAR BUMPER NEEDS REPAIR.
I KNOW WHO IT WAS.
DID I LET IT AFFECT MY ATTITUDE?
DON'T BE SILLY.

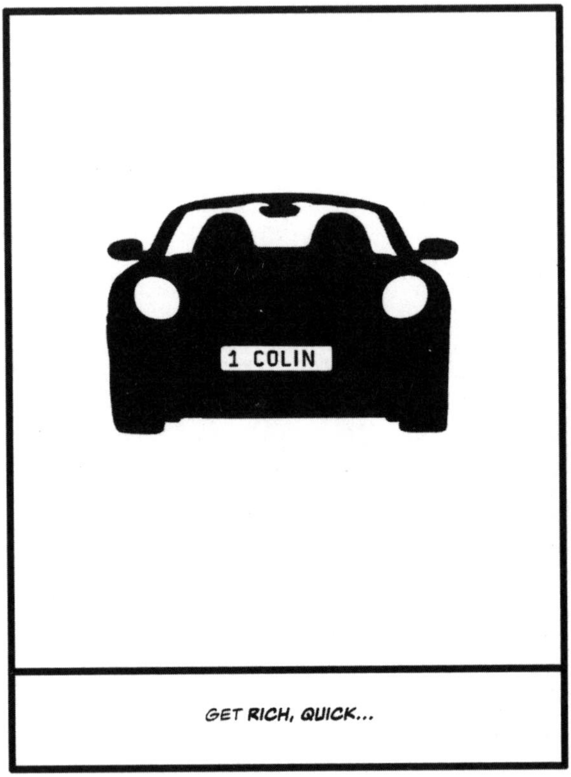
1 COLIN
GET RICH, QUICK...

...THAT'S THE **GOAL**.

GET RICH EARLY IN LIFE SO YOU CAN SPEND THE REST OF IT DOING THE THINGS THAT YOU WANT TO DO.

WHEN I GET PROMOTED OUT, WHEN I'M RUNNING MY OWN SALES OFFICE, I'LL BE ONE STEP CLOSER TO BEING ABLE TO GET A MORTGAGE APPROVED ON A HOUSE.

**PROPERTY**. BUY TO LET. THAT'S THE **KEY**. THAT'S THE KEY TO IT **ALL**.

BUY A HOUSE, DIVIDE IT UP, FILL IT WITH TENANTS.

LET THEM WORK FOR YOU, LET THEM PAY YOUR MORTGAGE OFF.

THEN YOU BUY ANOTHER HOUSE, AND ANOTHER, UNTIL YOU NEVER HAVE TO LIFT A FINGER TO EARN YOUR LIVING.

COMPLETE FINANCIAL INDEPENDENCE.

WHAT'S THE ALTERNATIVE? YOU GONNA WORK AND SAVE ALL YOUR LIFE?

DON'T BE RIDICULOUS.

THERE'S NO WORK FOR A START. NOTHING FOR THE AVERAGE JOE ANYWAY...

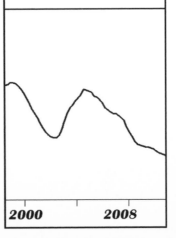

**2000**          **2008**

...UNLESS YOU WANT TO WORK IN THE SERVICE INDUSTRY OR TRY YOUR LUCK IN THE PUBLIC SECTOR.

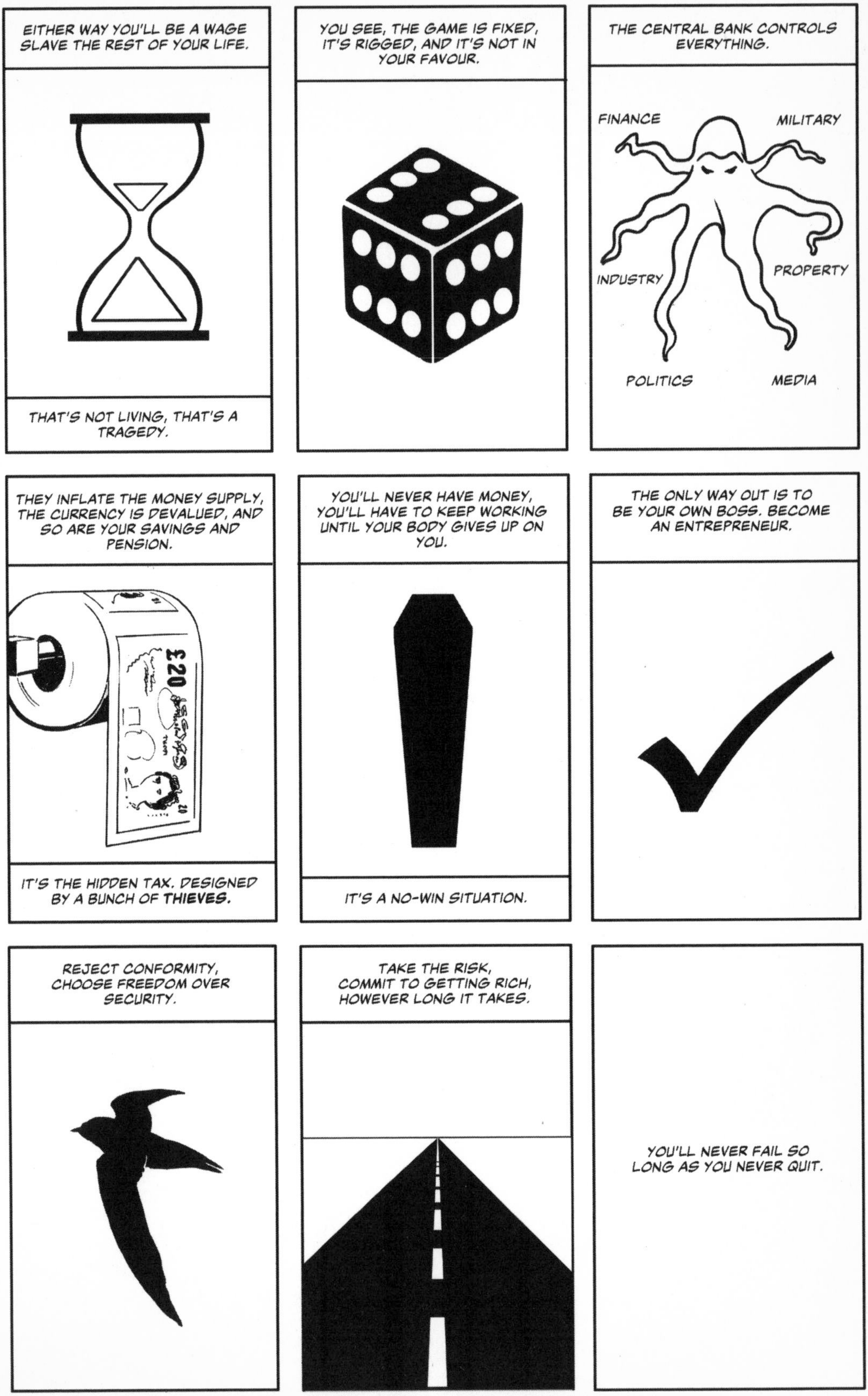

EITHER WAY YOU'LL BE A WAGE SLAVE THE REST OF YOUR LIFE.

THAT'S NOT LIVING, THAT'S A TRAGEDY.

YOU SEE, THE GAME IS FIXED, IT'S RIGGED, AND IT'S NOT IN YOUR FAVOUR.

THE CENTRAL BANK CONTROLS EVERYTHING.

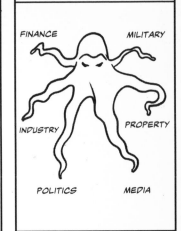

FINANCE

MILITARY

INDUSTRY

PROPERTY

POLITICS

MEDIA

THEY INFLATE THE MONEY SUPPLY, THE CURRENCY IS DEVALUED, AND SO ARE YOUR SAVINGS AND PENSION.

IT'S THE HIDDEN TAX. DESIGNED BY A BUNCH OF **THIEVES**.

YOU'LL NEVER HAVE MONEY, YOU'LL HAVE TO KEEP WORKING UNTIL YOUR BODY GIVES UP ON YOU.

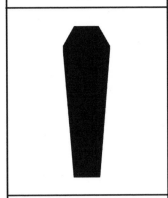

IT'S A NO-WIN SITUATION.

THE ONLY WAY OUT IS TO BE YOUR OWN BOSS. BECOME AN ENTREPRENEUR.

REJECT CONFORMITY, CHOOSE FREEDOM OVER SECURITY.

TAKE THE RISK, COMMIT TO GETTING RICH, HOWEVER LONG IT TAKES.

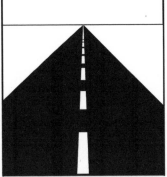

YOU'LL NEVER FAIL SO LONG AS YOU NEVER QUIT.

ASHLEY AND I HEAD STRAIGHT TOWARD THE RESIDENTIAL NEIGHBOURHOODS
SPREAD OUT ACROSS THE HILLS THAT OVERLOOK THE TOWN
CENTRE AND SEAFRONT.

I NEED **ASHLEY** TO MAKE **SIX** SALES A DAY
FOR **FIVE** STRAIGHT DAYS TO BE SURE OF **PROMOTION.**

IT'S A LOT OF WORK, BUT HE'S CAPABLE.
HE JUST NEEDS TO BE PUT IN THE RIGHT FRAME OF MIND.

HE SIMPLY NEEDS
TO BE TOLD ABOUT THE **OPPORTUNITY.**

IN A COUPLE OF HOURS HE'LL BE
PUTTY IN MY HANDS.

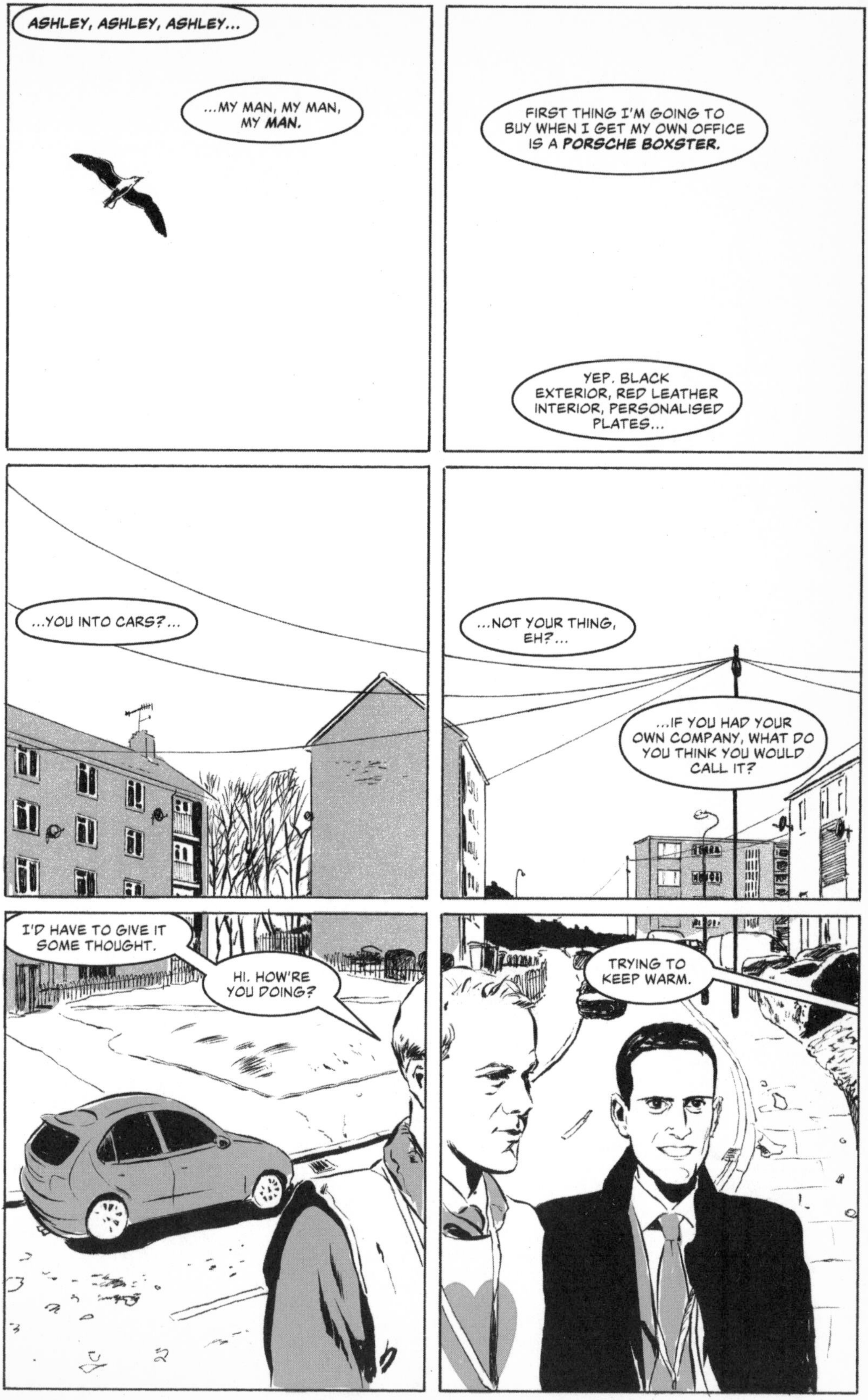
ASHLEY, ASHLEY, ASHLEY...
...MY MAN, MY MAN, MY **MAN.**
FIRST THING I'M GOING TO BUY WHEN I GET MY OWN OFFICE IS A **PORSCHE BOXSTER.**
YEP. BLACK EXTERIOR, RED LEATHER INTERIOR, PERSONALISED PLATES...
...YOU INTO CARS?...
...NOT YOUR THING, EH?...
...IF YOU HAD YOUR OWN COMPANY, WHAT DO YOU THINK YOU WOULD CALL IT?
I'D HAVE TO GIVE IT SOME THOUGHT.
HI. HOW'RE YOU DOING?
TRYING TO KEEP WARM.

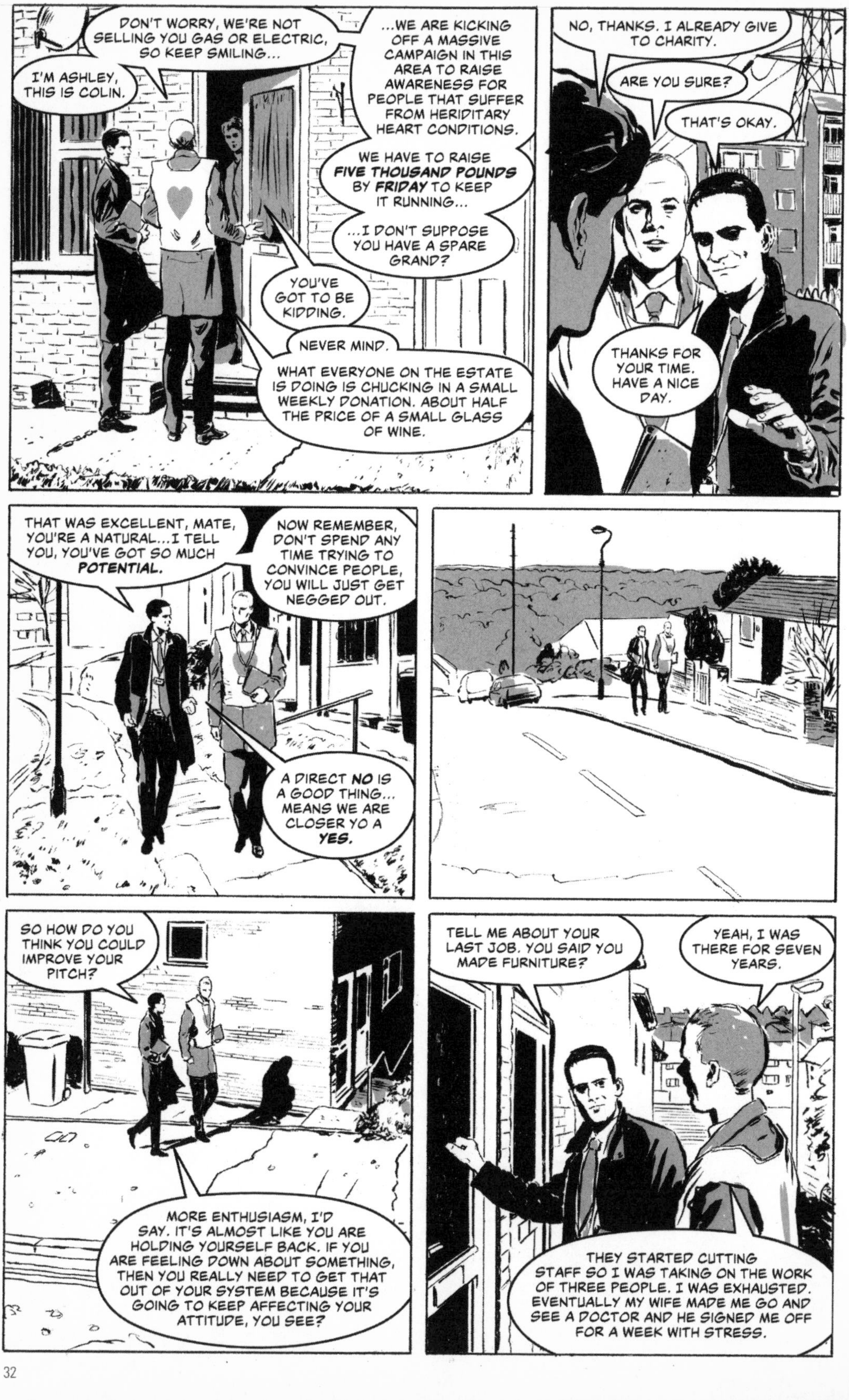
I'M ASHLEY, THIS IS COLIN.
DON'T WORRY, WE'RE NOT SELLING YOU GAS OR ELECTRIC, SO KEEP SMILING...
...WE ARE KICKING OFF A MASSIVE CAMPAIGN IN THIS AREA TO RAISE AWARENESS FOR PEOPLE THAT SUFFER FROM HERIDITARY HEART CONDITIONS.
WE HAVE TO RAISE FIVE THOUSAND POUNDS BY FRIDAY TO KEEP IT RUNNING...
...I DON'T SUPPOSE YOU HAVE A SPARE GRAND?
YOU'VE GOT TO BE KIDDING.
NEVER MIND.
WHAT EVERYONE ON THE ESTATE IS DOING IS CHUCKING IN A SMALL WEEKLY DONATION. ABOUT HALF THE PRICE OF A SMALL GLASS OF WINE.
NO, THANKS. I ALREADY GIVE TO CHARITY.
ARE YOU SURE?
THAT'S OKAY.
THANKS FOR YOUR TIME. HAVE A NICE DAY.
THAT WAS EXCELLENT, MATE, YOU'RE A NATURAL...I TELL YOU, YOU'VE GOT SO MUCH POTENTIAL.
NOW REMEMBER, DON'T SPEND ANY TIME TRYING TO CONVINCE PEOPLE, YOU WILL JUST GET NEGGED OUT.
A DIRECT NO IS A GOOD THING... MEANS WE ARE CLOSER YO A YES.
SO HOW DO YOU THINK YOU COULD IMPROVE YOUR PITCH?
MORE ENTHUSIASM, I'D SAY. IT'S ALMOST LIKE YOU ARE HOLDING YOURSELF BACK. IF YOU ARE FEELING DOWN ABOUT SOMETHING, THEN YOU REALLY NEED TO GET THAT OUT OF YOUR SYSTEM BECAUSE IT'S GOING TO KEEP AFFECTING YOUR ATTITUDE, YOU SEE?
TELL ME ABOUT YOUR LAST JOB. YOU SAID YOU MADE FURNITURE?
YEAH, I WAS THERE FOR SEVEN YEARS.
THEY STARTED CUTTING STAFF SO I WAS TAKING ON THE WORK OF THREE PEOPLE. I WAS EXHAUSTED. EVENTUALLY MY WIFE MADE ME GO AND SEE A DOCTOR AND HE SIGNED ME OFF FOR A WEEK WITH STRESS.

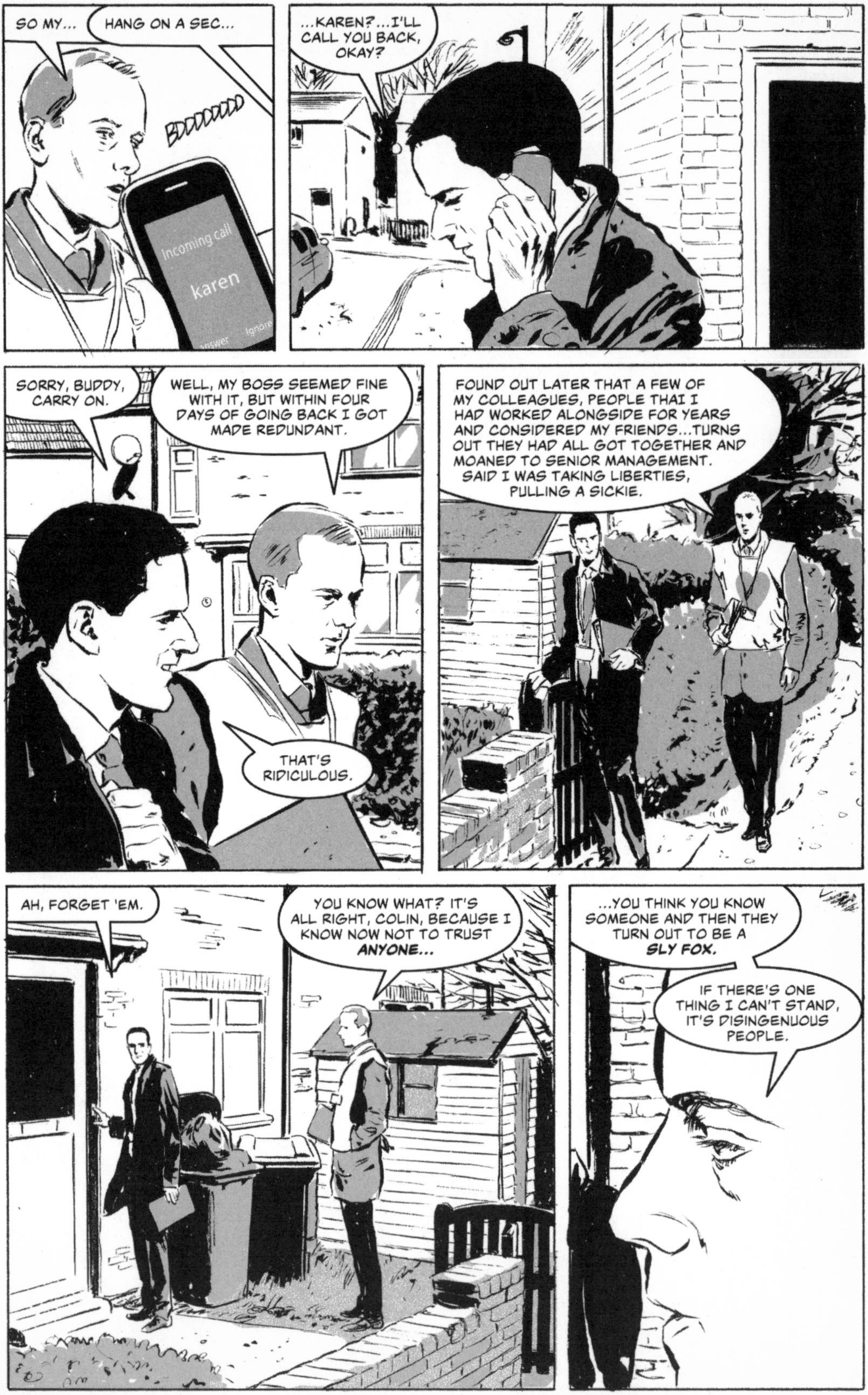
SO MY...
HANG ON A SEC...
BDDDDDDDD
Incoming call
karen
answer
ignore
...KAREN?...I'LL CALL YOU BACK, OKAY?
SORRY, BUDDY, CARRY ON.
WELL, MY BOSS SEEMED FINE WITH IT, BUT WITHIN FOUR DAYS OF GOING BACK I GOT MADE REDUNDANT.
THAT'S RIDICULOUS.
FOUND OUT LATER THAT A FEW OF MY COLLEAGUES, PEOPLE THAI I HAD WORKED ALONGSIDE FOR YEARS AND CONSIDERED MY FRIENDS...TURNS OUT THEY HAD ALL GOT TOGETHER AND MOANED TO SENIOR MANAGEMENT. SAID I WAS TAKING LIBERTIES, PULLING A SICKIE.
AH, FORGET 'EM.
YOU KNOW WHAT? IT'S ALL RIGHT, COLIN, BECAUSE I KNOW NOW NOT TO TRUST **ANYONE...**
...YOU THINK YOU KNOW SOMEONE AND THEN THEY TURN OUT TO BE A **SLY FOX.**
IF THERE'S ONE THING I CAN'T STAND, IT'S DISINGENUOUS PEOPLE.

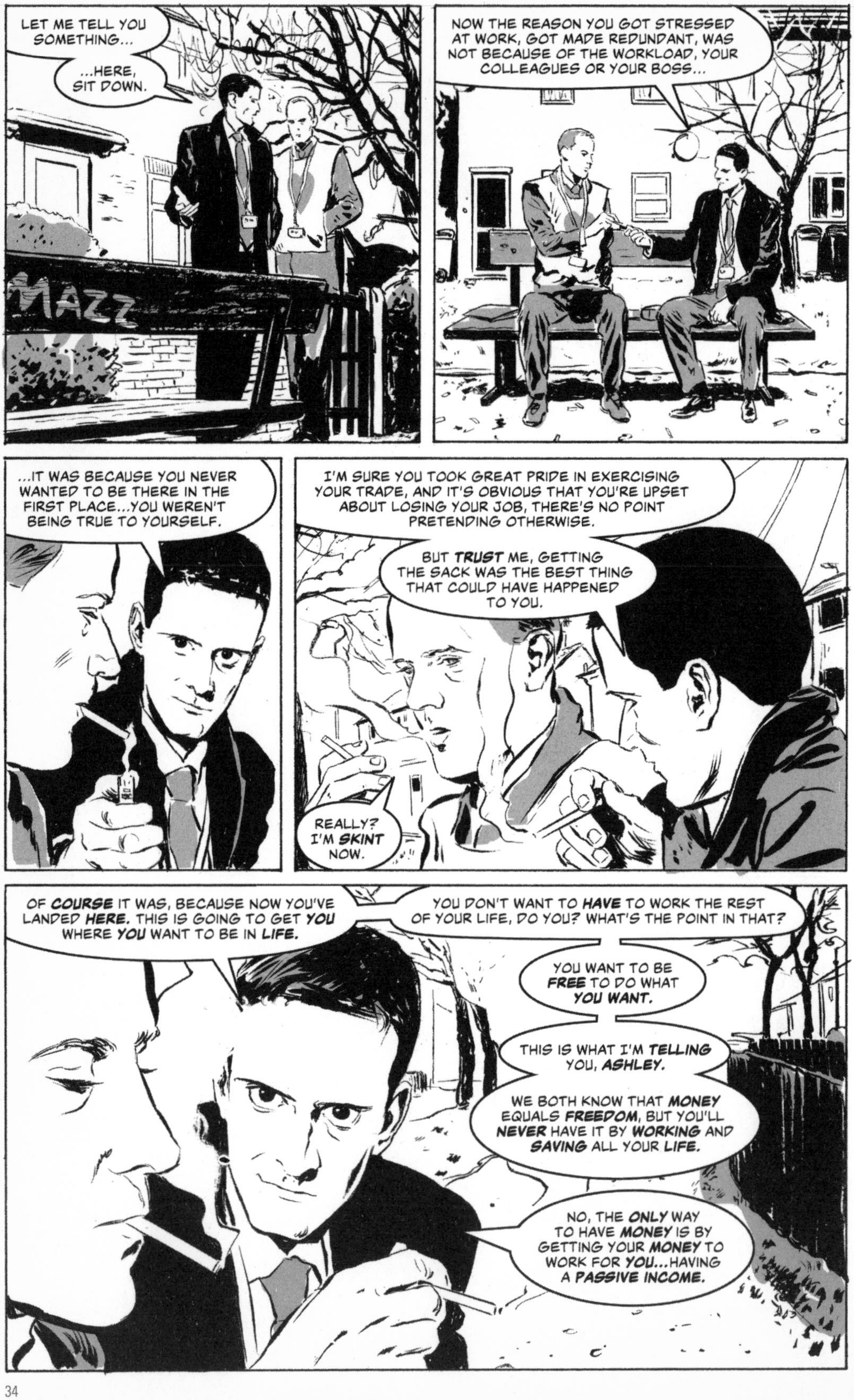
LET ME TELL YOU SOMETHING...
...HERE, SIT DOWN.
NOW THE REASON YOU GOT STRESSED AT WORK, GOT MADE REDUNDANT, WAS NOT BECAUSE OF THE WORKLOAD, YOUR COLLEAGUES OR YOUR BOSS...
...IT WAS BECAUSE YOU NEVER WANTED TO BE THERE IN THE FIRST PLACE...YOU WEREN'T BEING TRUE TO YOURSELF.
I'M SURE YOU TOOK GREAT PRIDE IN EXERCISING YOUR TRADE, AND IT'S OBVIOUS THAT YOU'RE UPSET ABOUT LOSING YOUR JOB, THERE'S NO POINT PRETENDING OTHERWISE.
BUT TRUST ME, GETTING THE SACK WAS THE BEST THING THAT COULD HAVE HAPPENED TO YOU.
REALLY? I'M SKINT NOW.
OF COURSE IT WAS, BECAUSE NOW YOU'VE LANDED HERE. THIS IS GOING TO GET YOU WHERE YOU WANT TO BE IN LIFE.
YOU DON'T WANT TO HAVE TO WORK THE REST OF YOUR LIFE, DO YOU? WHAT'S THE POINT IN THAT?
YOU WANT TO BE FREE TO DO WHAT YOU WANT.
THIS IS WHAT I'M TELLING YOU, ASHLEY.
WE BOTH KNOW THAT MONEY EQUALS FREEDOM, BUT YOU'LL NEVER HAVE IT BY WORKING AND SAVING ALL YOUR LIFE.
NO, THE ONLY WAY TO HAVE MONEY IS BY GETTING YOUR MONEY TO WORK FOR YOU...HAVING A PASSIVE INCOME.

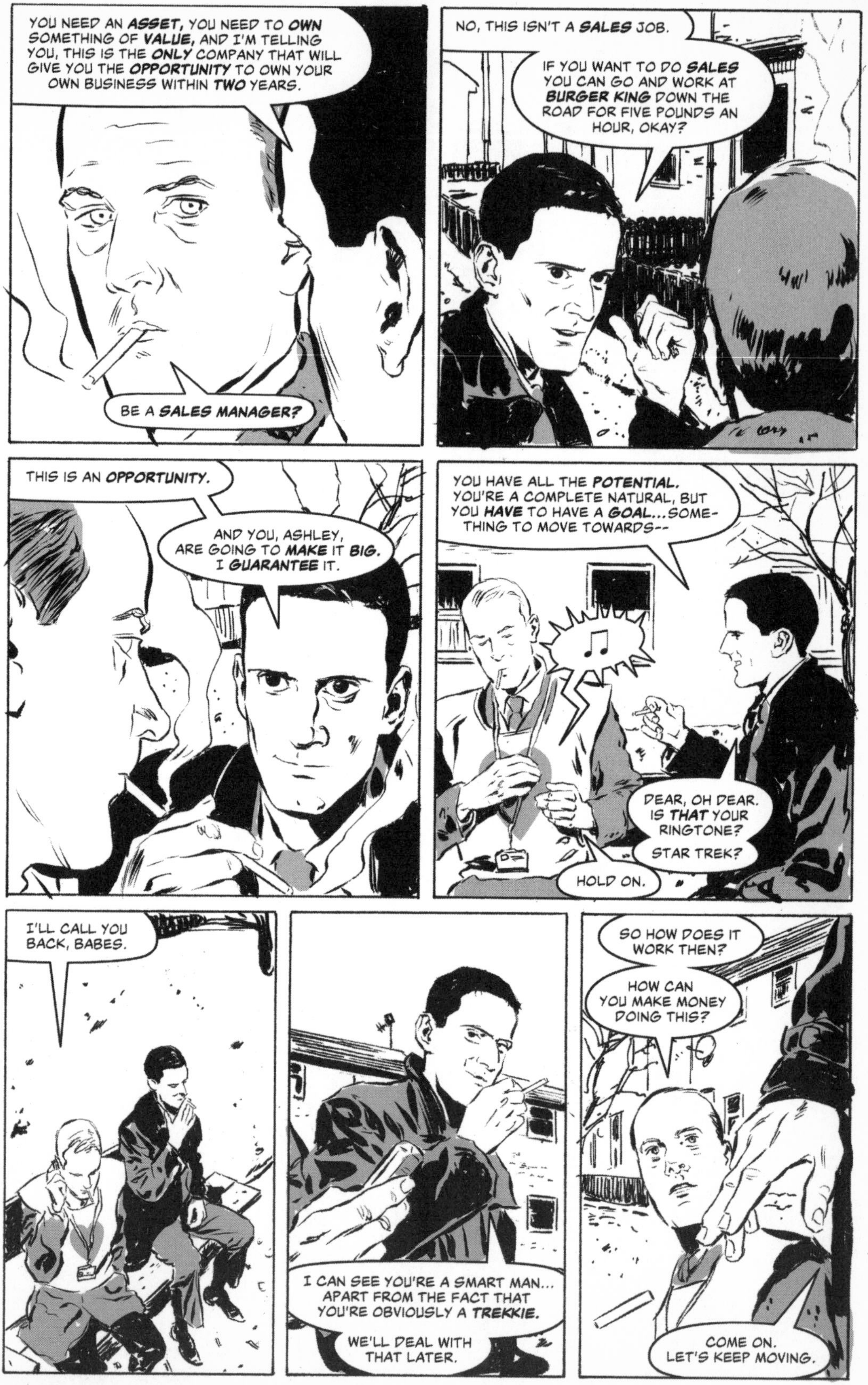
YOU NEED AN ASSET, YOU NEED TO OWN SOMETHING OF VALUE, AND I'M TELLING YOU, THIS IS THE ONLY COMPANY THAT WILL GIVE YOU THE OPPORTUNITY TO OWN YOUR OWN BUSINESS WITHIN TWO YEARS.
BE A SALES MANAGER?
NO, THIS ISN'T A SALES JOB.
IF YOU WANT TO DO SALES YOU CAN GO AND WORK AT BURGER KING DOWN THE ROAD FOR FIVE POUNDS AN HOUR, OKAY?
THIS IS AN OPPORTUNITY.
AND YOU, ASHLEY, ARE GOING TO MAKE IT BIG. I GUARANTEE IT.
YOU HAVE ALL THE POTENTIAL. YOU'RE A COMPLETE NATURAL, BUT YOU HAVE TO HAVE A GOAL...SOMETHING TO MOVE TOWARDS--
♫
DEAR, OH DEAR. IS THAT YOUR RINGTONE?
STAR TREK?
HOLD ON.
I'LL CALL YOU BACK, BABES.
I CAN SEE YOU'RE A SMART MAN... APART FROM THE FACT THAT YOU'RE OBVIOUSLY A TREKKIE.
WE'LL DEAL WITH THAT LATER.
SO HOW DOES IT WORK THEN?
HOW CAN YOU MAKE MONEY DOING THIS?
COME ON. LET'S KEEP MOVING.

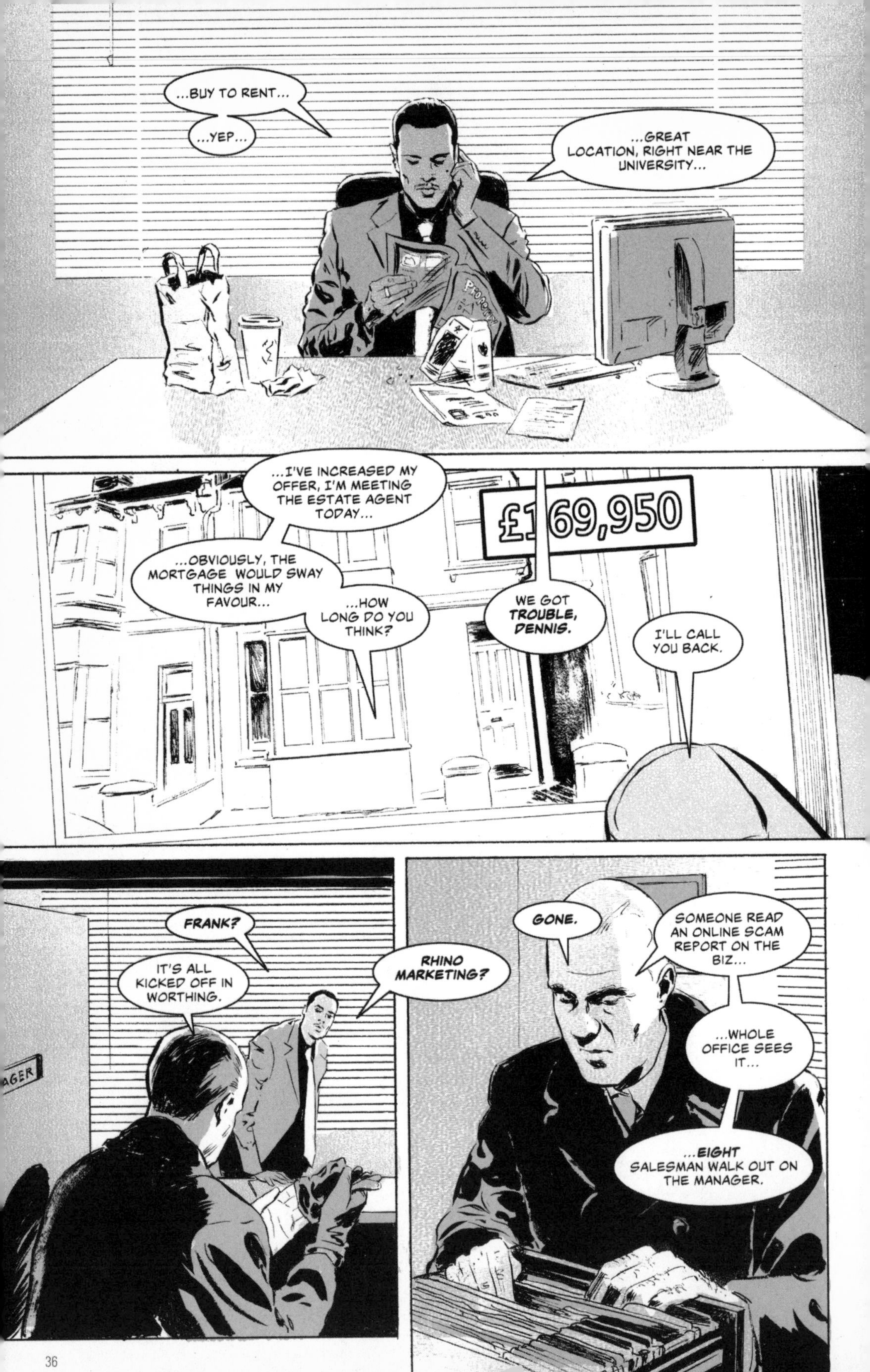
...BUY TO RENT...
...YEP...
...GREAT LOCATION, RIGHT NEAR THE UNIVERSITY...
...I'VE INCREASED MY OFFER, I'M MEETING THE ESTATE AGENT TODAY...
...OBVIOUSLY, THE MORTGAGE WOULD SWAY THINGS IN MY FAVOUR...
...HOW LONG DO YOU THINK?
£169,950
WE GOT **TROUBLE, DENNIS.**
I'LL CALL YOU BACK.
**FRANK?**
IT'S ALL KICKED OFF IN WORTHING.
**RHINO MARKETING?**
**GONE.**
SOMEONE READ AN ONLINE SCAM REPORT ON THE BIZ...
...WHOLE OFFICE SEES IT...
...**EIGHT** SALESMAN WALK OUT ON THE MANAGER.

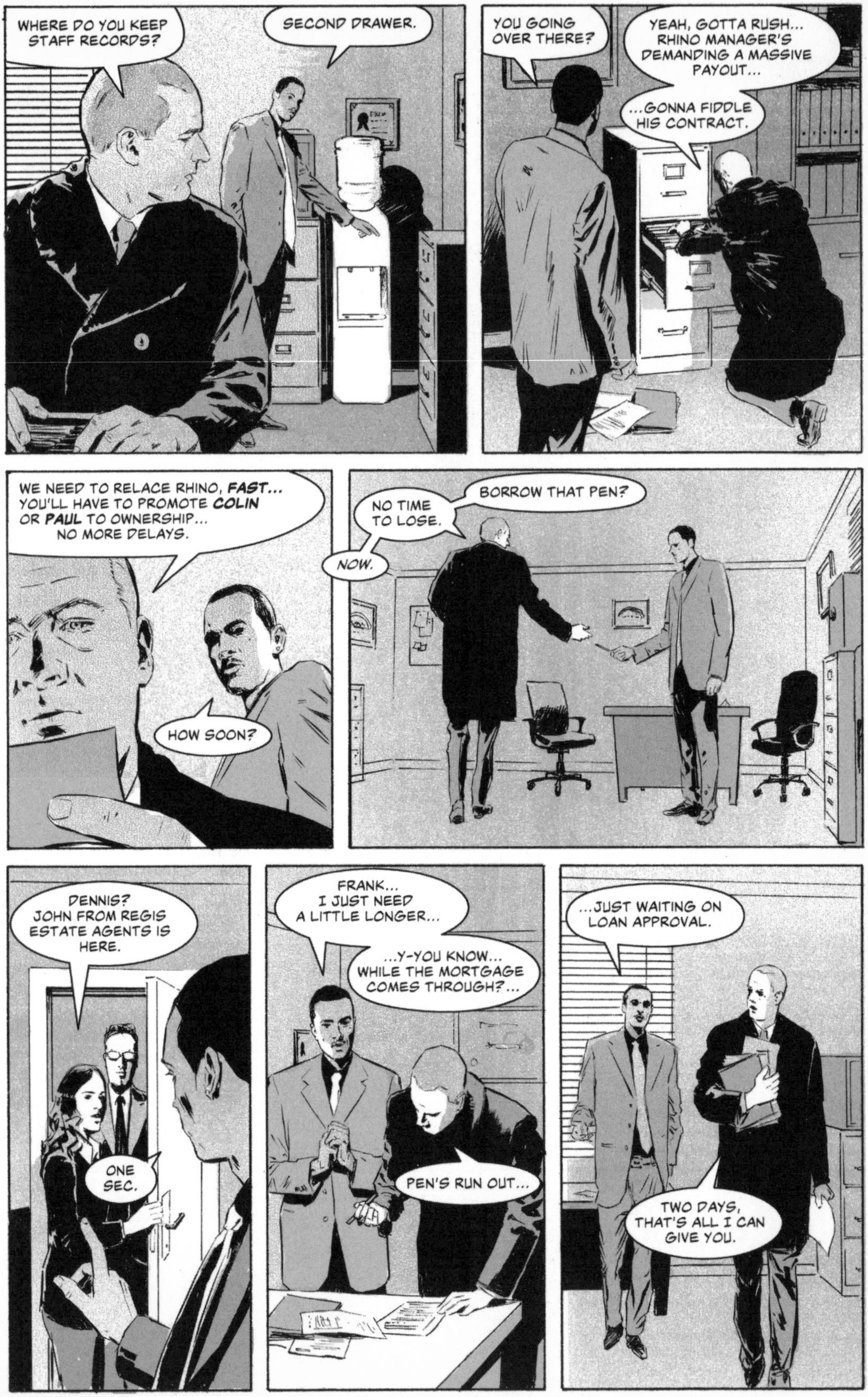
WHERE DO YOU KEEP STAFF RECORDS?
SECOND DRAWER.
YOU GOING OVER THERE?
YEAH, GOTTA RUSH... RHINO MANAGER'S DEMANDING A MASSIVE PAYOUT...
...GONNA FIDDLE HIS CONTRACT.
WE NEED TO RELACE RHINO, FAST... YOU'LL HAVE TO PROMOTE COLIN OR PAUL TO OWNERSHIP... NO MORE DELAYS.
HOW SOON?
NO TIME TO LOSE.
NOW.
BORROW THAT PEN?
DENNIS? JOHN FROM REGIS ESTATE AGENTS IS HERE.
ONE SEC.
FRANK... I JUST NEED A LITTLE LONGER...
...Y-YOU KNOW... WHILE THE MORTGAGE COMES THROUGH?...
PEN'S RUN OUT...
...JUST WAITING ON LOAN APPROVAL.
TWO DAYS, THAT'S ALL I CAN GIVE YOU.

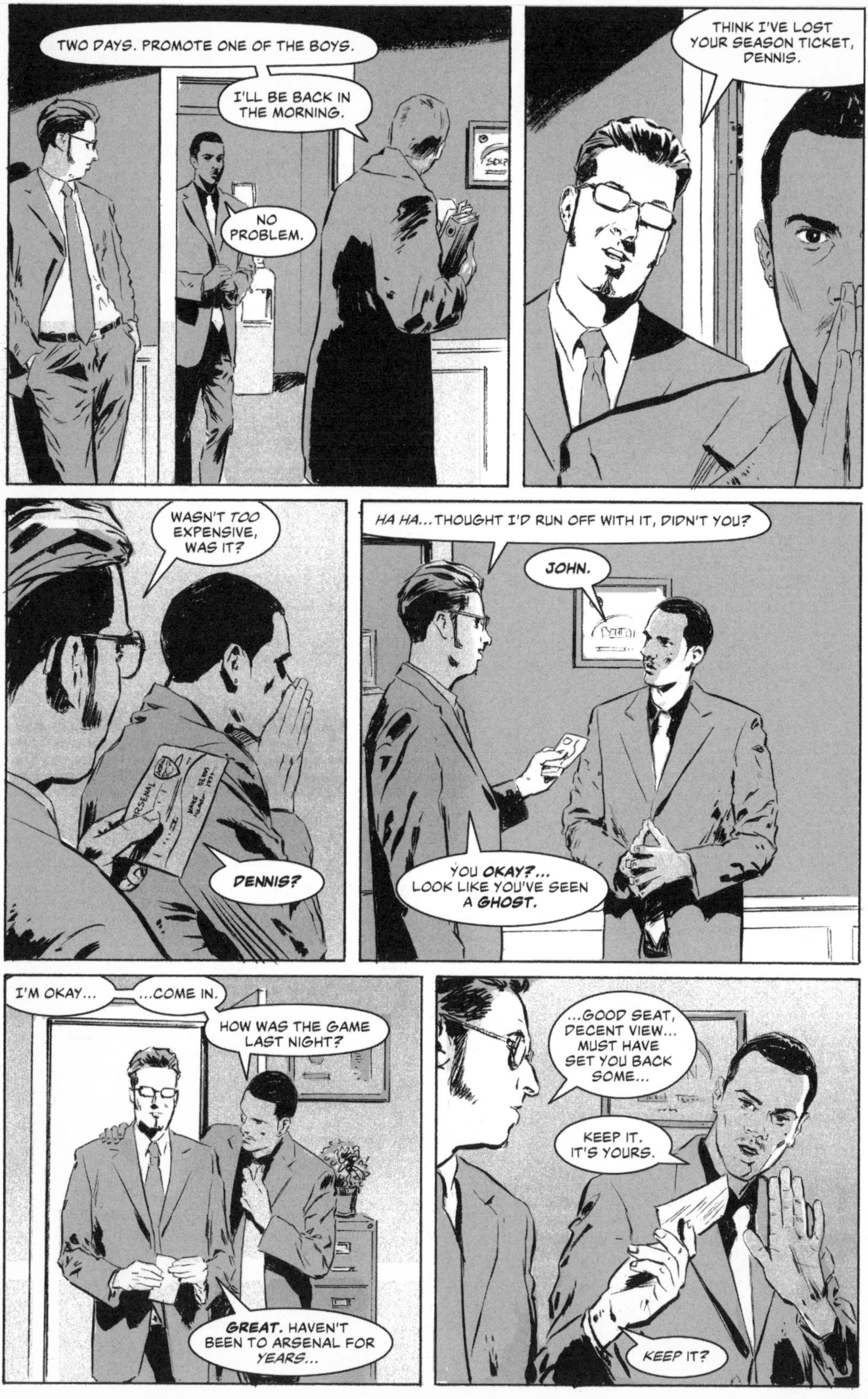
TWO DAYS. PROMOTE ONE OF THE BOYS.
I'LL BE BACK IN THE MORNING.
NO PROBLEM.
THINK I'VE LOST YOUR SEASON TICKET, DENNIS.
WASN'T *TOO* EXPENSIVE, WAS IT?
**DENNIS?**
*HA HA...* THOUGHT I'D RUN OFF WITH IT, DIDN'T YOU?
**JOHN.**
YOU **OKAY?...** LOOK LIKE YOU'VE SEEN A **GHOST.**
I'M OKAY...
...COME IN.
HOW WAS THE GAME LAST NIGHT?
**GREAT.** HAVEN'T BEEN TO ARSENAL FOR *YEARS...*
...GOOD SEAT, DECENT VIEW... MUST HAVE SET YOU BACK SOME...
KEEP IT. IT'S YOURS.
KEEP IT?

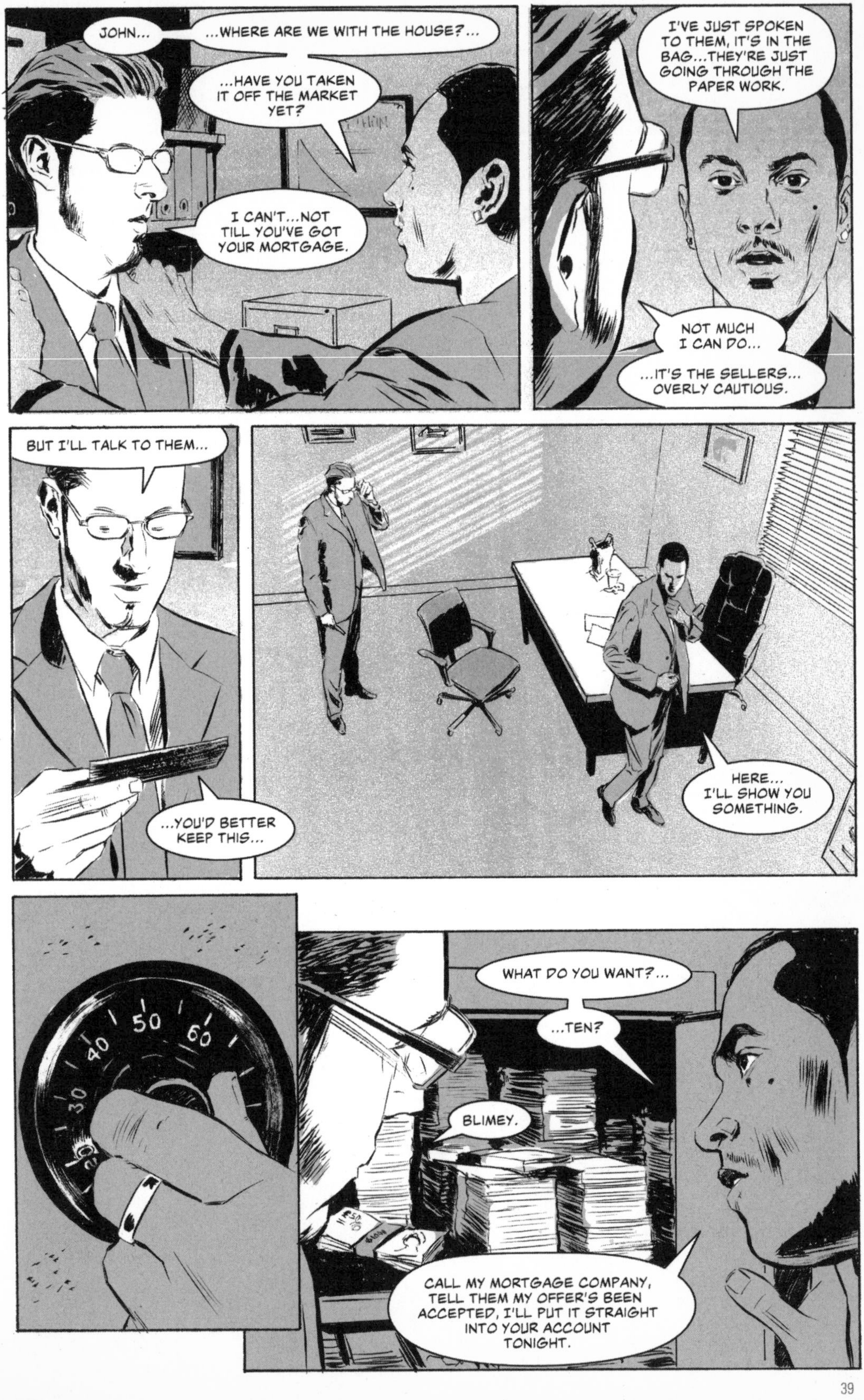
JOHN...
...WHERE ARE WE WITH THE HOUSE?...
...HAVE YOU TAKEN IT OFF THE MARKET YET?
I CAN'T...NOT TILL YOU'VE GOT YOUR MORTGAGE.
I'VE JUST SPOKEN TO THEM, IT'S IN THE BAG...THEY'RE JUST GOING THROUGH THE PAPER WORK.
NOT MUCH I CAN DO...
...IT'S THE SELLERS... OVERLY CAUTIOUS.
BUT I'LL TALK TO THEM...
...YOU'D BETTER KEEP THIS...
HERE... I'LL SHOW YOU SOMETHING.
WHAT DO YOU WANT?...
...TEN?
BLIMEY.
CALL MY MORTGAGE COMPANY, TELL THEM MY OFFER'S BEEN ACCEPTED, I'LL PUT IT STRAIGHT INTO YOUR ACCOUNT TONIGHT.

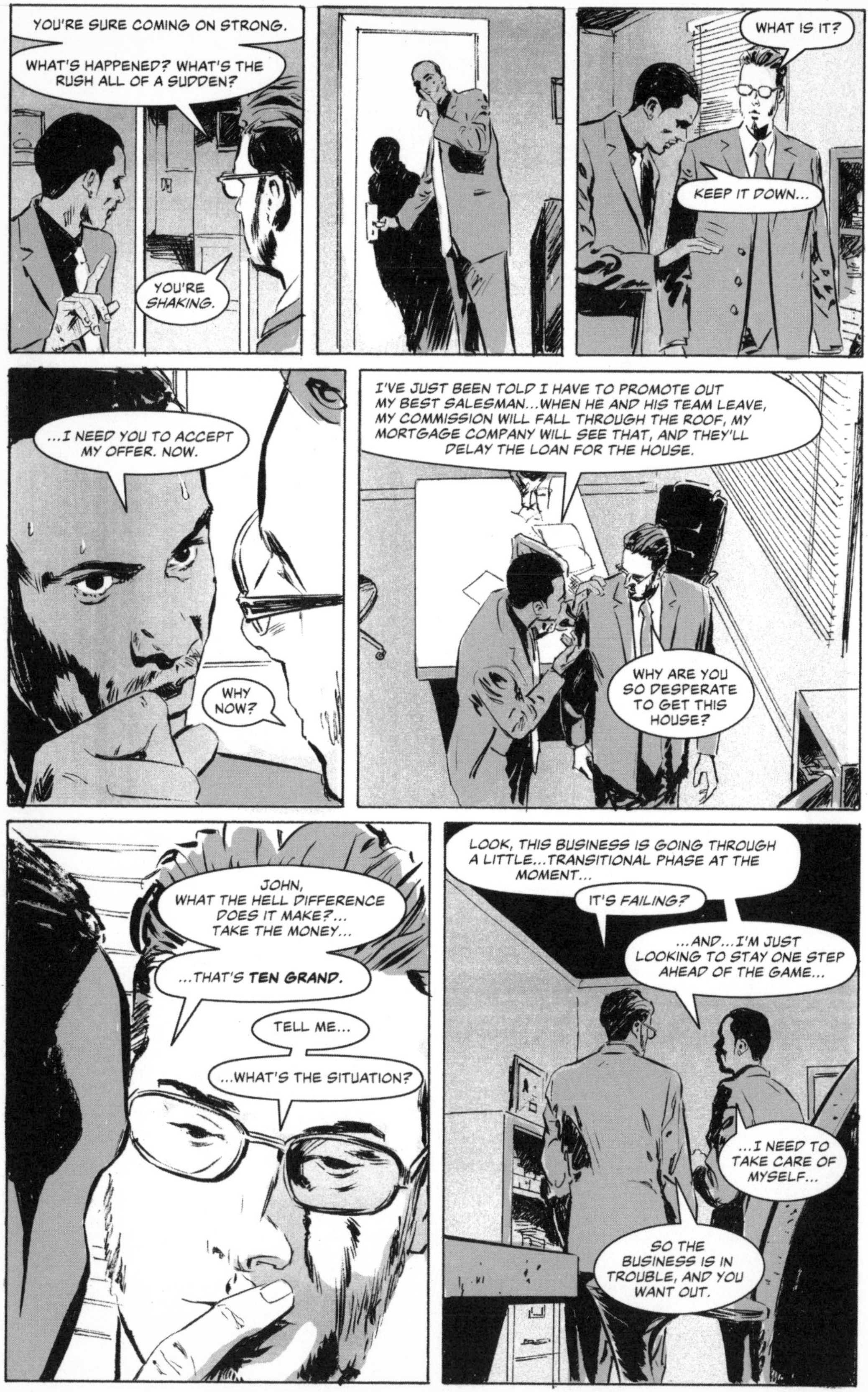
YOU'RE SURE COMING ON STRONG.
WHAT'S HAPPENED? WHAT'S THE RUSH ALL OF A SUDDEN?
YOU'RE SHAKING.
WHAT IS IT?
KEEP IT DOWN...
...I NEED YOU TO ACCEPT MY OFFER. NOW.
WHY NOW?
I'VE JUST BEEN TOLD I HAVE TO PROMOTE OUT MY BEST SALESMAN...WHEN HE AND HIS TEAM LEAVE, MY COMMISSION WILL FALL THROUGH THE ROOF, MY MORTGAGE COMPANY WILL SEE THAT, AND THEY'LL DELAY THE LOAN FOR THE HOUSE.
WHY ARE YOU SO DESPERATE TO GET THIS HOUSE?
JOHN, WHAT THE HELL DIFFERENCE DOES IT MAKE?... TAKE THE MONEY...
...THAT'S **TEN GRAND.**
TELL ME...
...WHAT'S THE SITUATION?
LOOK, THIS BUSINESS IS GOING THROUGH A LITTLE...TRANSITIONAL PHASE AT THE MOMENT...
IT'S FAILING?
...AND...I'M JUST LOOKING TO STAY ONE STEP AHEAD OF THE GAME...
...I NEED TO TAKE CARE OF MYSELF...
SO THE BUSINESS IS IN TROUBLE, AND YOU WANT OUT.

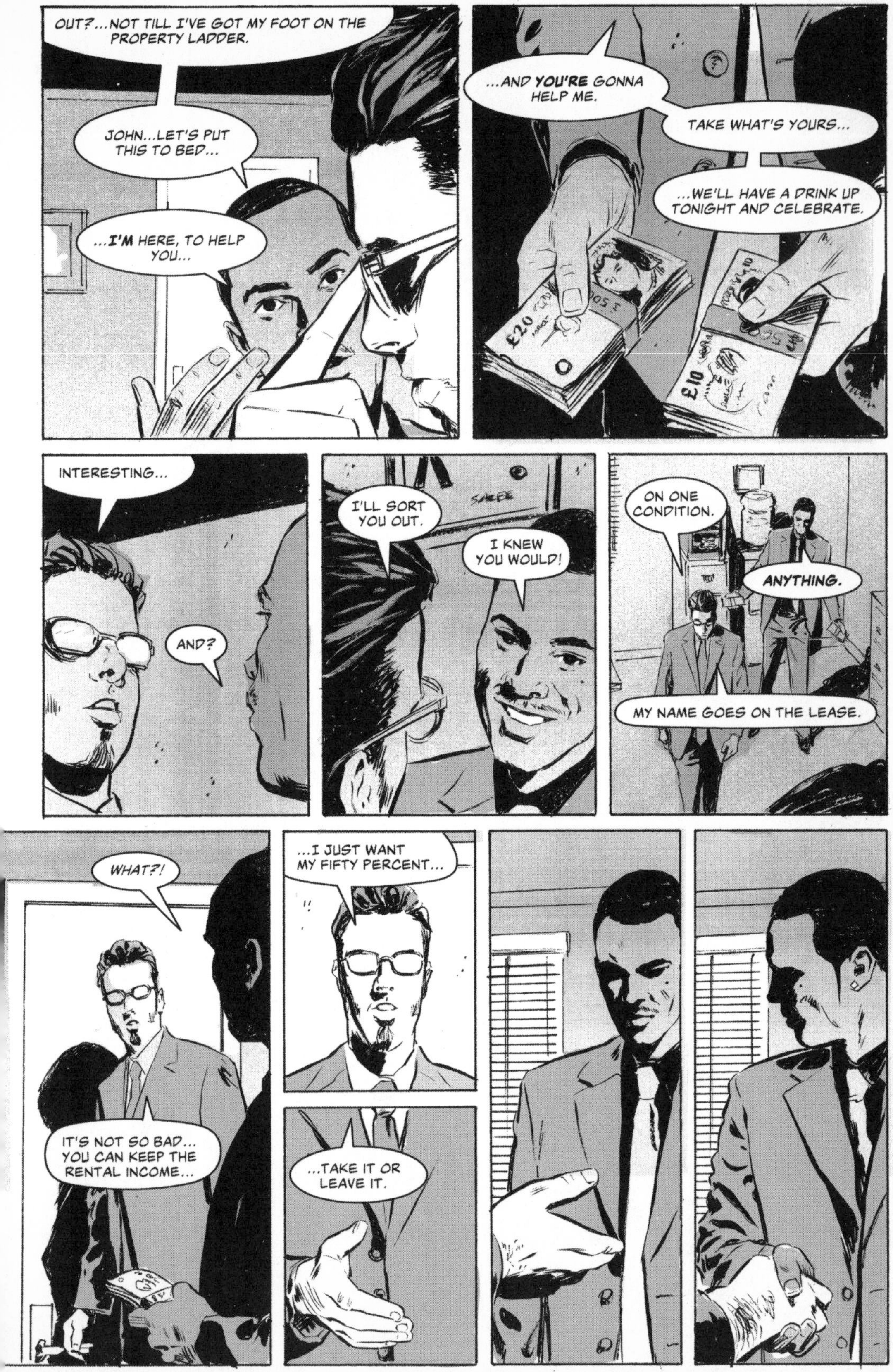
OUT?...NOT TILL I'VE GOT MY FOOT ON THE PROPERTY LADDER.
JOHN...LET'S PUT THIS TO BED...
...I'M HERE, TO HELP YOU...
...AND YOU'RE GONNA HELP ME.
TAKE WHAT'S YOURS...
...WE'LL HAVE A DRINK UP TONIGHT AND CELEBRATE.
INTERESTING...
AND?
I'LL SORT YOU OUT.
I KNEW YOU WOULD!
ON ONE CONDITION.
ANYTHING.
MY NAME GOES ON THE LEASE.
WHAT?!
IT'S NOT SO BAD... YOU CAN KEEP THE RENTAL INCOME...
...I JUST WANT MY FIFTY PERCENT...
...TAKE IT OR LEAVE IT.

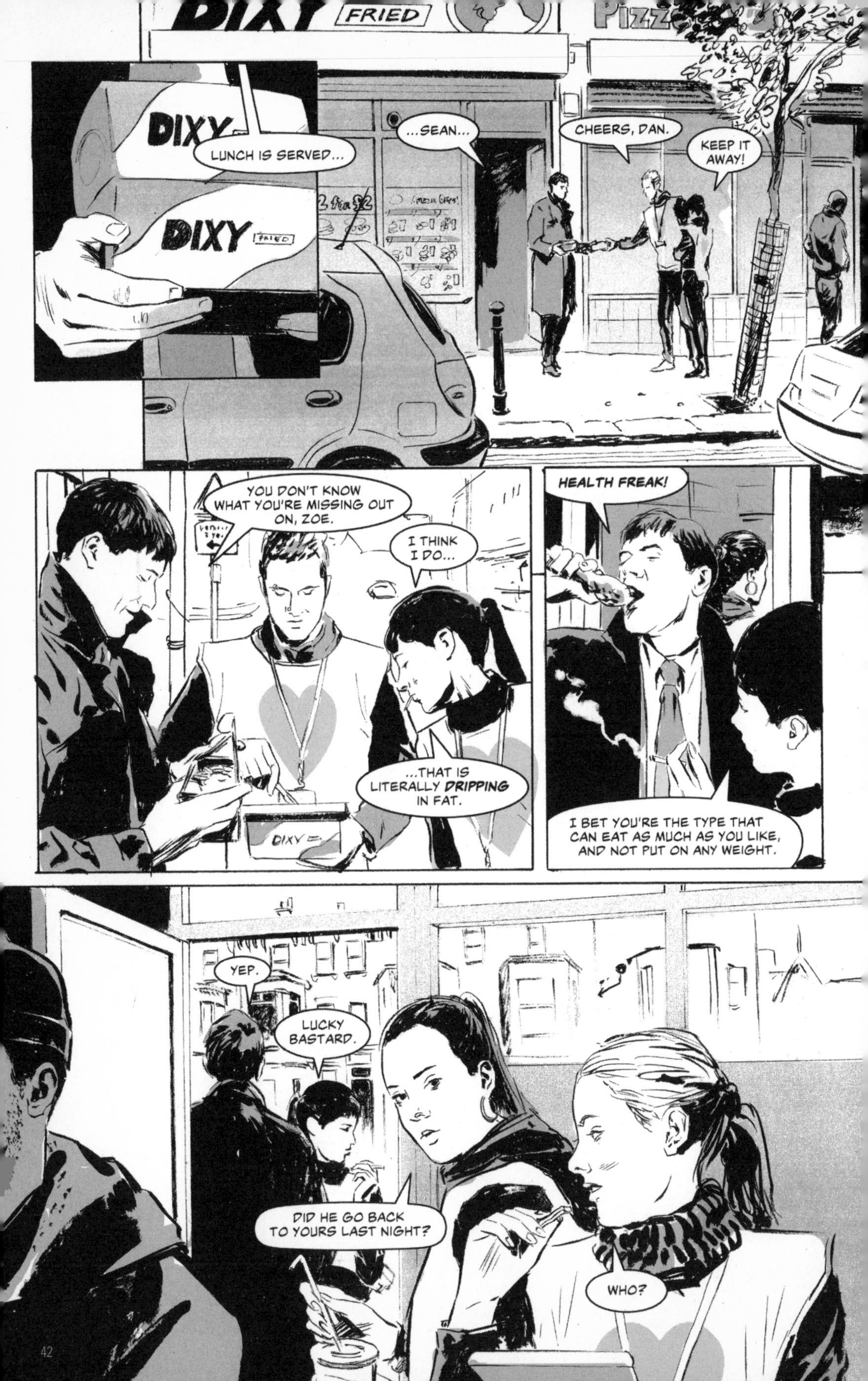
DIXY
FRIED
DIXY
LUNCH IS SERVED...
DIXY
...SEAN...
CHEERS, DAN.
KEEP IT AWAY!
YOU DON'T KNOW WHAT YOU'RE MISSING OUT ON, ZOE.
I THINK I DO...
...THAT IS LITERALLY DRIPPING IN FAT.
DIXY
HEALTH FREAK!
I BET YOU'RE THE TYPE THAT CAN EAT AS MUCH AS YOU LIKE, AND NOT PUT ON ANY WEIGHT.
YEP.
LUCKY BASTARD.
DID HE GO BACK TO YOURS LAST NIGHT?
WHO?

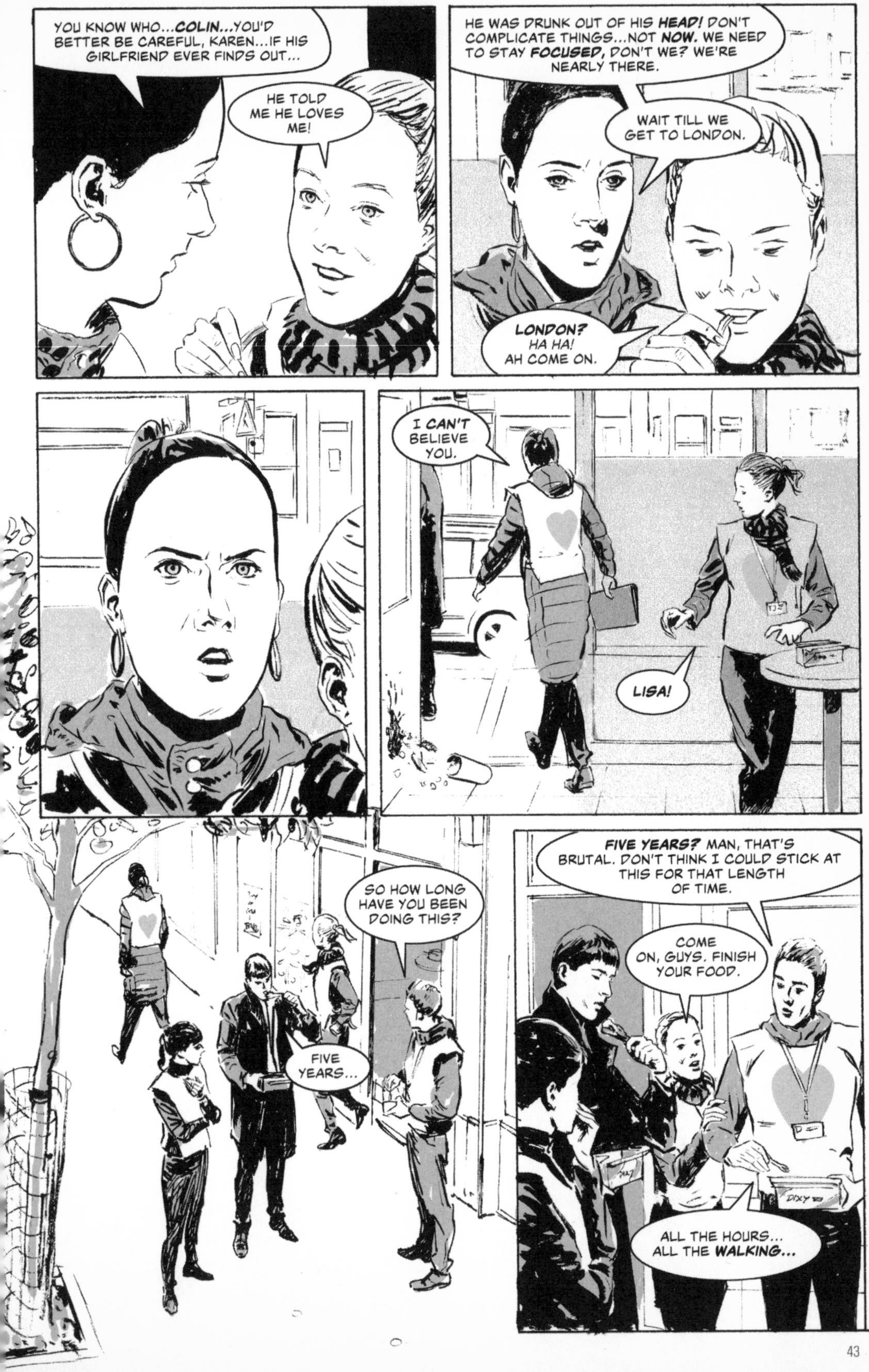
YOU KNOW WHO...COLIN...YOU'D BETTER BE CAREFUL, KAREN...IF HIS GIRLFRIEND EVER FINDS OUT...
HE TOLD ME HE LOVES ME!
HE WAS DRUNK OUT OF HIS HEAD! DON'T COMPLICATE THINGS...NOT NOW. WE NEED TO STAY FOCUSED, DON'T WE? WE'RE NEARLY THERE.
WAIT TILL WE GET TO LONDON.
LONDON? HA HA! AH COME ON.
I CAN'T BELIEVE YOU.
LISA!
SO HOW LONG HAVE YOU BEEN DOING THIS?
FIVE YEARS...
FIVE YEARS? MAN, THAT'S BRUTAL. DON'T THINK I COULD STICK AT THIS FOR THAT LENGTH OF TIME.
COME ON, GUYS. FINISH YOUR FOOD.
ALL THE HOURS... ALL THE WALKING...

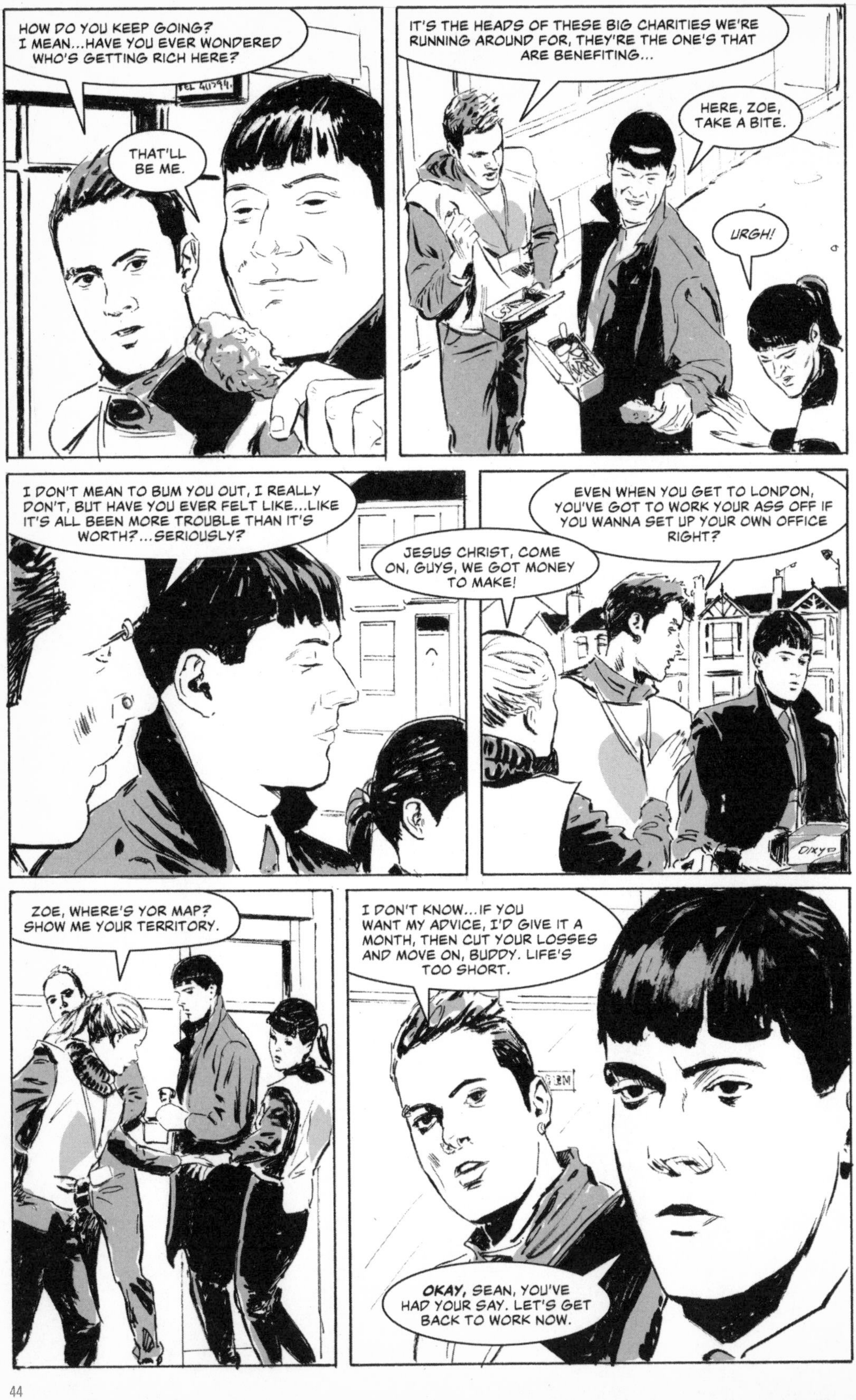

HOW DO YOU KEEP GOING? I MEAN...HAVE YOU EVER WONDERED WHO'S GETTING RICH HERE?
THAT'LL BE ME.
IT'S THE HEADS OF THESE BIG CHARITIES WE'RE RUNNING AROUND FOR, THEY'RE THE ONE'S THAT ARE BENEFITING...
HERE, ZOE, TAKE A BITE.
URGH!
I DON'T MEAN TO BUM YOU OUT, I REALLY DON'T, BUT HAVE YOU EVER FELT LIKE...LIKE IT'S ALL BEEN MORE TROUBLE THAN IT'S WORTH?...SERIOUSLY?
EVEN WHEN YOU GET TO LONDON, YOU'VE GOT TO WORK YOUR ASS OFF IF YOU WANNA SET UP YOUR OWN OFFICE RIGHT?
JESUS CHRIST, COME ON, GUYS, WE GOT MONEY TO MAKE!
ZOE, WHERE'S YOR MAP? SHOW ME YOUR TERRITORY.
I DON'T KNOW...IF YOU WANT MY ADVICE, I'D GIVE IT A MONTH, THEN CUT YOUR LOSSES AND MOVE ON, BUDDY. LIFE'S TOO SHORT.
OKAY, SEAN, YOU'VE HAD YOUR SAY. LET'S GET BACK TO WORK NOW.

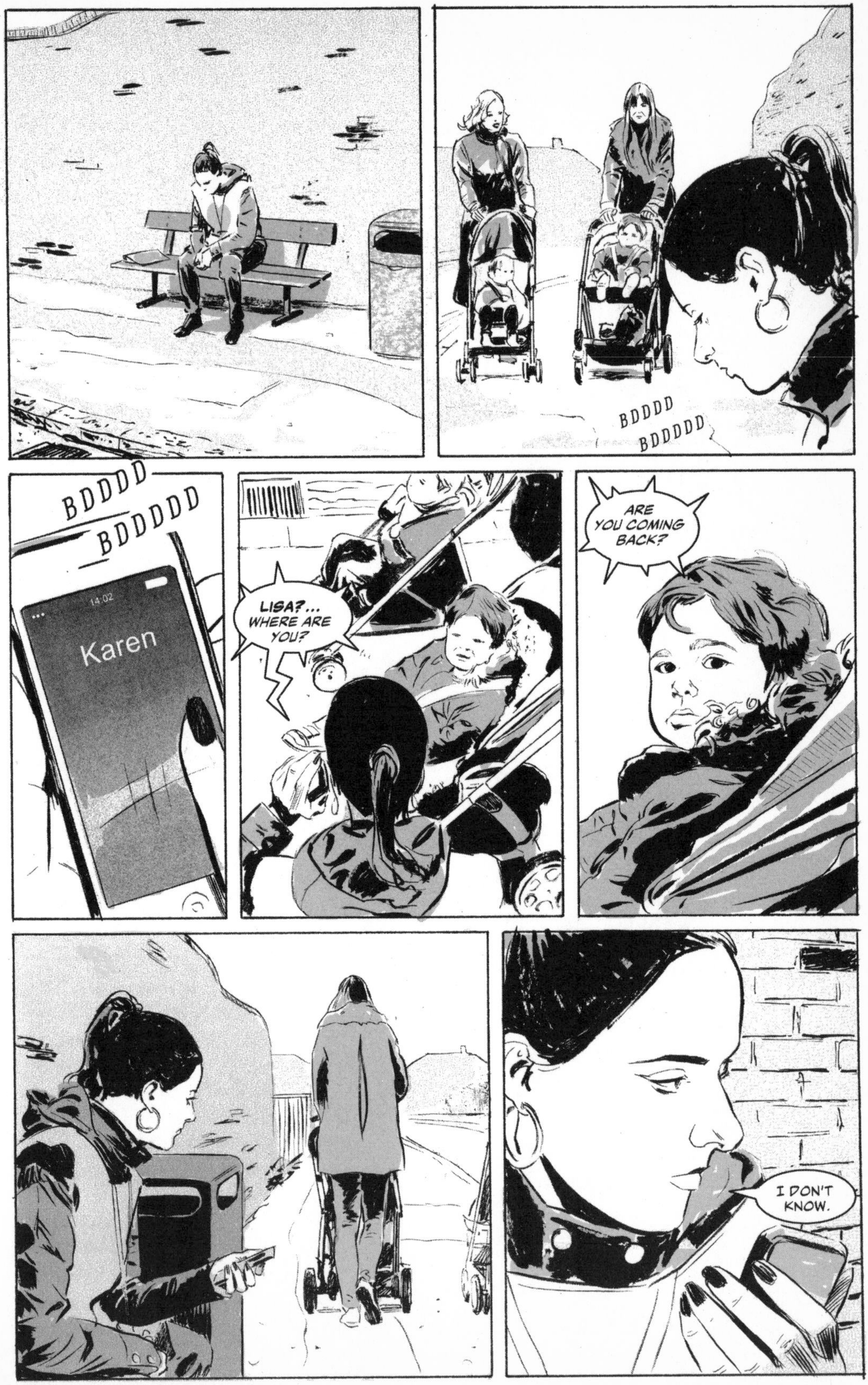
BDDDD
BDDDDD
BDDDD
BDDDDD
14:02
Karen
LISA?... WHERE ARE YOU?
ARE YOU COMING BACK?
I DON'T KNOW.

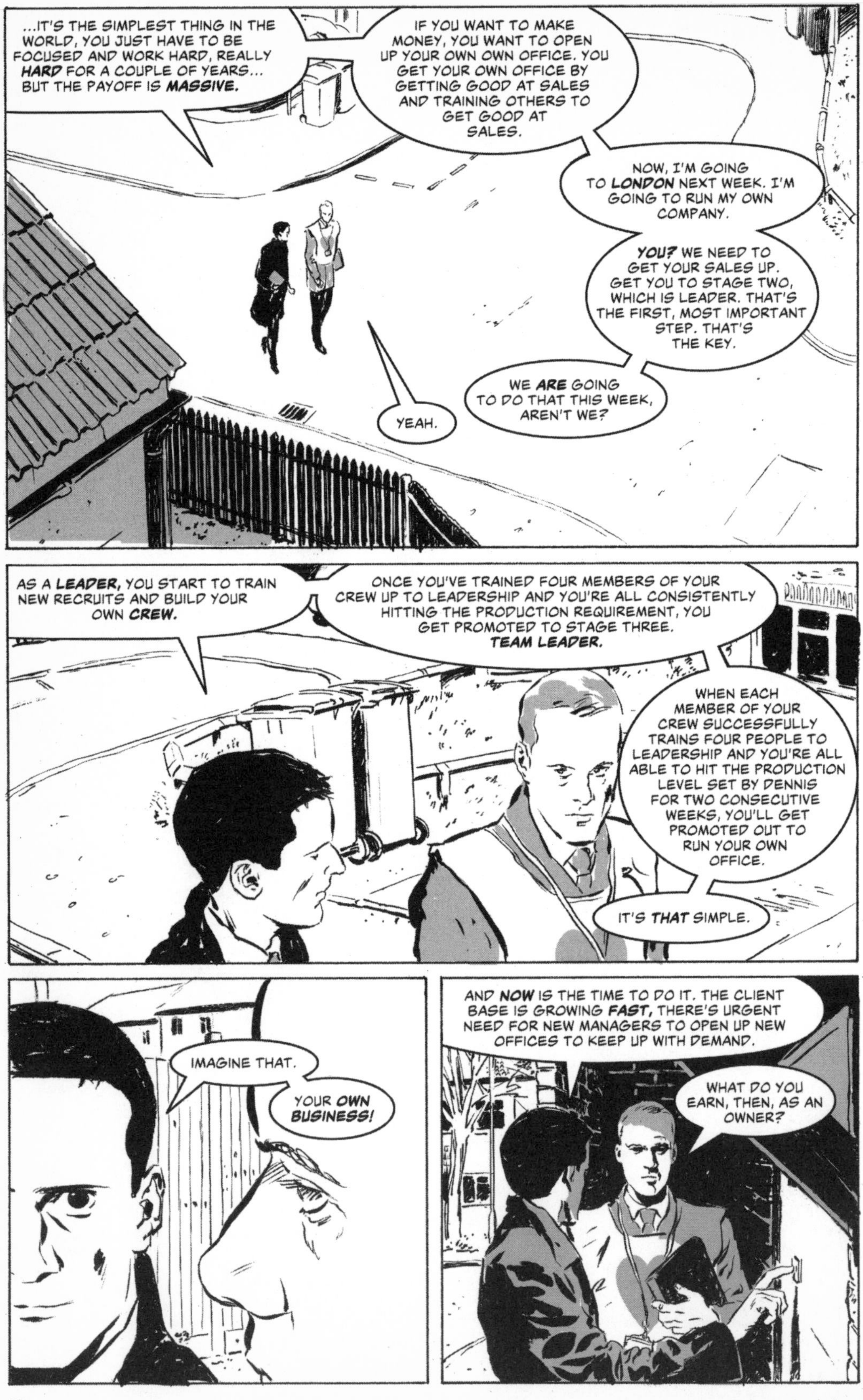
...IT'S THE SIMPLEST THING IN THE WORLD, YOU JUST HAVE TO BE FOCUSED AND WORK HARD, REALLY HARD FOR A COUPLE OF YEARS... BUT THE PAYOFF IS MASSIVE.
IF YOU WANT TO MAKE MONEY, YOU WANT TO OPEN UP YOUR OWN OWN OFFICE. YOU GET YOUR OWN OFFICE BY GETTING GOOD AT SALES AND TRAINING OTHERS TO GET GOOD AT SALES.
NOW, I'M GOING TO LONDON NEXT WEEK. I'M GOING TO RUN MY OWN COMPANY.
YOU? WE NEED TO GET YOUR SALES UP. GET YOU TO STAGE TWO, WHICH IS LEADER. THAT'S THE FIRST, MOST IMPORTANT STEP. THAT'S THE KEY.
WE ARE GOING TO DO THAT THIS WEEK, AREN'T WE?
YEAH.
AS A LEADER, YOU START TO TRAIN NEW RECRUITS AND BUILD YOUR OWN CREW.
ONCE YOU'VE TRAINED FOUR MEMBERS OF YOUR CREW UP TO LEADERSHIP AND YOU'RE ALL CONSISTENTLY HITTING THE PRODUCTION REQUIREMENT, YOU GET PROMOTED TO STAGE THREE. TEAM LEADER.
WHEN EACH MEMBER OF YOUR CREW SUCCESSFULLY TRAINS FOUR PEOPLE TO LEADERSHIP AND YOU'RE ALL ABLE TO HIT THE PRODUCTION LEVEL SET BY DENNIS FOR TWO CONSECUTIVE WEEKS, YOU'LL GET PROMOTED OUT TO RUN YOUR OWN OFFICE.
IT'S THAT SIMPLE.
IMAGINE THAT.
YOUR OWN BUSINESS!
AND NOW IS THE TIME TO DO IT. THE CLIENT BASE IS GROWING FAST, THERE'S URGENT NEED FOR NEW MANAGERS TO OPEN UP NEW OFFICES TO KEEP UP WITH DEMAND.
WHAT DO YOU EARN, THEN, AS AN OWNER?

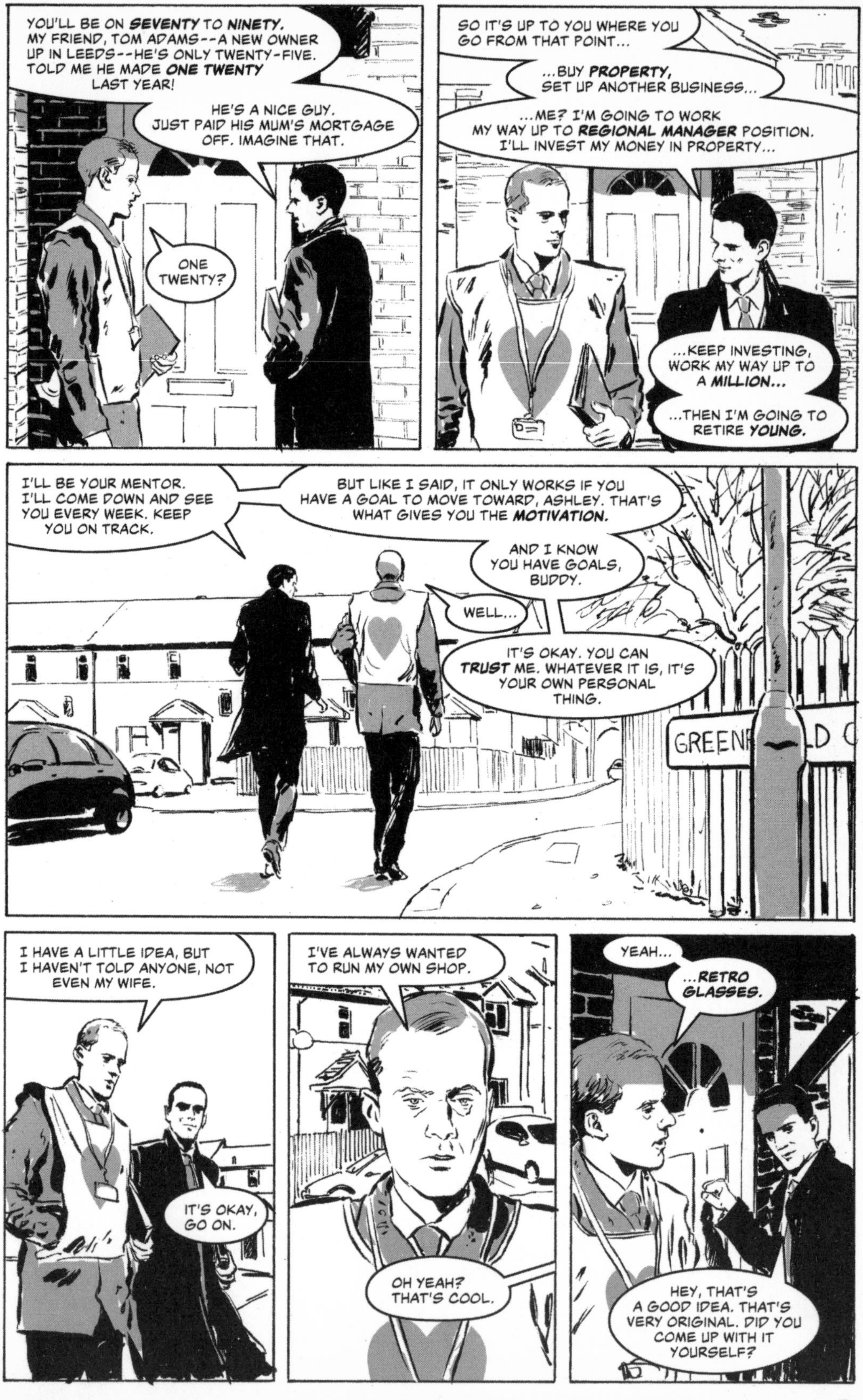
YOU'LL BE ON SEVENTY TO NINETY. MY FRIEND, TOM ADAMS--A NEW OWNER UP IN LEEDS--HE'S ONLY TWENTY-FIVE. TOLD ME HE MADE ONE TWENTY LAST YEAR!
HE'S A NICE GUY. JUST PAID HIS MUM'S MORTGAGE OFF. IMAGINE THAT.
ONE TWENTY?
SO IT'S UP TO YOU WHERE YOU GO FROM THAT POINT...
...BUY PROPERTY, SET UP ANOTHER BUSINESS...
...ME? I'M GOING TO WORK MY WAY UP TO REGIONAL MANAGER POSITION. I'LL INVEST MY MONEY IN PROPERTY...
...KEEP INVESTING, WORK MY WAY UP TO A MILLION...
...THEN I'M GOING TO RETIRE YOUNG.
I'LL BE YOUR MENTOR. I'LL COME DOWN AND SEE YOU EVERY WEEK. KEEP YOU ON TRACK.
BUT LIKE I SAID, IT ONLY WORKS IF YOU HAVE A GOAL TO MOVE TOWARD, ASHLEY. THAT'S WHAT GIVES YOU THE MOTIVATION.
AND I KNOW YOU HAVE GOALS, BUDDY.
WELL...
IT'S OKAY. YOU CAN TRUST ME. WHATEVER IT IS, IT'S YOUR OWN PERSONAL THING.
GREENF
I HAVE A LITTLE IDEA, BUT I HAVEN'T TOLD ANYONE, NOT EVEN MY WIFE.
IT'S OKAY, GO ON.
I'VE ALWAYS WANTED TO RUN MY OWN SHOP.
OH YEAH? THAT'S COOL.
YEAH...
...RETRO GLASSES.
HEY, THAT'S A GOOD IDEA. THAT'S VERY ORIGINAL. DID YOU COME UP WITH IT YOURSELF?

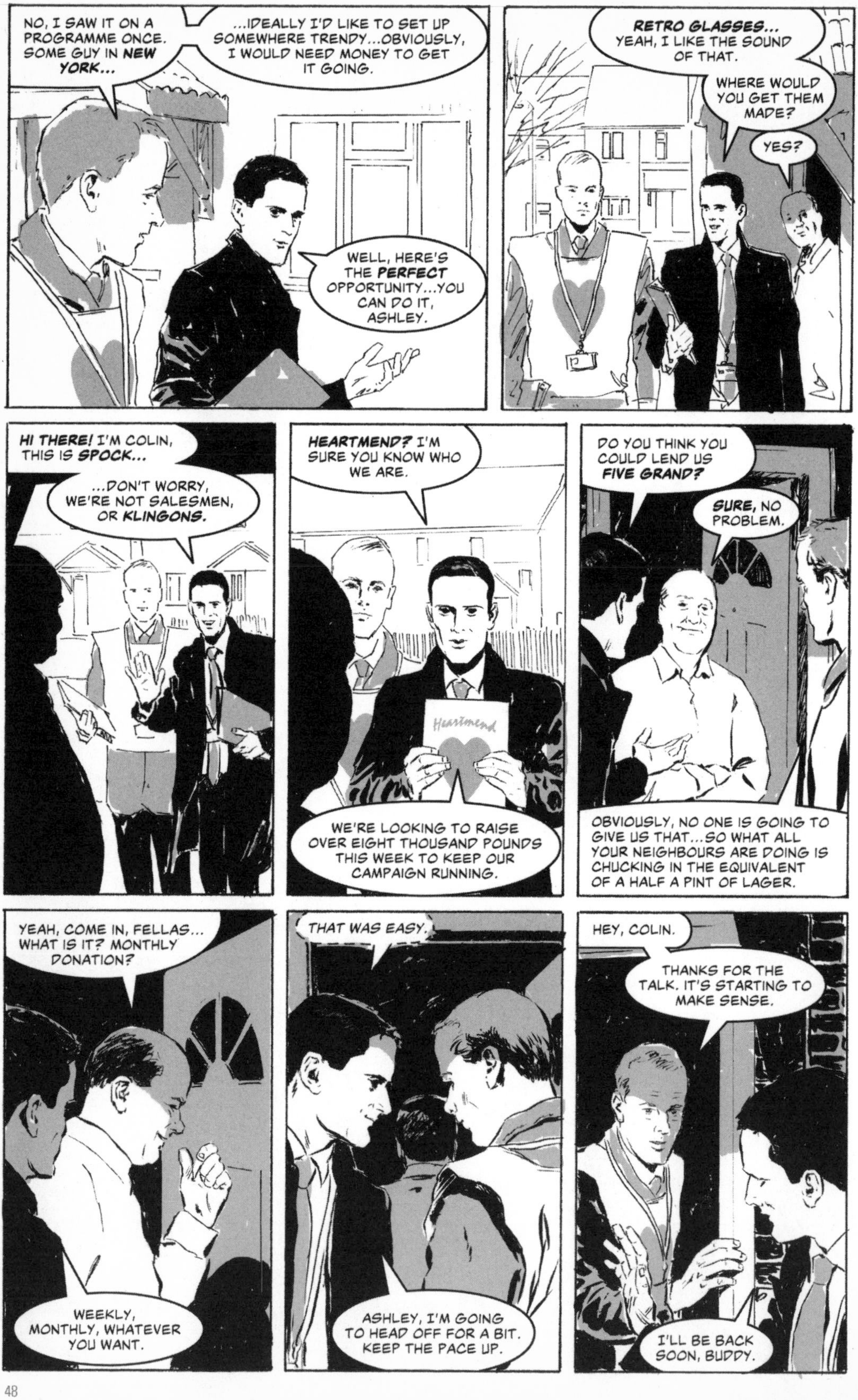
NO, I SAW IT ON A PROGRAMME ONCE. SOME GUY IN NEW YORK...
...IDEALLY I'D LIKE TO SET UP SOMEWHERE TRENDY...OBVIOUSLY, I WOULD NEED MONEY TO GET IT GOING.
WELL, HERE'S THE PERFECT OPPORTUNITY...YOU CAN DO IT, ASHLEY.
RETRO GLASSES... YEAH, I LIKE THE SOUND OF THAT.
WHERE WOULD YOU GET THEM MADE?
YES?
HI THERE! I'M COLIN, THIS IS SPOCK...
...DON'T WORRY, WE'RE NOT SALESMEN, OR KLINGONS.
HEARTMEND? I'M SURE YOU KNOW WHO WE ARE.
Heartmend
WE'RE LOOKING TO RAISE OVER EIGHT THOUSAND POUNDS THIS WEEK TO KEEP OUR CAMPAIGN RUNNING.
DO YOU THINK YOU COULD LEND US FIVE GRAND?
SURE, NO PROBLEM.
OBVIOUSLY, NO ONE IS GOING TO GIVE US THAT...SO WHAT ALL YOUR NEIGHBOURS ARE DOING IS CHUCKING IN THE EQUIVALENT OF A HALF A PINT OF LAGER.
YEAH, COME IN, FELLAS... WHAT IS IT? MONTHLY DONATION?
WEEKLY, MONTHLY, WHATEVER YOU WANT.
THAT WAS EASY.
ASHLEY, I'M GOING TO HEAD OFF FOR A BIT. KEEP THE PACE UP.
HEY, COLIN.
THANKS FOR THE TALK. IT'S STARTING TO MAKE SENSE.
I'LL BE BACK SOON, BUDDY.

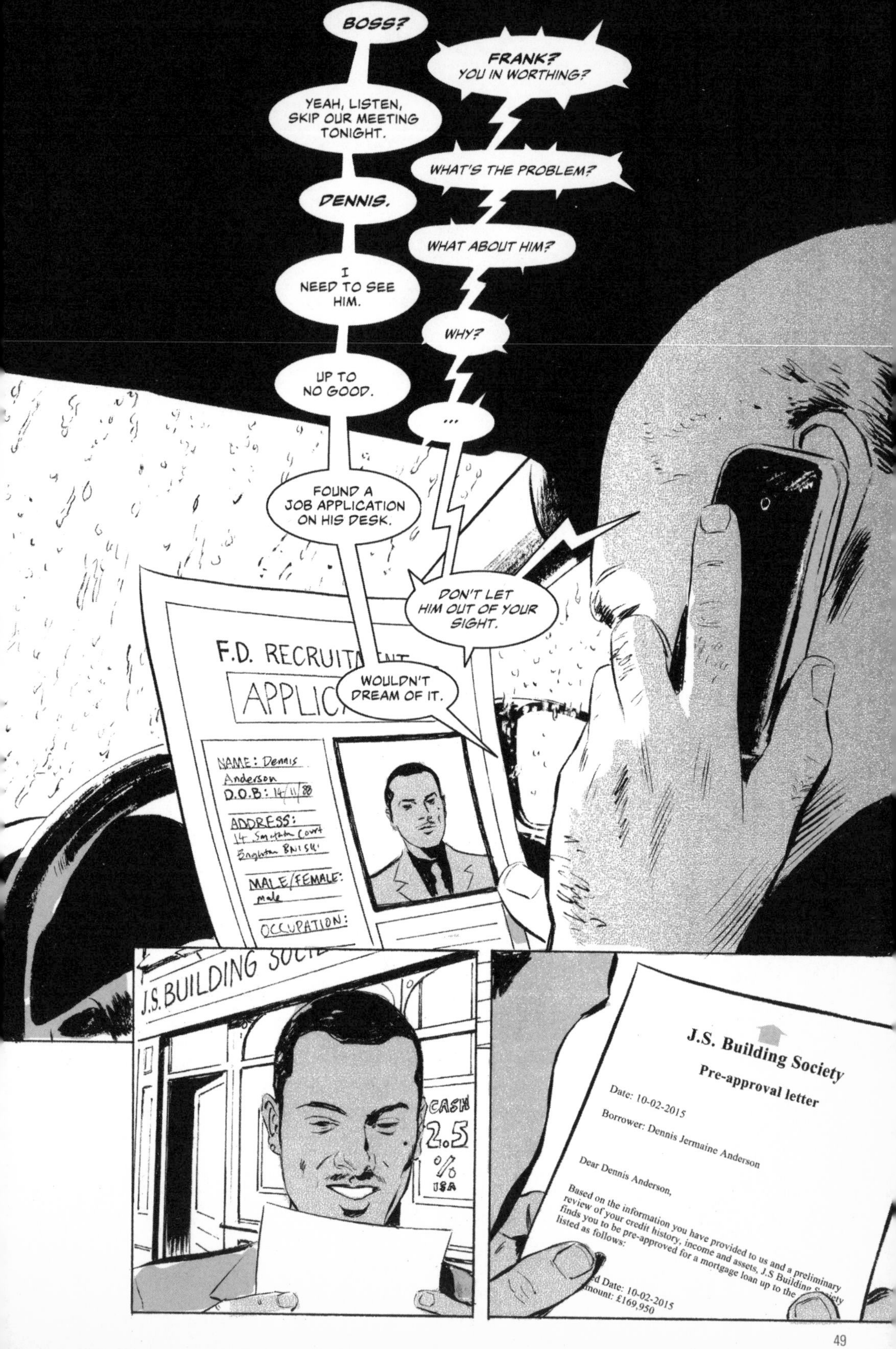
BOSS?
FRANK? YOU IN WORTHING?
YEAH, LISTEN, SKIP OUR MEETING TONIGHT.
WHAT'S THE PROBLEM?
DENNIS.
WHAT ABOUT HIM?
I NEED TO SEE HIM.
WHY?
UP TO NO GOOD.
...
FOUND A JOB APPLICATION ON HIS DESK.
DON'T LET HIM OUT OF YOUR SIGHT.
WOULDN'T DREAM OF IT.
F.D. RECRUITM
APPLIC
NAME: Dennis Anderson
D.O.B: 14/11/88
ADDRESS:
MALE/FEMALE: male
OCCUPATION:
J.S. BUILDING SOCIE
CASH
2.5
%
J.S. Building Society
Pre-approval letter
Date: 10-02-2015
Borrower: Dennis Jermaine Anderson
Dear Dennis Anderson,
Based on the information you have provided to us and a preliminary review of your credit history, income and assets, J.S Building Society finds you to be pre-approved for a mortgage loan up to the
d Date: 10-02-2015
mount: £169,950

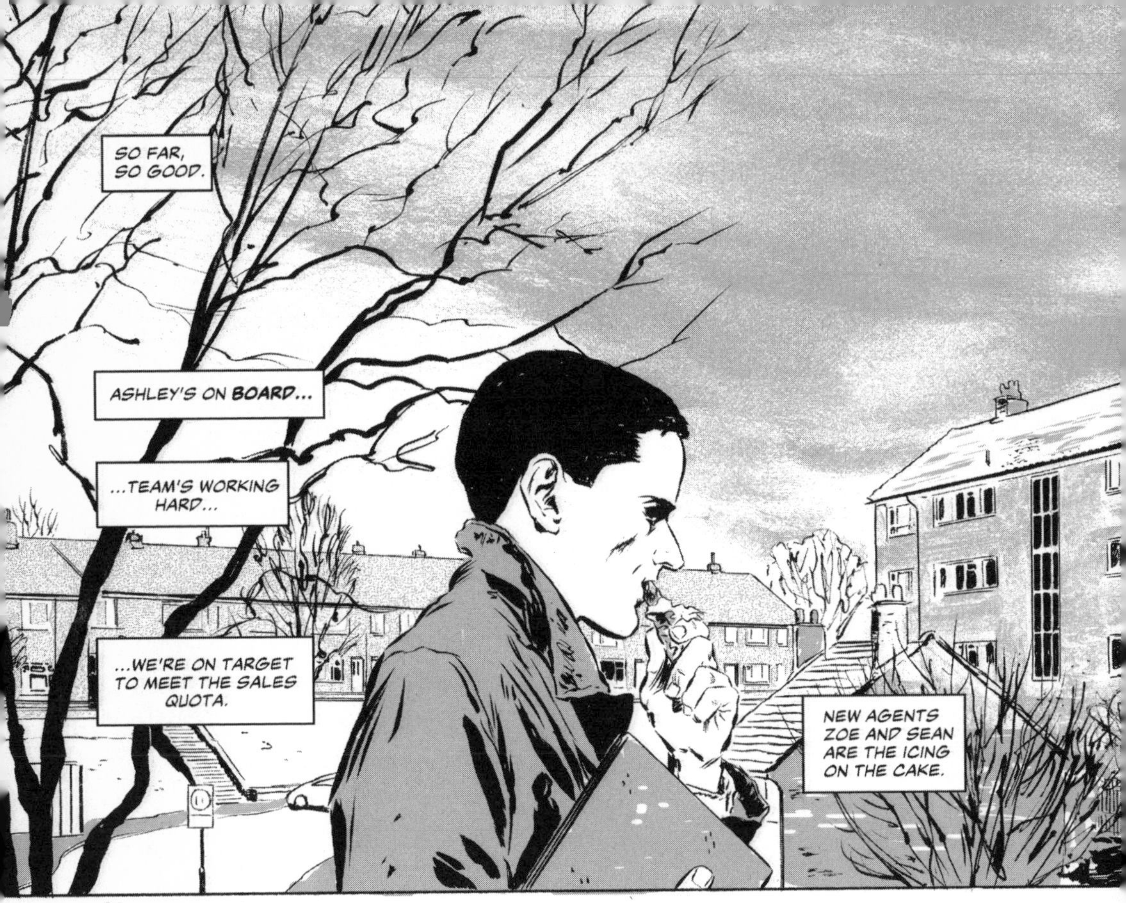
SO FAR, SO GOOD.
ASHLEY'S ON **BOARD...**
...TEAM'S WORKING HARD...
...WE'RE ON TARGET TO MEET THE SALES QUOTA.
NEW AGENTS ZOE AND SEAN ARE THE ICING ON THE CAKE.

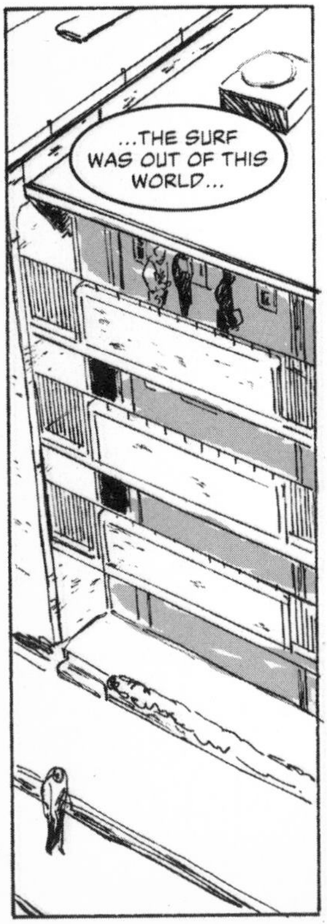
...THE SURF WAS OUT OF THIS WORLD...

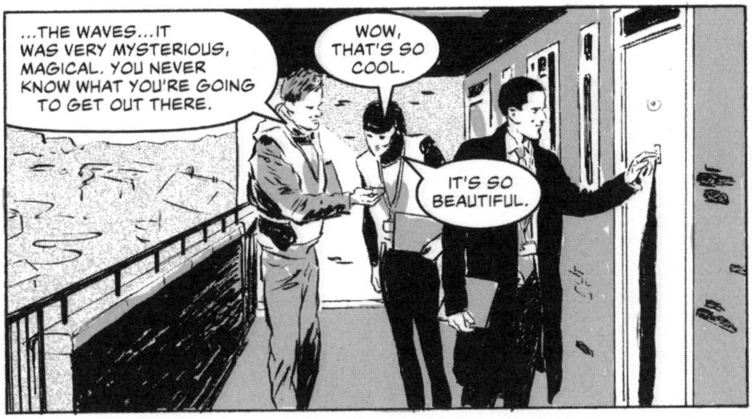
...THE WAVES...IT WAS VERY MYSTERIOUS, MAGICAL. YOU NEVER KNOW WHAT YOU'RE GOING TO GET OUT THERE.
WOW, THAT'S SO COOL.
IT'S SO BEAUTIFUL.

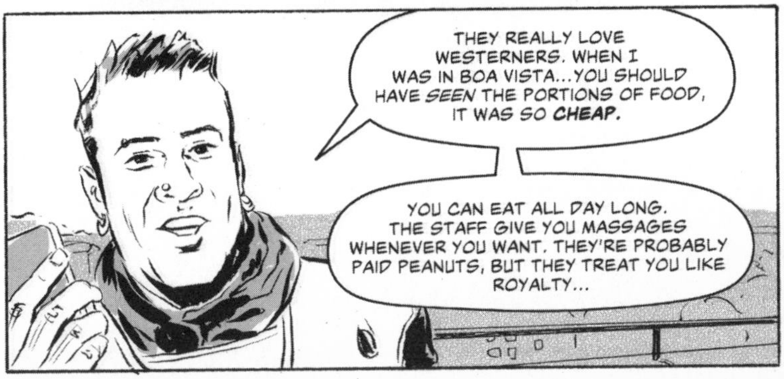
THEY REALLY LOVE WESTERNERS. WHEN I WAS IN BOA VISTA...YOU SHOULD HAVE *SEEN* THE PORTIONS OF FOOD, IT WAS SO **CHEAP.**
YOU CAN EAT ALL DAY LONG. THE STAFF GIVE YOU MASSAGES WHENEVER YOU WANT. THEY'RE PROBABLY PAID PEANUTS, BUT THEY TREAT YOU LIKE ROYALTY...

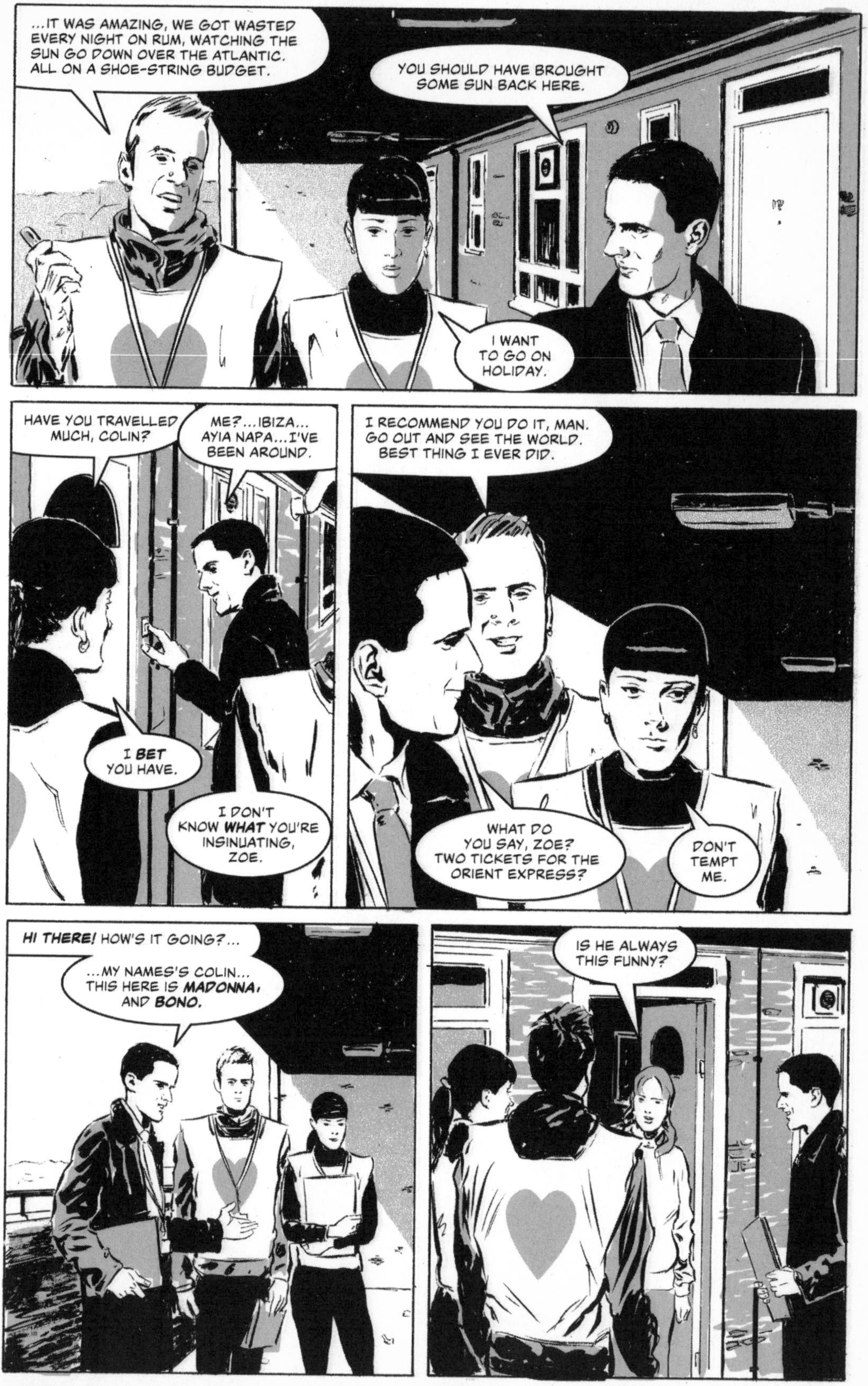
...IT WAS AMAZING, WE GOT WASTED EVERY NIGHT ON RUM, WATCHING THE SUN GO DOWN OVER THE ATLANTIC. ALL ON A SHOE-STRING BUDGET.
YOU SHOULD HAVE BROUGHT SOME SUN BACK HERE.
I WANT TO GO ON HOLIDAY.
HAVE YOU TRAVELLED MUCH, COLIN?
ME?...IBIZA... AYIA NAPA...I'VE BEEN AROUND.
I BET YOU HAVE.
I DON'T KNOW WHAT YOU'RE INSINUATING, ZOE.
I RECOMMEND YOU DO IT, MAN. GO OUT AND SEE THE WORLD. BEST THING I EVER DID.
WHAT DO YOU SAY, ZOE? TWO TICKETS FOR THE ORIENT EXPRESS?
DON'T TEMPT ME.
HI THERE! HOW'S IT GOING?...
...MY NAMES'S COLIN... THIS HERE IS MADONNA, AND BONO.
IS HE ALWAYS THIS FUNNY?

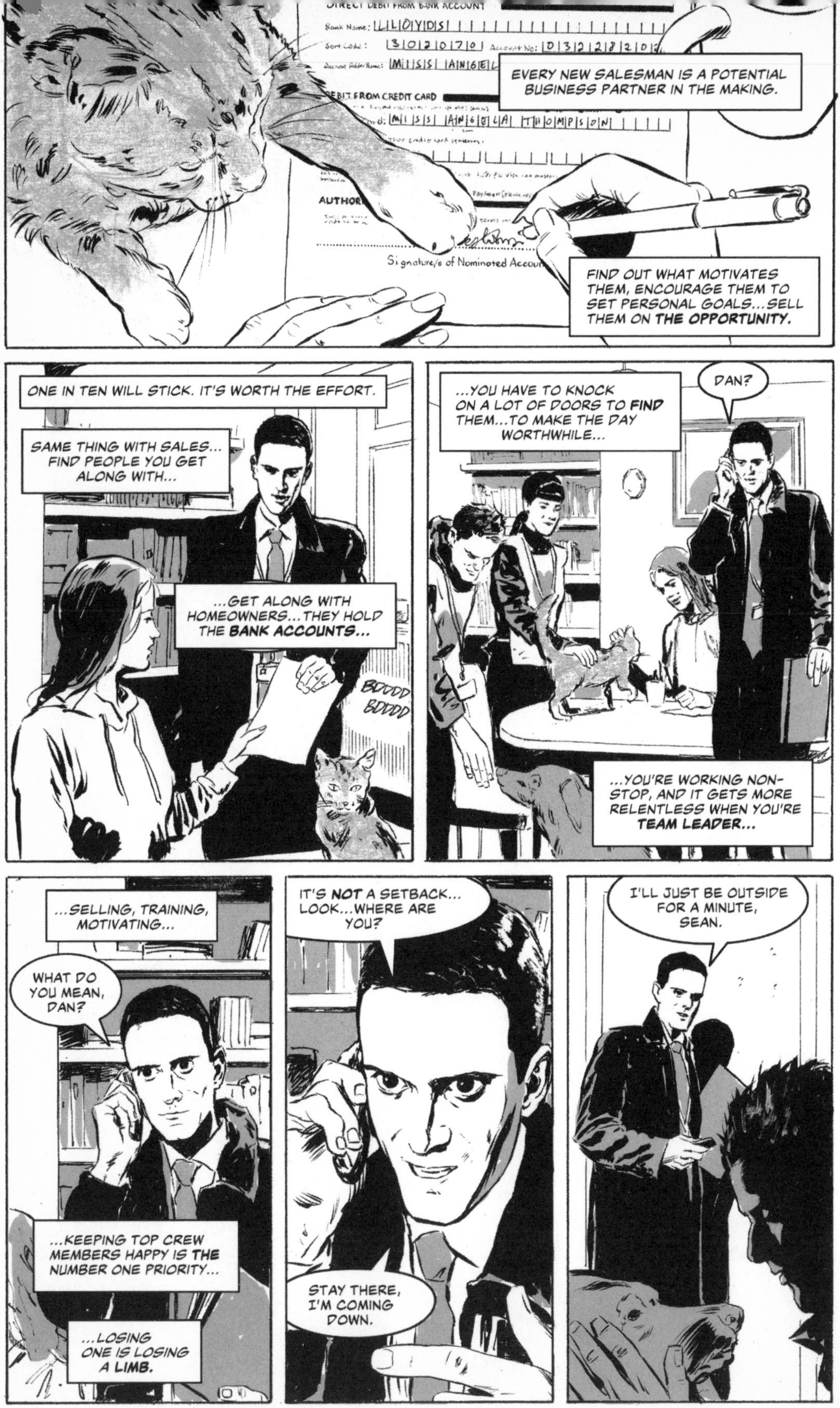

DIRECT DEBIT FROM BANK ACCOUNT
Bank Name: LLOYDS
EVERY NEW SALESMAN IS A POTENTIAL BUSINESS PARTNER IN THE MAKING.
MISS ANGELA THOMPSON
FIND OUT WHAT MOTIVATES THEM, ENCOURAGE THEM TO SET PERSONAL GOALS... SELL THEM ON THE OPPORTUNITY.
ONE IN TEN WILL STICK. IT'S WORTH THE EFFORT.
SAME THING WITH SALES... FIND PEOPLE YOU GET ALONG WITH...
...GET ALONG WITH HOMEOWNERS... THEY HOLD THE BANK ACCOUNTS...
BDDDD BDDDD
...YOU HAVE TO KNOCK ON A LOT OF DOORS TO FIND THEM... TO MAKE THE DAY WORTHWHILE...
DAN?
...YOU'RE WORKING NON-STOP, AND IT GETS MORE RELENTLESS WHEN YOU'RE TEAM LEADER...
...SELLING, TRAINING, MOTIVATING...
WHAT DO YOU MEAN, DAN?
...KEEPING TOP CREW MEMBERS HAPPY IS THE NUMBER ONE PRIORITY...
...LOSING ONE IS LOSING A LIMB.
IT'S NOT A SETBACK... LOOK... WHERE ARE YOU?
STAY THERE, I'M COMING DOWN.
I'LL JUST BE OUTSIDE FOR A MINUTE, SEAN.

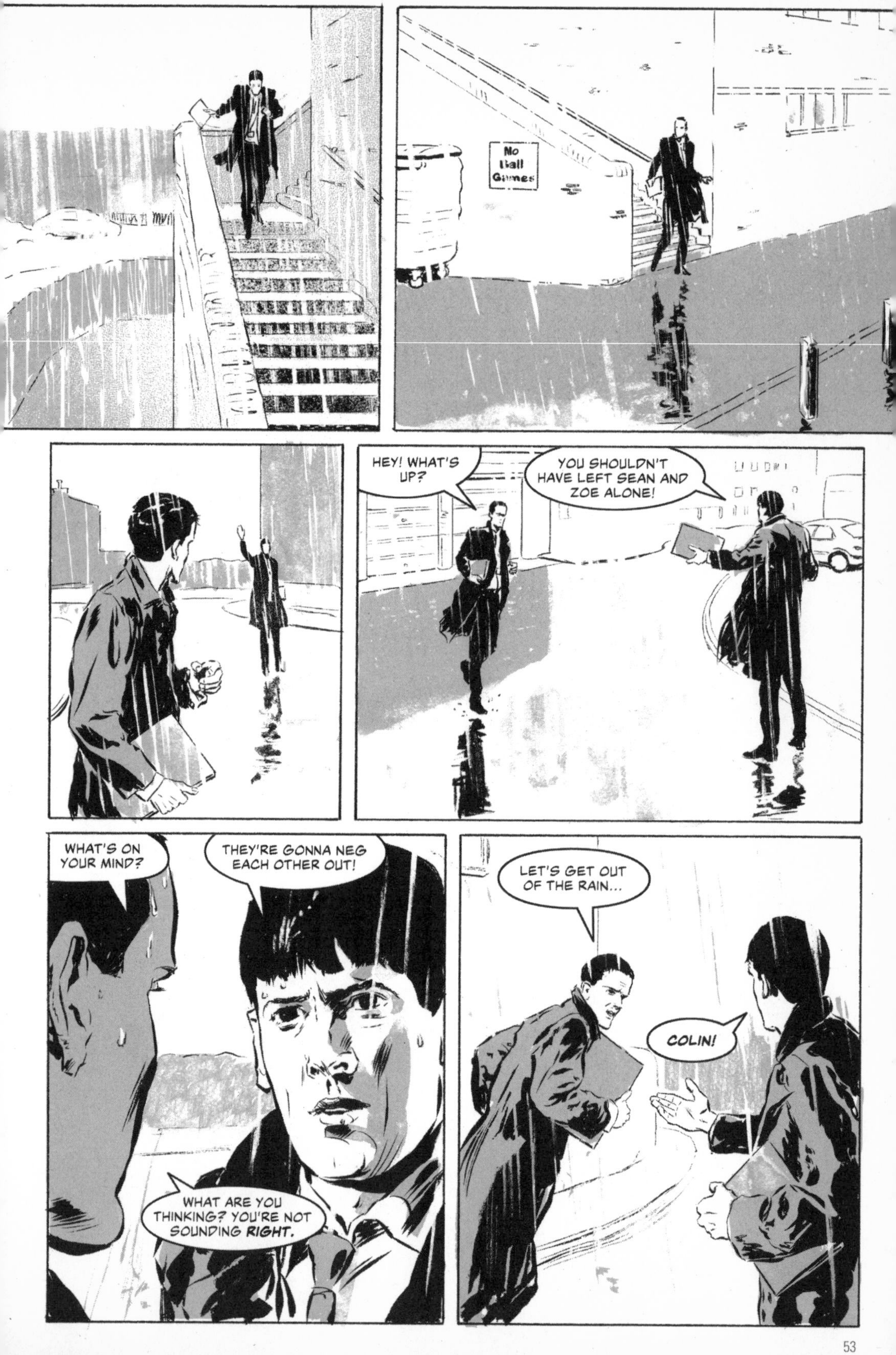
No Ball Games
HEY! WHAT'S UP?
YOU SHOULDN'T HAVE LEFT SEAN AND ZOE ALONE!
WHAT'S ON YOUR MIND?
THEY'RE GONNA NEG EACH OTHER OUT!
WHAT ARE YOU THINKING? YOU'RE NOT SOUNDING **RIGHT.**
LET'S GET OUT OF THE RAIN...
COLIN!

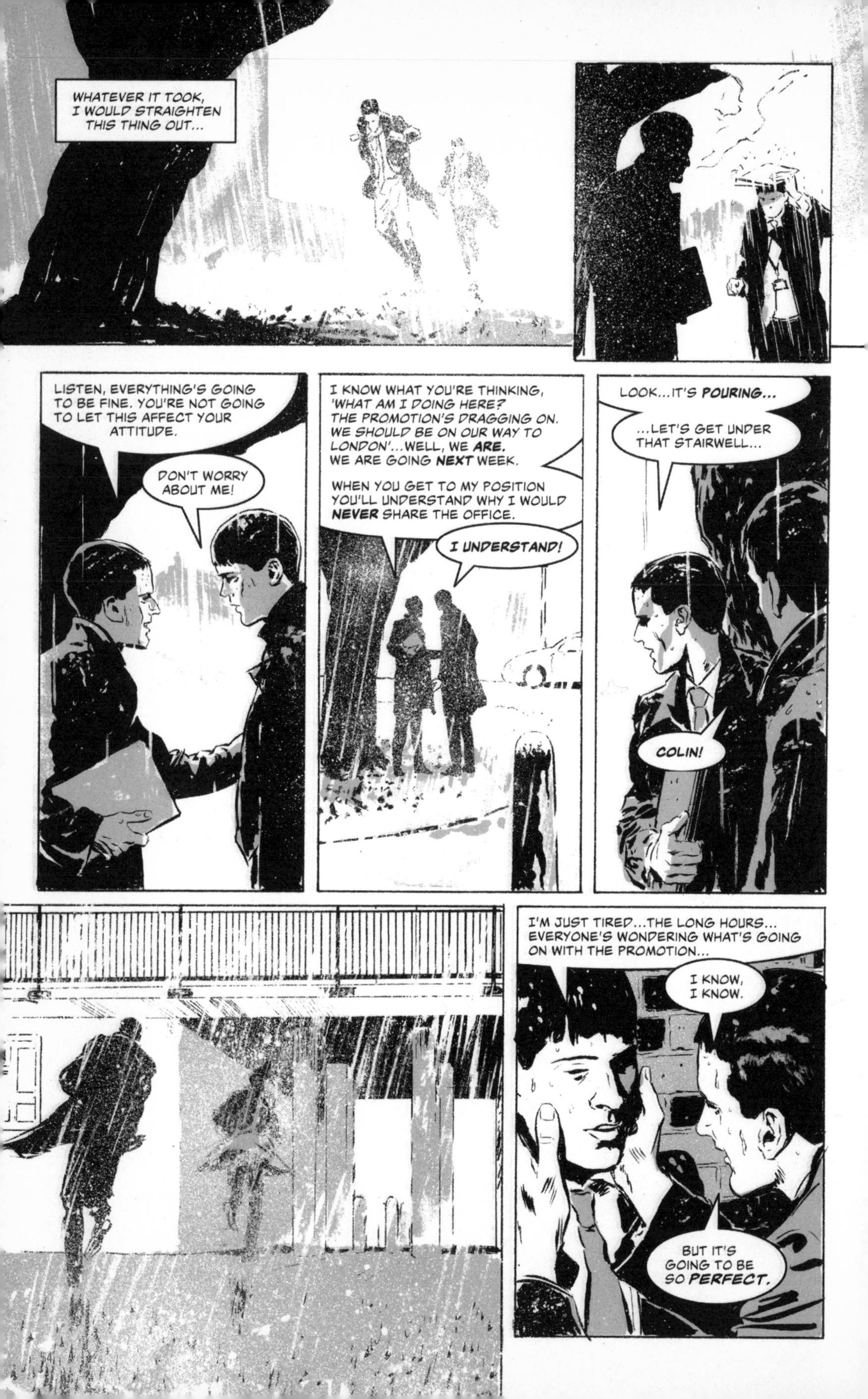
WHATEVER IT TOOK, I WOULD STRAIGHTEN THIS THING OUT...
LISTEN, EVERYTHING'S GOING TO BE FINE. YOU'RE NOT GOING TO LET THIS AFFECT YOUR ATTITUDE.
DON'T WORRY ABOUT ME!
I KNOW WHAT YOU'RE THINKING, 'WHAT AM I DOING HERE? THE PROMOTION'S DRAGGING ON. WE SHOULD BE ON OUR WAY TO LONDON'...WELL, WE ARE. WE ARE GOING NEXT WEEK.
WHEN YOU GET TO MY POSITION YOU'LL UNDERSTAND WHY I WOULD NEVER SHARE THE OFFICE.
I UNDERSTAND!
LOOK...IT'S POURING...
...LET'S GET UNDER THAT STAIRWELL...
COLIN!
I'M JUST TIRED...THE LONG HOURS... EVERYONE'S WONDERING WHAT'S GOING ON WITH THE PROMOTION...
I KNOW, I KNOW.
BUT IT'S GOING TO BE SO PERFECT.

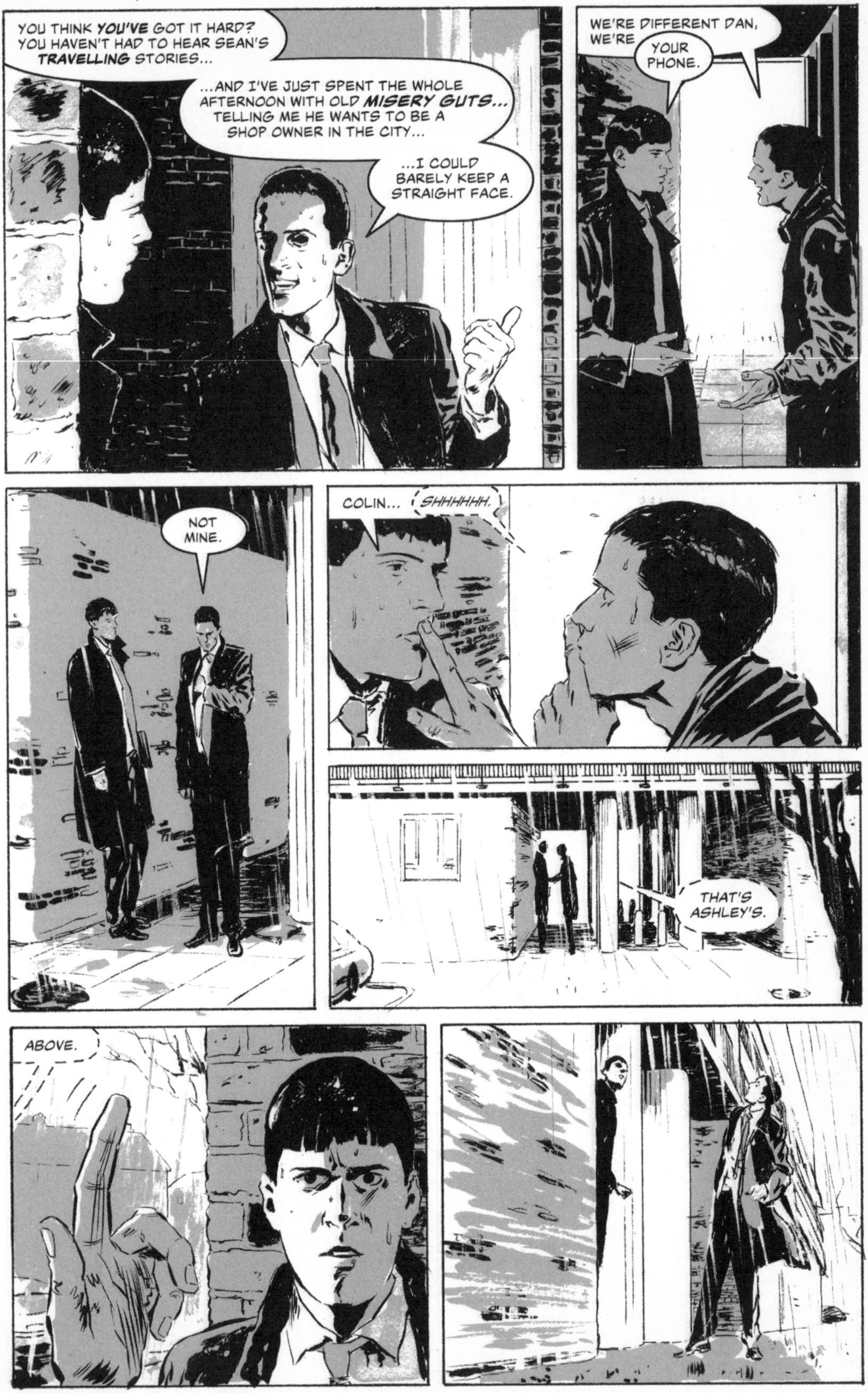
YOU THINK YOU'VE GOT IT HARD? YOU HAVEN'T HAD TO HEAR SEAN'S TRAVELLING STORIES...
...AND I'VE JUST SPENT THE WHOLE AFTERNOON WITH OLD MISERY GUTS... TELLING ME HE WANTS TO BE A SHOP OWNER IN THE CITY...
...I COULD BARELY KEEP A STRAIGHT FACE.
WE'RE DIFFERENT DAN, WE'RE
YOUR PHONE.
NOT MINE.
COLIN...
SHHHHHH.
THAT'S ASHLEY'S.
ABOVE.

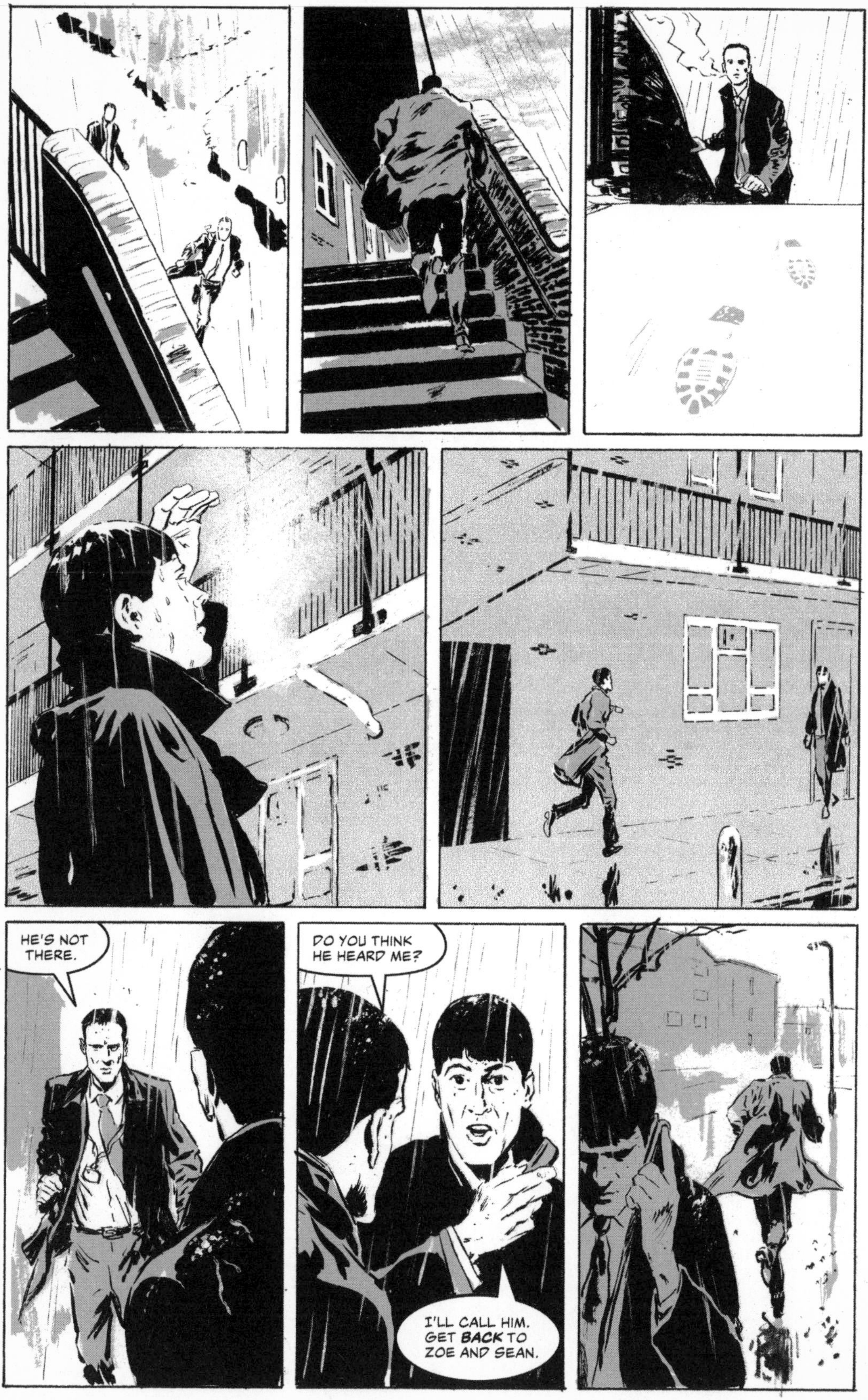
HE'S NOT THERE.
DO YOU THINK HE HEARD ME?
I'LL CALL HIM. GET BACK TO ZOE AND SEAN.

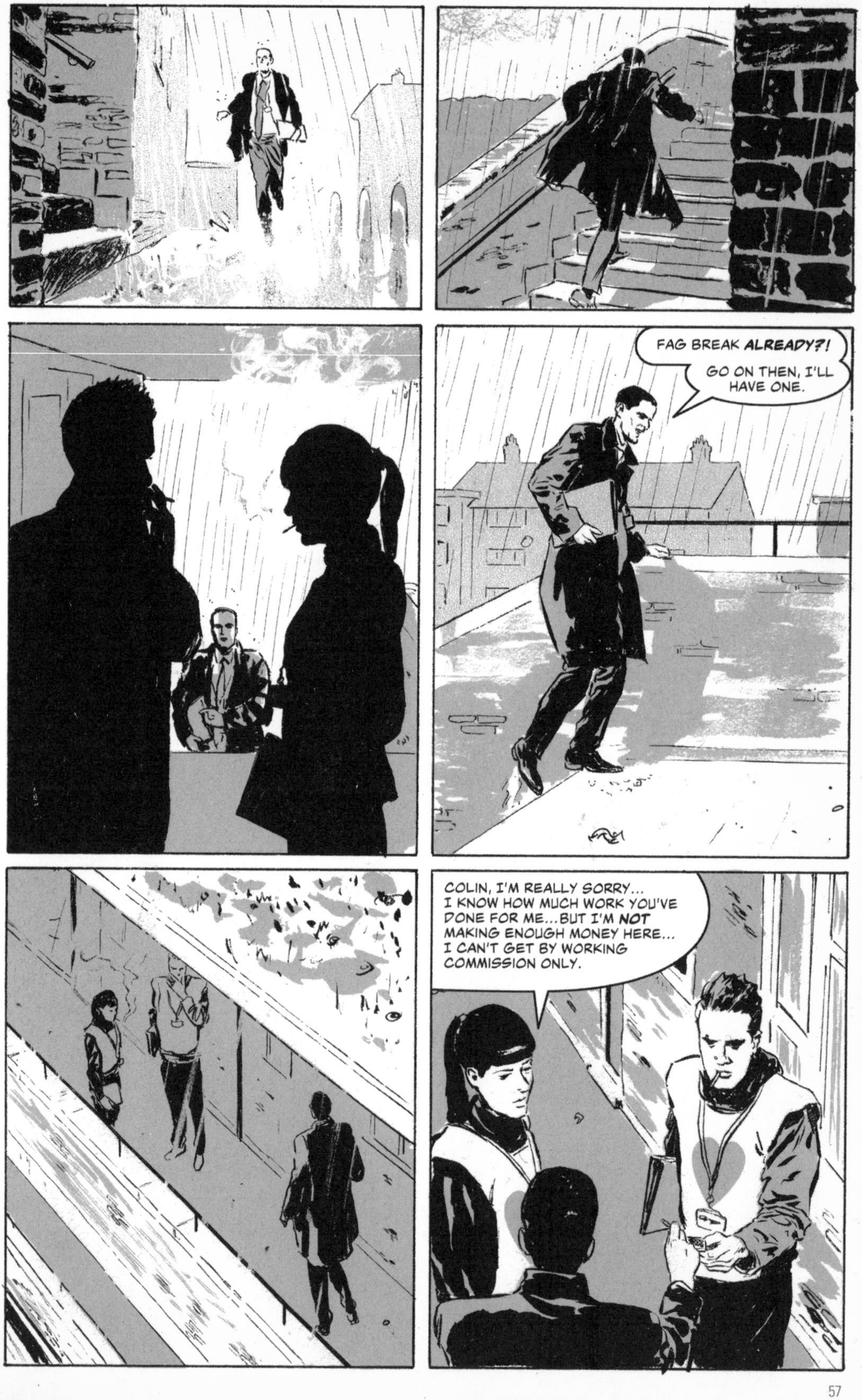
FAG BREAK ALREADY?!
GO ON THEN, I'LL HAVE ONE.
COLIN, I'M REALLY SORRY... I KNOW HOW MUCH WORK YOU'VE DONE FOR ME...BUT I'M NOT MAKING ENOUGH MONEY HERE... I CAN'T GET BY WORKING COMMISSION ONLY.

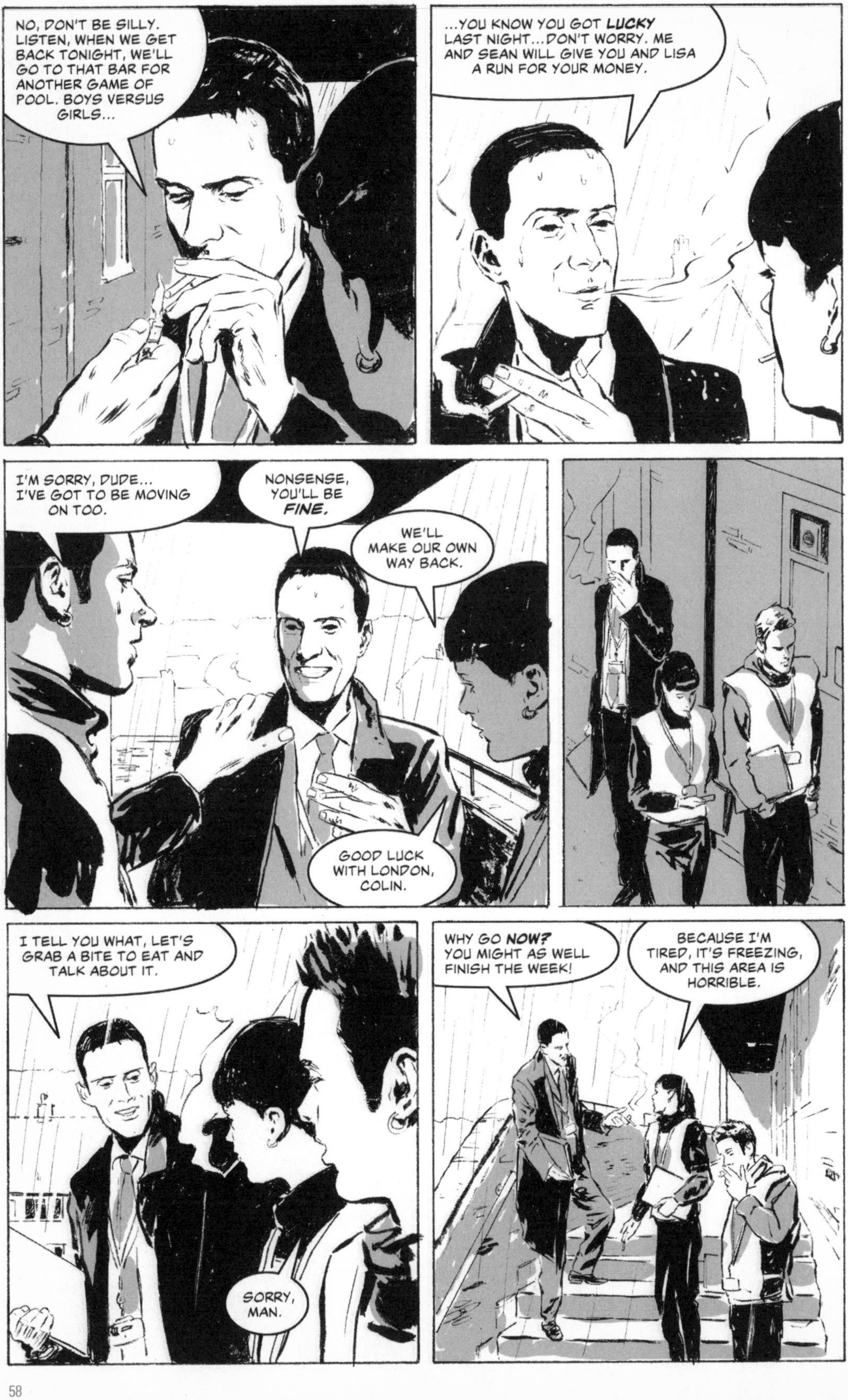
NO, DON'T BE SILLY. LISTEN, WHEN WE GET BACK TONIGHT, WE'LL GO TO THAT BAR FOR ANOTHER GAME OF POOL. BOYS VERSUS GIRLS...
...YOU KNOW YOU GOT **LUCKY** LAST NIGHT...DON'T WORRY. ME AND SEAN WILL GIVE YOU AND LISA A RUN FOR YOUR MONEY.
I'M SORRY, DUDE... I'VE GOT TO BE MOVING ON TOO.
NONSENSE, YOU'LL BE **FINE.**
WE'LL MAKE OUR OWN WAY BACK.
GOOD LUCK WITH LONDON, COLIN.
I TELL YOU WHAT, LET'S GRAB A BITE TO EAT AND TALK ABOUT IT.
SORRY, MAN.
WHY GO **NOW?** YOU MIGHT AS WELL FINISH THE WEEK!
BECAUSE I'M TIRED, IT'S FREEZING, AND THIS AREA IS HORRIBLE.

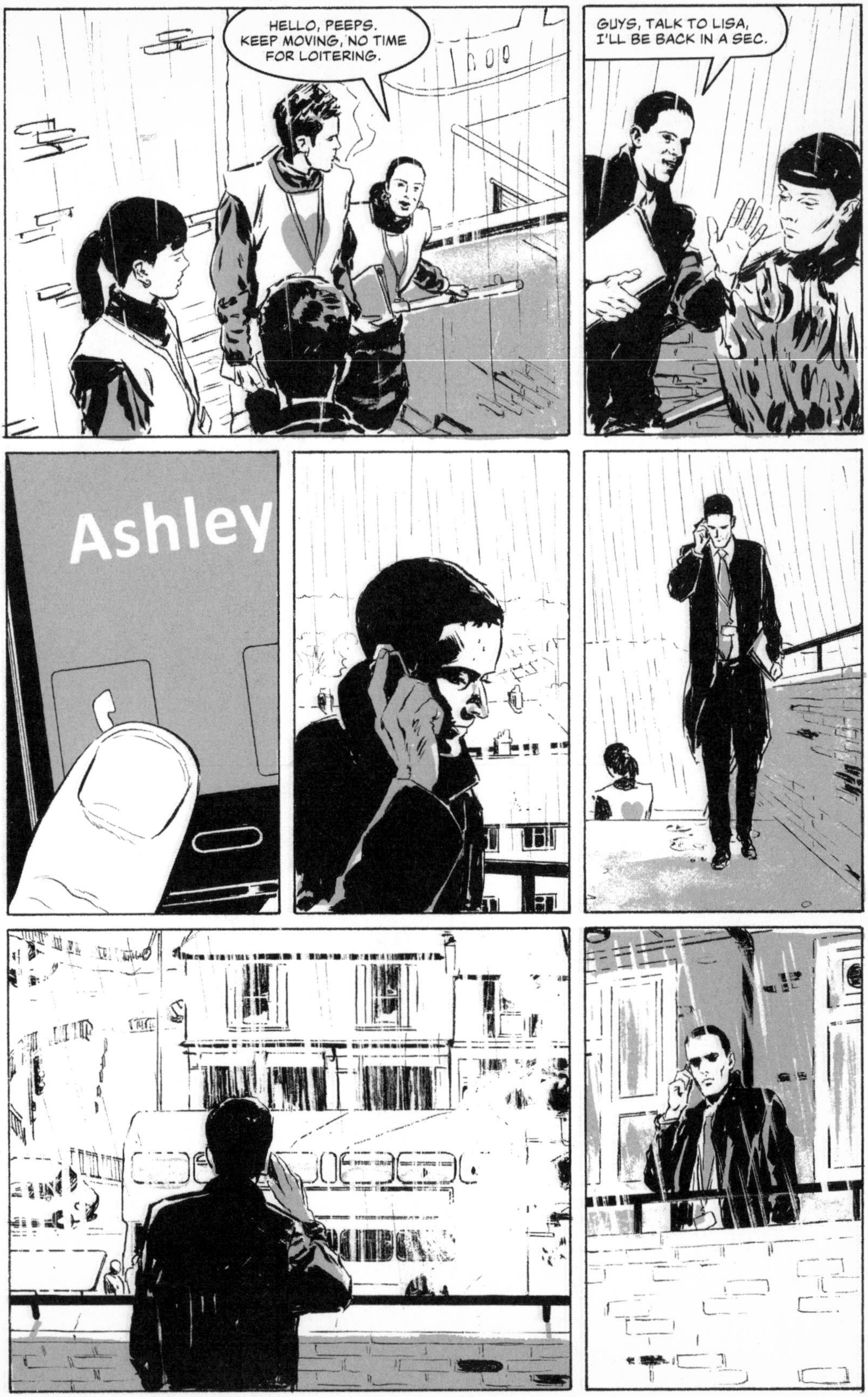
HELLO, PEEPS. KEEP MOVING, NO TIME FOR LOITERING.
GUYS, TALK TO LISA, I'LL BE BACK IN A SEC.
Ashley

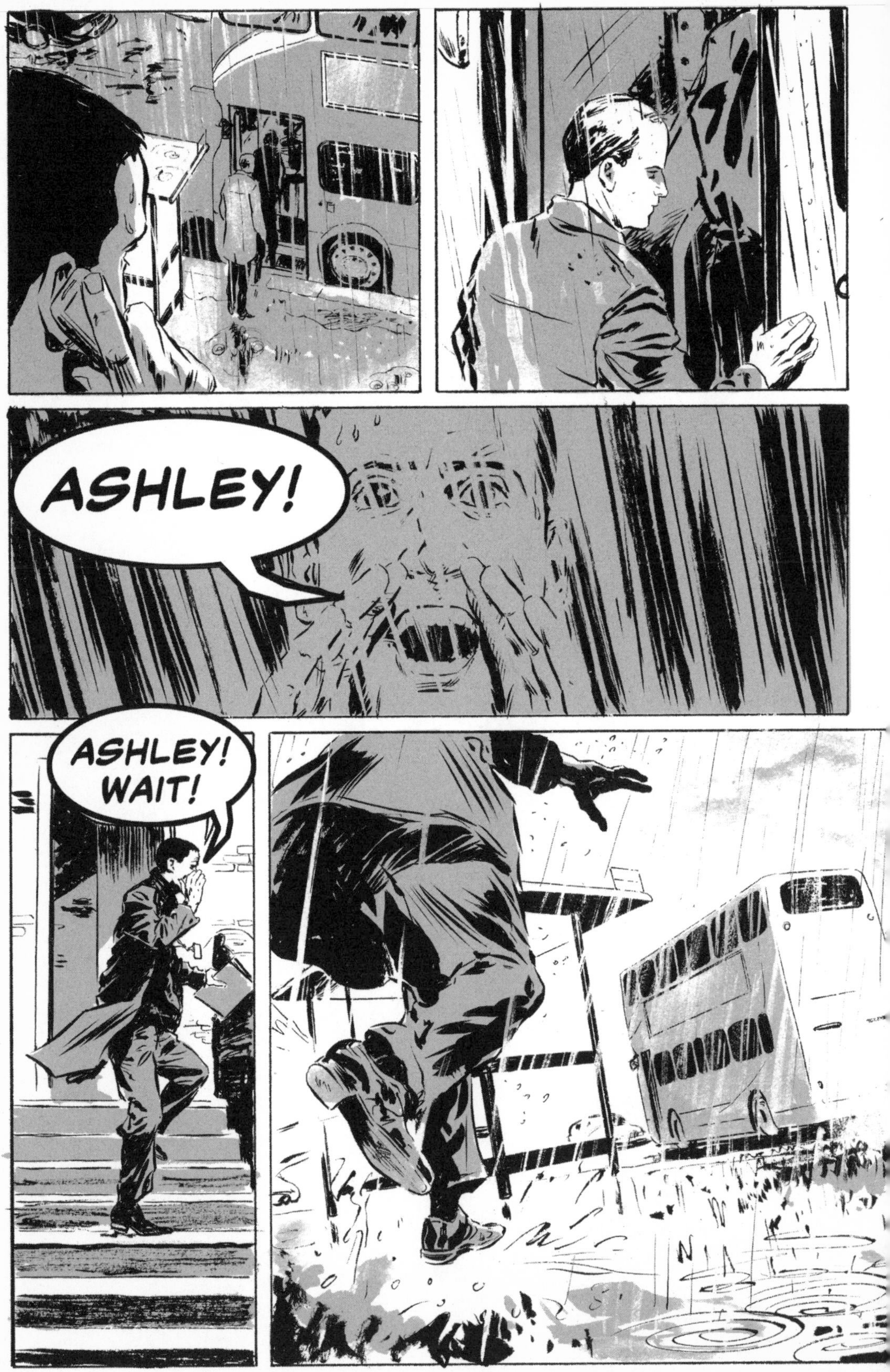
ASHLEY!
ASHLEY! WAIT!

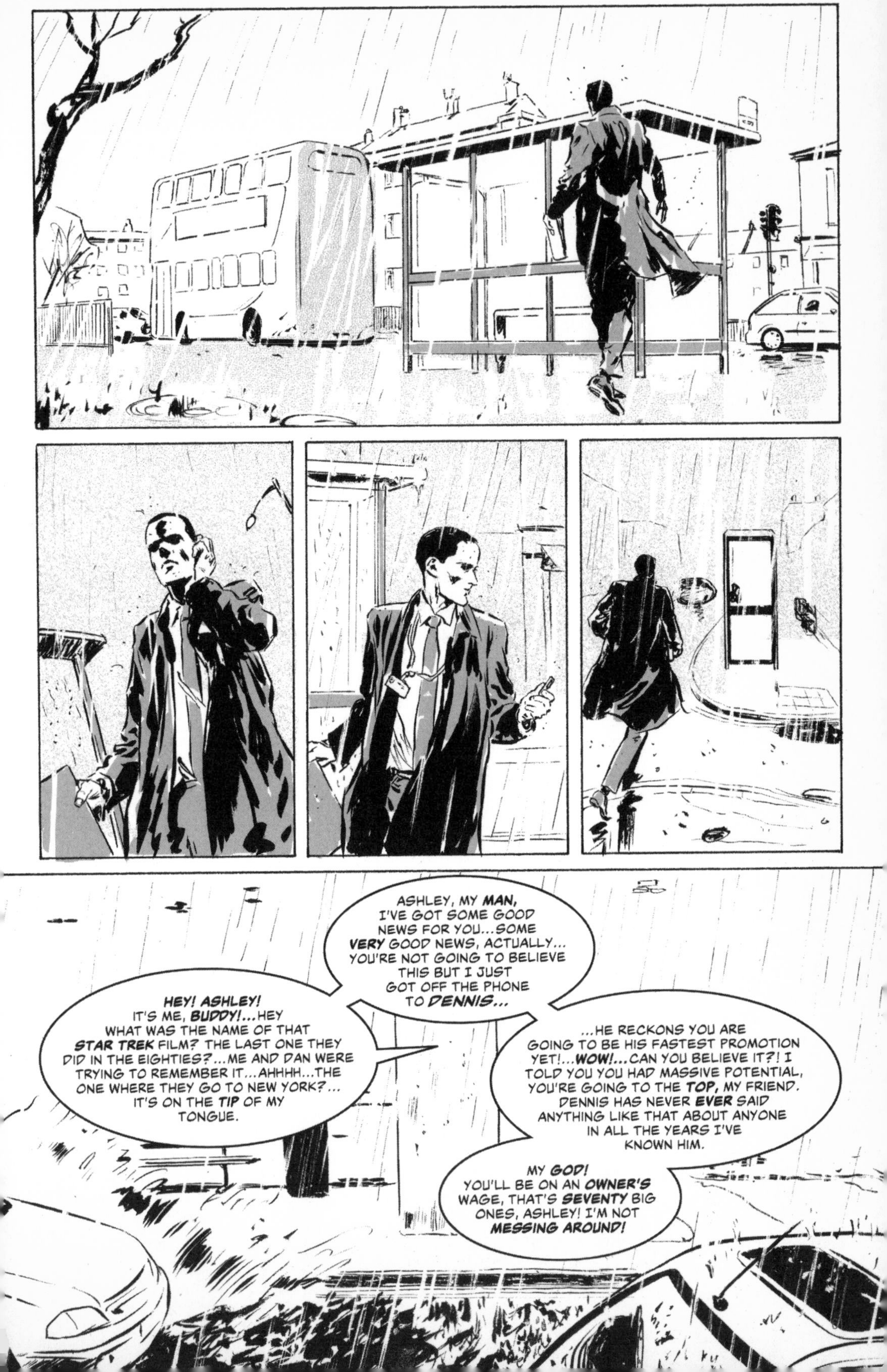

ASHLEY, MY MAN, I'VE GOT SOME GOOD NEWS FOR YOU...SOME VERY GOOD NEWS, ACTUALLY... YOU'RE NOT GOING TO BELIEVE THIS BUT I JUST GOT OFF THE PHONE TO DENNIS...
HEY! ASHLEY! IT'S ME, BUDDY!...HEY WHAT WAS THE NAME OF THAT STAR TREK FILM? THE LAST ONE THEY DID IN THE EIGHTIES?...ME AND DAN WERE TRYING TO REMEMBER IT...AHHHH...THE ONE WHERE THEY GO TO NEW YORK?... IT'S ON THE TIP OF MY TONGUE.
...HE RECKONS YOU ARE GOING TO BE HIS FASTEST PROMOTION YET!...WOW!...CAN YOU BELIEVE IT?! I TOLD YOU YOU HAD MASSIVE POTENTIAL, YOU'RE GOING TO THE TOP, MY FRIEND. DENNIS HAS NEVER EVER SAID ANYTHING LIKE THAT ABOUT ANYONE IN ALL THE YEARS I'VE KNOWN HIM.
MY GOD! YOU'LL BE ON AN OWNER'S WAGE, THAT'S SEVENTY BIG ONES, ASHLEY! I'M NOT MESSING AROUND!

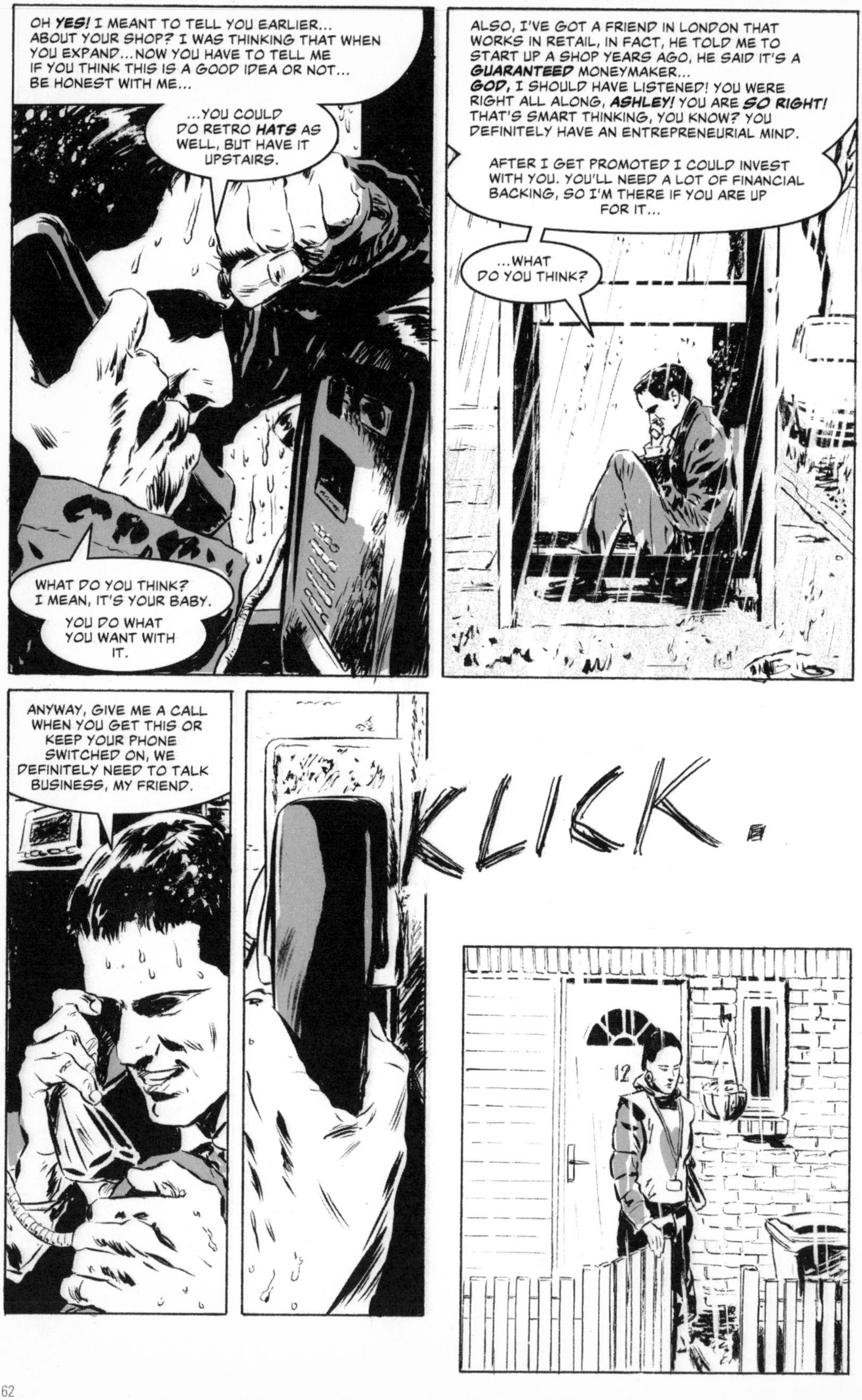

OH **YES!** I MEANT TO TELL YOU EARLIER... ABOUT YOUR SHOP? I WAS THINKING THAT WHEN YOU EXPAND...NOW YOU HAVE TO TELL ME IF YOU THINK THIS IS A GOOD IDEA OR NOT... BE HONEST WITH ME...
...YOU COULD DO RETRO **HATS** AS WELL, BUT HAVE IT UPSTAIRS.
WHAT DO YOU THINK? I MEAN, IT'S YOUR BABY.
YOU DO WHAT YOU WANT WITH IT.
ALSO, I'VE GOT A FRIEND IN LONDON THAT WORKS IN RETAIL, IN FACT, HE TOLD ME TO START UP A SHOP YEARS AGO, HE SAID IT'S A **GUARANTEED** MONEYMAKER... **GOD,** I SHOULD HAVE LISTENED! YOU WERE RIGHT ALL ALONG, **ASHLEY!** YOU ARE **SO RIGHT!** THAT'S SMART THINKING, YOU KNOW? YOU DEFINITELY HAVE AN ENTREPRENEURIAL MIND.
AFTER I GET PROMOTED I COULD INVEST WITH YOU. YOU'LL NEED A LOT OF FINANCIAL BACKING, SO I'M THERE IF YOU ARE UP FOR IT...
...WHAT DO YOU THINK?
ANYWAY, GIVE ME A CALL WHEN YOU GET THIS OR KEEP YOUR PHONE SWITCHED ON, WE DEFINITELY NEED TO TALK BUSINESS, MY FRIEND.
KLICK.
12

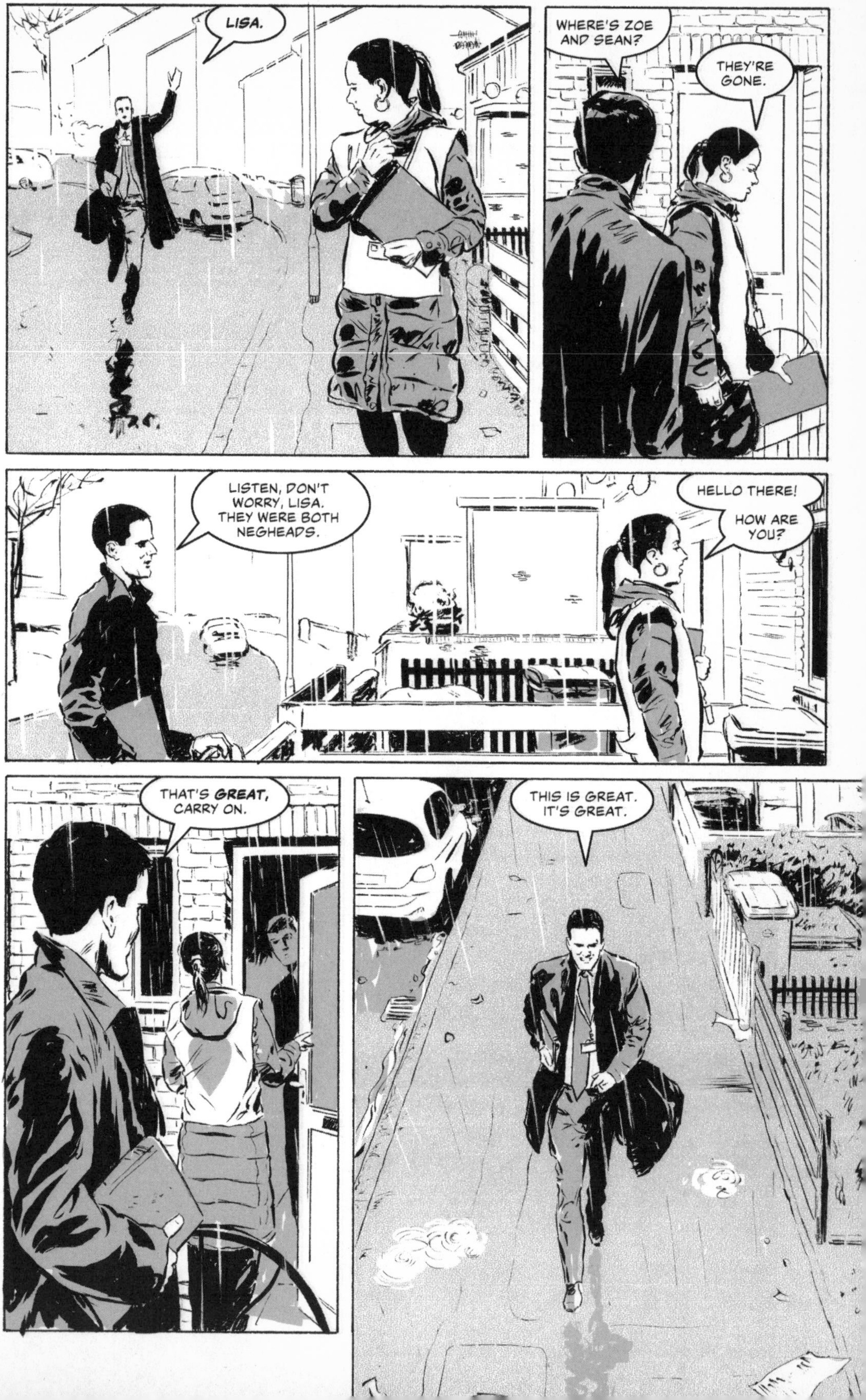
LISA.
WHERE'S ZOE AND SEAN?
THEY'RE GONE.
LISTEN, DON'T WORRY, LISA. THEY WERE BOTH NEGHEADS.
HELLO THERE!
HOW ARE YOU?
THAT'S **GREAT,** CARRY ON.
THIS IS GREAT. IT'S GREAT.

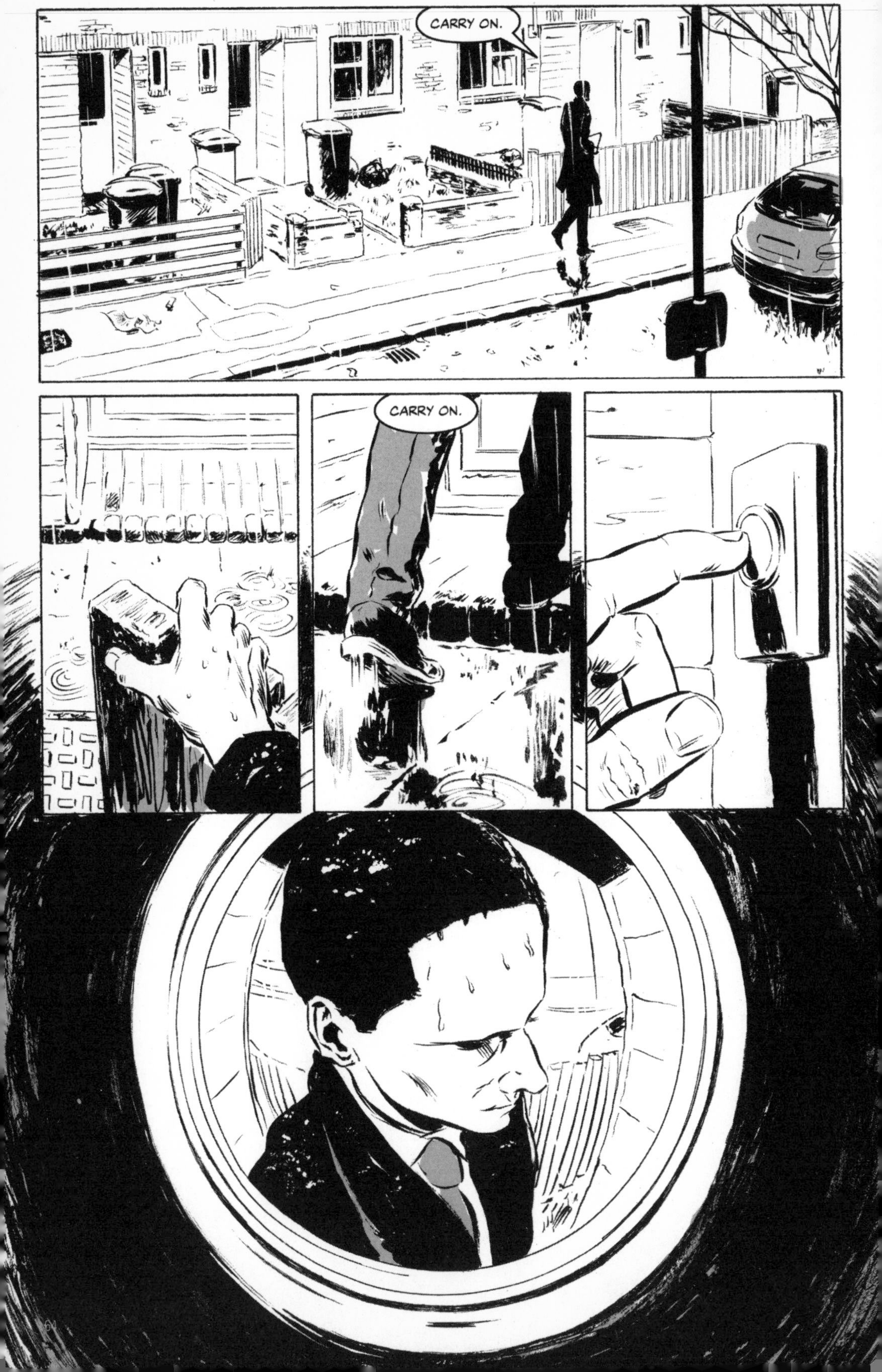
CARRY ON.
CARRY ON.

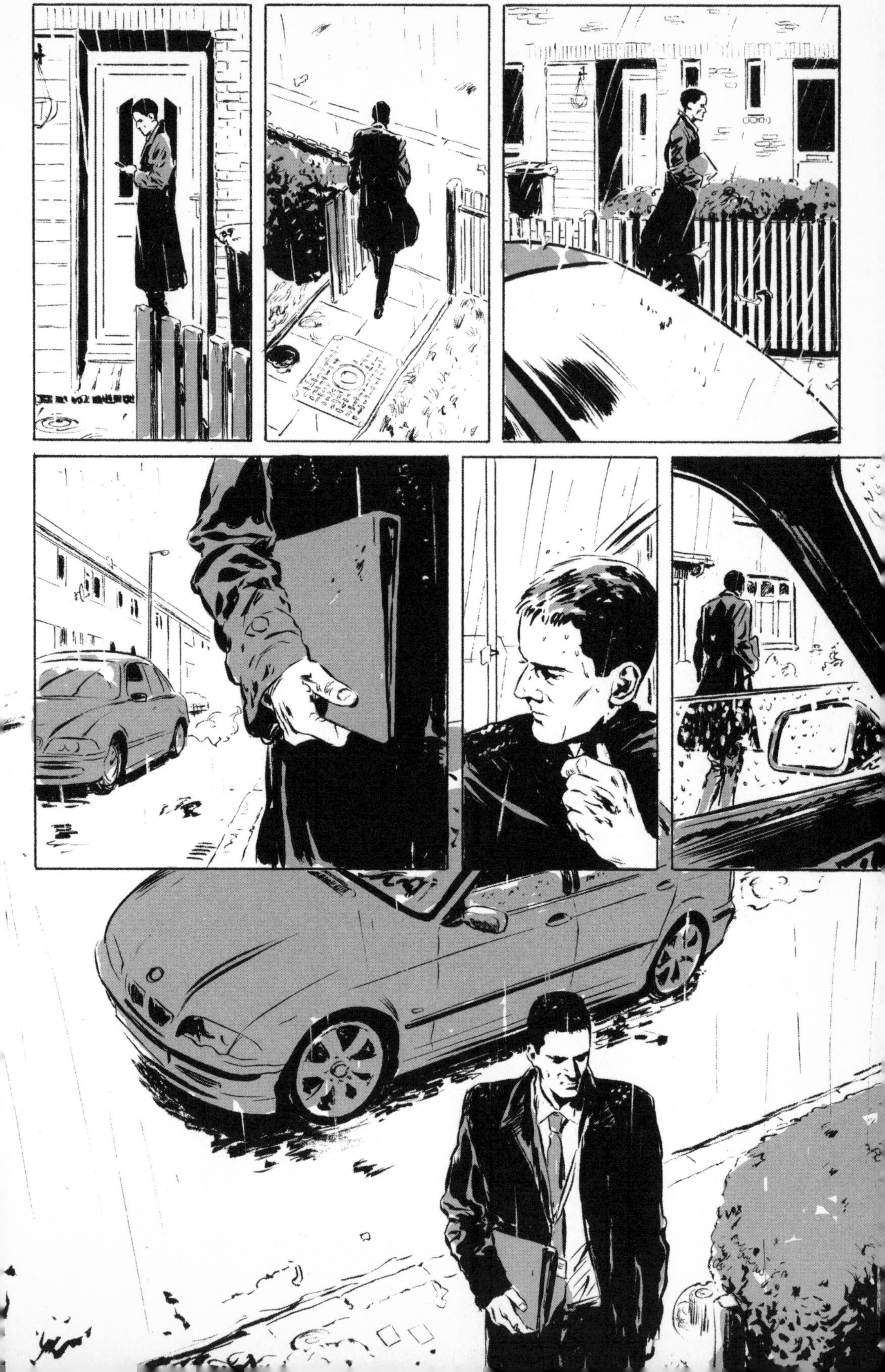

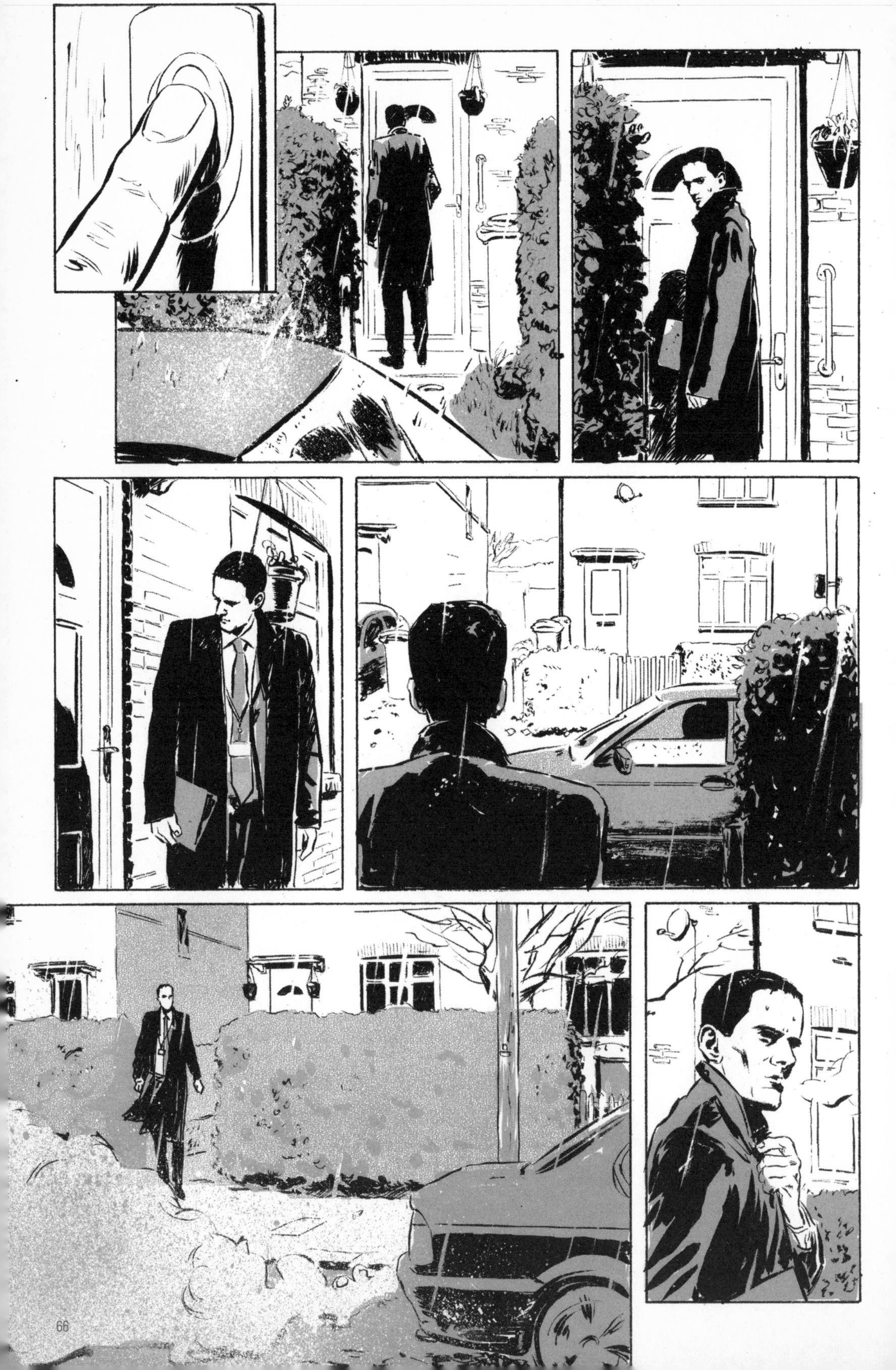

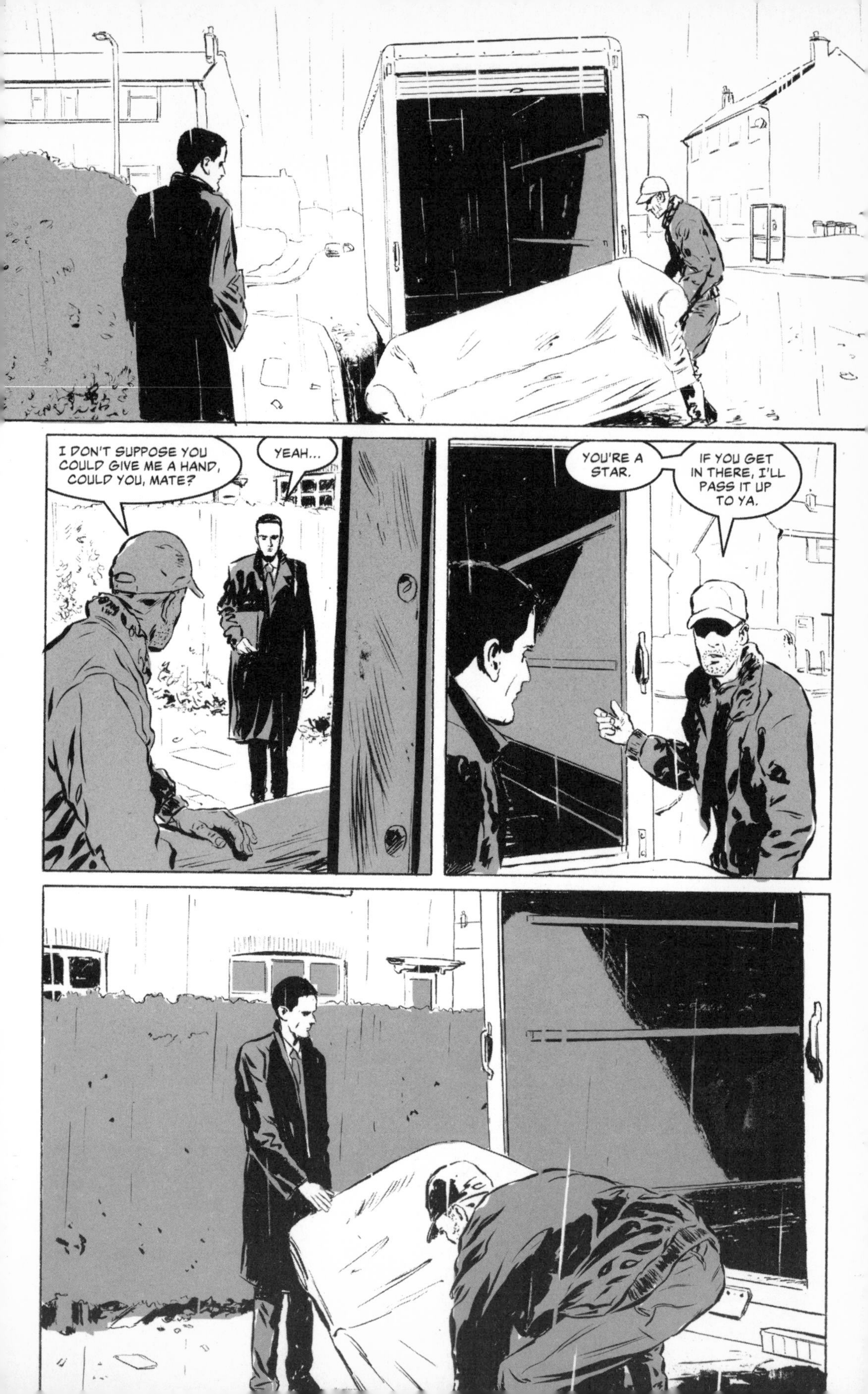
I DON'T SUPPOSE YOU COULD GIVE ME A HAND, COULD YOU, MATE?
YEAH...
YOU'RE A STAR.
IF YOU GET IN THERE, I'LL PASS IT UP TO YA.

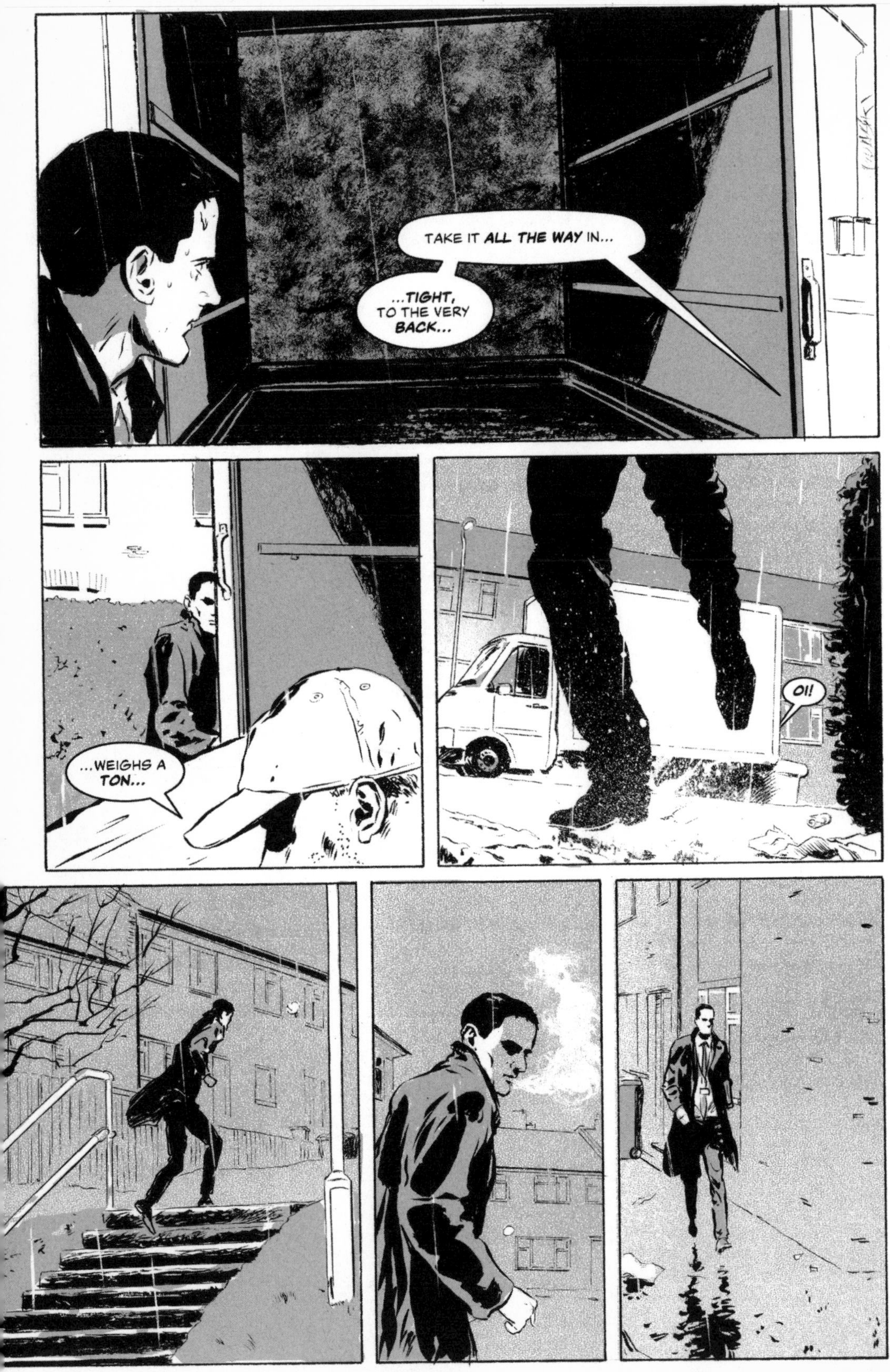
TAKE IT ALL THE WAY IN...
...TIGHT, TO THE VERY BACK...
...WEIGHS A TON...
OI!

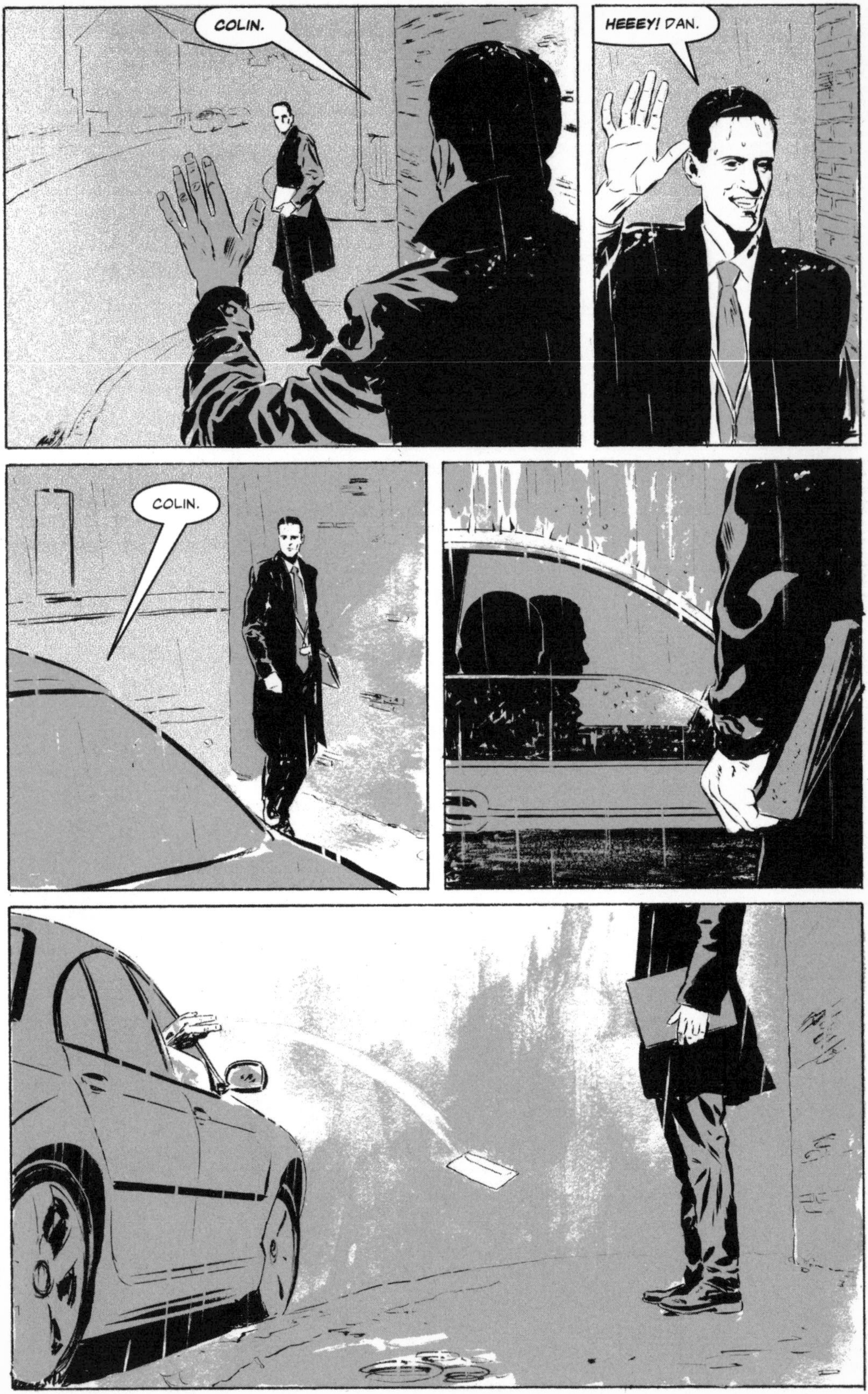
COLIN.
HEEEY! DAN.
COLIN.

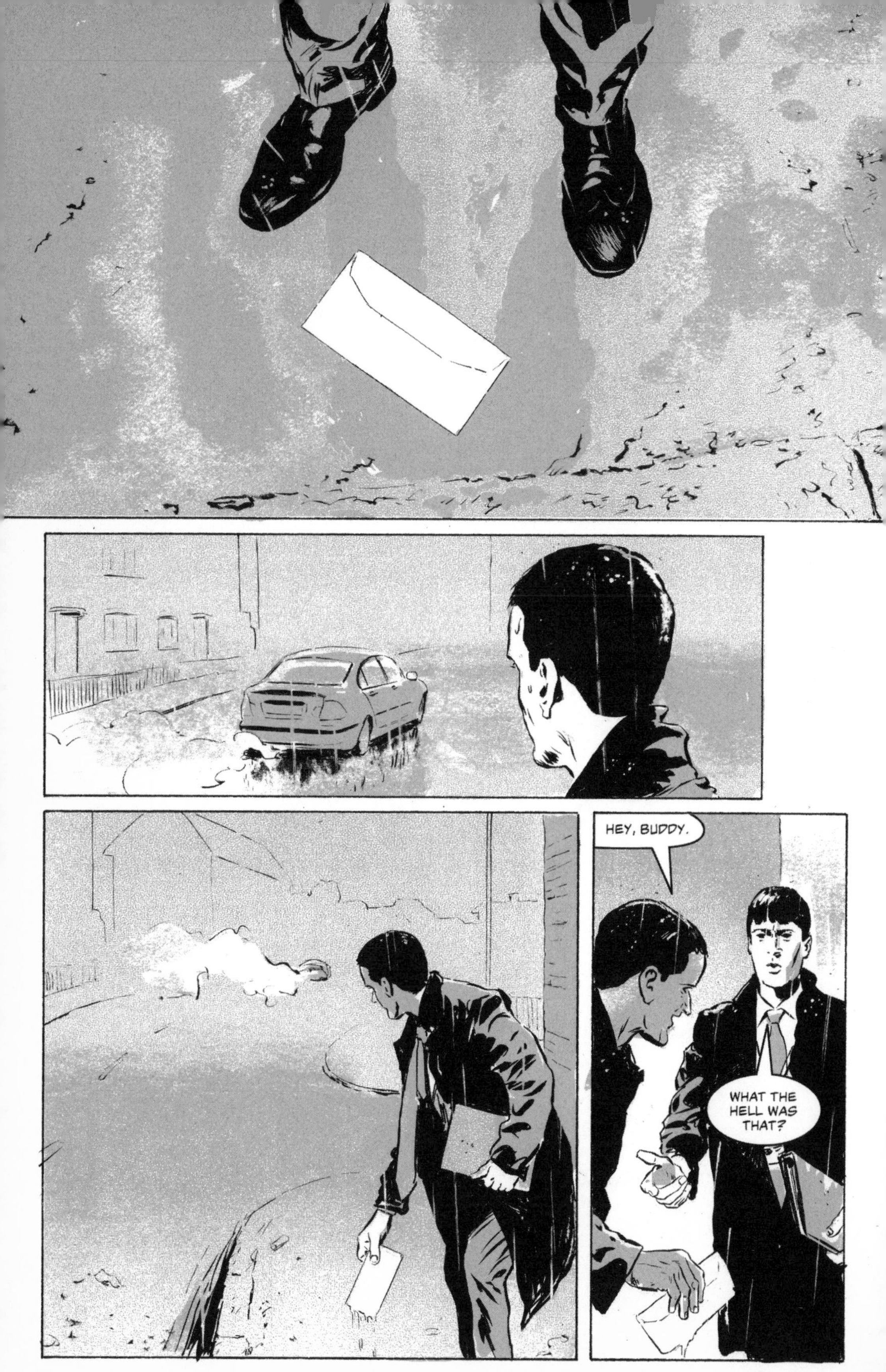
HEY, BUDDY.
WHAT THE HELL WAS THAT?

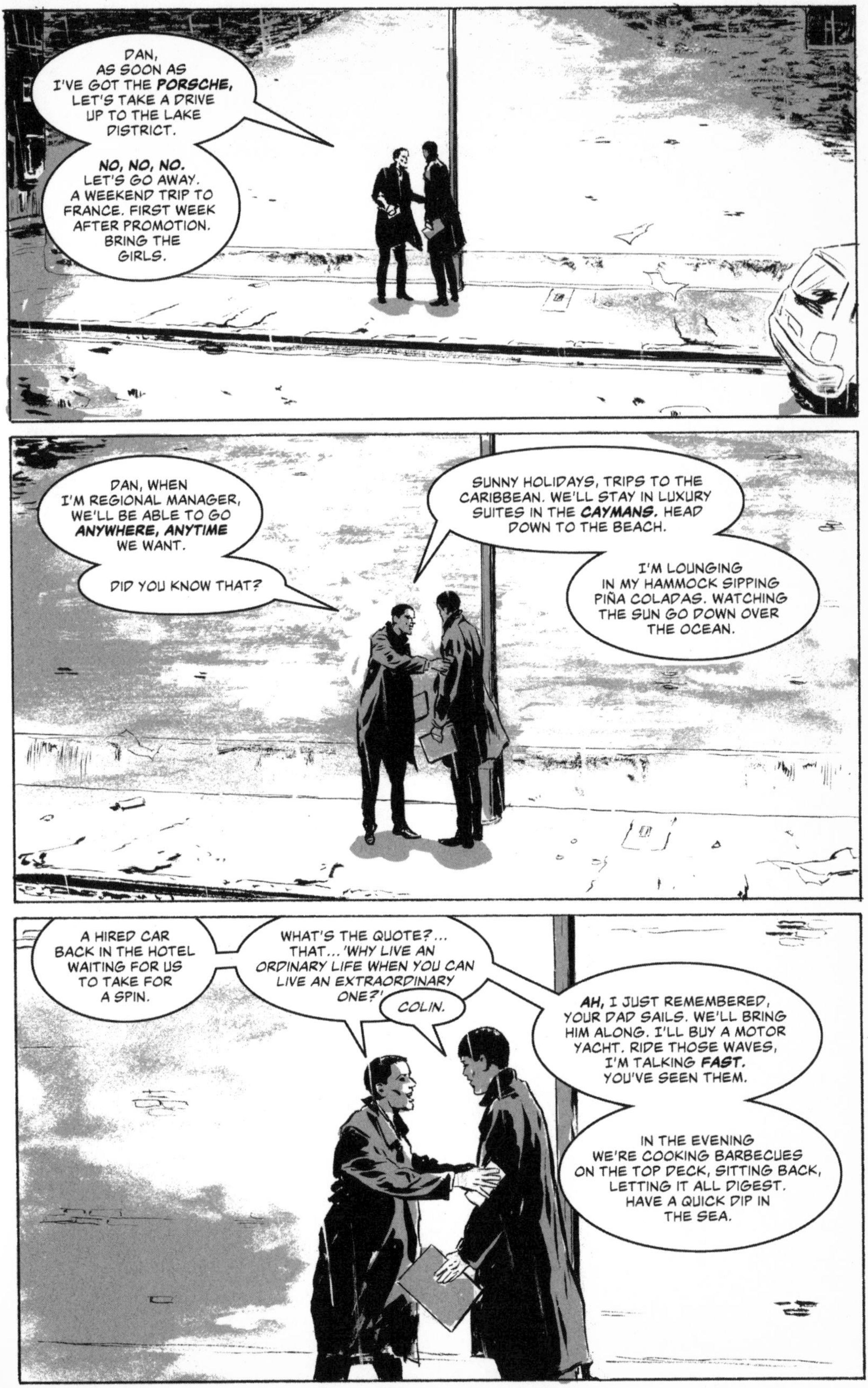
DAN, AS SOON AS I'VE GOT THE **PORSCHE,** LET'S TAKE A DRIVE UP TO THE LAKE DISTRICT.
**NO, NO, NO.** LET'S GO AWAY. A WEEKEND TRIP TO FRANCE. FIRST WEEK AFTER PROMOTION. BRING THE GIRLS.
DAN, WHEN I'M REGIONAL MANAGER, WE'LL BE ABLE TO GO **ANYWHERE, ANYTIME** WE WANT.
DID YOU KNOW THAT?
SUNNY HOLIDAYS, TRIPS TO THE CARIBBEAN. WE'LL STAY IN LUXURY SUITES IN THE **CAYMANS.** HEAD DOWN TO THE BEACH.
I'M LOUNGING IN MY HAMMOCK SIPPING PIÑA COLADAS. WATCHING THE SUN GO DOWN OVER THE OCEAN.
A HIRED CAR BACK IN THE HOTEL WAITING FOR US TO TAKE FOR A SPIN.
WHAT'S THE QUOTE?... THAT... 'WHY LIVE AN ORDINARY LIFE WHEN YOU CAN LIVE AN EXTRAORDINARY ONE?'
COLIN.
**AH,** I JUST REMEMBERED, YOUR DAD SAILS. WE'LL BRING HIM ALONG. I'LL BUY A MOTOR YACHT. RIDE THOSE WAVES, I'M TALKING **FAST.** YOU'VE SEEN THEM.
IN THE EVENING WE'RE COOKING BARBECUES ON THE TOP DECK, SITTING BACK, LETTING IT ALL DIGEST. HAVE A QUICK DIP IN THE SEA.

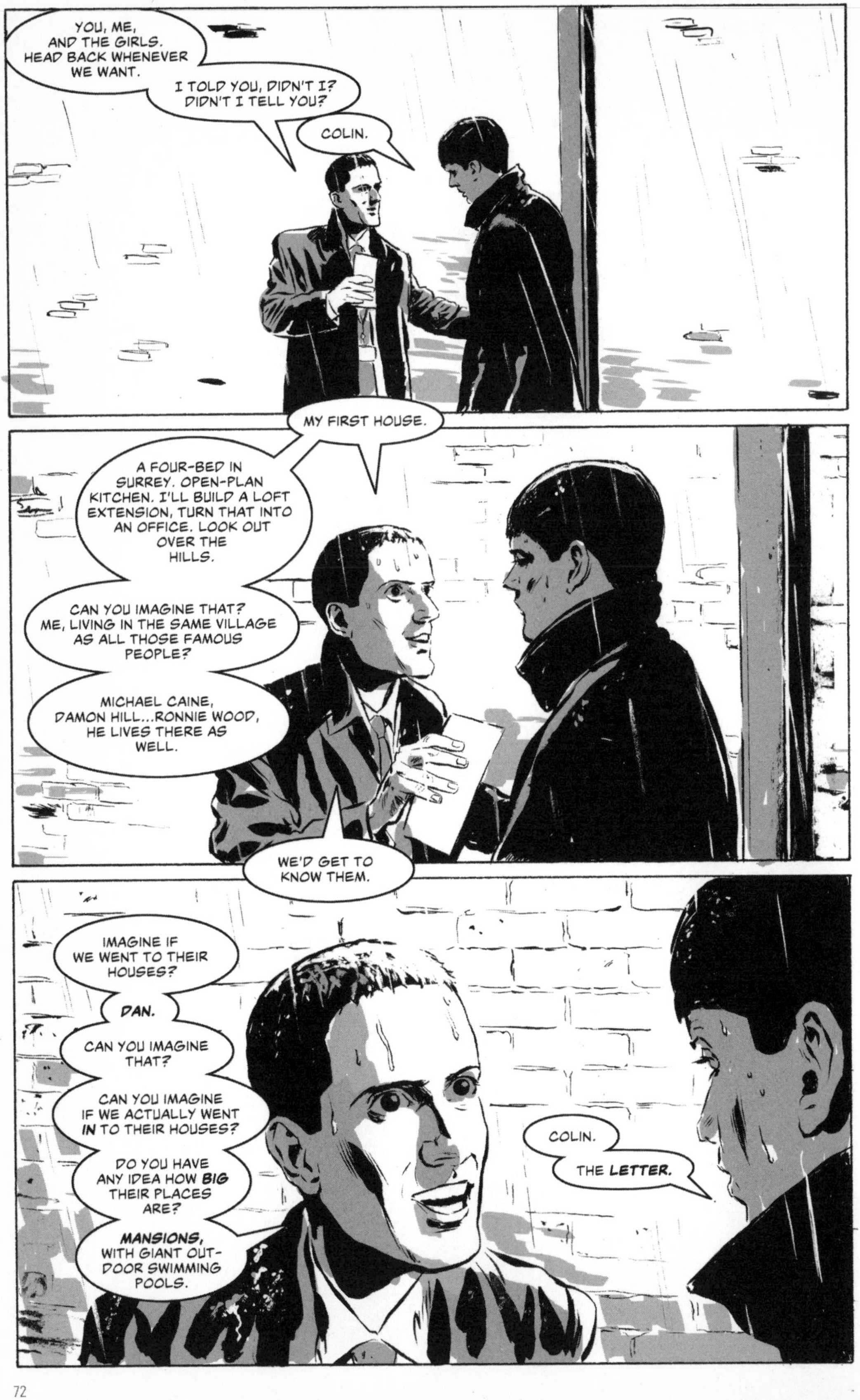
YOU, ME, AND THE GIRLS. HEAD BACK WHENEVER WE WANT.
I TOLD YOU, DIDN'T I? DIDN'T I TELL YOU?
COLIN.
MY FIRST HOUSE.
A FOUR-BED IN SURREY. OPEN-PLAN KITCHEN. I'LL BUILD A LOFT EXTENSION, TURN THAT INTO AN OFFICE. LOOK OUT OVER THE HILLS.
CAN YOU IMAGINE THAT? ME, LIVING IN THE SAME VILLAGE AS ALL THOSE FAMOUS PEOPLE?
MICHAEL CAINE, DAMON HILL...RONNIE WOOD, HE LIVES THERE AS WELL.
WE'D GET TO KNOW THEM.
IMAGINE IF WE WENT TO THEIR HOUSES?
DAN.
CAN YOU IMAGINE THAT?
CAN YOU IMAGINE IF WE ACTUALLY WENT IN TO THEIR HOUSES?
DO YOU HAVE ANY IDEA HOW BIG THEIR PLACES ARE?
MANSIONS, WITH GIANT OUT-DOOR SWIMMING POOLS.
COLIN.
THE LETTER.

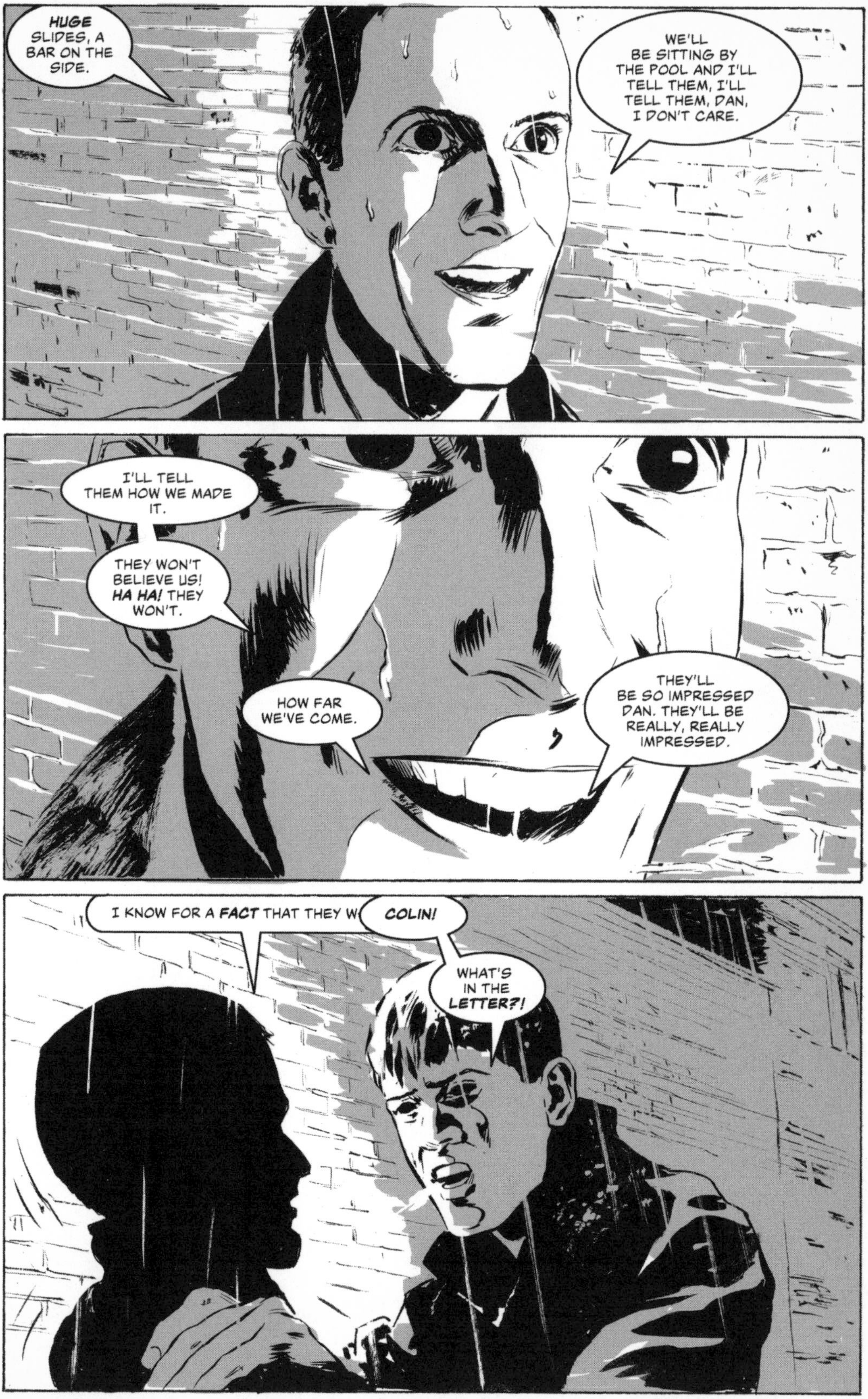
HUGE SLIDES, A BAR ON THE SIDE.
WE'LL BE SITTING BY THE POOL AND I'LL TELL THEM, I'LL TELL THEM, DAN, I DON'T CARE.
I'LL TELL THEM HOW WE MADE IT.
THEY WON'T BELIEVE US! HA HA! THEY WON'T.
HOW FAR WE'VE COME.
THEY'LL BE SO IMPRESSED DAN. THEY'LL BE REALLY, REALLY IMPRESSED.
I KNOW FOR A FACT THAT THEY W
COLIN!
WHAT'S IN THE LETTER?!

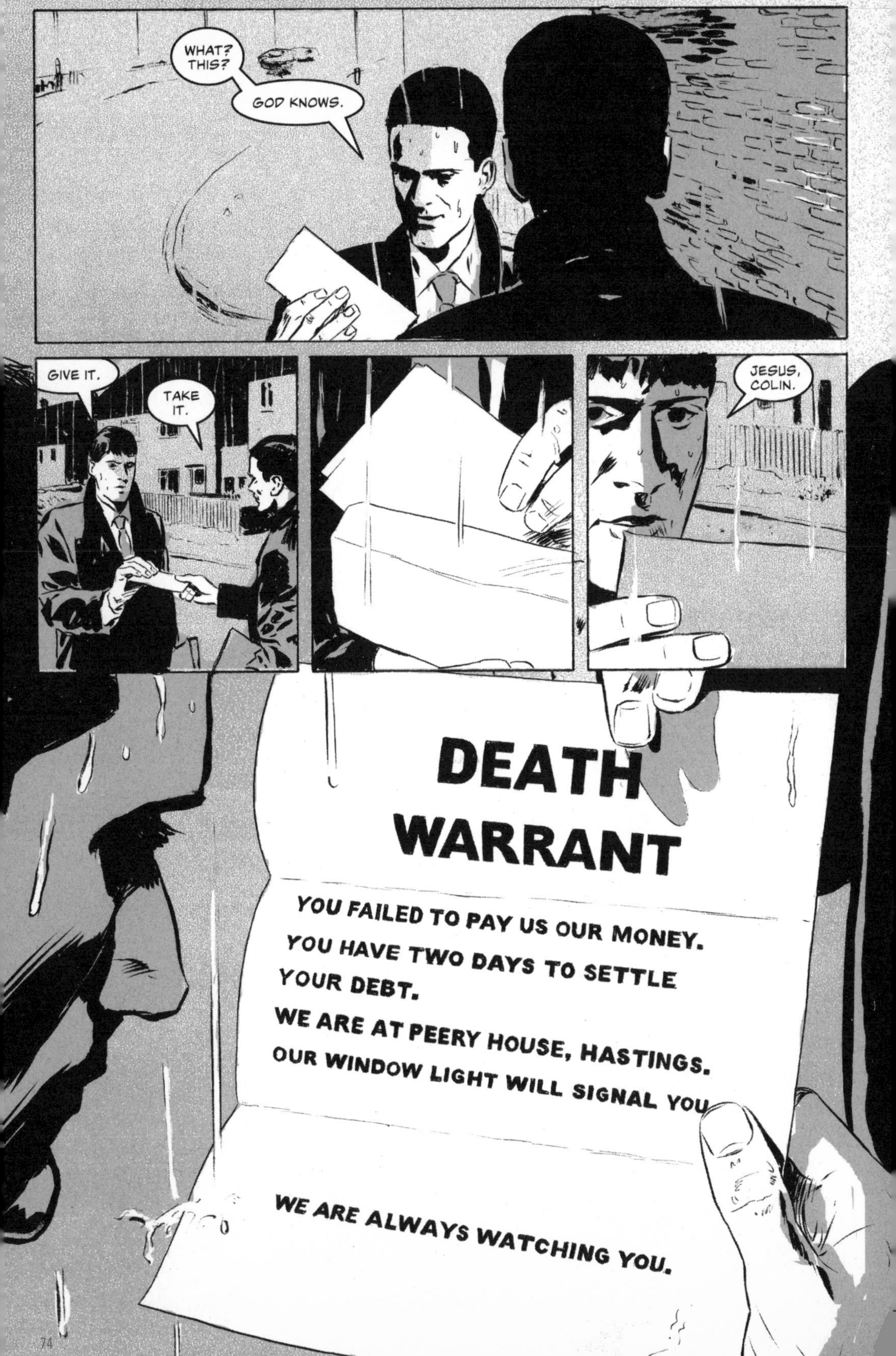
WHAT? THIS?
GOD KNOWS.
GIVE IT.
TAKE IT.
JESUS, COLIN.
DEATH WARRANT
YOU FAILED TO PAY US OUR MONEY.
YOU HAVE TWO DAYS TO SETTLE YOUR DEBT.
WE ARE AT PEERY HOUSE, HASTINGS.
OUR WINDOW LIGHT WILL SIGNAL YOU
WE ARE ALWAYS WATCHING YOU.

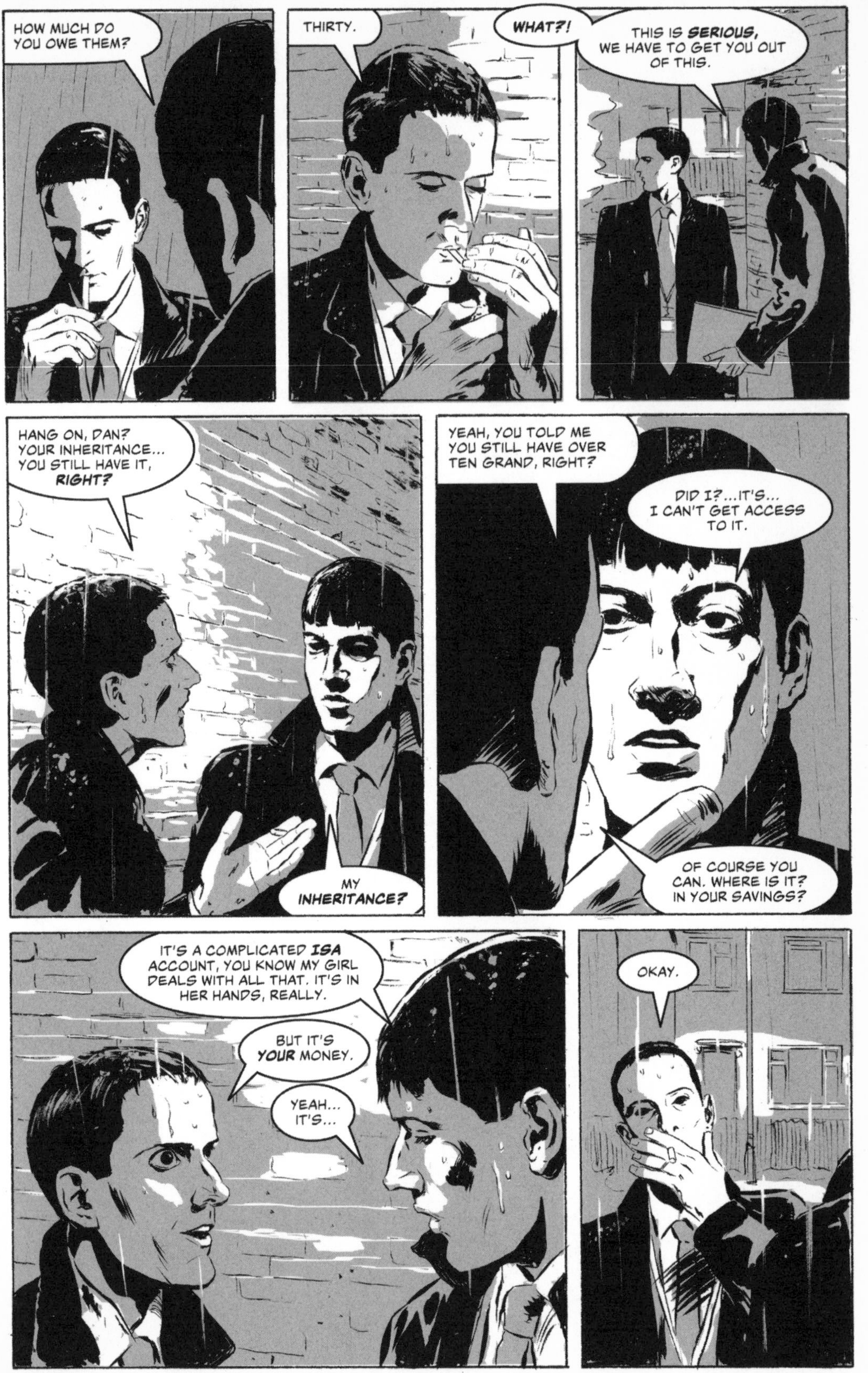
HOW MUCH DO YOU OWE THEM?
THIRTY.
WHAT?!
THIS IS SERIOUS, WE HAVE TO GET YOU OUT OF THIS.
HANG ON, DAN? YOUR INHERITANCE... YOU STILL HAVE IT, RIGHT?
MY INHERITANCE?
YEAH, YOU TOLD ME YOU STILL HAVE OVER TEN GRAND, RIGHT?
DID I?...IT'S... I CAN'T GET ACCESS TO IT.
OF COURSE YOU CAN. WHERE IS IT? IN YOUR SAVINGS?
IT'S A COMPLICATED ISA ACCOUNT, YOU KNOW MY GIRL DEALS WITH ALL THAT. IT'S IN HER HANDS, REALLY.
BUT IT'S YOUR MONEY.
YEAH... IT'S...
OKAY.

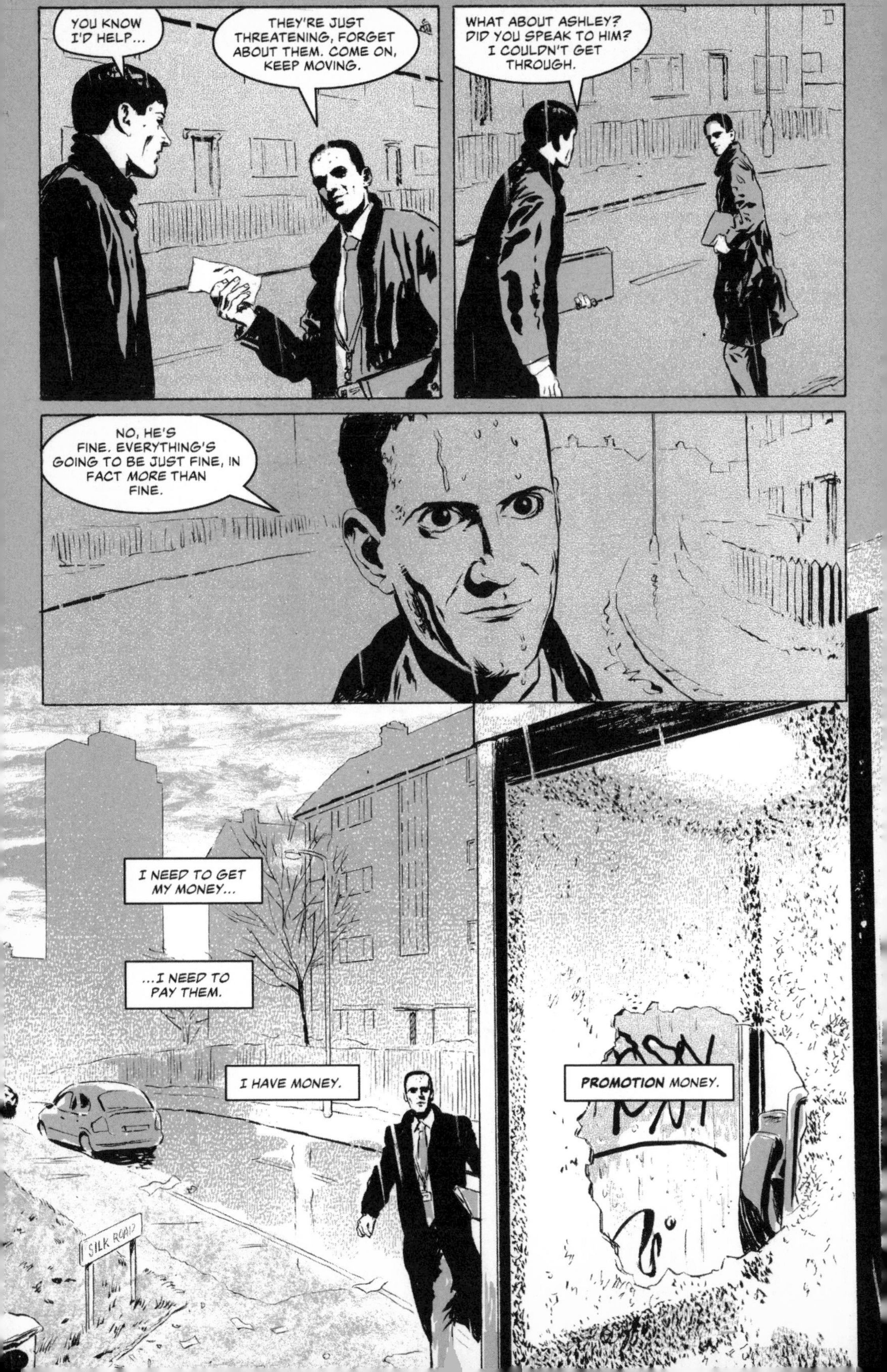
YOU KNOW I'D HELP...
THEY'RE JUST THREATENING, FORGET ABOUT THEM. COME ON, KEEP MOVING.
WHAT ABOUT ASHLEY? DID YOU SPEAK TO HIM? I COULDN'T GET THROUGH.
NO, HE'S FINE. EVERYTHING'S GOING TO BE JUST FINE, IN FACT MORE THAN FINE.
I NEED TO GET MY MONEY...
...I NEED TO PAY THEM.
I HAVE MONEY.
PROMOTION MONEY.
SILK ROAD

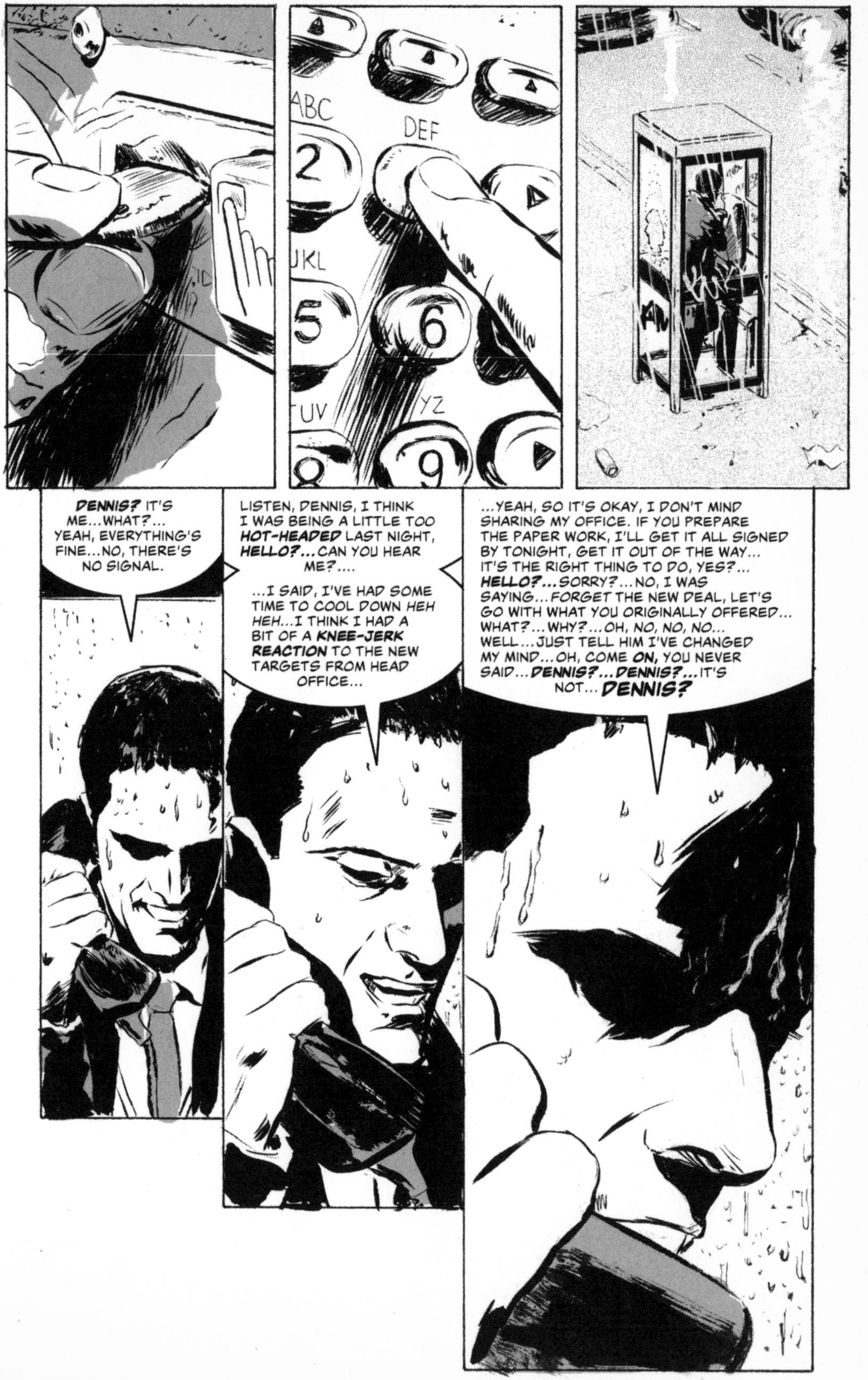
ABC
DEF
JKL
TUV
YZ
DENNIS? IT'S ME...WHAT?... YEAH, EVERYTHING'S FINE...NO, THERE'S NO SIGNAL.
LISTEN, DENNIS, I THINK I WAS BEING A LITTLE TOO HOT-HEADED LAST NIGHT, HELLO?... CAN YOU HEAR ME?....
...I SAID, I'VE HAD SOME TIME TO COOL DOWN HEH HEH...I THINK I HAD A BIT OF A KNEE-JERK REACTION TO THE NEW TARGETS FROM HEAD OFFICE...
...YEAH, SO IT'S OKAY, I DON'T MIND SHARING MY OFFICE. IF YOU PREPARE THE PAPER WORK, I'LL GET IT ALL SIGNED BY TONIGHT, GET IT OUT OF THE WAY... IT'S THE RIGHT THING TO DO, YES?... HELLO?... SORRY?... NO, I WAS SAYING... FORGET THE NEW DEAL, LET'S GO WITH WHAT YOU ORIGINALLY OFFERED... WHAT?... WHY?... OH, NO, NO, NO... WELL... JUST TELL HIM I'VE CHANGED MY MIND... OH, COME ON, YOU NEVER SAID... DENNIS?... DENNIS?... IT'S NOT... DENNIS?

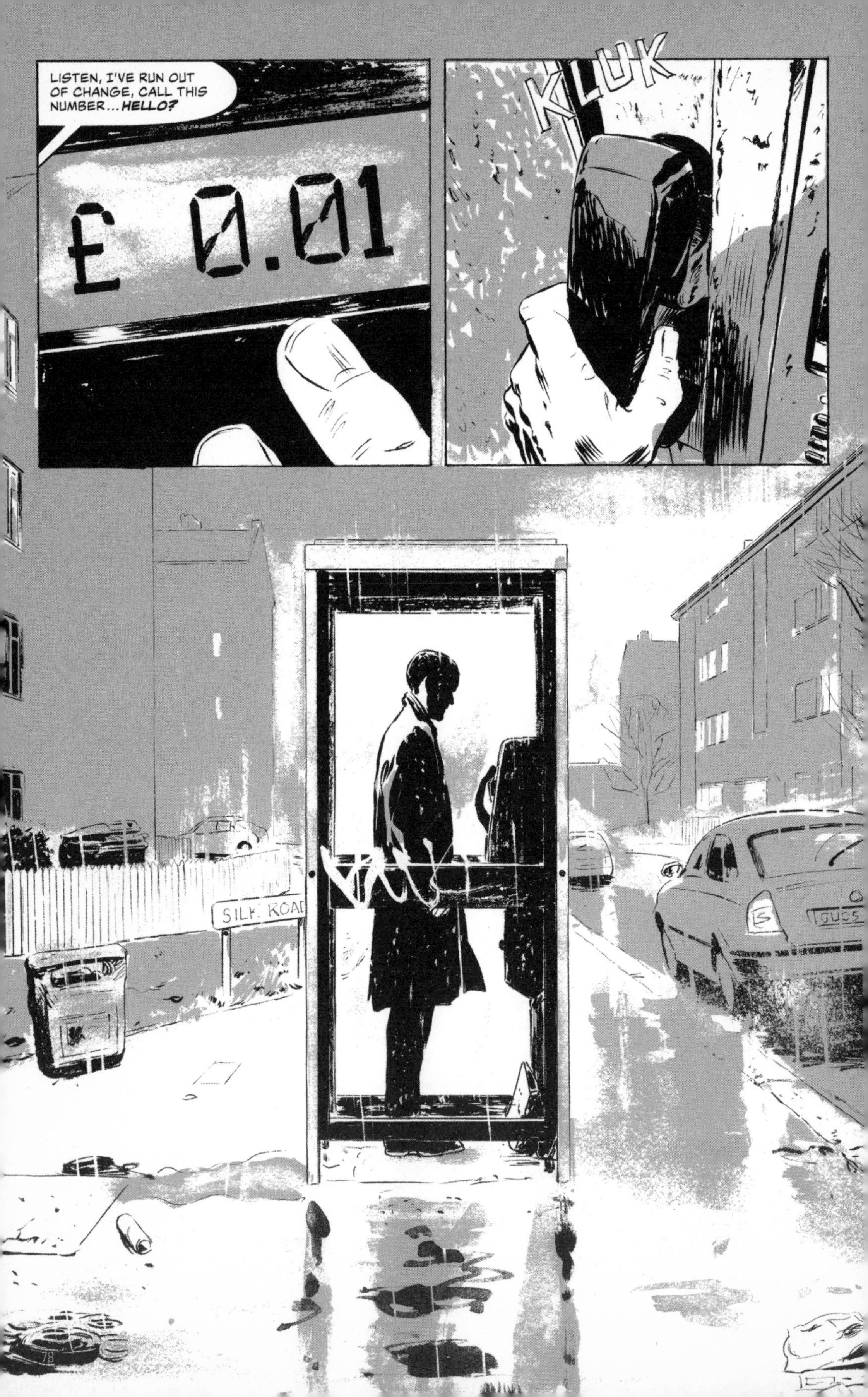
LISTEN, I'VE RUN OUT OF CHANGE, CALL THIS NUMBER... *HELLO?*
£ 0.01
KLUK
SILK ROAD

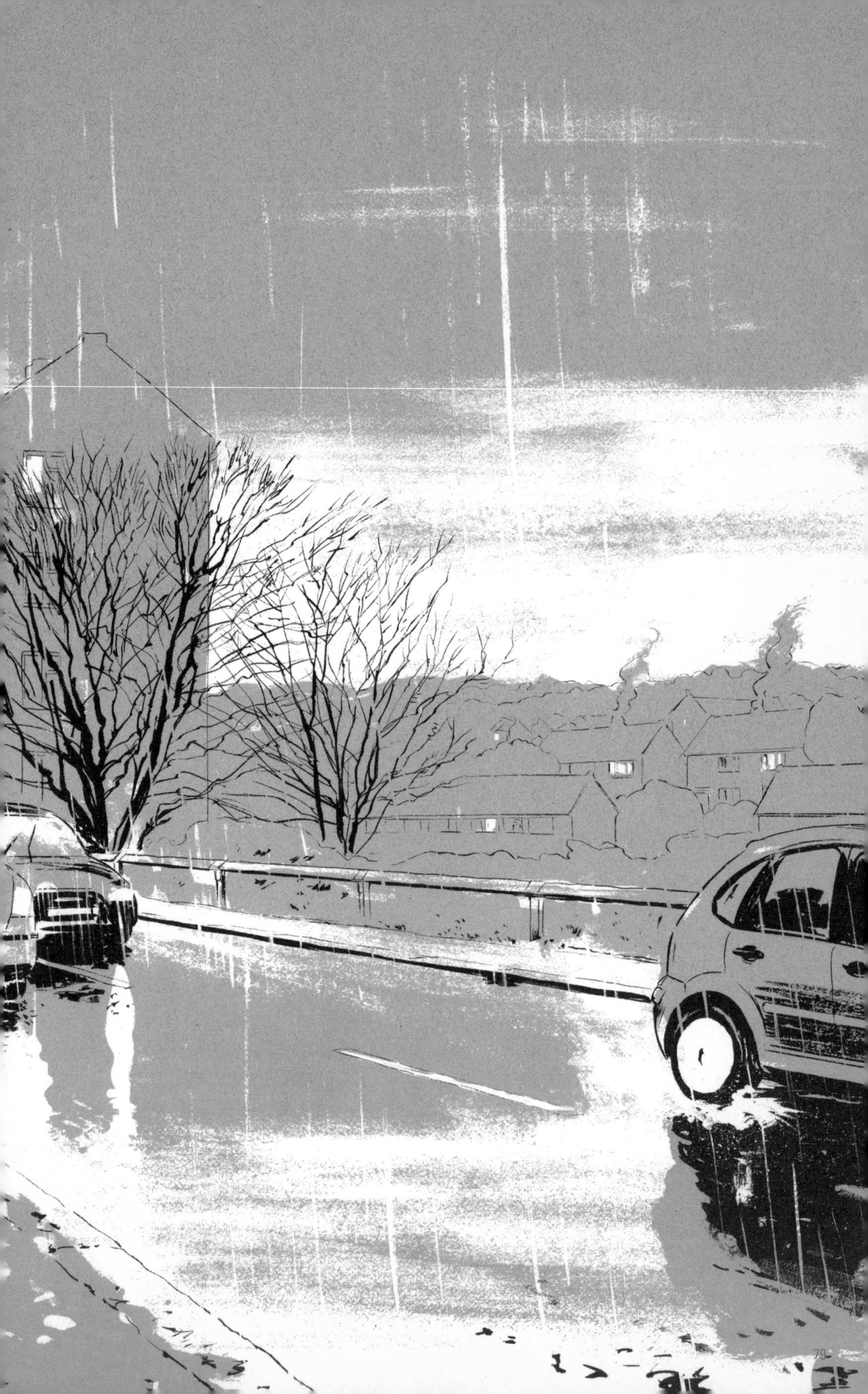

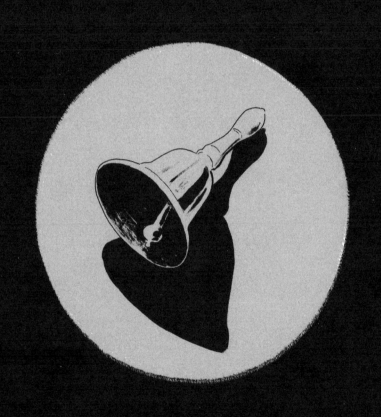

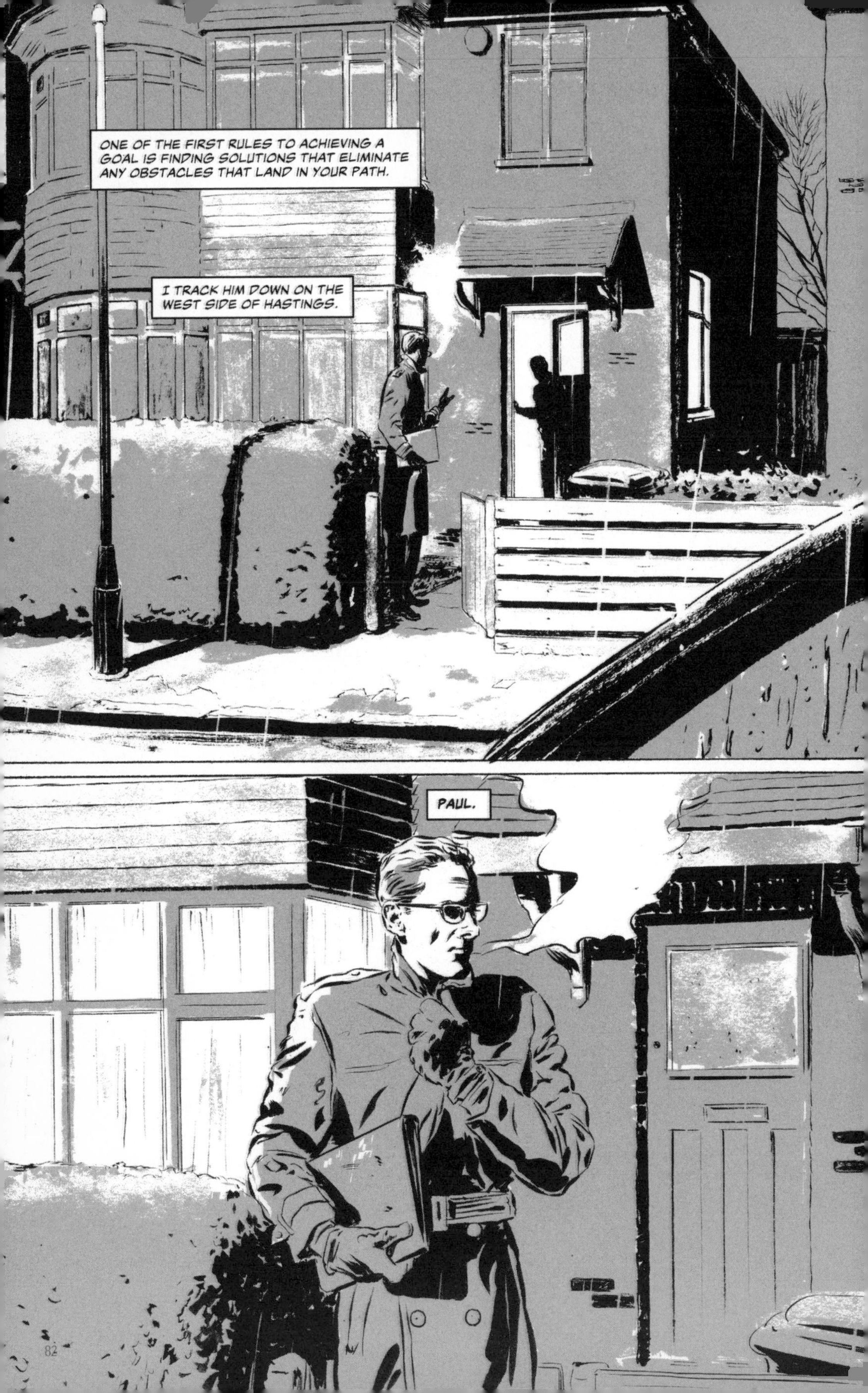
ONE OF THE FIRST RULES TO ACHIEVING A GOAL IS FINDING SOLUTIONS THAT ELIMINATE ANY OBSTACLES THAT LAND IN YOUR PATH.
I TRACK HIM DOWN ON THE WEST SIDE OF HASTINGS.
PAUL.

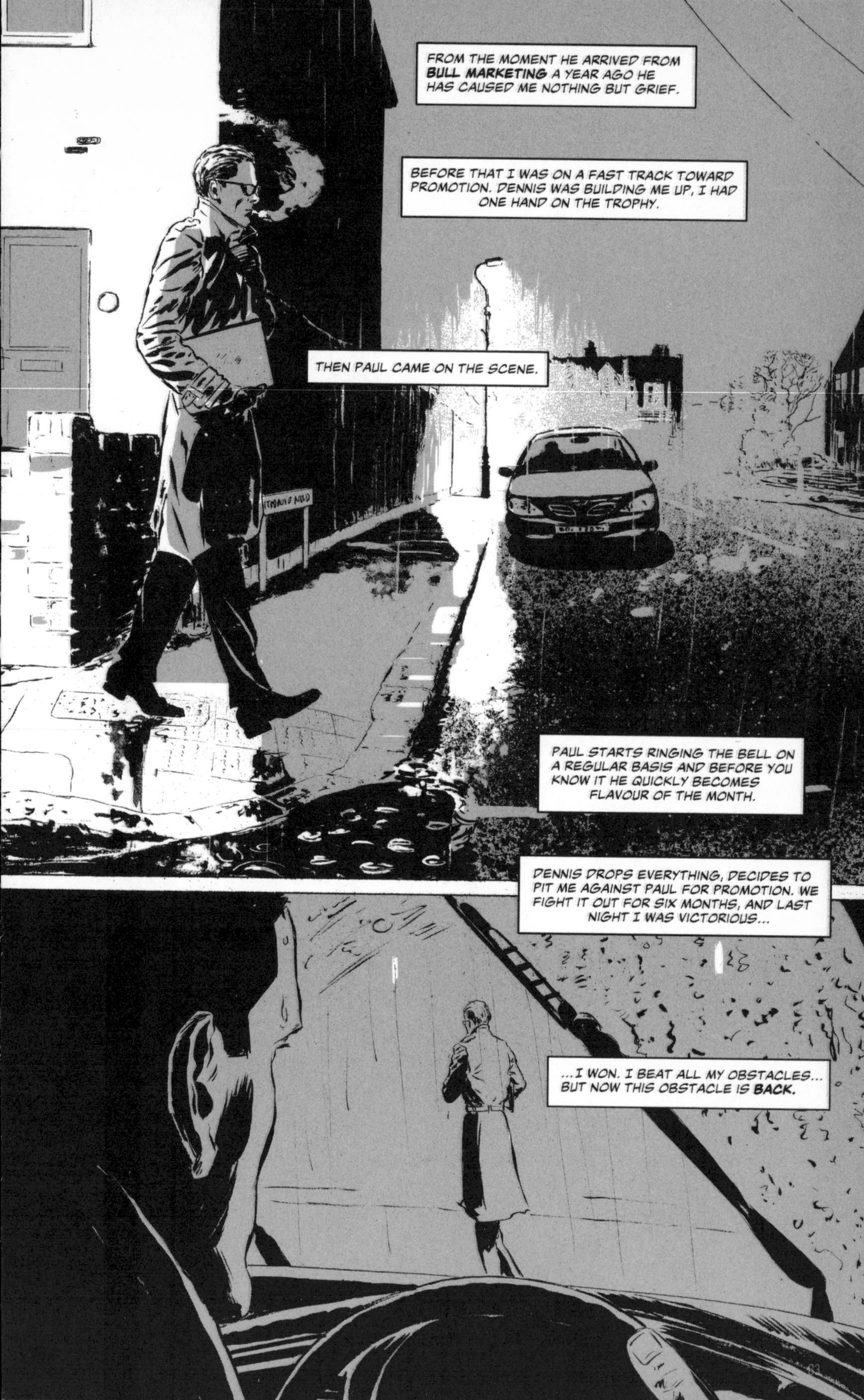
FROM THE MOMENT HE ARRIVED FROM BULL MARKETING A YEAR AGO HE HAS CAUSED ME NOTHING BUT GRIEF.
BEFORE THAT I WAS ON A FAST TRACK TOWARD PROMOTION. DENNIS WAS BUILDING ME UP, I HAD ONE HAND ON THE TROPHY.
THEN PAUL CAME ON THE SCENE.
PAUL STARTS RINGING THE BELL ON A REGULAR BASIS AND BEFORE YOU KNOW IT HE QUICKLY BECOMES FLAVOUR OF THE MONTH.
DENNIS DROPS EVERYTHING, DECIDES TO PIT ME AGAINST PAUL FOR PROMOTION. WE FIGHT IT OUT FOR SIX MONTHS, AND LAST NIGHT I WAS VICTORIOUS...
...I WON. I BEAT ALL MY OBSTACLES... BUT NOW THIS OBSTACLE IS BACK.

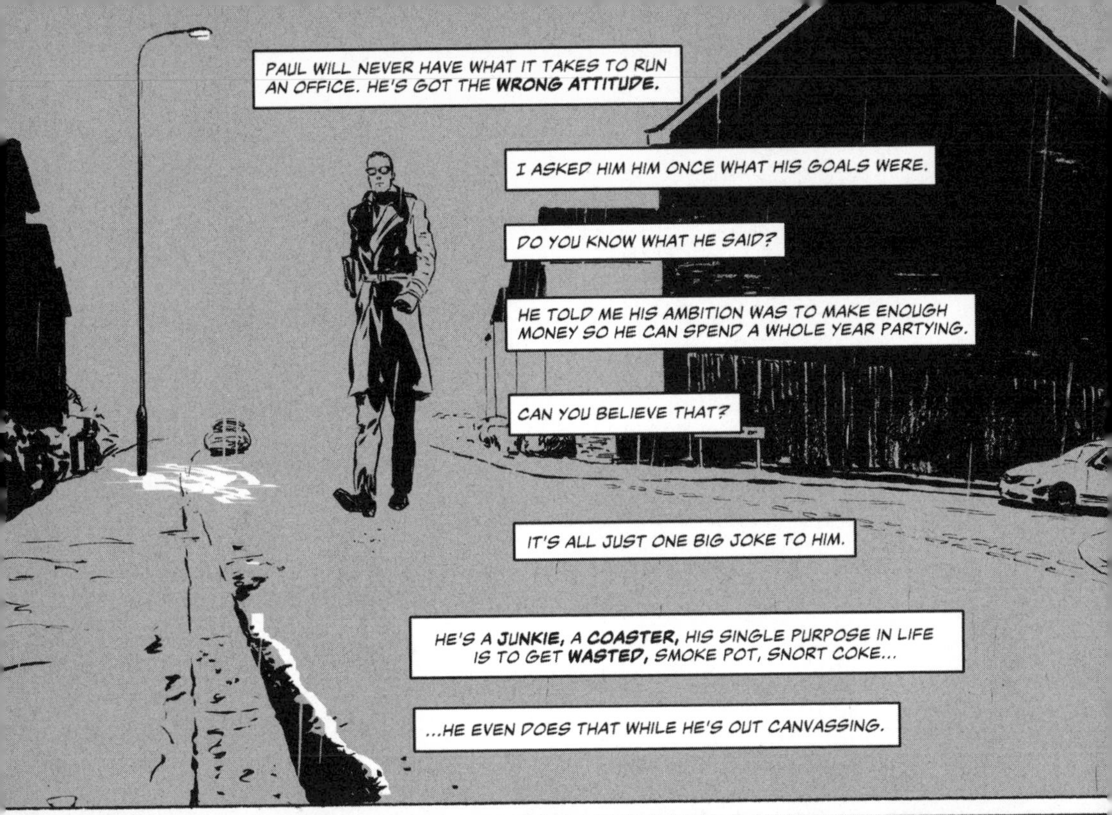
PAUL WILL NEVER HAVE WHAT IT TAKES TO RUN AN OFFICE. HE'S GOT THE WRONG ATTITUDE.
I ASKED HIM HIM ONCE WHAT HIS GOALS WERE.
DO YOU KNOW WHAT HE SAID?
HE TOLD ME HIS AMBITION WAS TO MAKE ENOUGH MONEY SO HE CAN SPEND A WHOLE YEAR PARTYING.
CAN YOU BELIEVE THAT?
IT'S ALL JUST ONE BIG JOKE TO HIM.
HE'S A JUNKIE, A COASTER, HIS SINGLE PURPOSE IN LIFE IS TO GET WASTED, SMOKE POT, SNORT COKE...
...HE EVEN DOES THAT WHILE HE'S OUT CANVASSING.

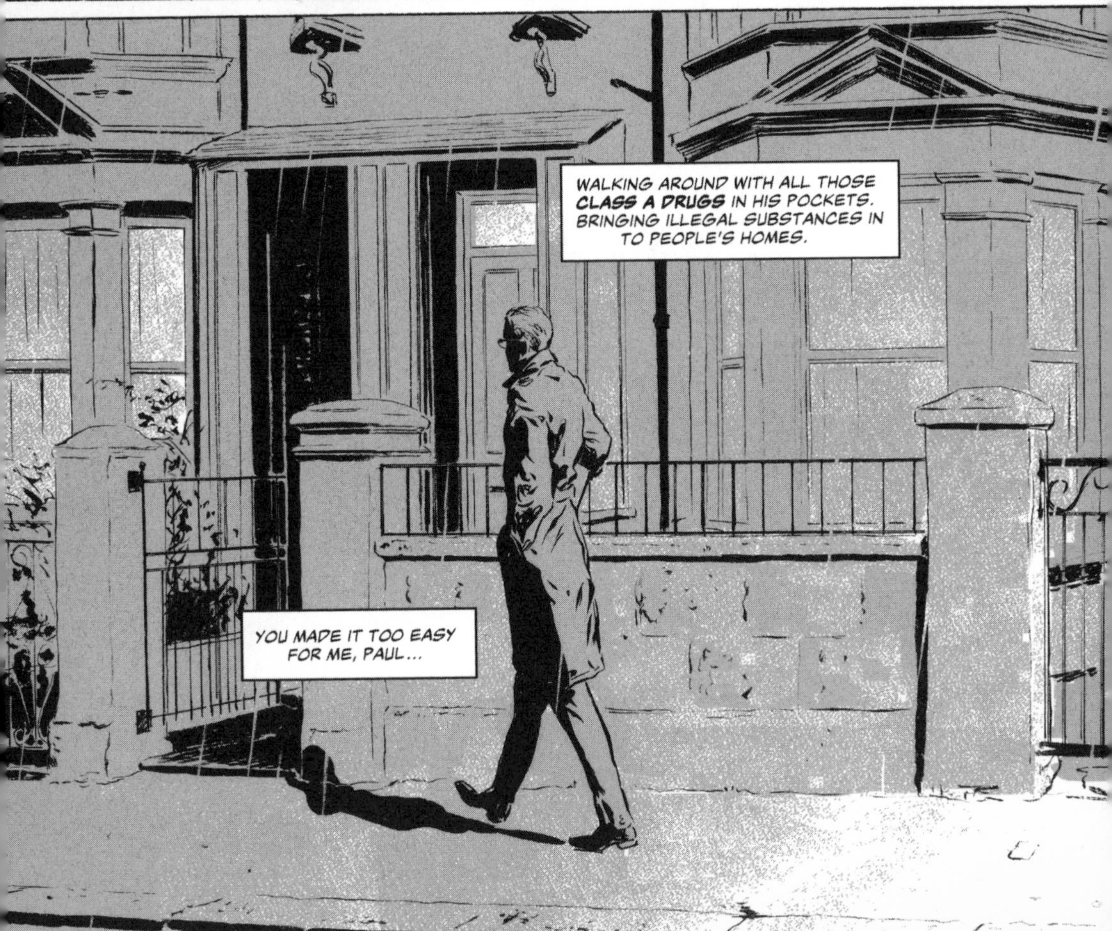
WALKING AROUND WITH ALL THOSE CLASS A DRUGS IN HIS POCKETS. BRINGING ILLEGAL SUBSTANCES IN TO PEOPLE'S HOMES.
YOU MADE IT TOO EASY FOR ME, PAUL...

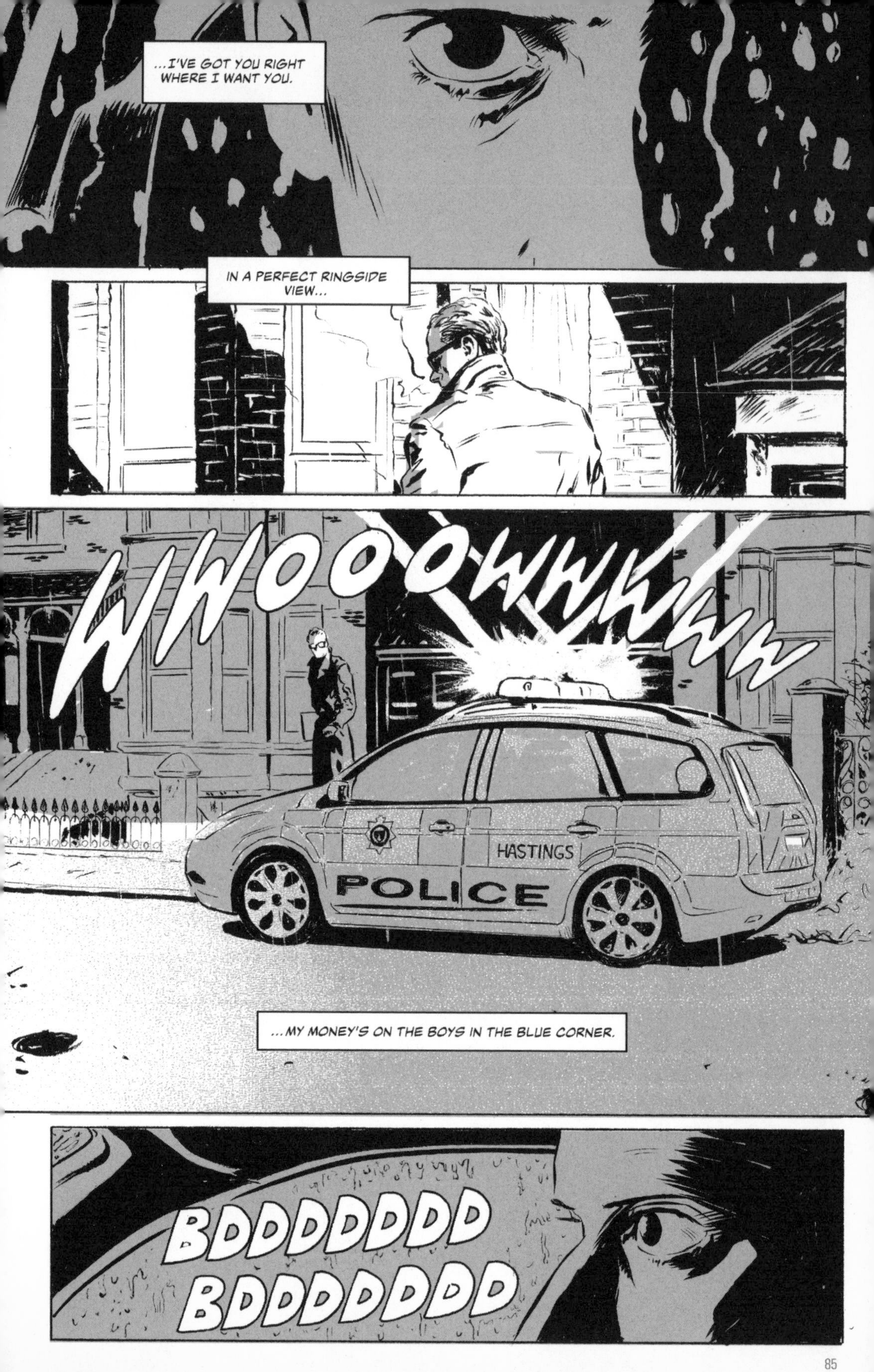
...I'VE GOT YOU RIGHT WHERE I WANT YOU.
IN A PERFECT RINGSIDE VIEW...
WHOOOWWWWW
HASTINGS
POLICE
...MY MONEY'S ON THE BOYS IN THE BLUE CORNER.
BDDDDDDD
BDDDDDDD

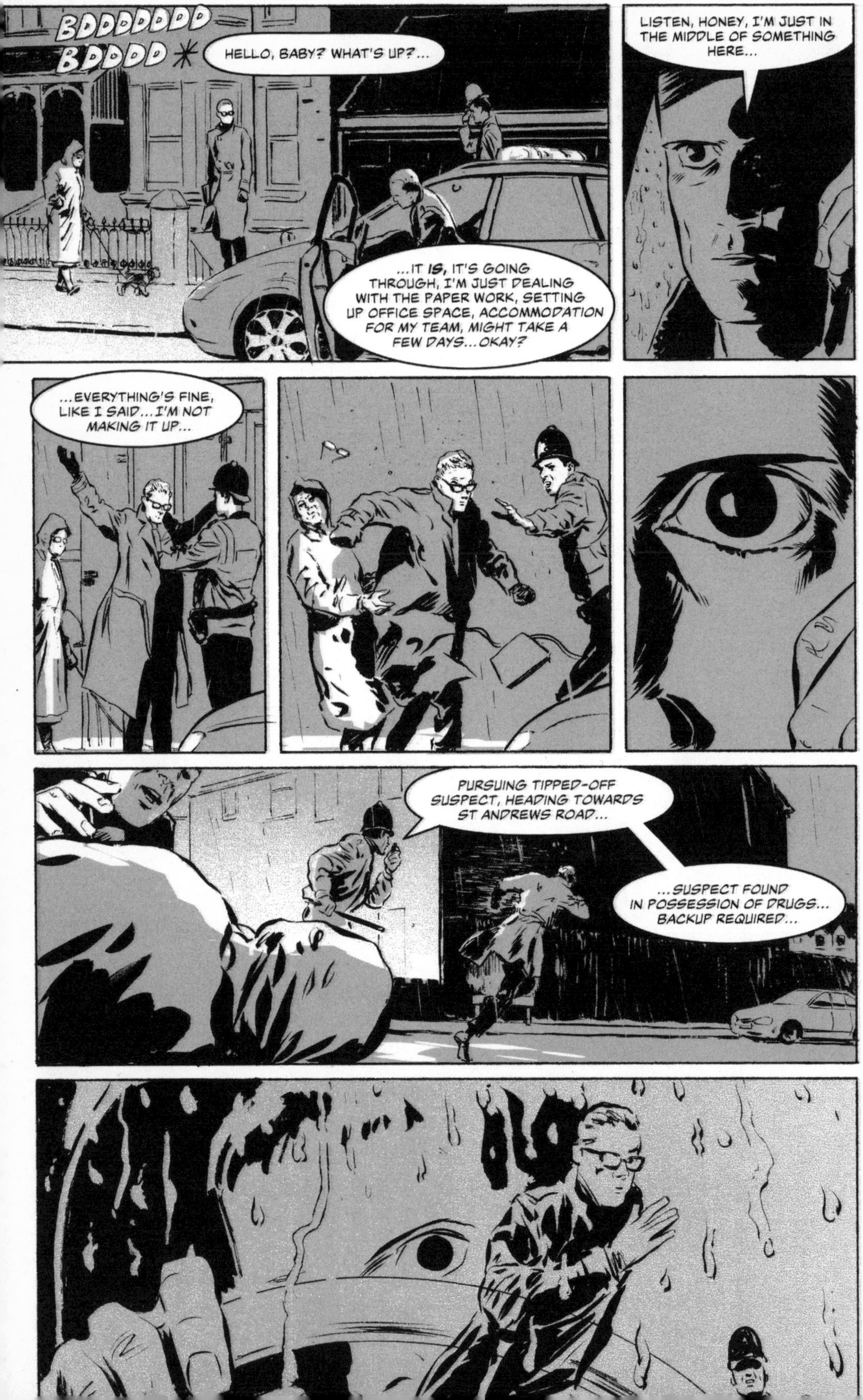
BDDDDDDD BDDDD
HELLO, BABY? WHAT'S UP?...
LISTEN, HONEY, I'M JUST IN THE MIDDLE OF SOMETHING HERE...
...IT IS, IT'S GOING THROUGH, I'M JUST DEALING WITH THE PAPER WORK, SETTING UP OFFICE SPACE, ACCOMMODATION FOR MY TEAM, MIGHT TAKE A FEW DAYS...OKAY?
...EVERYTHING'S FINE, LIKE I SAID...I'M NOT MAKING IT UP...
PURSUING TIPPED-OFF SUSPECT, HEADING TOWARDS ST ANDREWS ROAD...
...SUSPECT FOUND IN POSSESSION OF DRUGS... BACKUP REQUIRED...

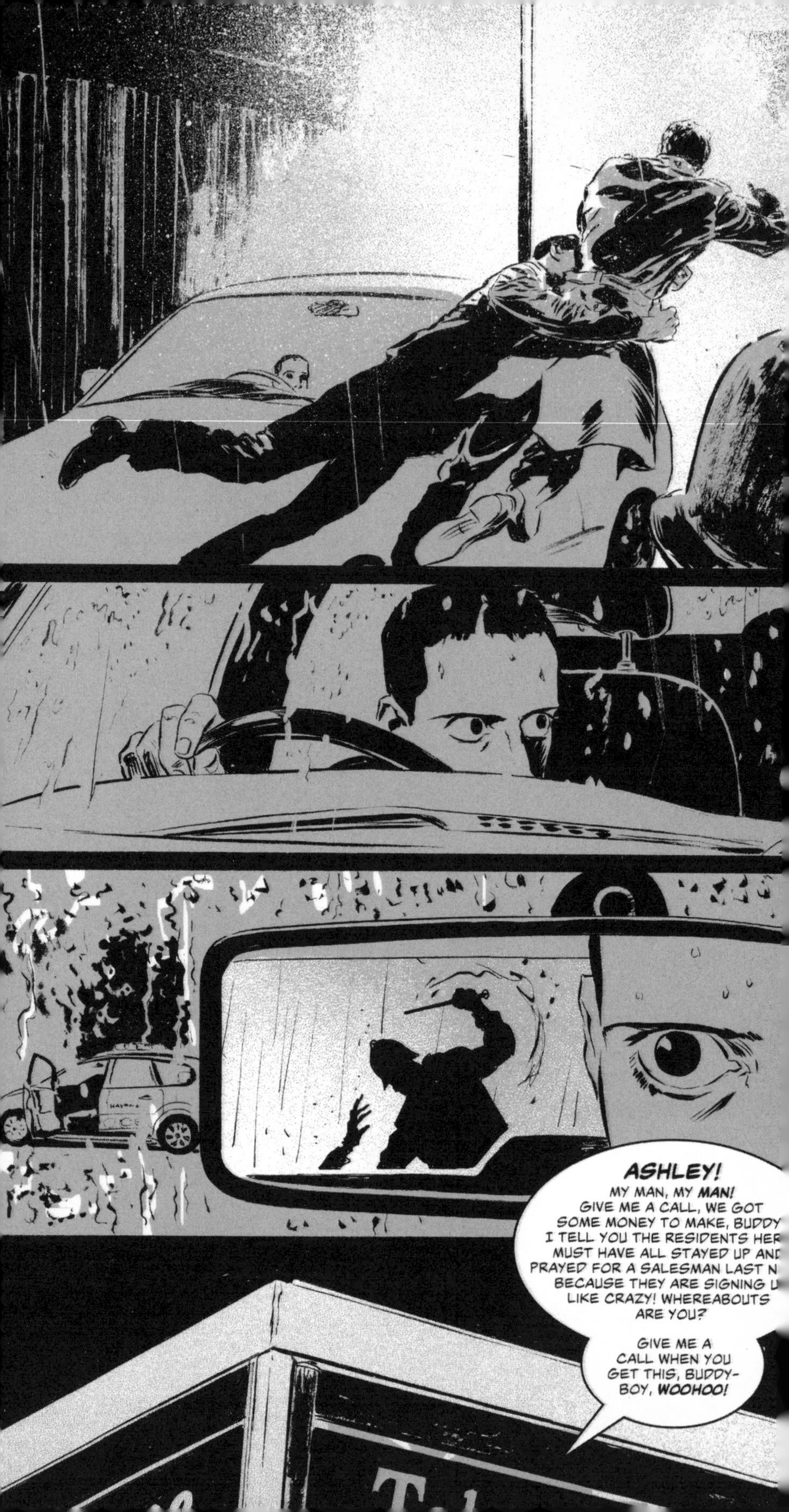
ASHLEY!
MY MAN, MY MAN!
GIVE ME A CALL, WE GOT
SOME MONEY TO MAKE, BUDDY
I TELL YOU THE RESIDENTS HER
MUST HAVE ALL STAYED UP AND
PRAYED FOR A SALESMAN LAST N
BECAUSE THEY ARE SIGNING U
LIKE CRAZY! WHEREABOUTS
ARE YOU?
GIVE ME A
CALL WHEN YOU
GET THIS, BUDDY-
BOY, WOOHOO!

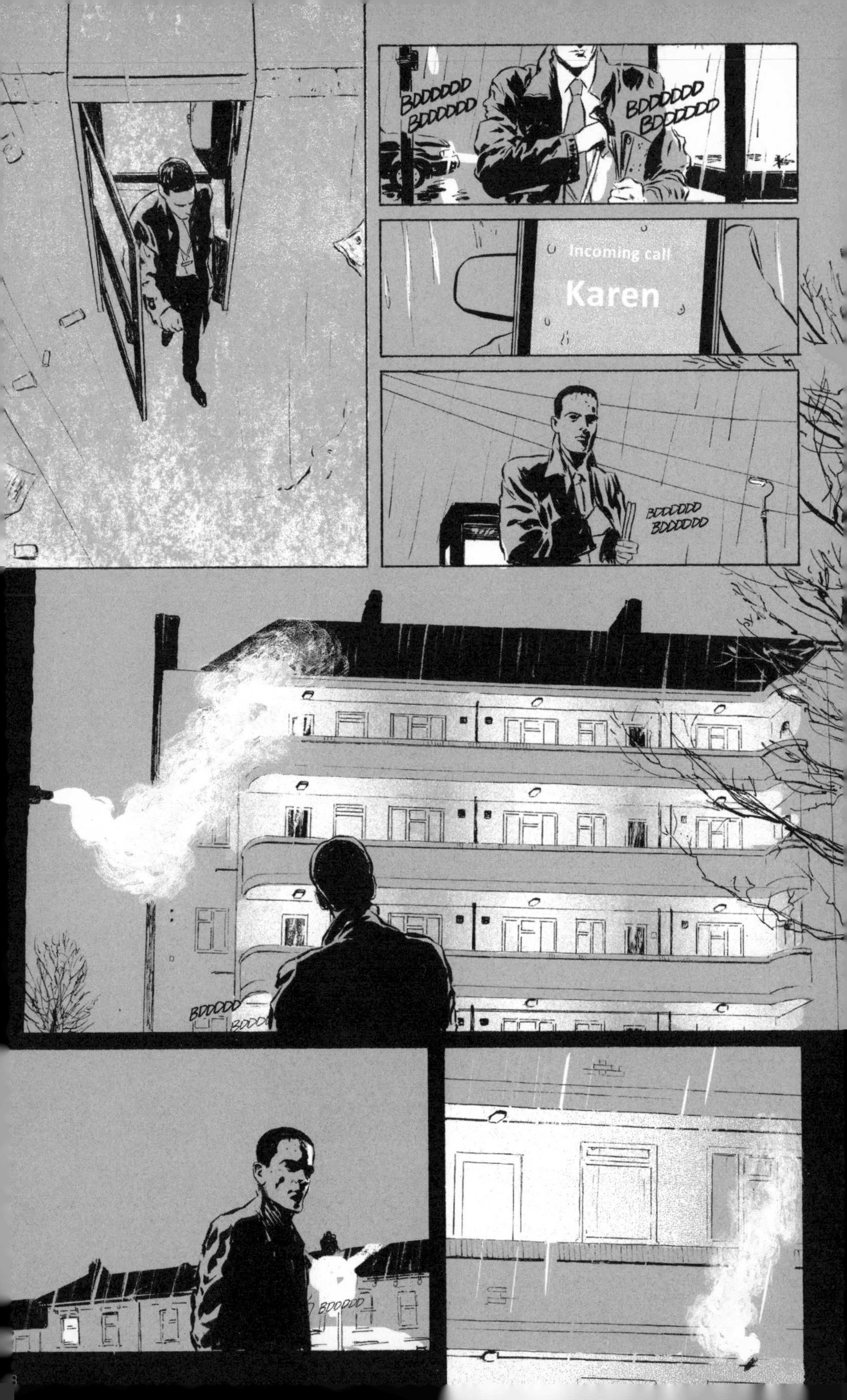
BDDDDDD
BDDDDDD
BDDDDDDD
BDDDDDDD
Incoming call
Karen
BDDDDDD
BDDDDDD
BDDDDD
BDDDD
BDDDDD

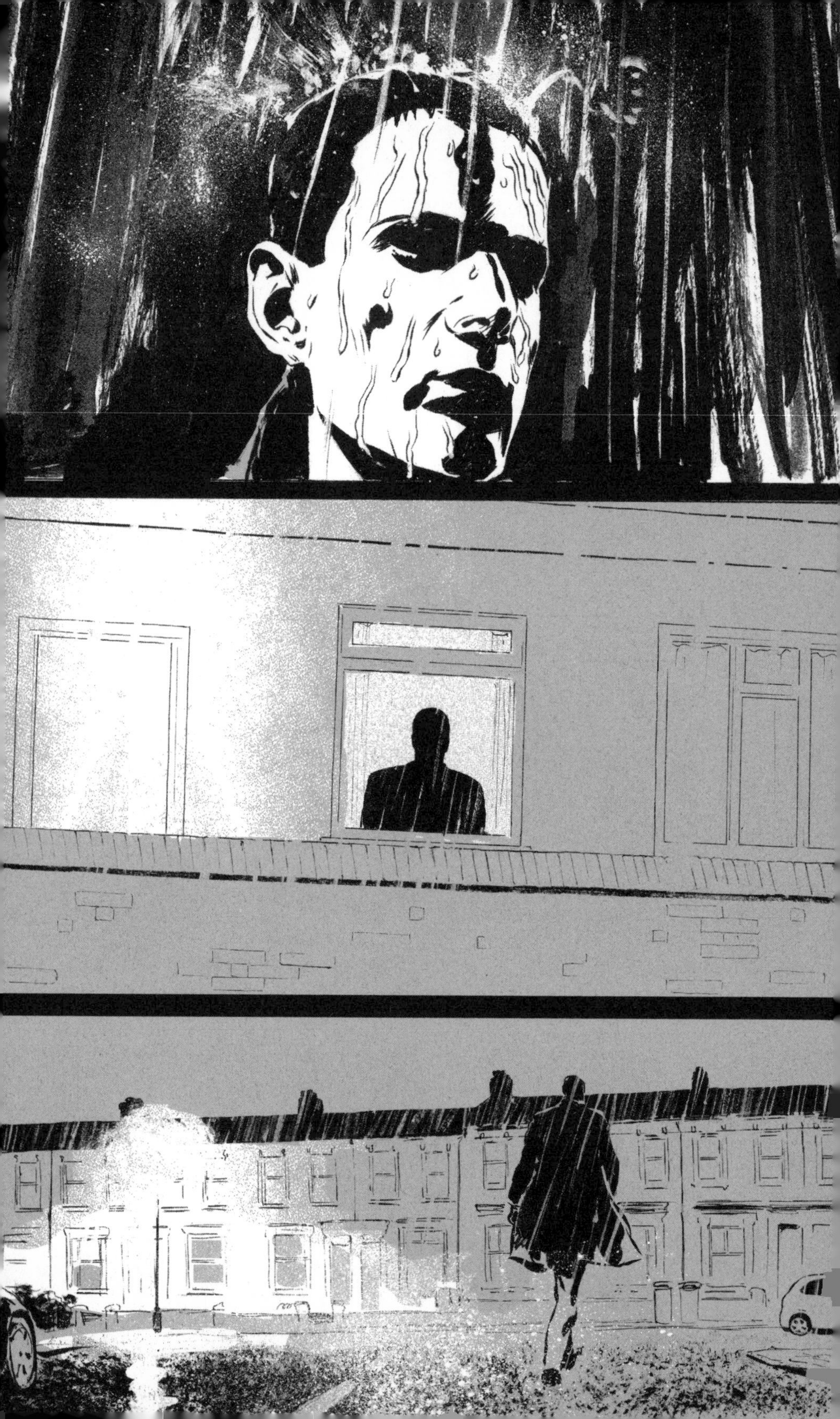

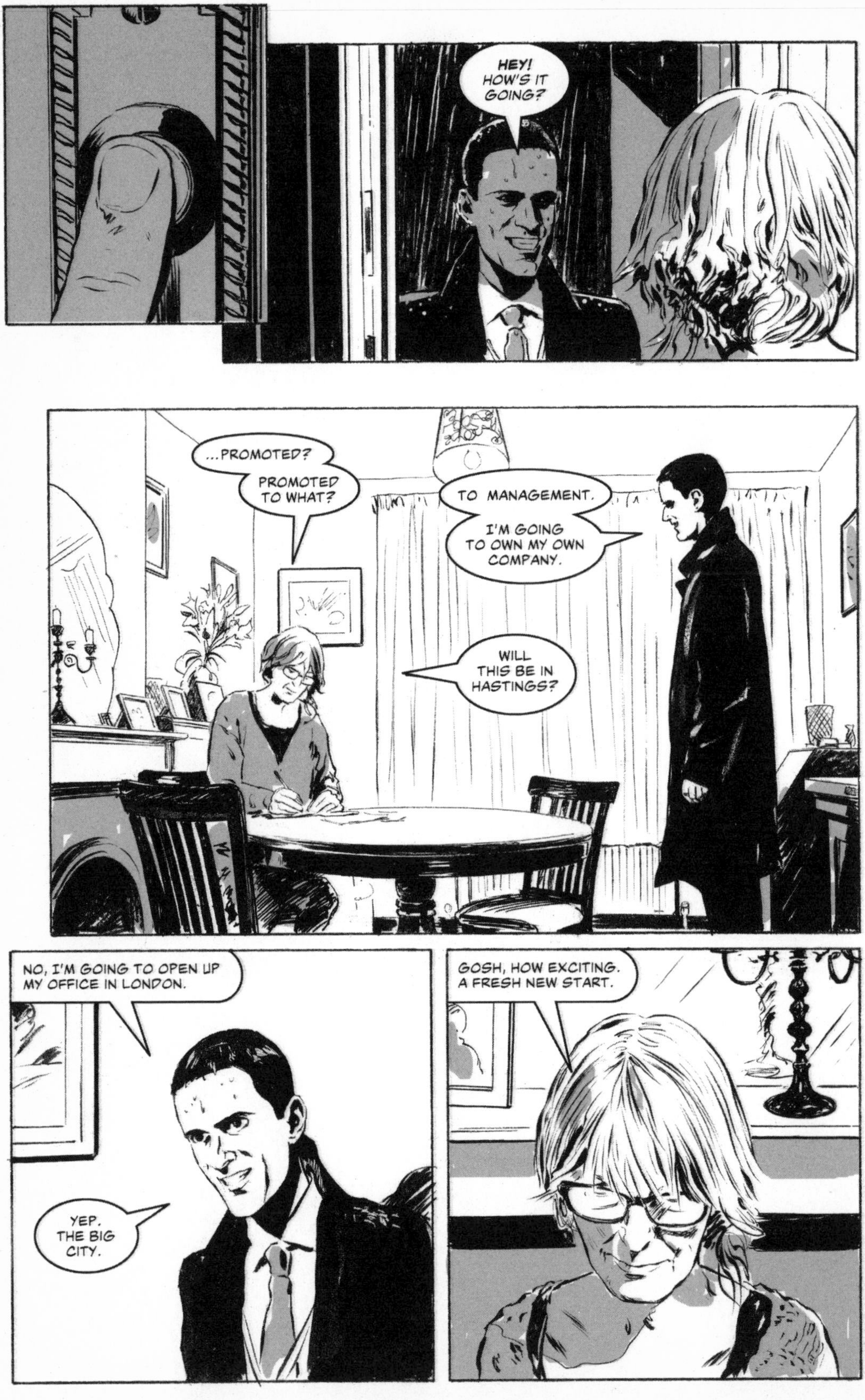
HEY! HOW'S IT GOING?
...PROMOTED?
PROMOTED TO WHAT?
TO MANAGEMENT.
I'M GOING TO OWN MY OWN COMPANY.
WILL THIS BE IN HASTINGS?
NO, I'M GOING TO OPEN UP MY OFFICE IN LONDON.
YEP. THE BIG CITY.
GOSH, HOW EXCITING. A FRESH NEW START.

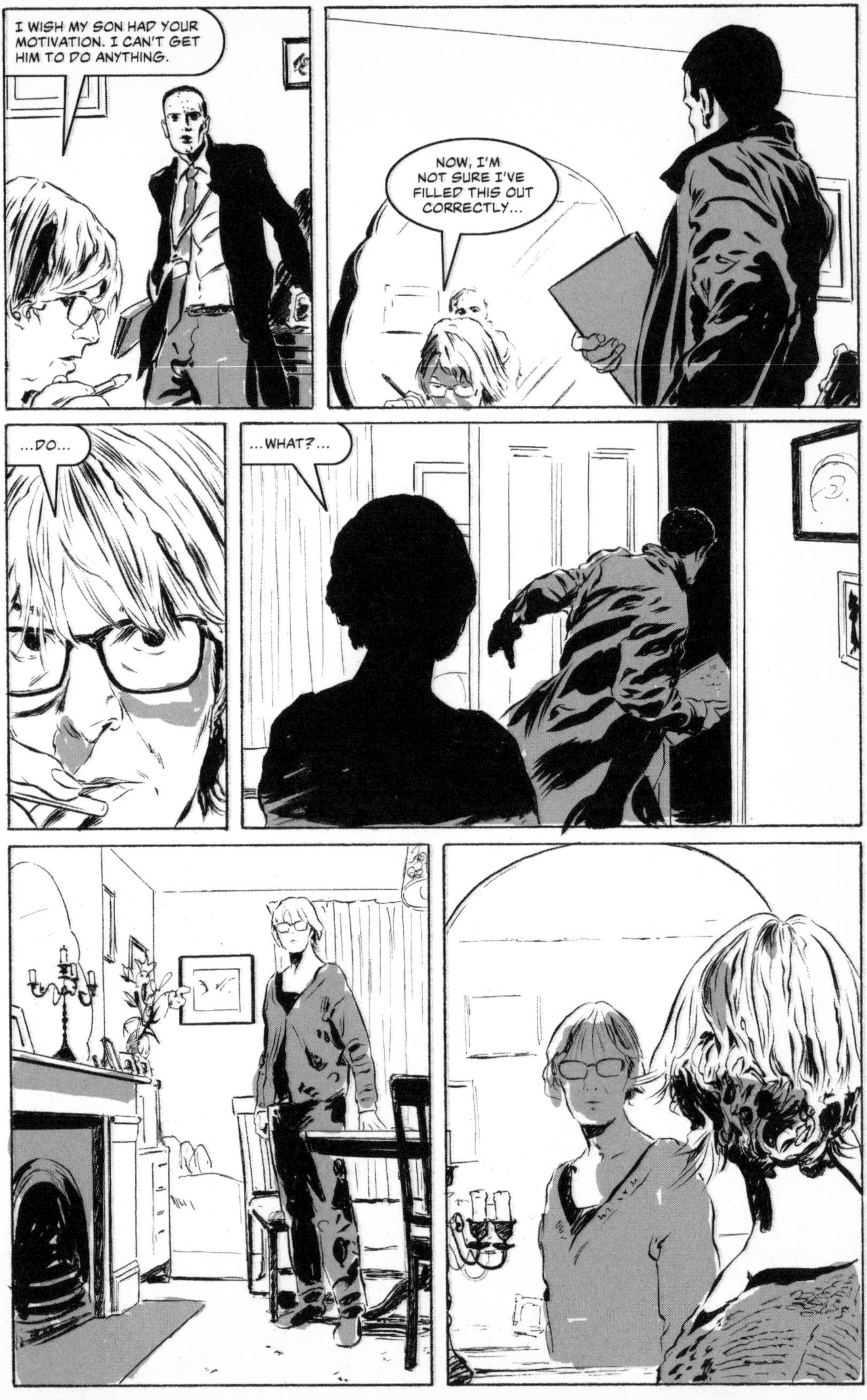
I WISH MY SON HAD YOUR MOTIVATION. I CAN'T GET HIM TO DO ANYTHING.
NOW, I'M NOT SURE I'VE FILLED THIS OUT CORRECTLY...
...DO...
...WHAT?...

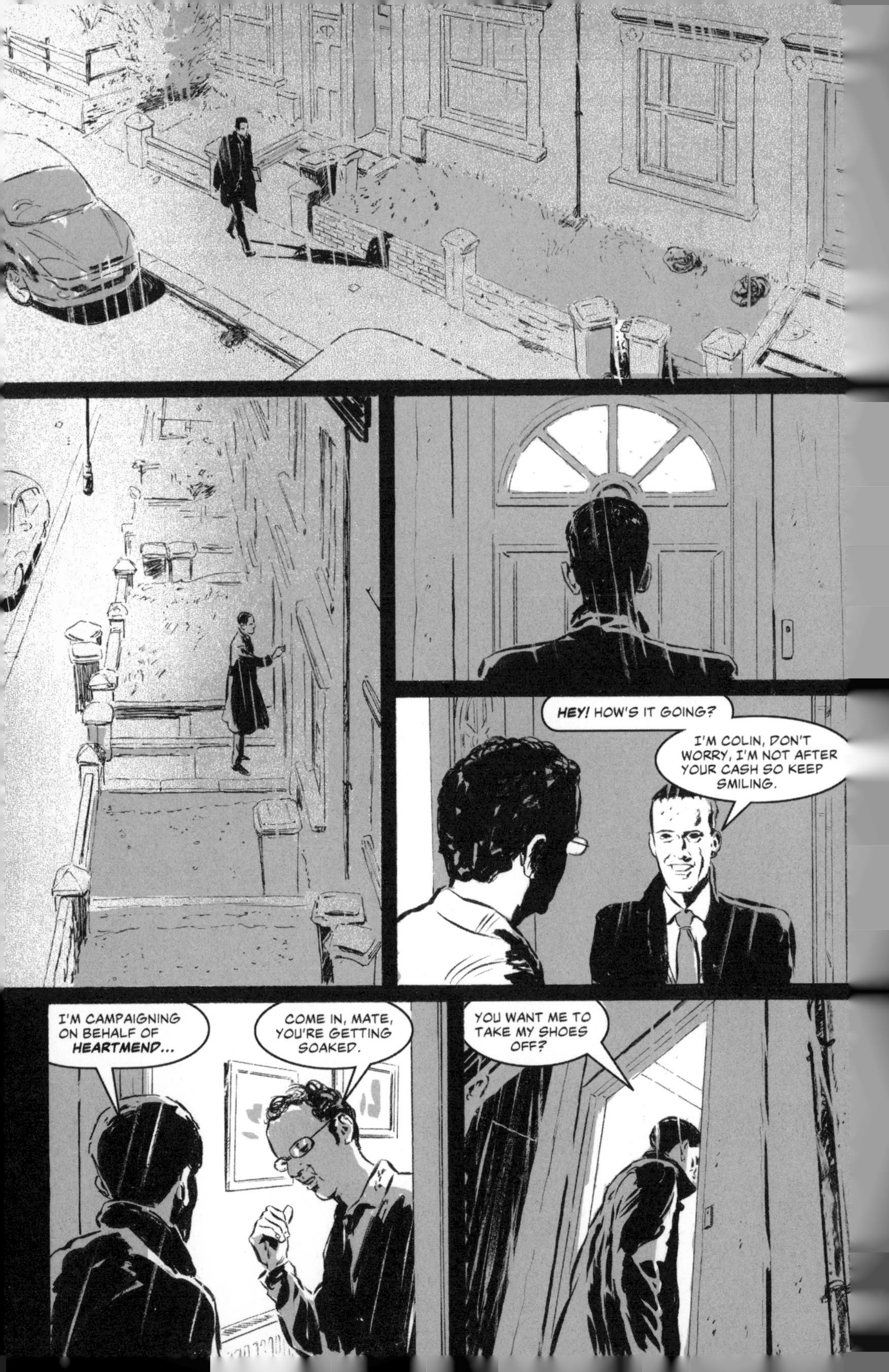
HEY! HOW'S IT GOING?
I'M COLIN, DON'T WORRY, I'M NOT AFTER YOUR CASH SO KEEP SMILING.
I'M CAMPAIGNING ON BEHALF OF HEARTMEND...
COME IN, MATE, YOU'RE GETTING SOAKED.
YOU WANT ME TO TAKE MY SHOES OFF?

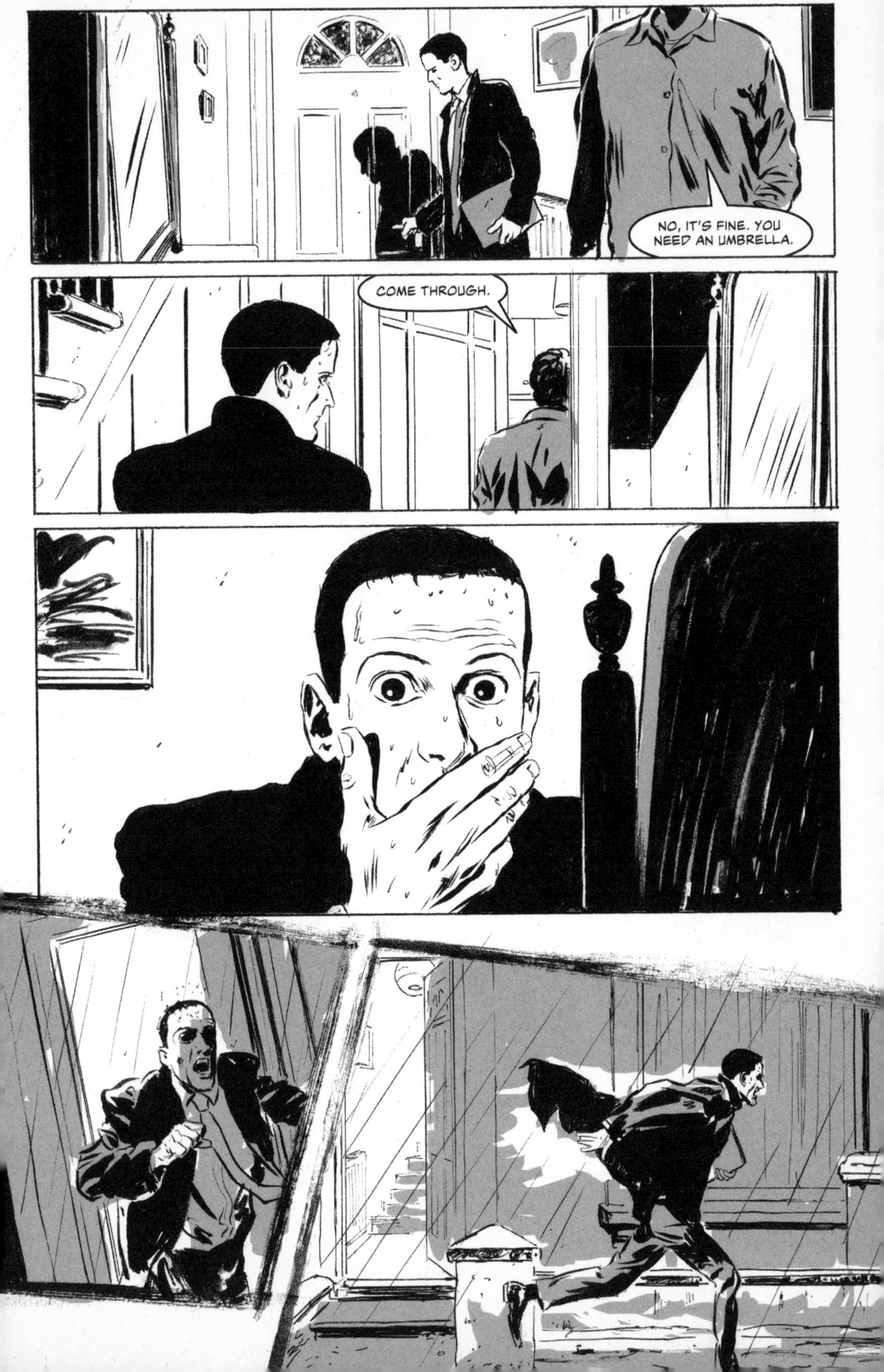
NO, IT'S FINE. YOU NEED AN UMBRELLA.
COME THROUGH.

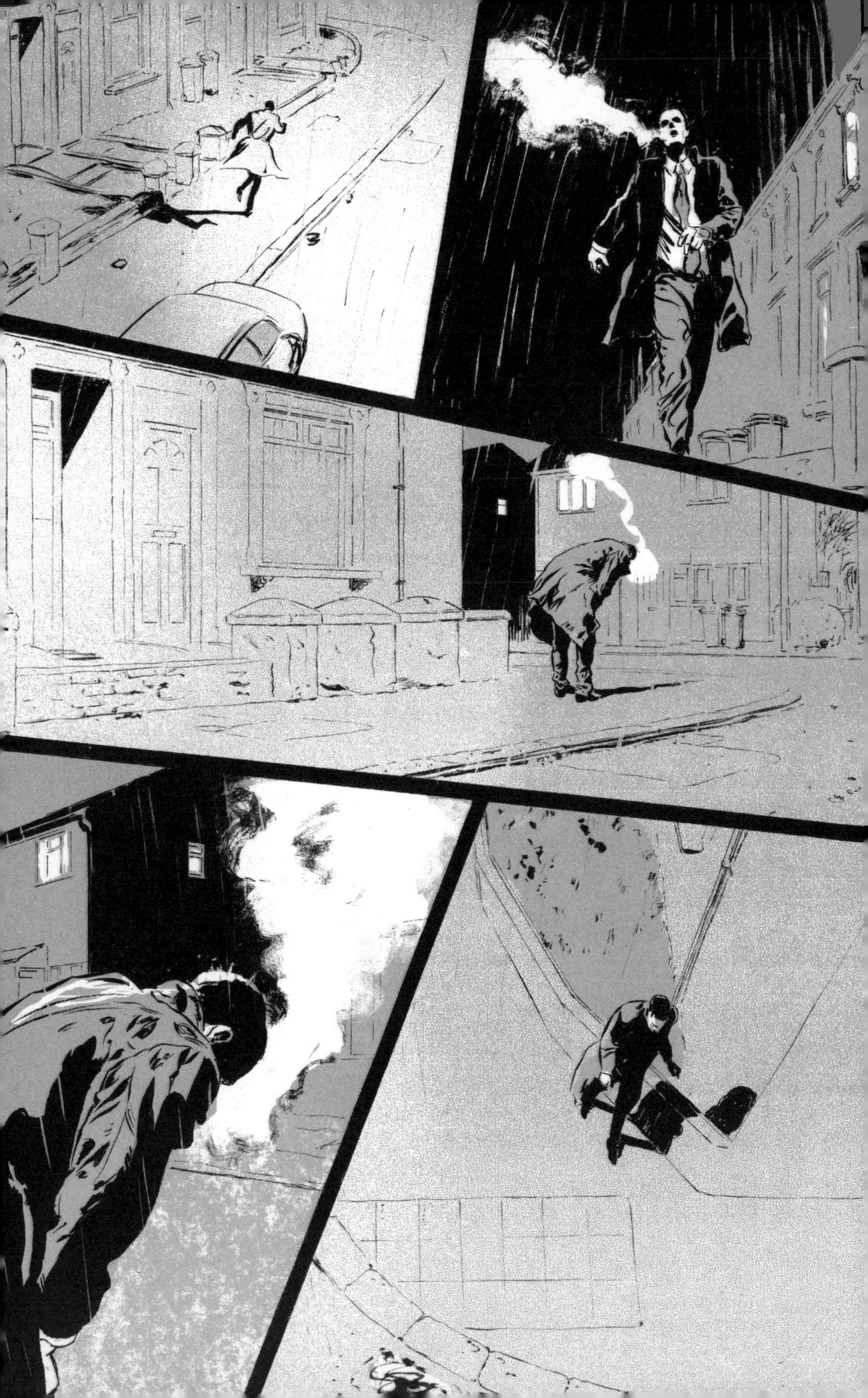

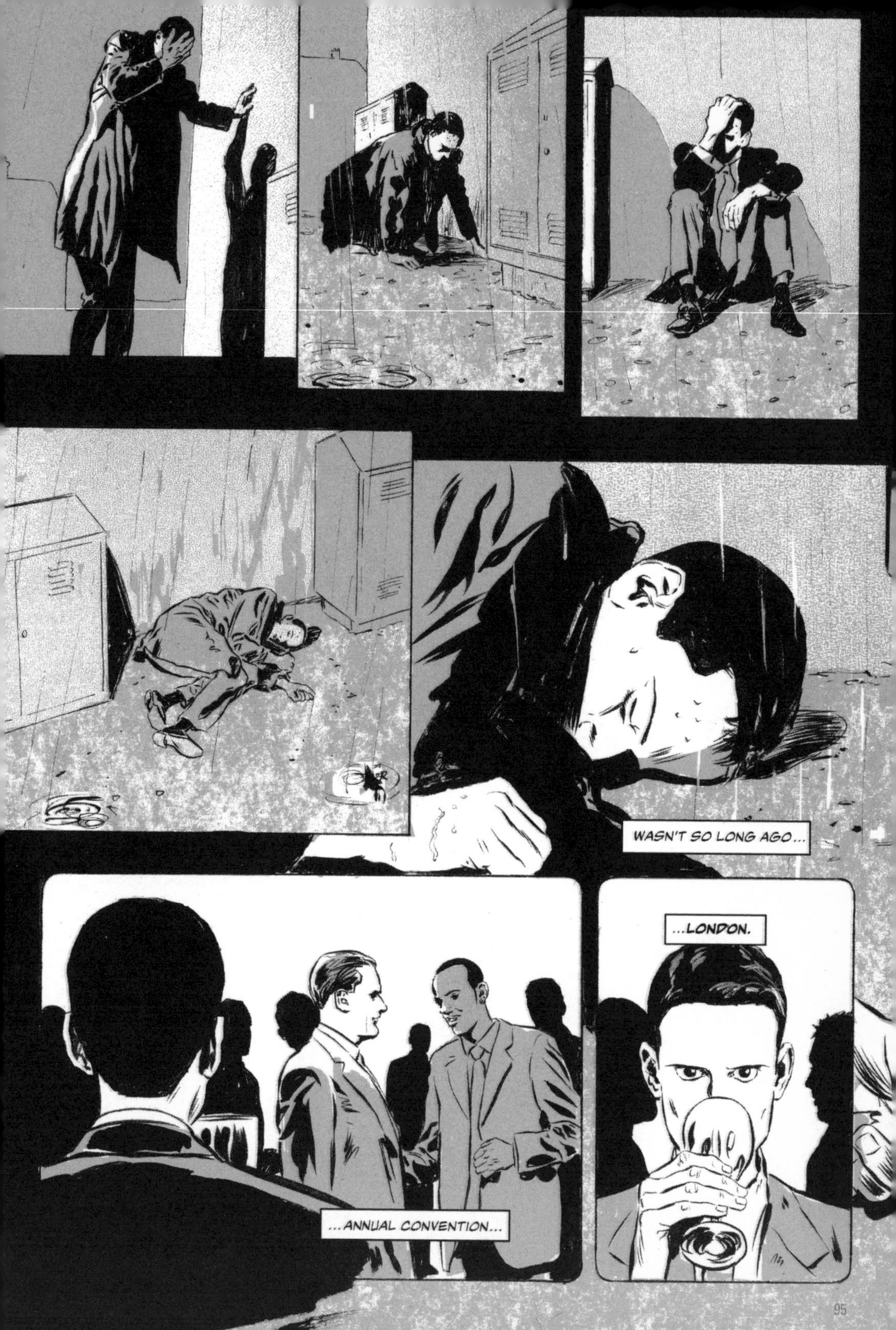
WASN'T SO LONG AGO...
...ANNUAL CONVENTION...
...LONDON.

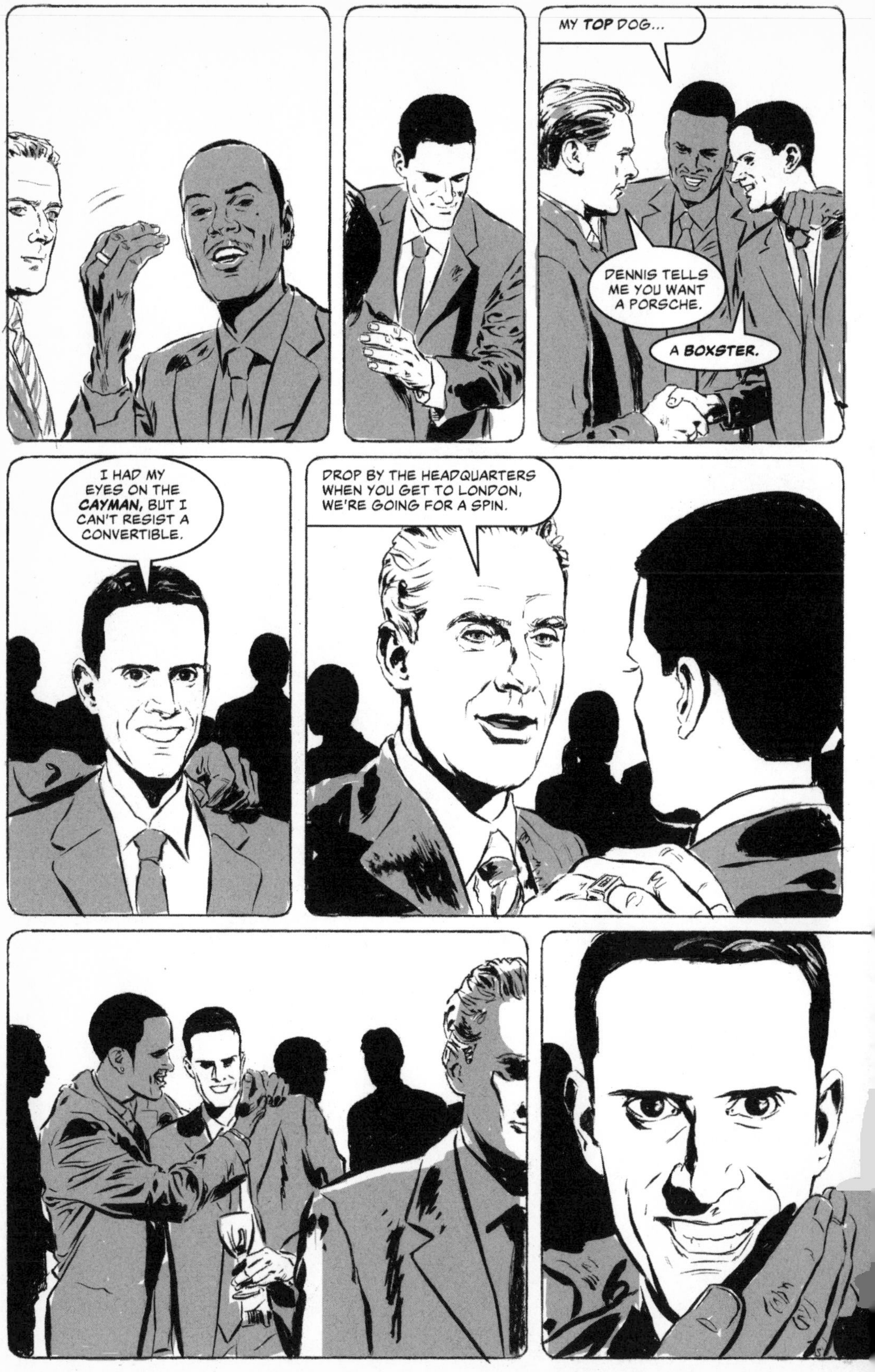
MY **TOP** DOG...
DENNIS TELLS ME YOU WANT A PORSCHE.
A **BOXSTER.**
I HAD MY EYES ON THE **CAYMAN,** BUT I CAN'T RESIST A CONVERTIBLE.
DROP BY THE HEADQUARTERS WHEN YOU GET TO LONDON, WE'RE GOING FOR A SPIN.

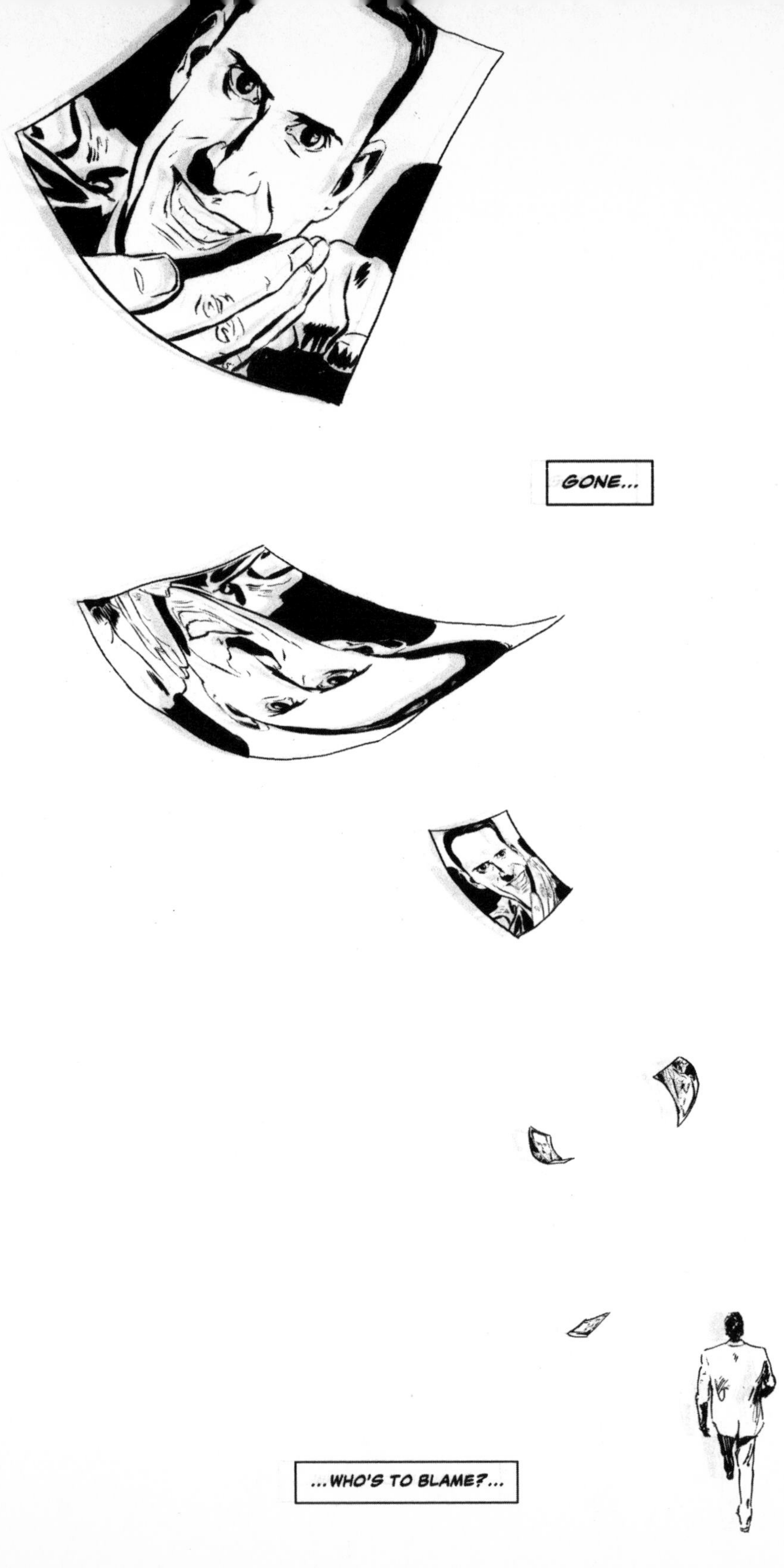
GONE...
...WHO'S TO BLAME?...

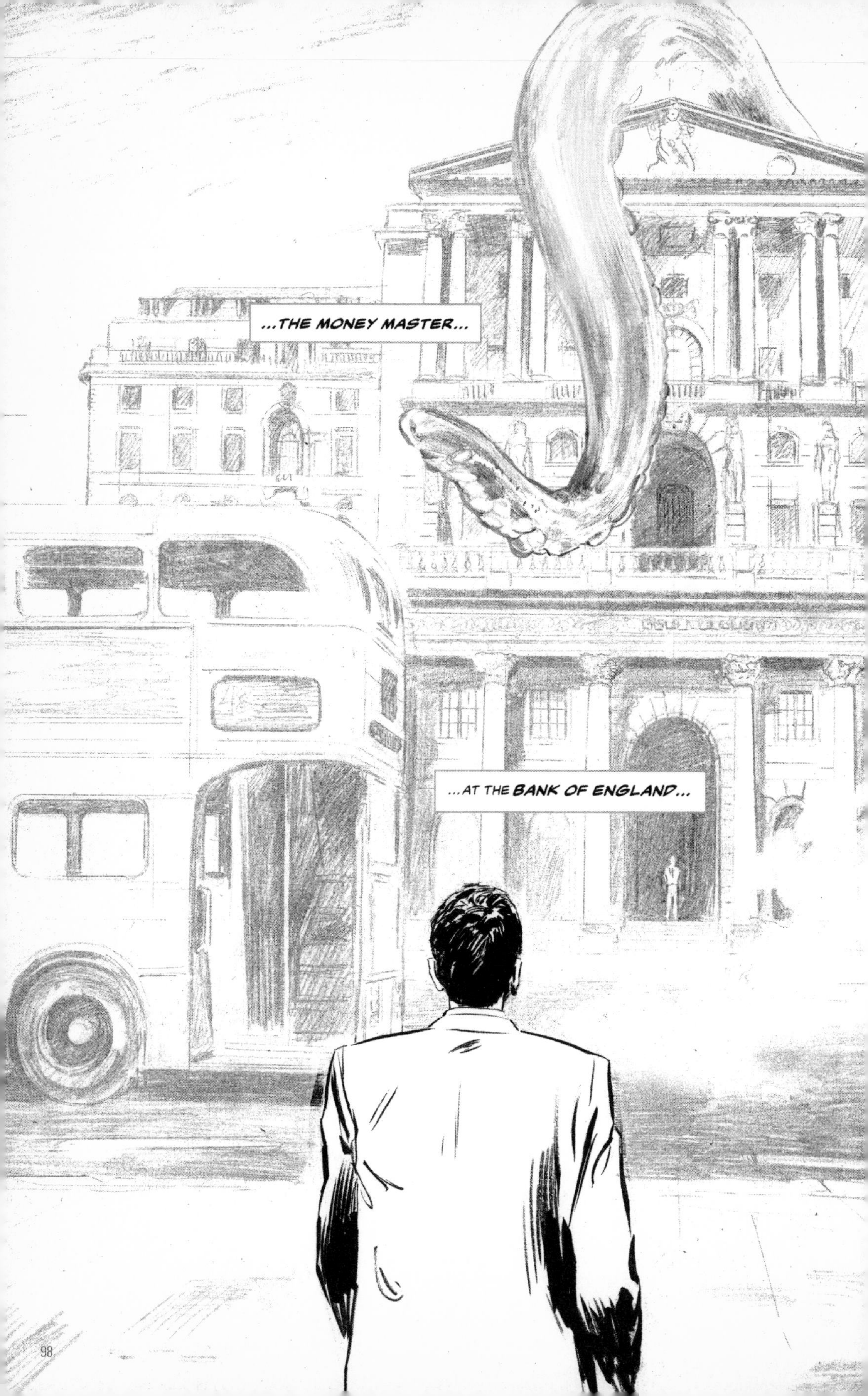
...THE MONEY MASTER...
...AT THE BANK OF ENGLAND...

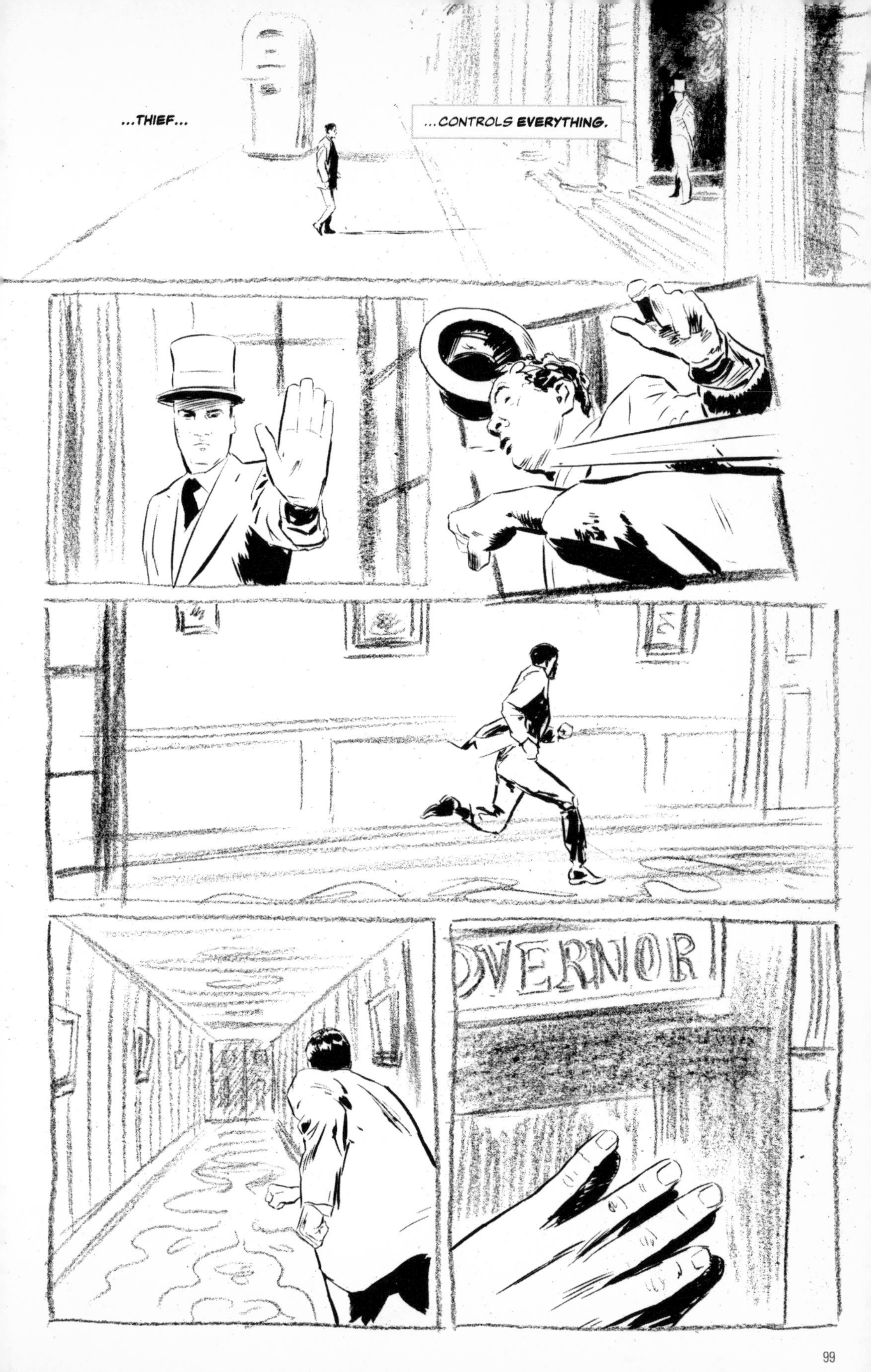
...THIEF...
...CONTROLS EVERYTHING.
OVERNOR

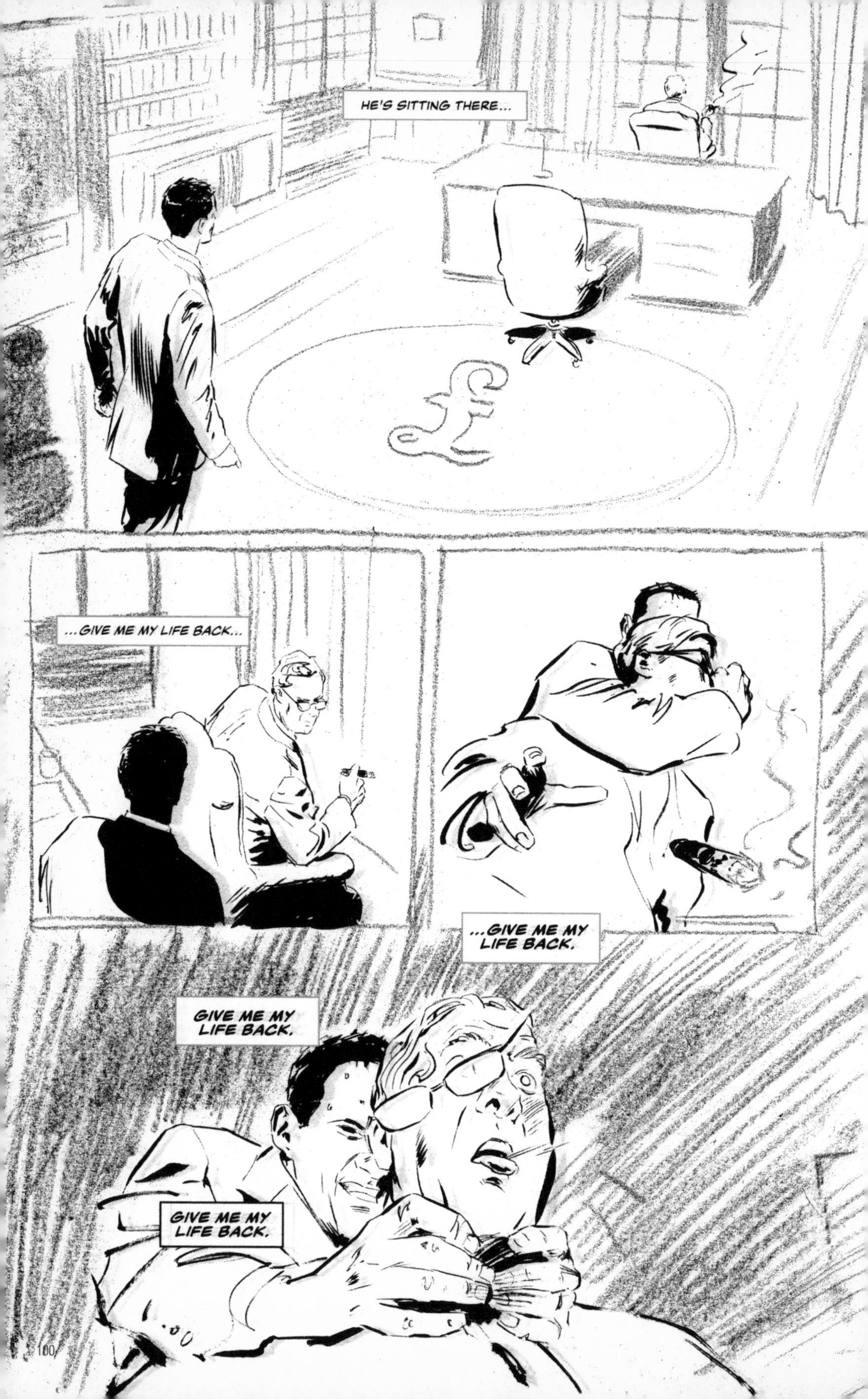
HE'S SITTING THERE...
...GIVE ME MY LIFE BACK...
...GIVE ME MY LIFE BACK.
GIVE ME MY LIFE BACK.
GIVE ME MY LIFE BACK.

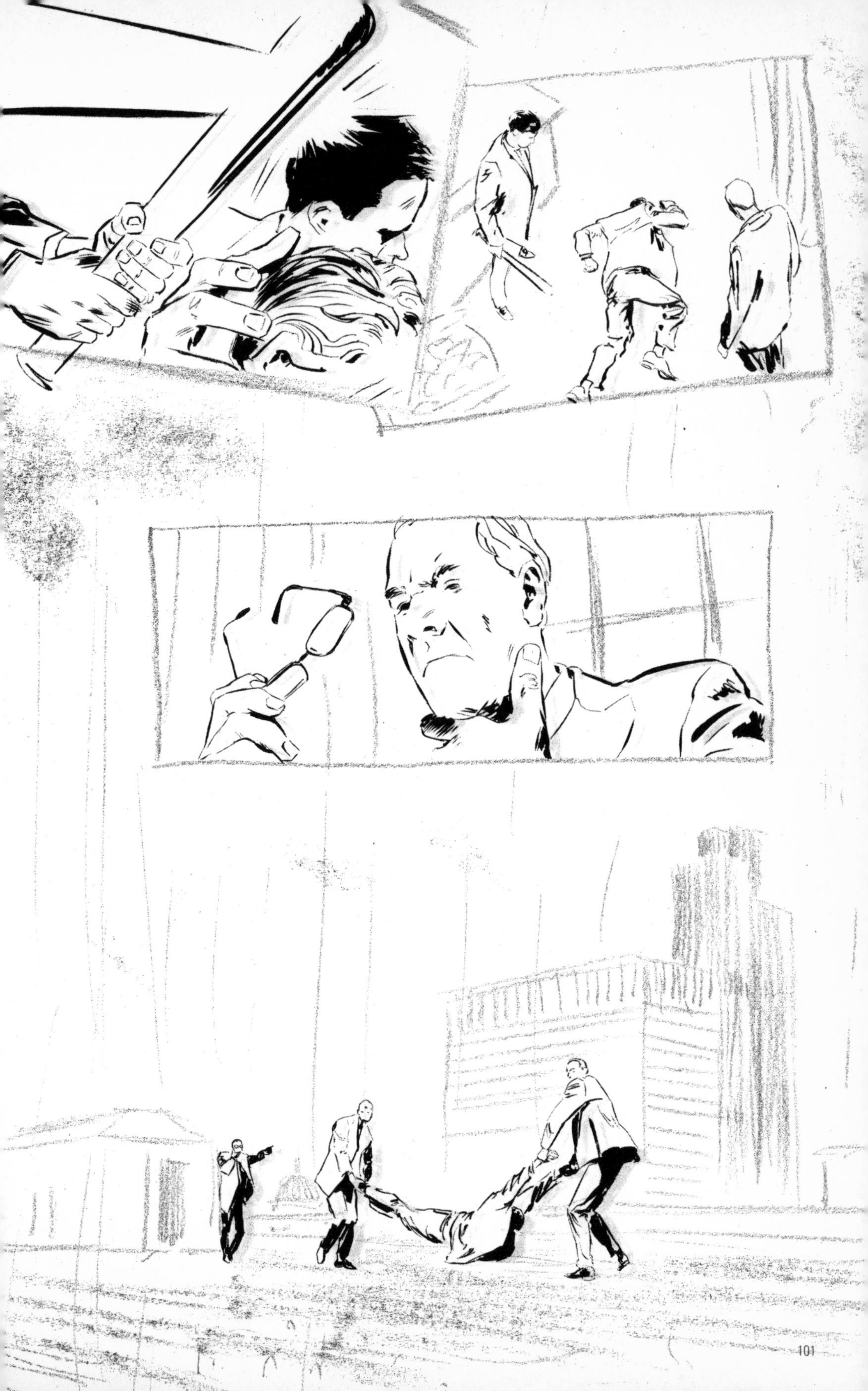

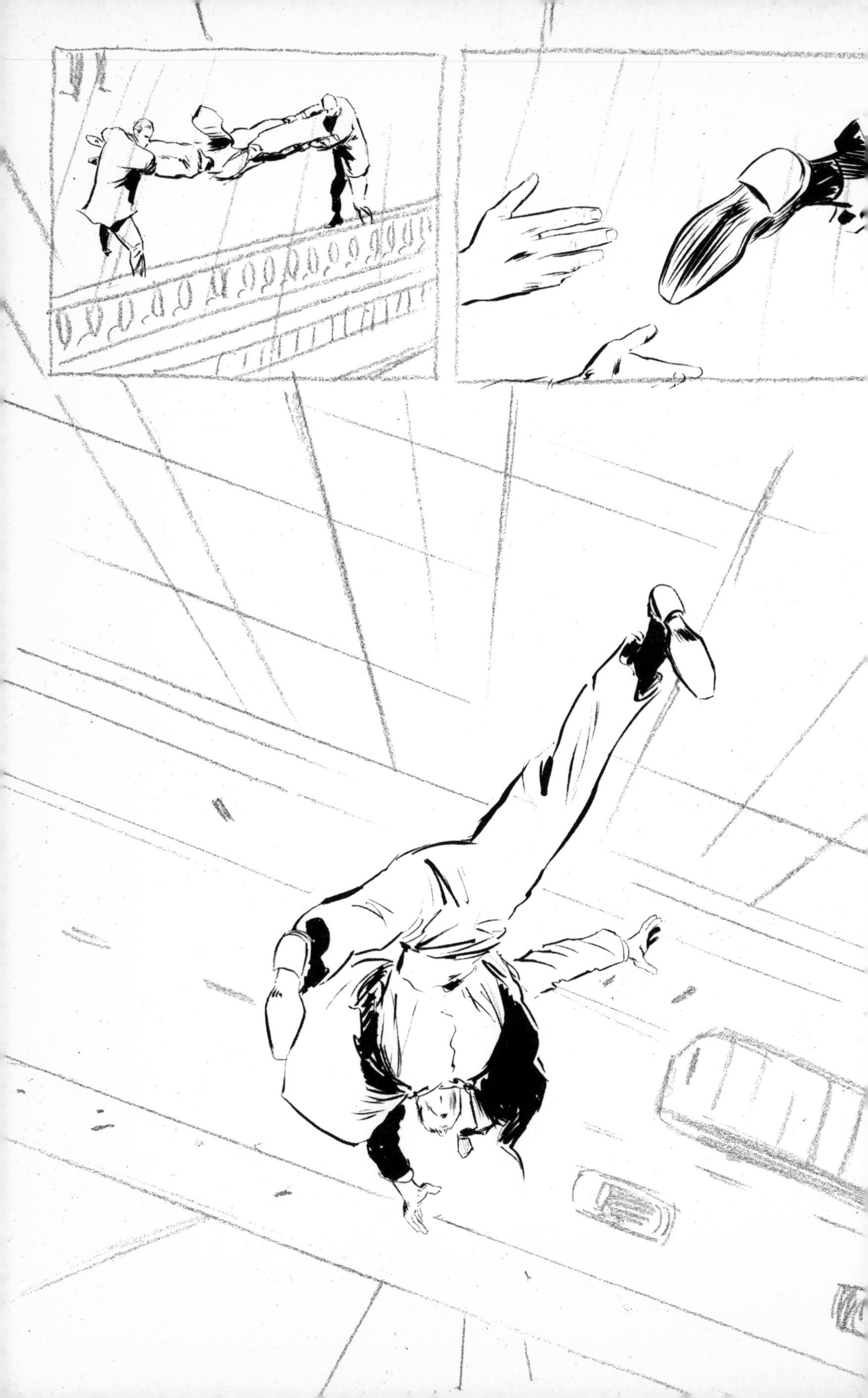

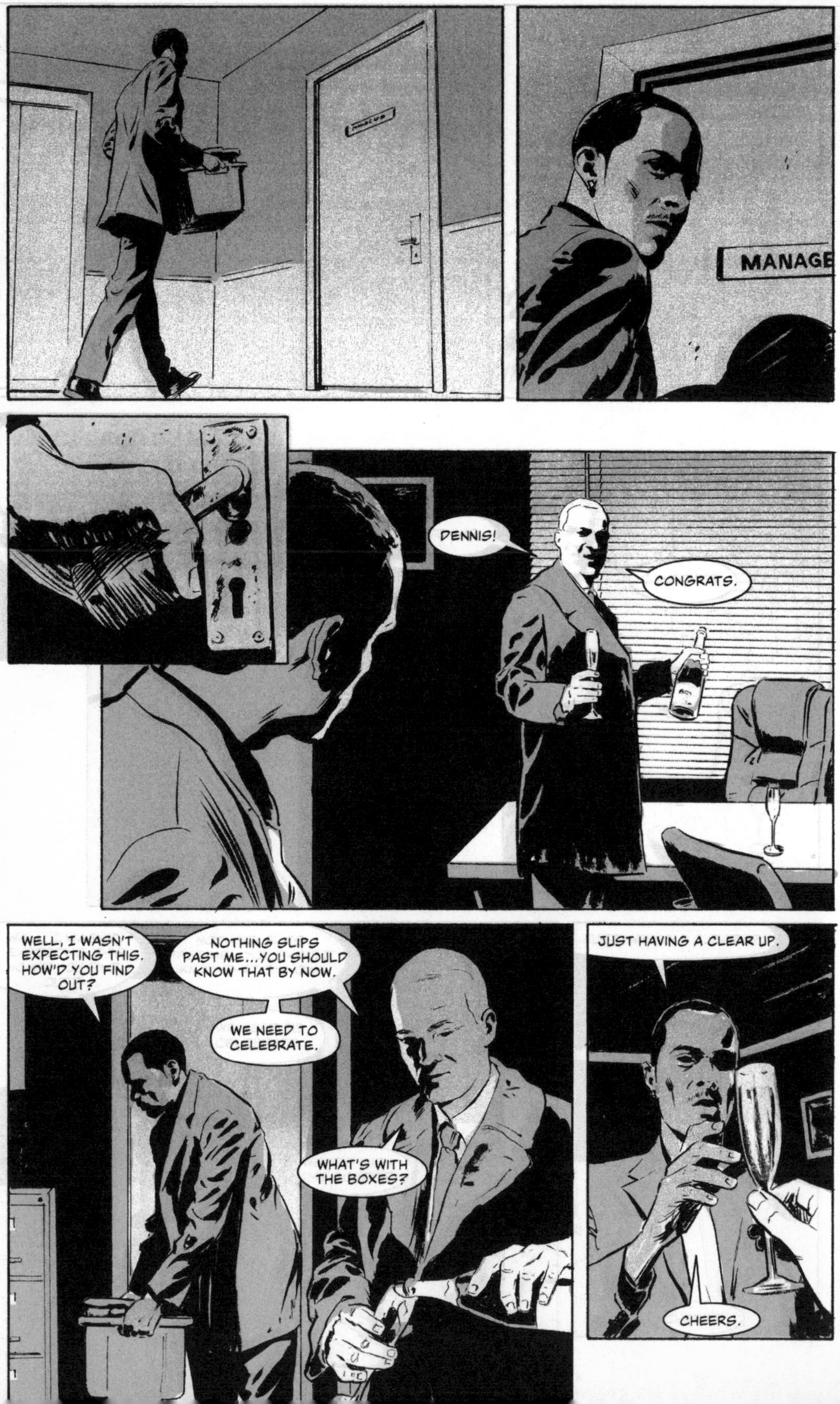
MANAGE
DENNIS!
CONGRATS.
WELL, I WASN'T EXPECTING THIS. HOW'D YOU FIND OUT?
NOTHING SLIPS PAST ME...YOU SHOULD KNOW THAT BY NOW.
WE NEED TO CELEBRATE.
WHAT'S WITH THE BOXES?
JUST HAVING A CLEAR UP.
CHEERS.

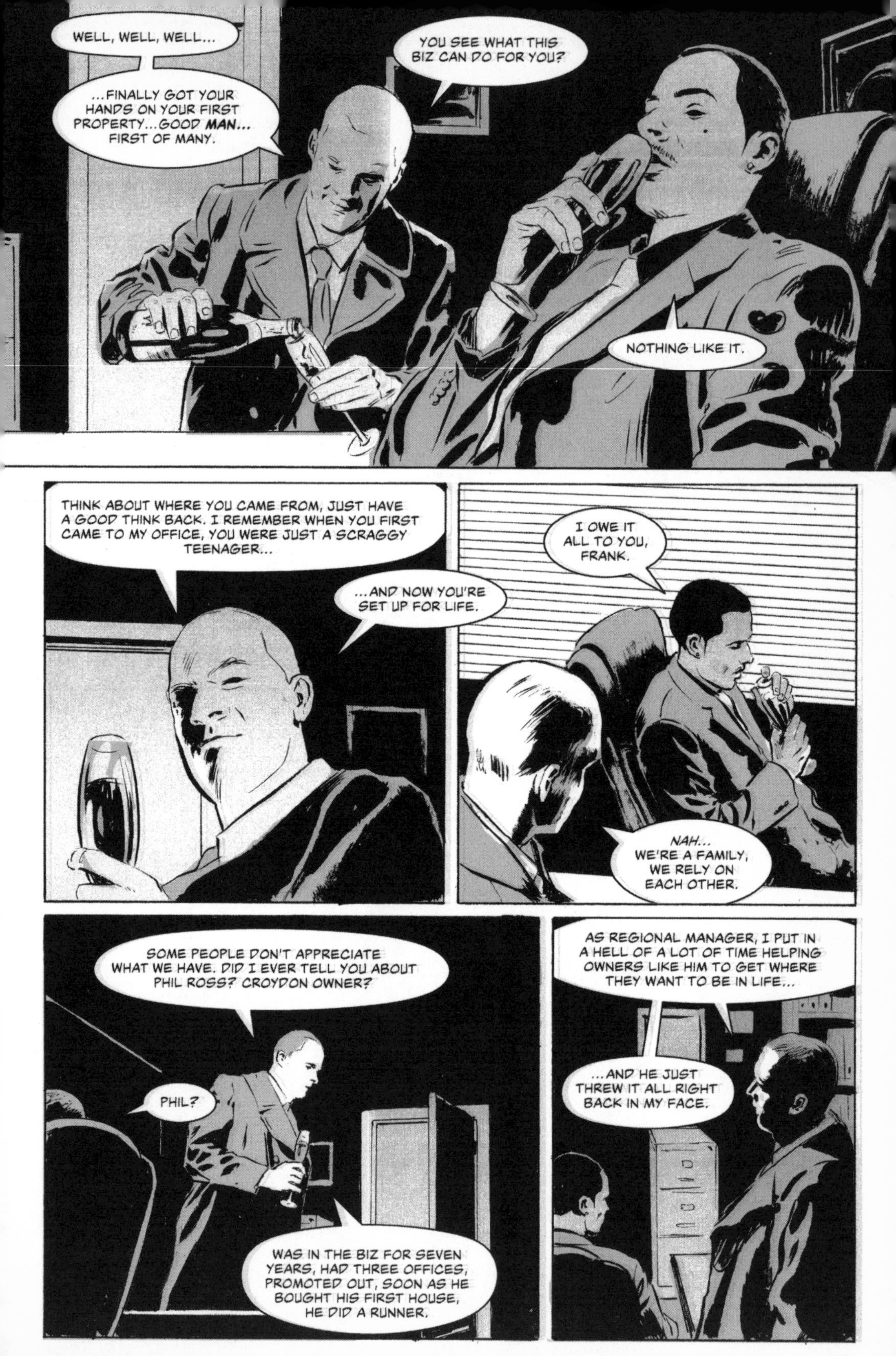
WELL, WELL, WELL...
...FINALLY GOT YOUR HANDS ON YOUR FIRST PROPERTY...GOOD **MAN...** FIRST OF MANY.
YOU SEE WHAT THIS BIZ CAN DO FOR YOU?
NOTHING LIKE IT.
THINK ABOUT WHERE YOU CAME FROM, JUST HAVE A GOOD THINK BACK. I REMEMBER WHEN YOU FIRST CAME TO MY OFFICE, YOU WERE JUST A SCRAGGY TEENAGER...
...AND NOW YOU'RE SET UP FOR LIFE.
I OWE IT ALL TO YOU, FRANK.
*NAH...* WE'RE A FAMILY, WE RELY ON EACH OTHER.
SOME PEOPLE DON'T APPRECIATE WHAT WE HAVE. DID I EVER TELL YOU ABOUT PHIL ROSS? CROYDON OWNER?
PHIL?
WAS IN THE BIZ FOR SEVEN YEARS, HAD THREE OFFICES, PROMOTED OUT, SOON AS HE BOUGHT HIS FIRST HOUSE, HE DID A RUNNER.
AS REGIONAL MANAGER, I PUT IN A HELL OF A LOT OF TIME HELPING OWNERS LIKE HIM TO GET WHERE THEY WANT TO BE IN LIFE...
...AND HE JUST THREW IT ALL RIGHT BACK IN MY FACE.

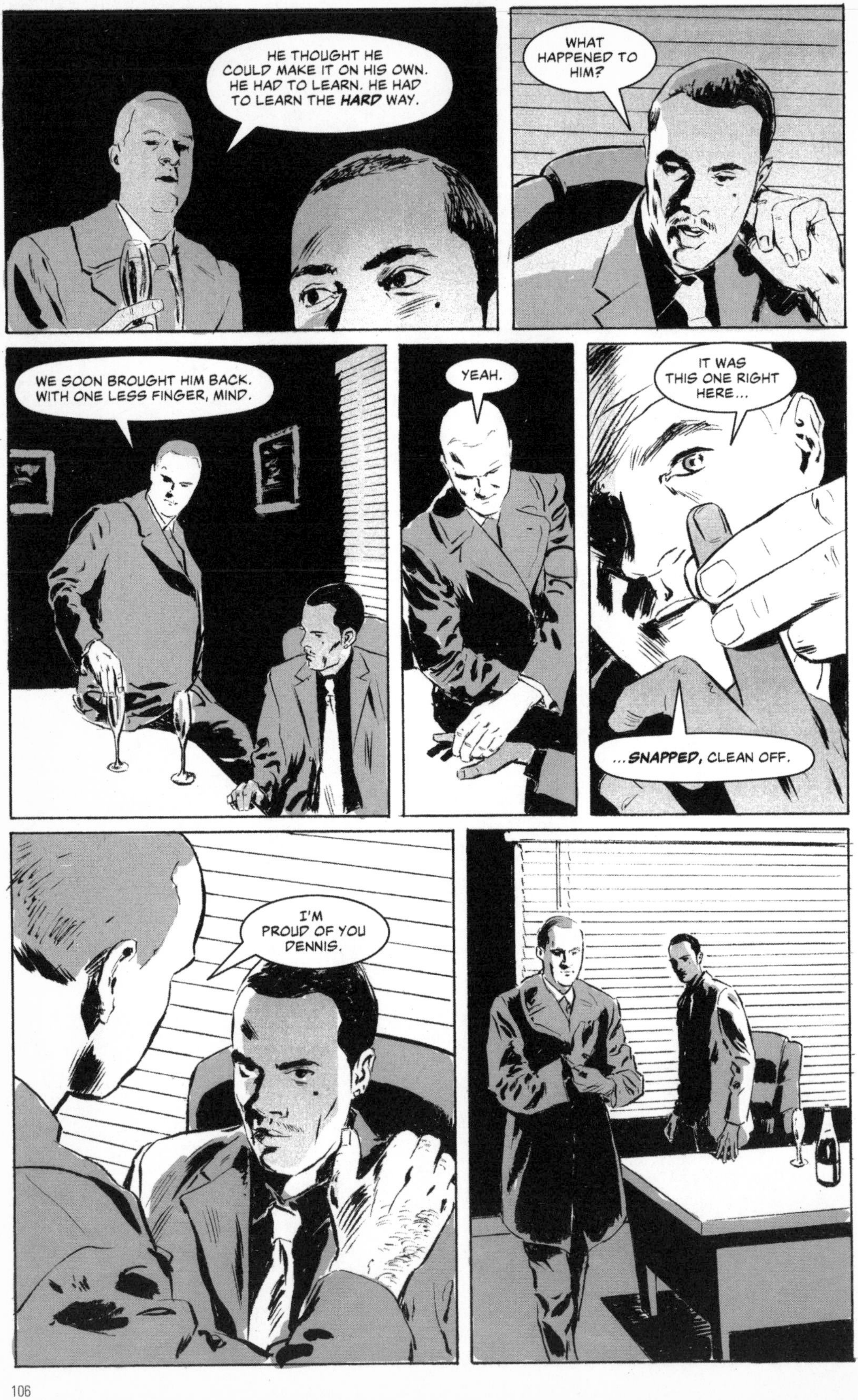
HE THOUGHT HE COULD MAKE IT ON HIS OWN. HE HAD TO LEARN. HE HAD TO LEARN THE **HARD** WAY.
WHAT HAPPENED TO HIM?
WE SOON BROUGHT HIM BACK. WITH ONE LESS FINGER, MIND.
YEAH.
IT WAS THIS ONE RIGHT HERE...
...**SNAPPED,** CLEAN OFF.
I'M PROUD OF YOU DENNIS.

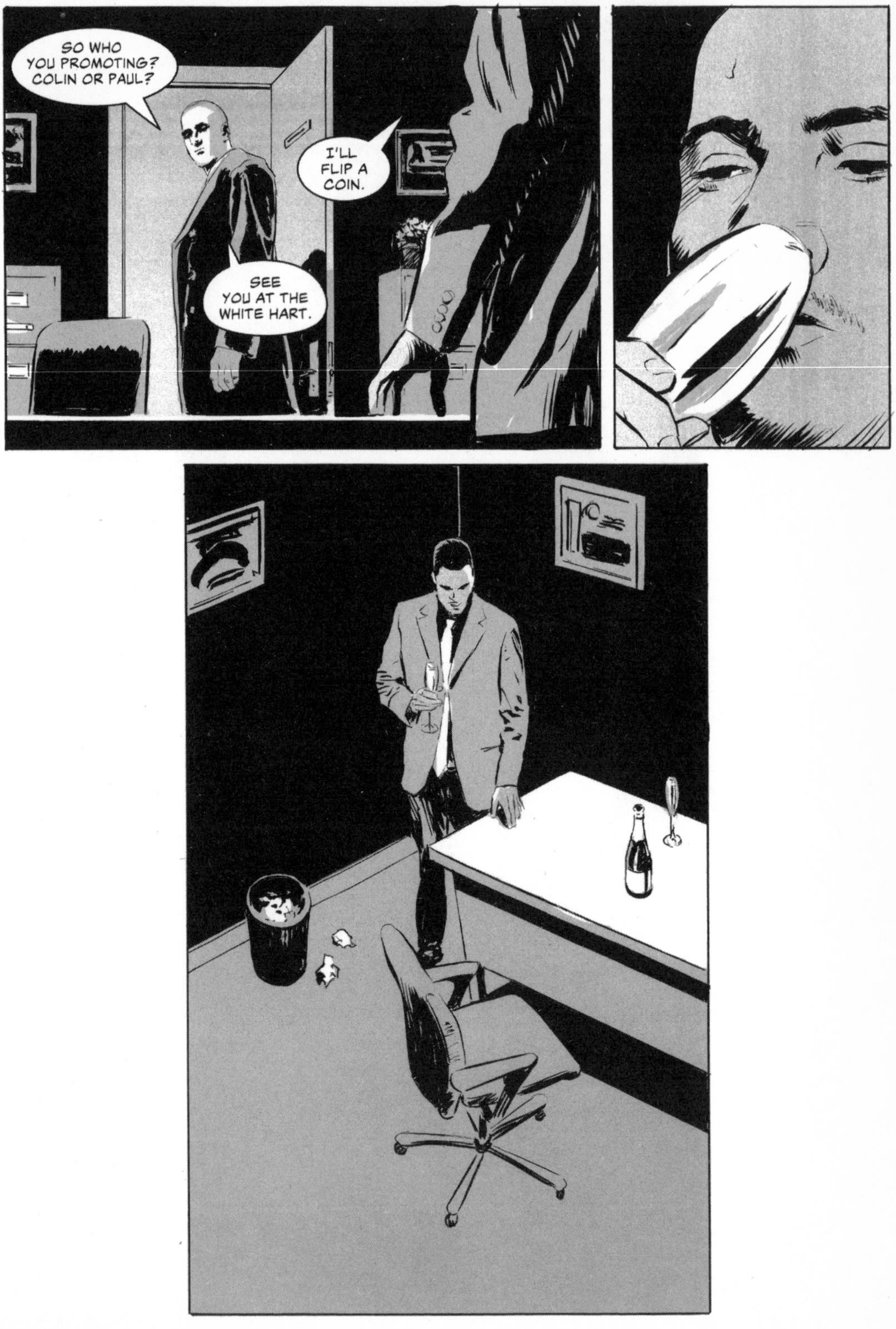
SO WHO YOU PROMOTING? COLIN OR PAUL?
I'LL FLIP A COIN.
SEE YOU AT THE WHITE HART.

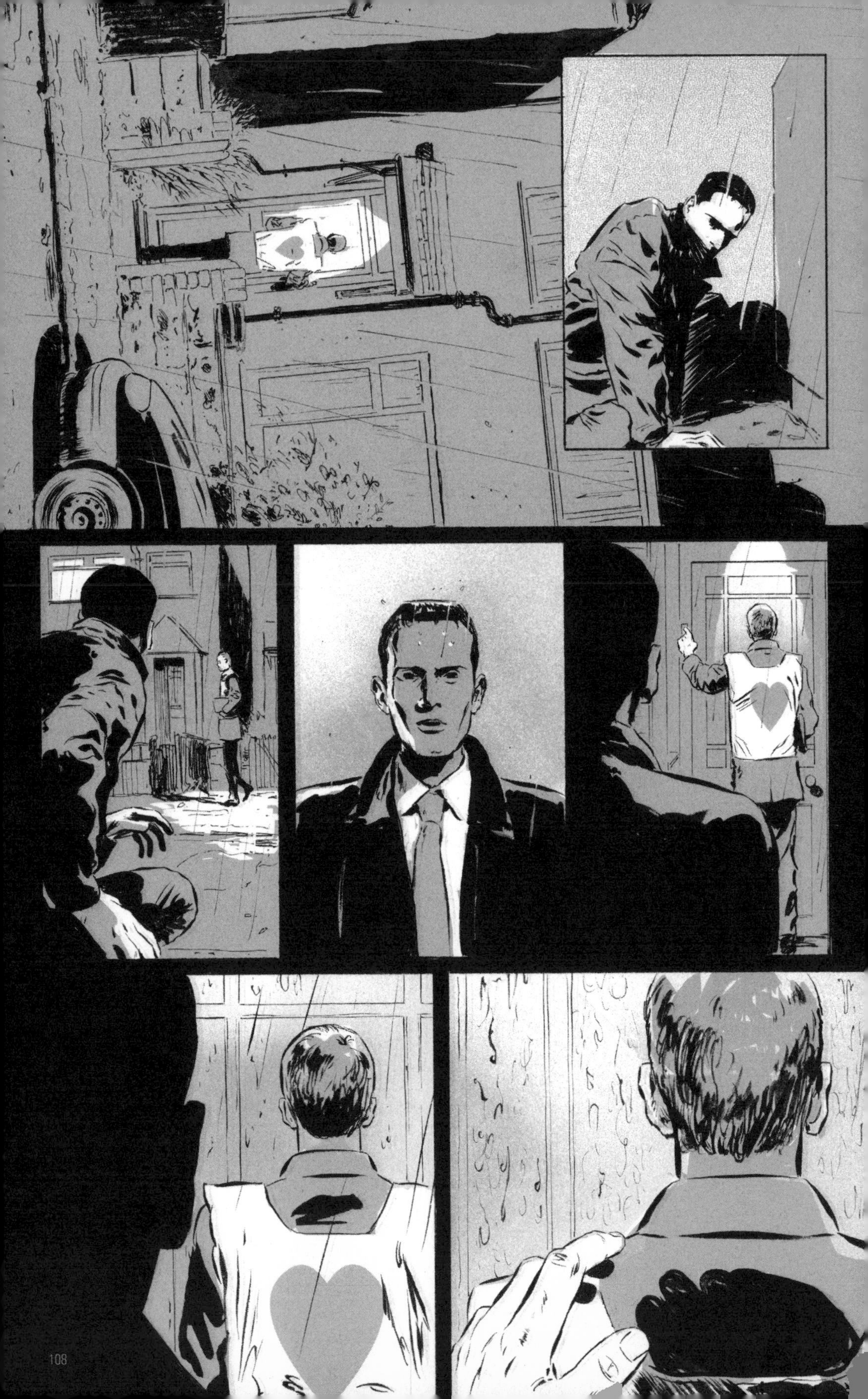

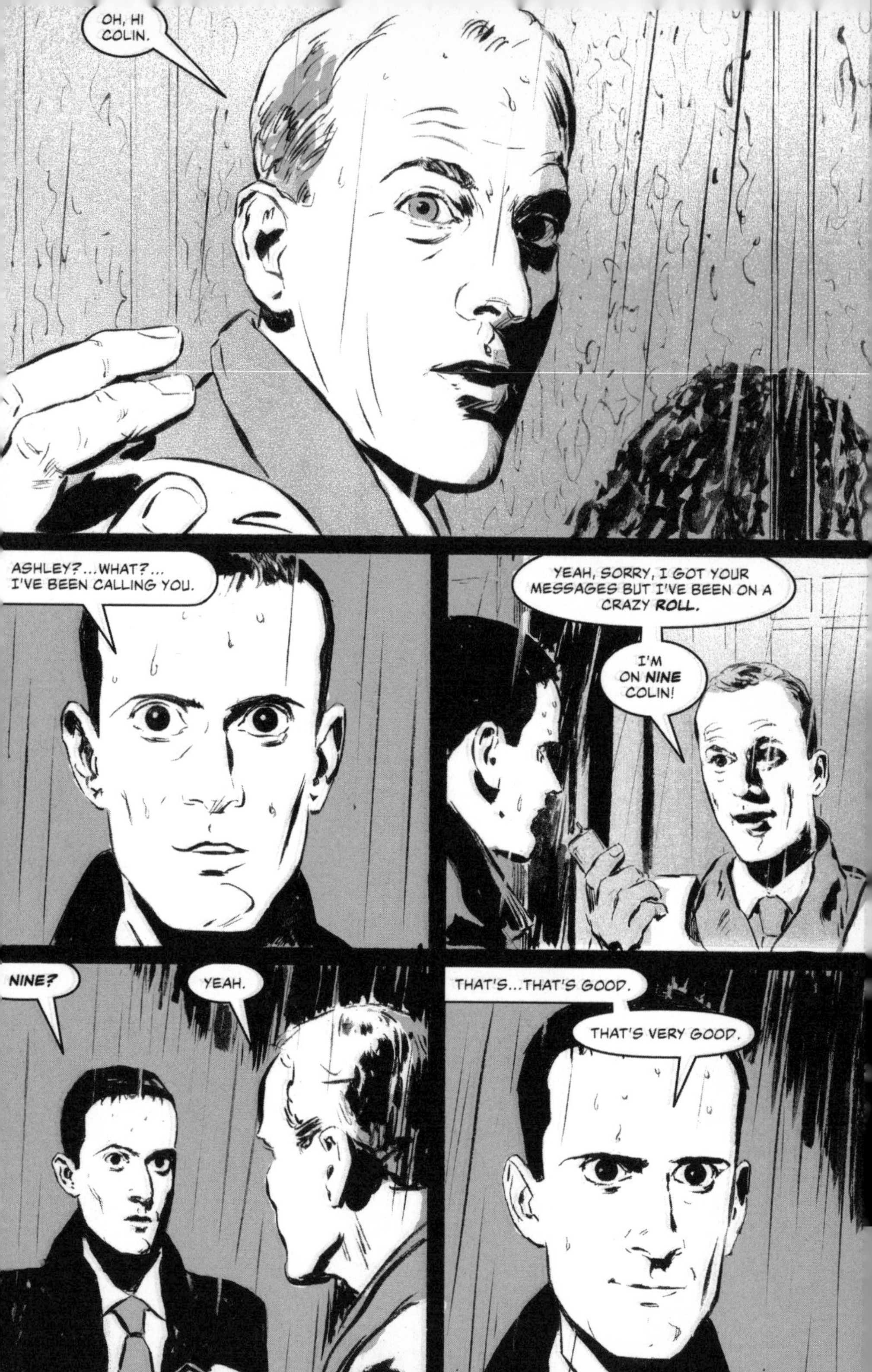

OH, HI COLIN.
ASHLEY?...WHAT?... I'VE BEEN CALLING YOU.
YEAH, SORRY, I GOT YOUR MESSAGES BUT I'VE BEEN ON A CRAZY **ROLL.**
I'M ON **NINE** COLIN!
**NINE?**
YEAH.
THAT'S...THAT'S GOOD.
THAT'S VERY GOOD.

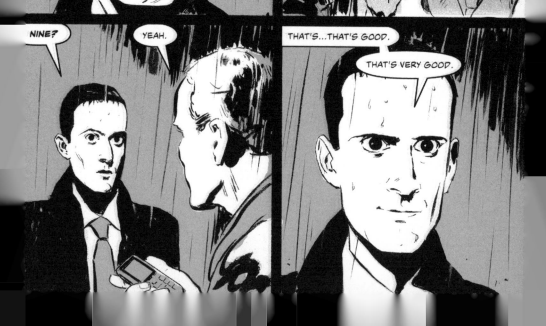

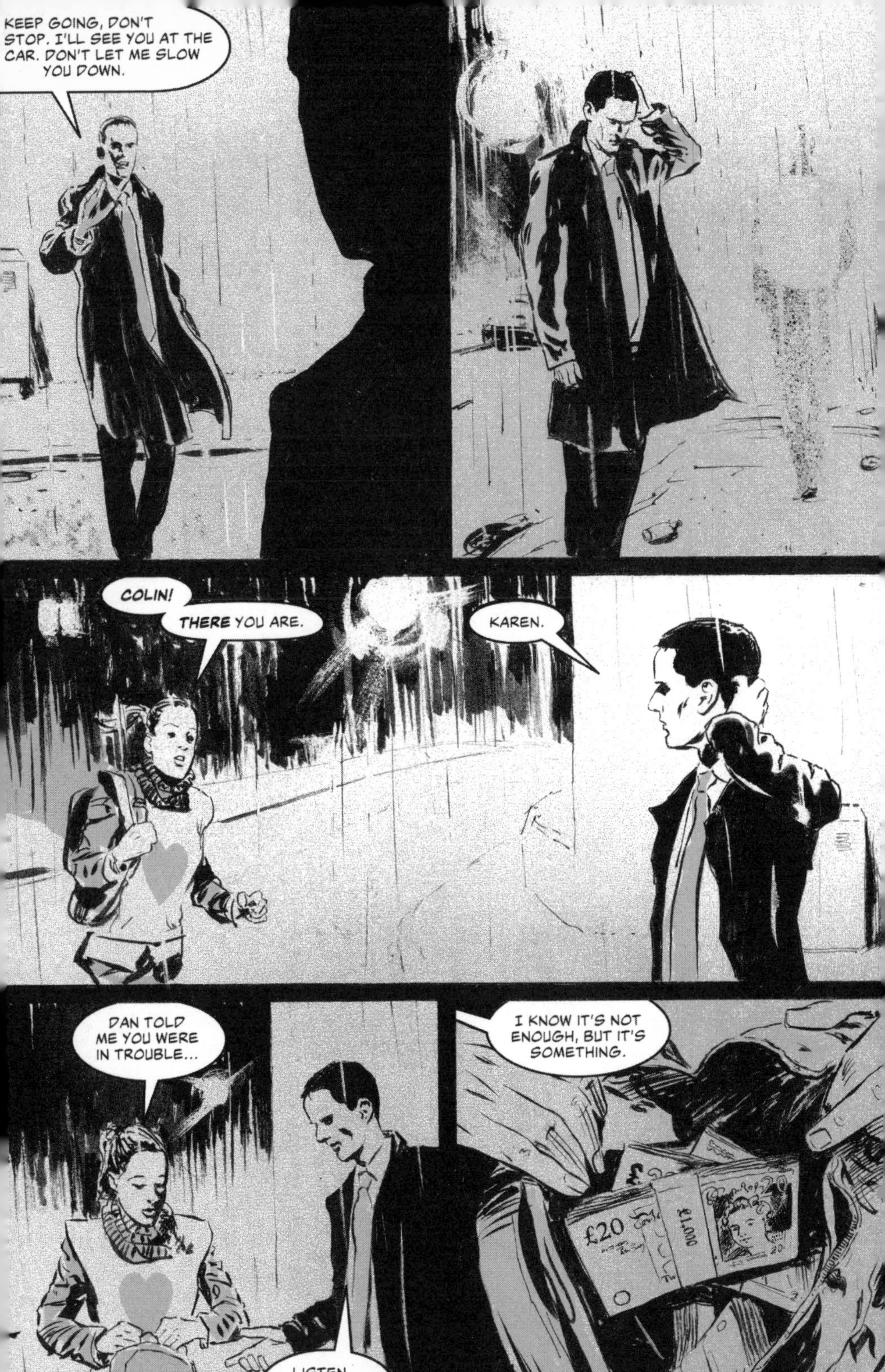
KEEP GOING, DON'T STOP. I'LL SEE YOU AT THE CAR. DON'T LET ME SLOW YOU DOWN.
COLIN!
THERE YOU ARE.
KAREN.
DAN TOLD ME YOU WERE IN TROUBLE...
LISTEN... ABOUT LAST NIGHT...
I KNOW IT'S NOT ENOUGH, BUT IT'S SOMETHING.

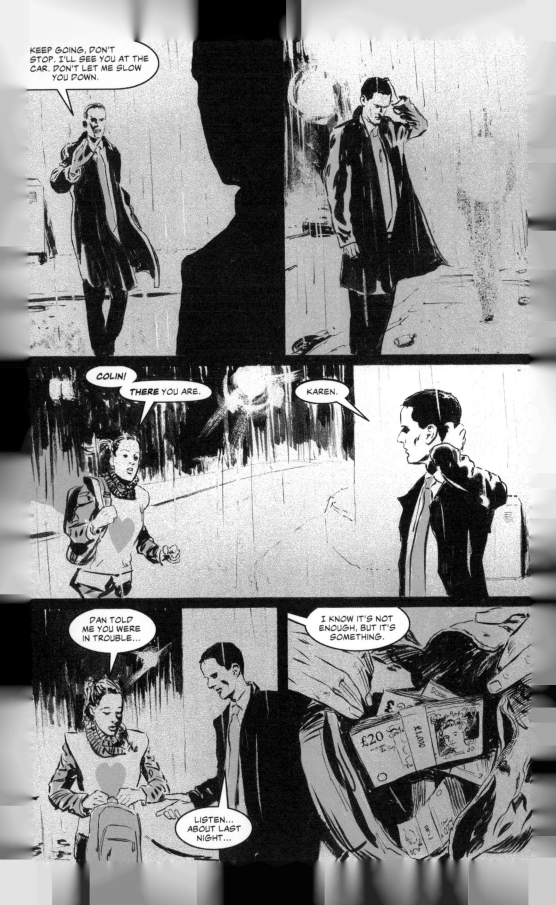

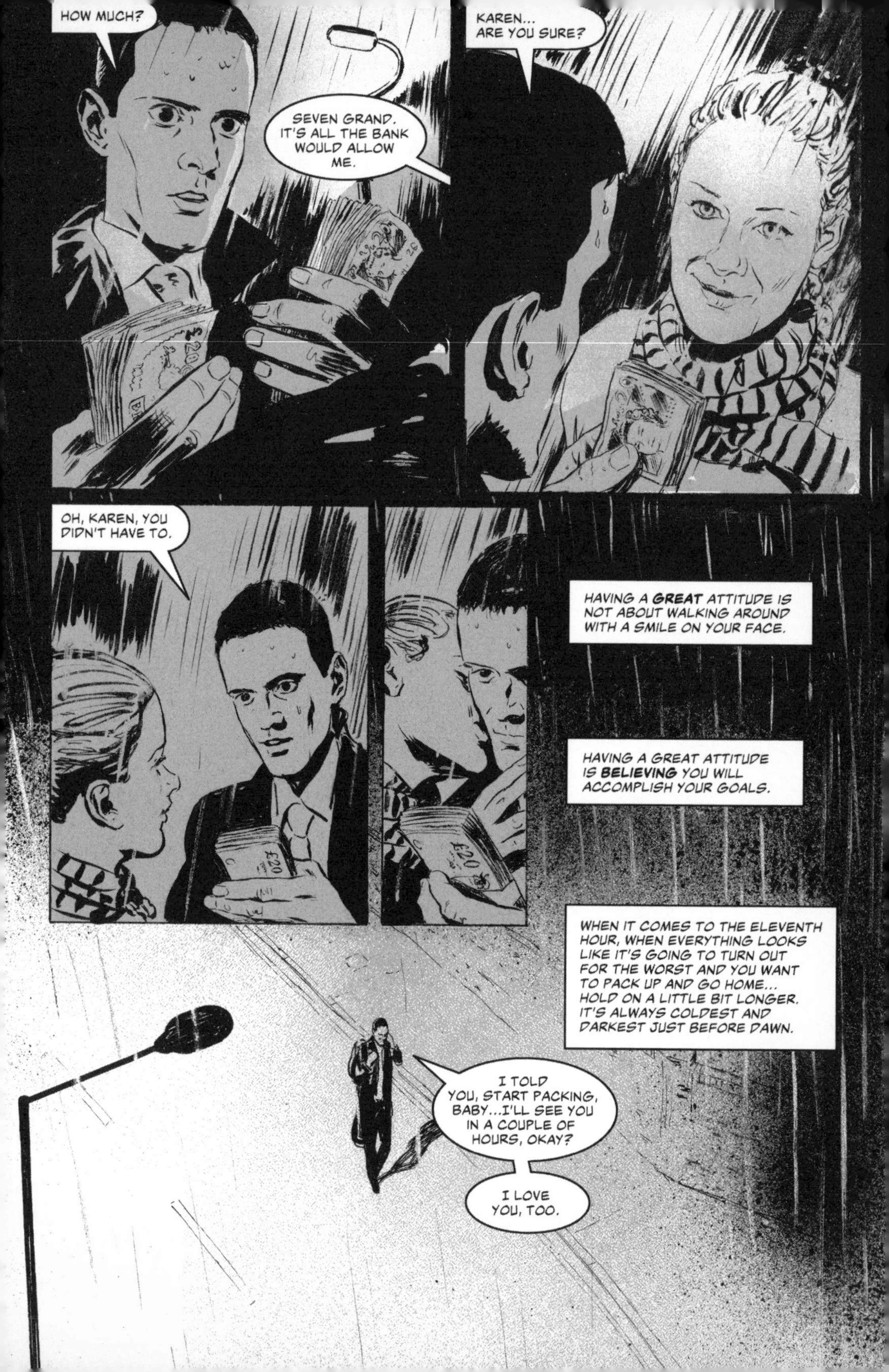
HOW MUCH?
SEVEN GRAND. IT'S ALL THE BANK WOULD ALLOW ME.
KAREN... ARE YOU SURE?
OH, KAREN, YOU DIDN'T HAVE TO.
HAVING A **GREAT** ATTITUDE IS NOT ABOUT WALKING AROUND WITH A SMILE ON YOUR FACE.
HAVING A GREAT ATTITUDE IS **BELIEVING** YOU WILL ACCOMPLISH YOUR GOALS.
WHEN IT COMES TO THE ELEVENTH HOUR, WHEN EVERYTHING LOOKS LIKE IT'S GOING TO TURN OUT FOR THE WORST AND YOU WANT TO PACK UP AND GO HOME... HOLD ON A LITTLE BIT LONGER. IT'S ALWAYS COLDEST AND DARKEST JUST BEFORE DAWN.
I TOLD YOU, START PACKING, BABY...I'LL SEE YOU IN A COUPLE OF HOURS, OKAY?
I LOVE YOU, TOO.

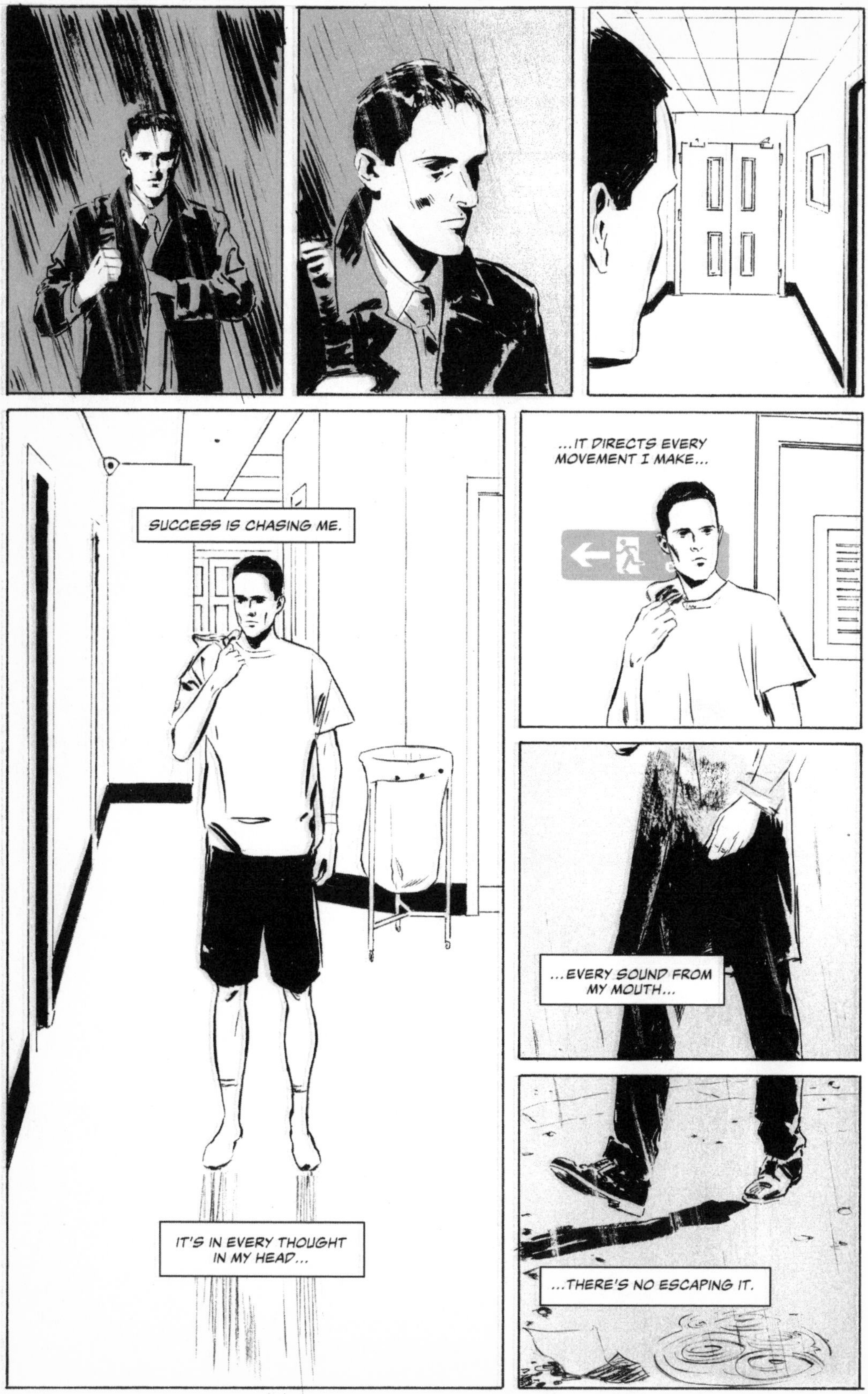
SUCCESS IS CHASING ME.
IT'S IN EVERY THOUGHT IN MY HEAD...
...IT DIRECTS EVERY MOVEMENT I MAKE...
...EVERY SOUND FROM MY MOUTH...
...THERE'S NO ESCAPING IT.

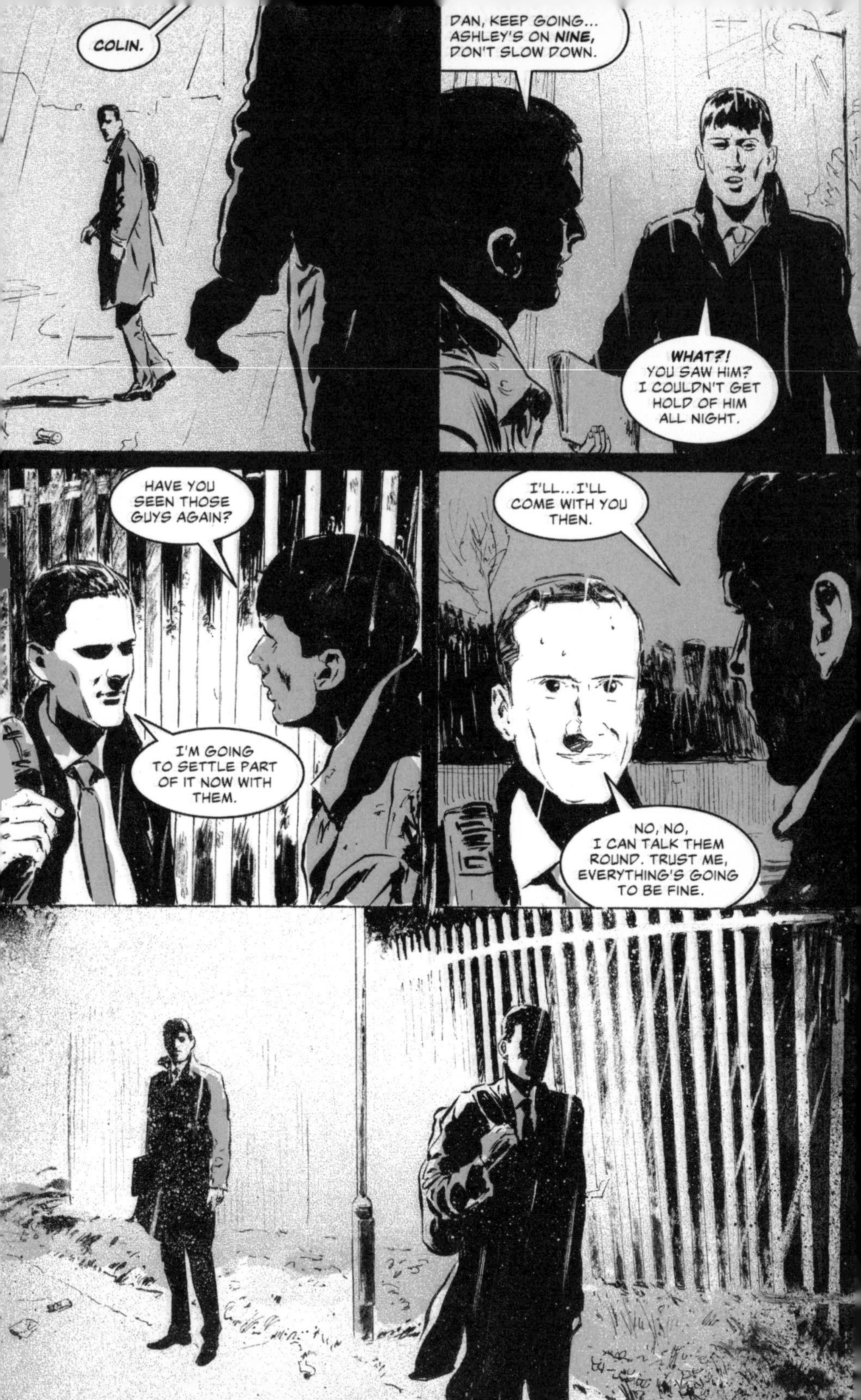
COLIN.
DAN, KEEP GOING... ASHLEY'S ON NINE, DON'T SLOW DOWN.
WHAT?! YOU SAW HIM? I COULDN'T GET HOLD OF HIM ALL NIGHT.
HAVE YOU SEEN THOSE GUYS AGAIN?
I'M GOING TO SETTLE PART OF IT NOW WITH THEM.
I'LL...I'LL COME WITH YOU THEN.
NO, NO, I CAN TALK THEM ROUND. TRUST ME, EVERYTHING'S GOING TO BE FINE.

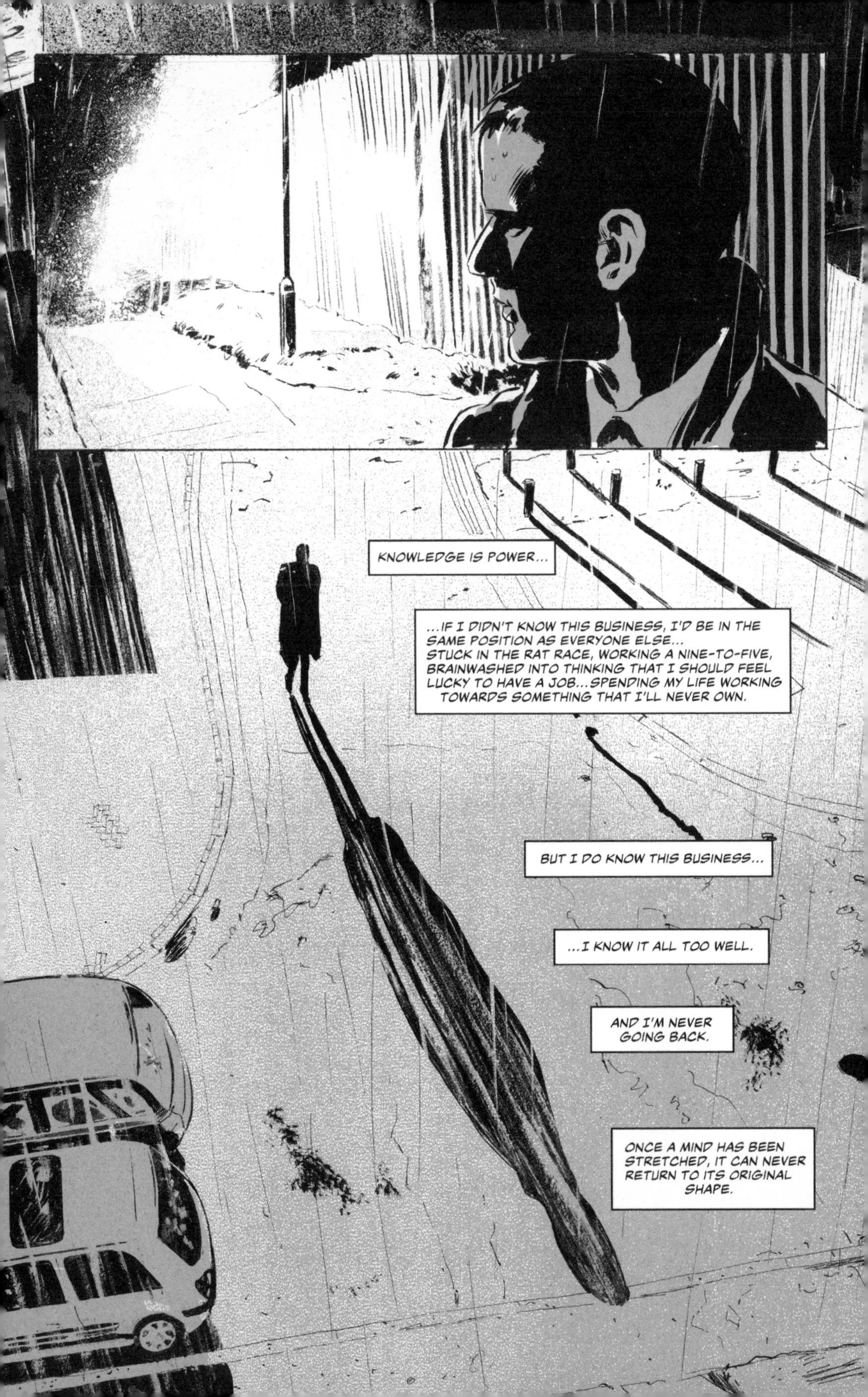
KNOWLEDGE IS POWER...
...IF I DIDN'T KNOW THIS BUSINESS, I'D BE IN THE SAME POSITION AS EVERYONE ELSE... STUCK IN THE RAT RACE, WORKING A NINE-TO-FIVE, BRAINWASHED INTO THINKING THAT I SHOULD FEEL LUCKY TO HAVE A JOB...SPENDING MY LIFE WORKING TOWARDS SOMETHING THAT I'LL NEVER OWN.
BUT I DO KNOW THIS BUSINESS...
...I KNOW IT ALL TOO WELL.
AND I'M NEVER GOING BACK.
ONCE A MIND HAS BEEN STRETCHED, IT CAN NEVER RETURN TO ITS ORIGINAL SHAPE.

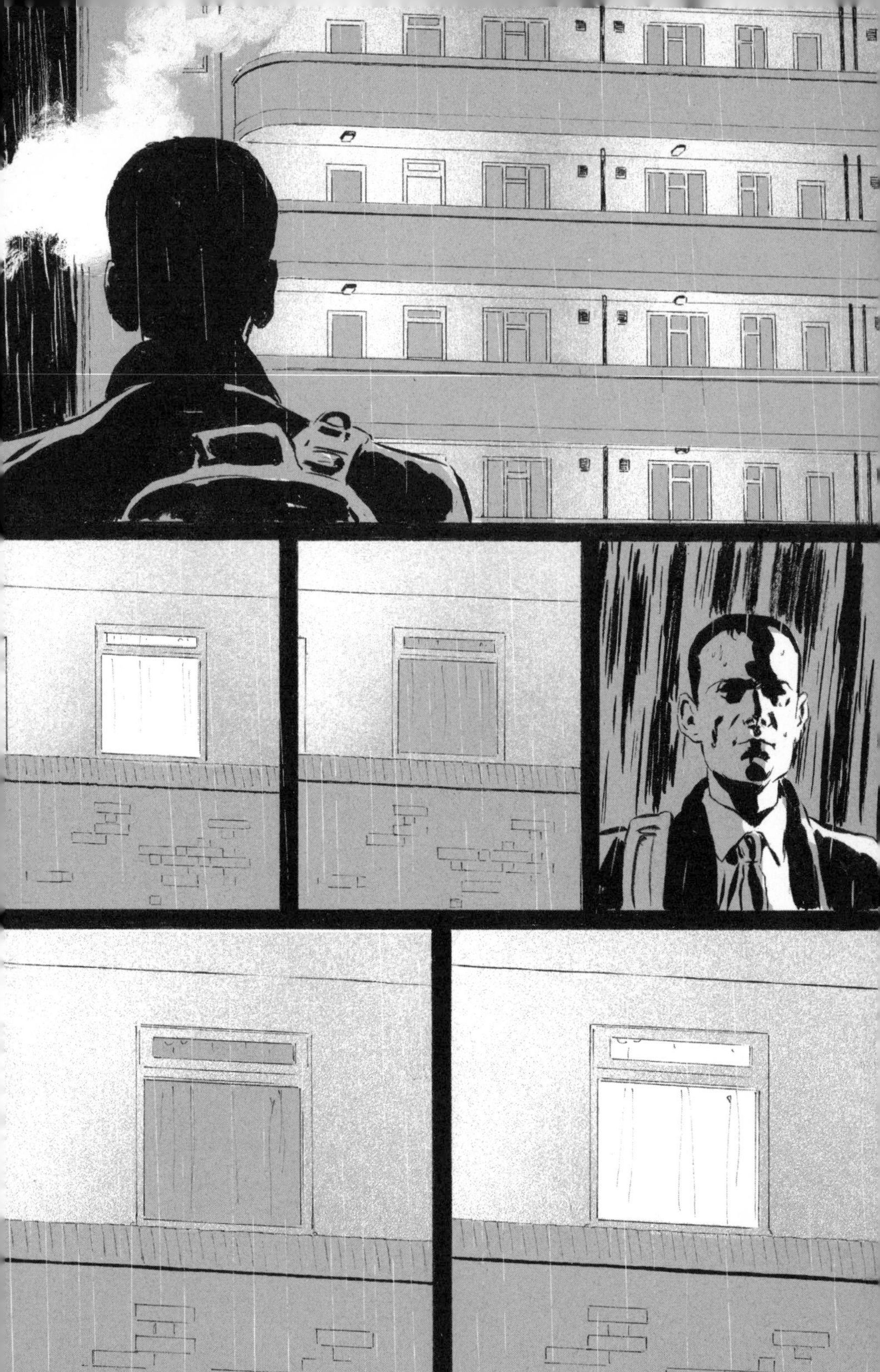

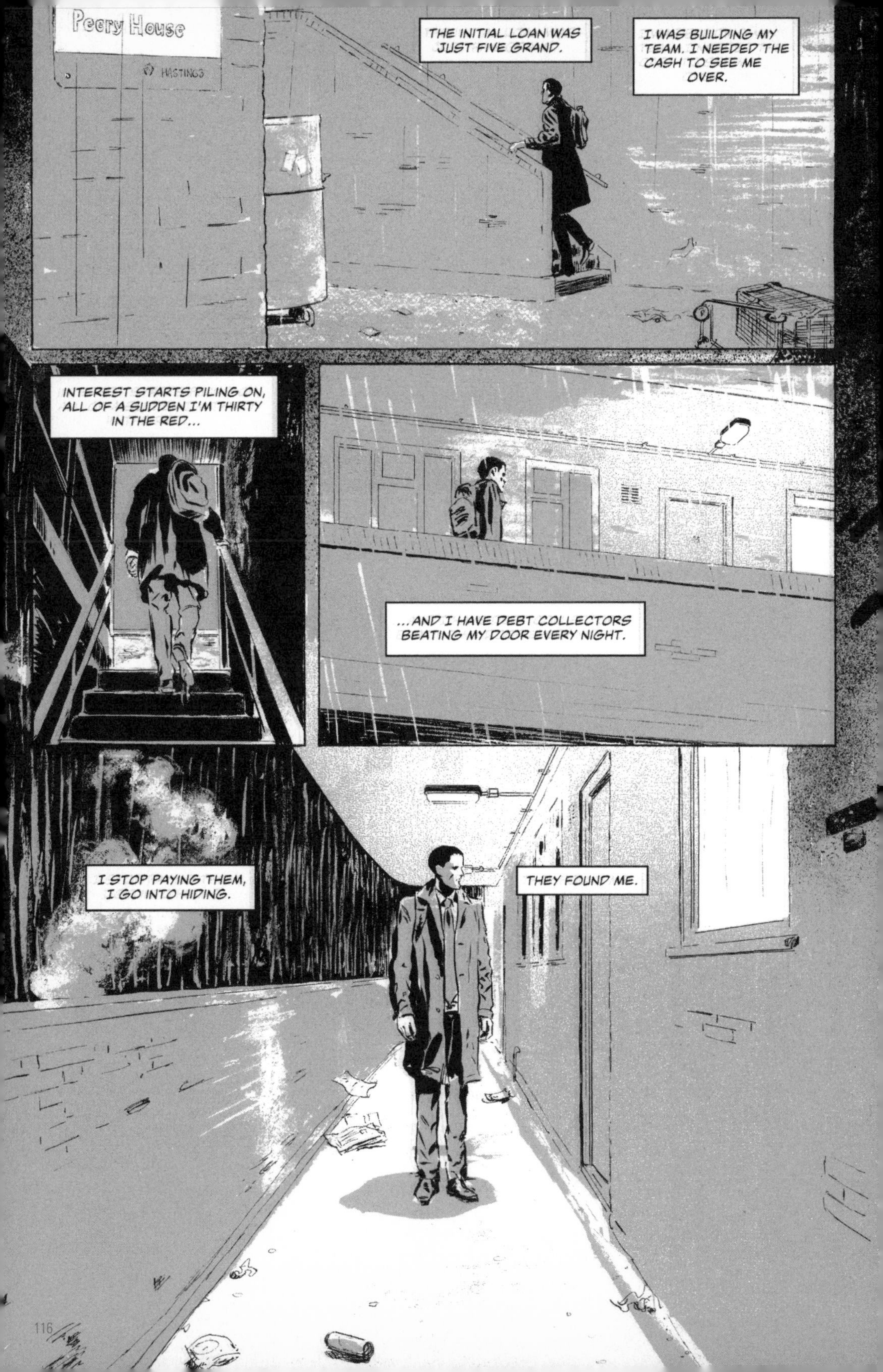
Peery House
HASTINGS
THE INITIAL LOAN WAS JUST FIVE GRAND.
I WAS BUILDING MY TEAM. I NEEDED THE CASH TO SEE ME OVER.
INTEREST STARTS PILING ON, ALL OF A SUDDEN I'M THIRTY IN THE RED...
...AND I HAVE DEBT COLLECTORS BEATING MY DOOR EVERY NIGHT.
I STOP PAYING THEM, I GO INTO HIDING.
THEY FOUND ME.

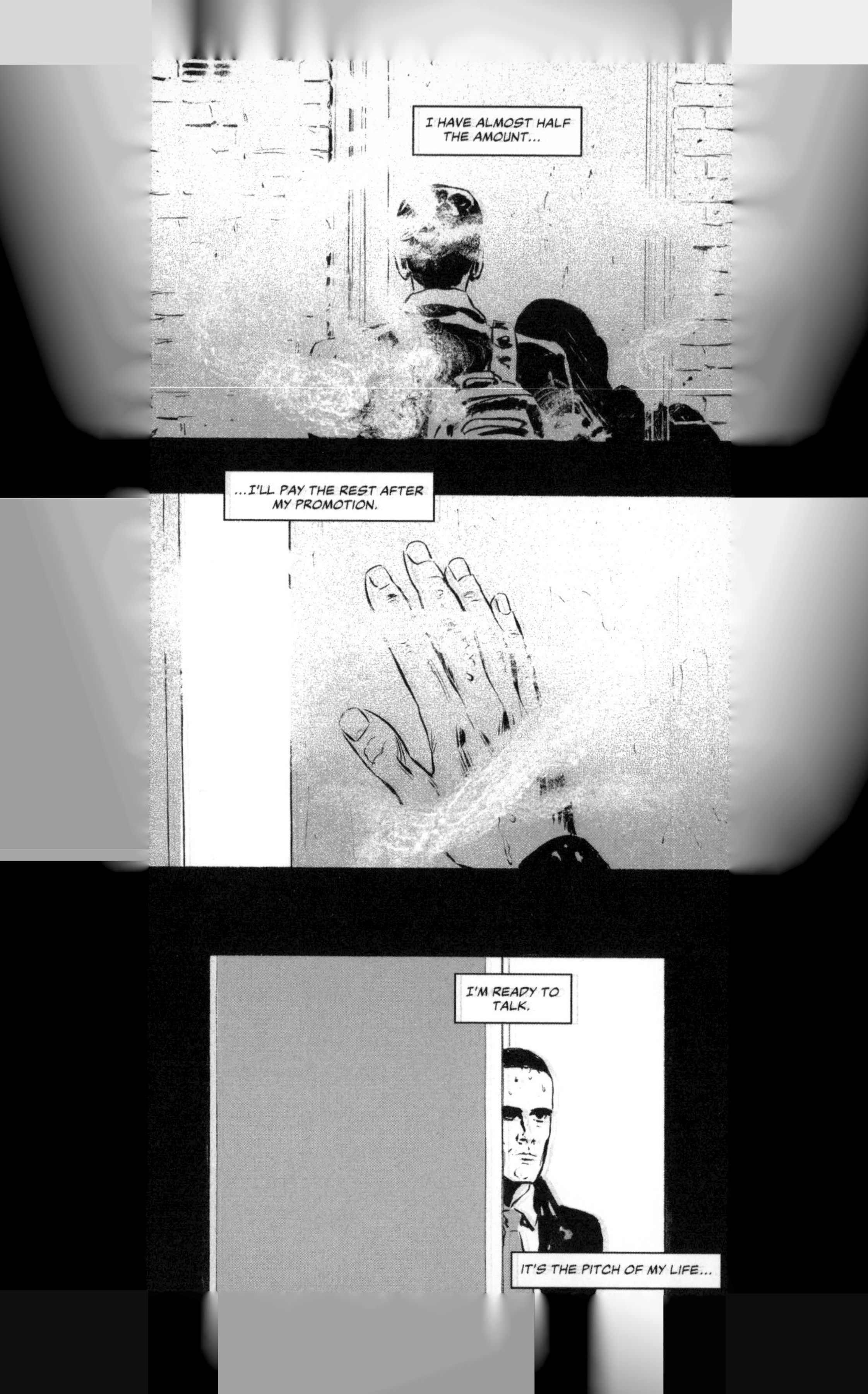
I HAVE ALMOST HALF THE AMOUNT...
...I'LL PAY THE REST AFTER MY PROMOTION.
I'M READY TO TALK.
IT'S THE PITCH OF MY LIFE...

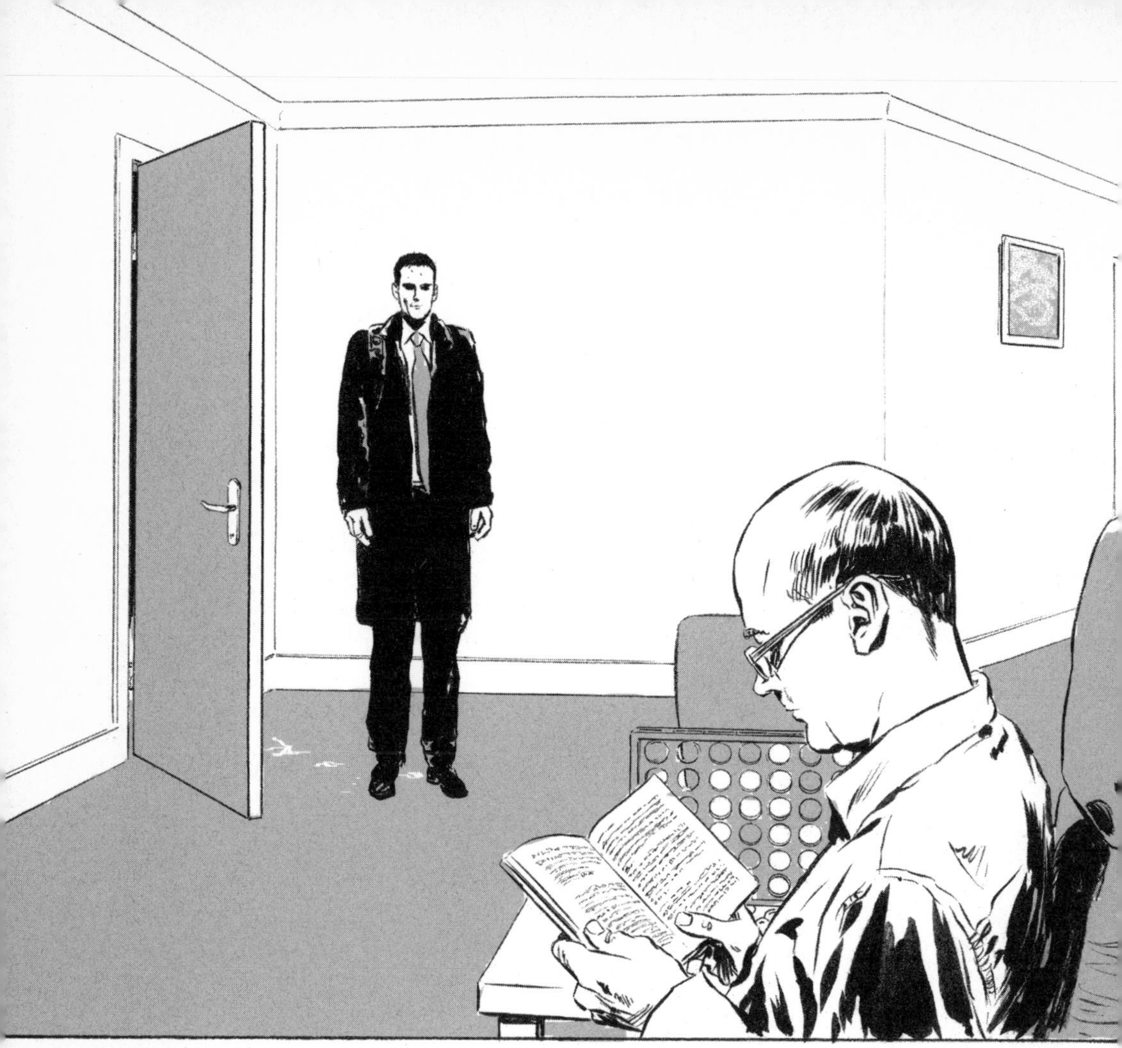

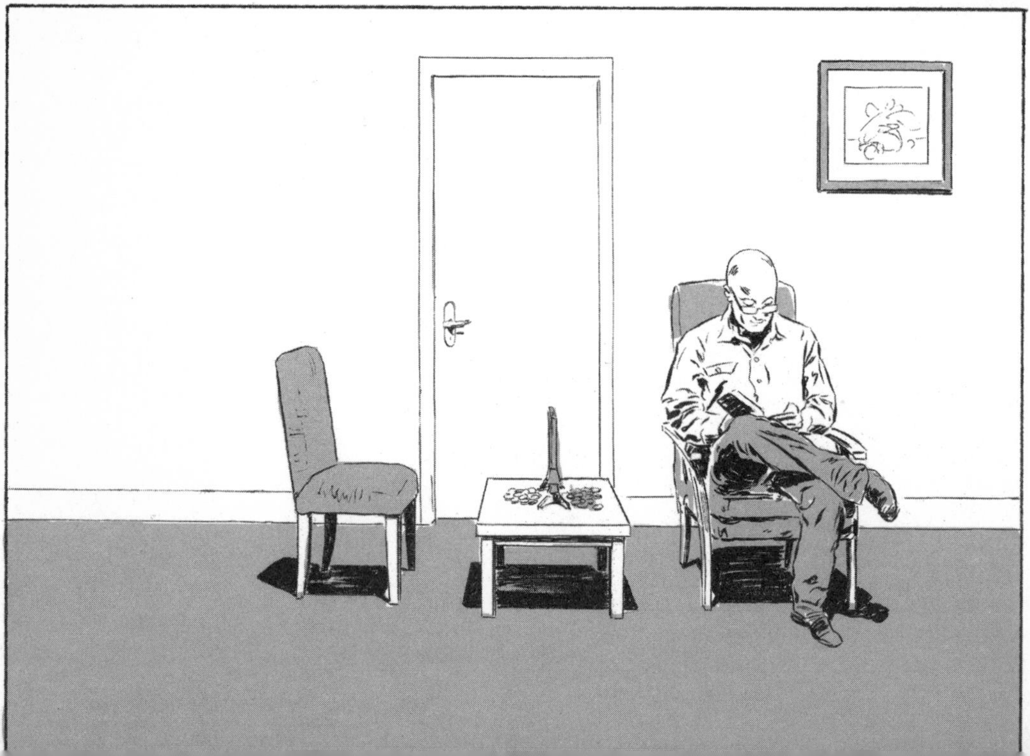

HELLO COLIN...

...DON'T WORRY,

I HAVEN'T GONE YET.

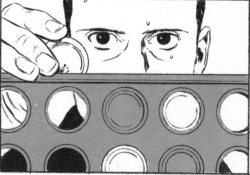

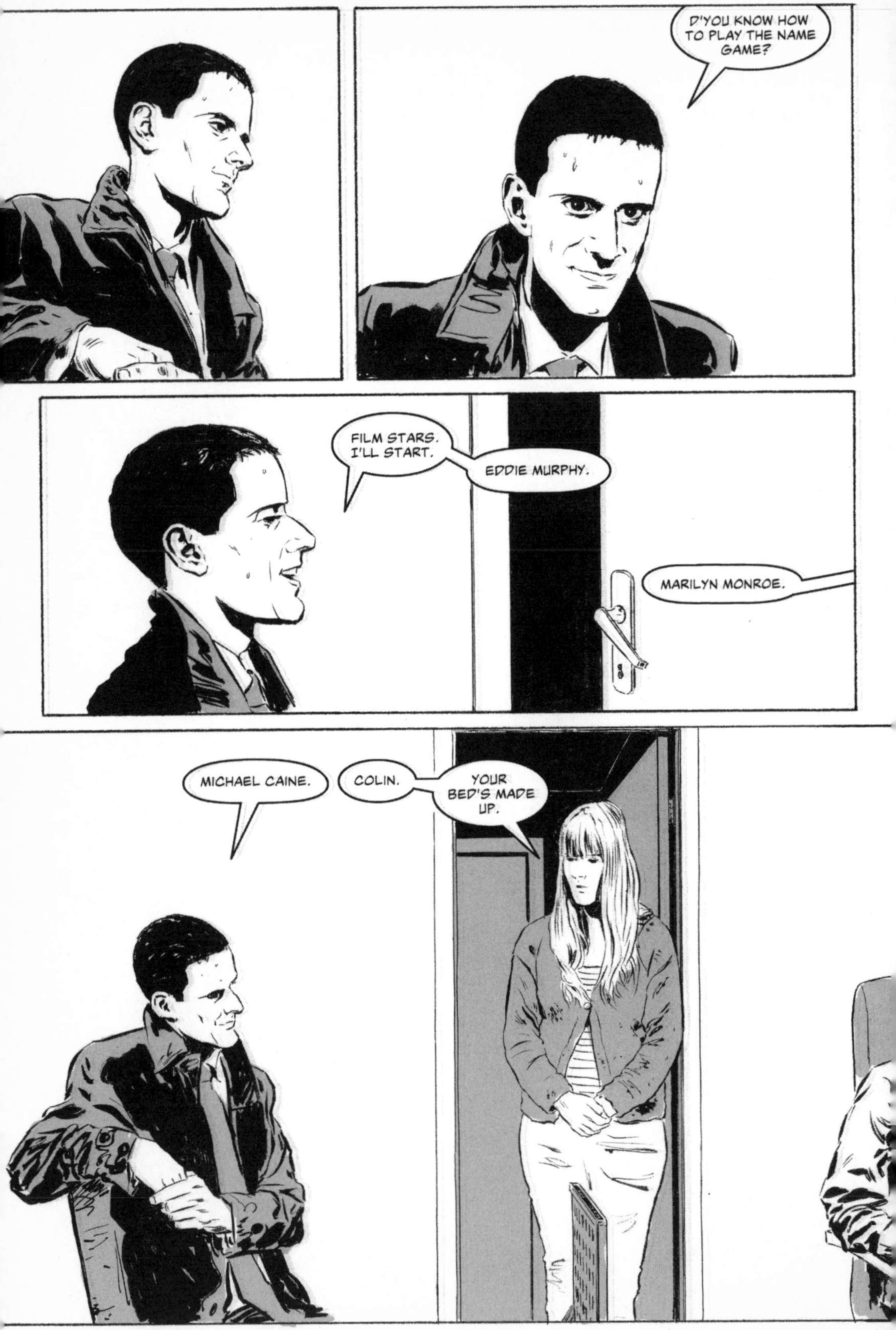
D'YOU KNOW HOW TO PLAY THE NAME GAME?
FILM STARS. I'LL START.
EDDIE MURPHY.
MARILYN MONROE.
MICHAEL CAINE.
COLIN.
YOUR BED'S MADE UP.

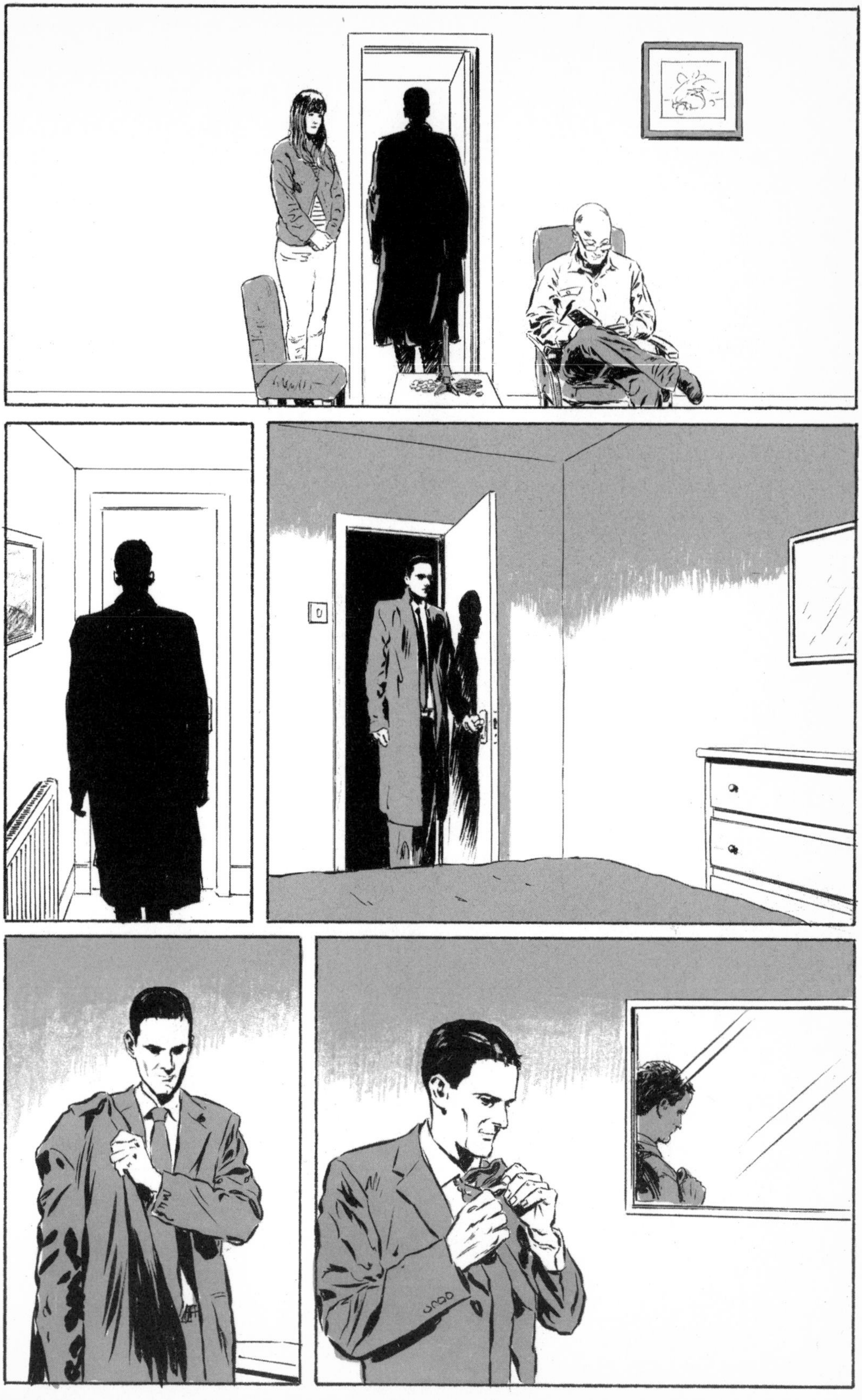

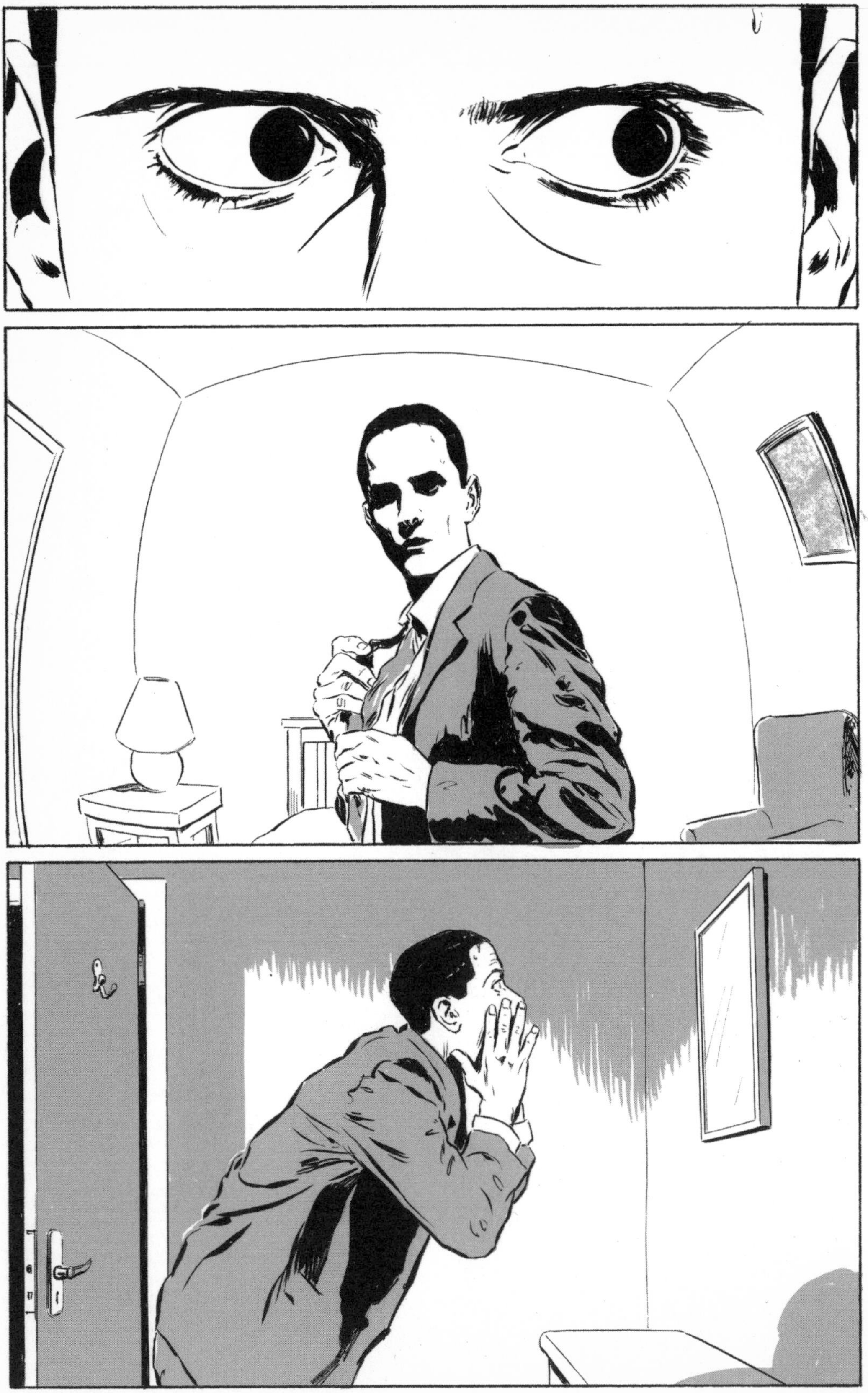

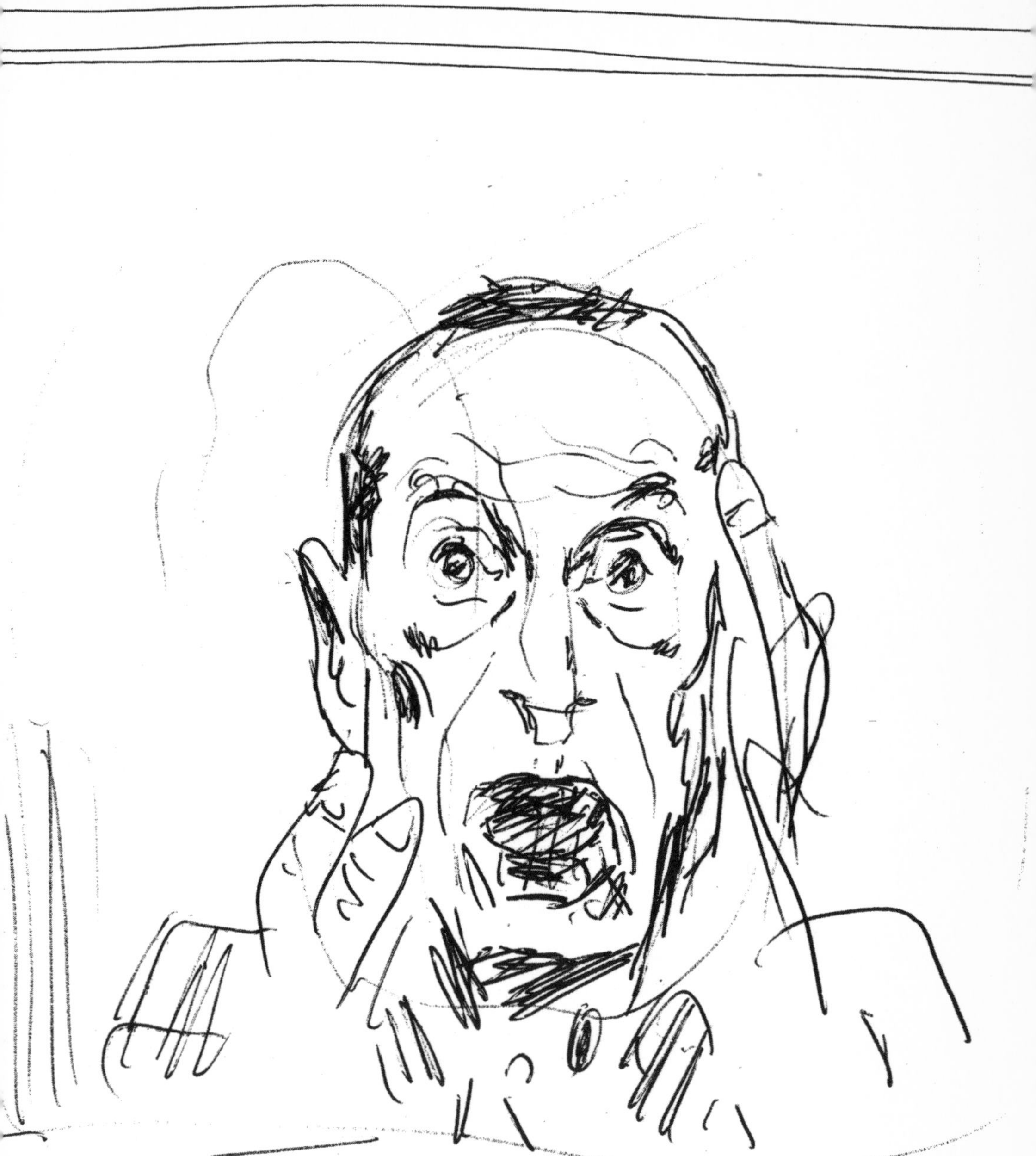

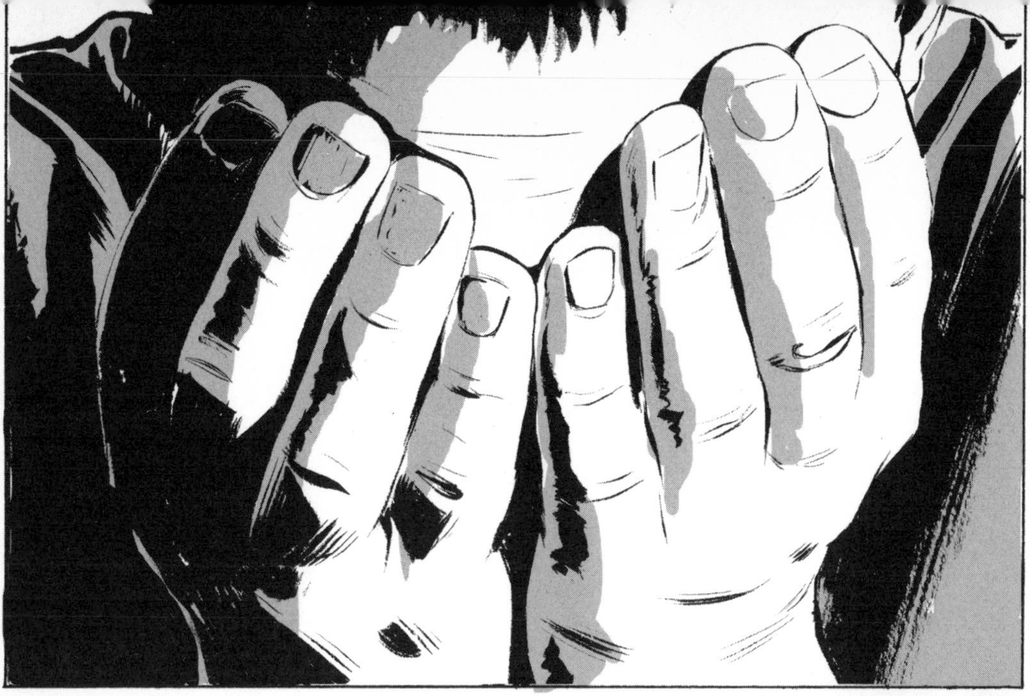

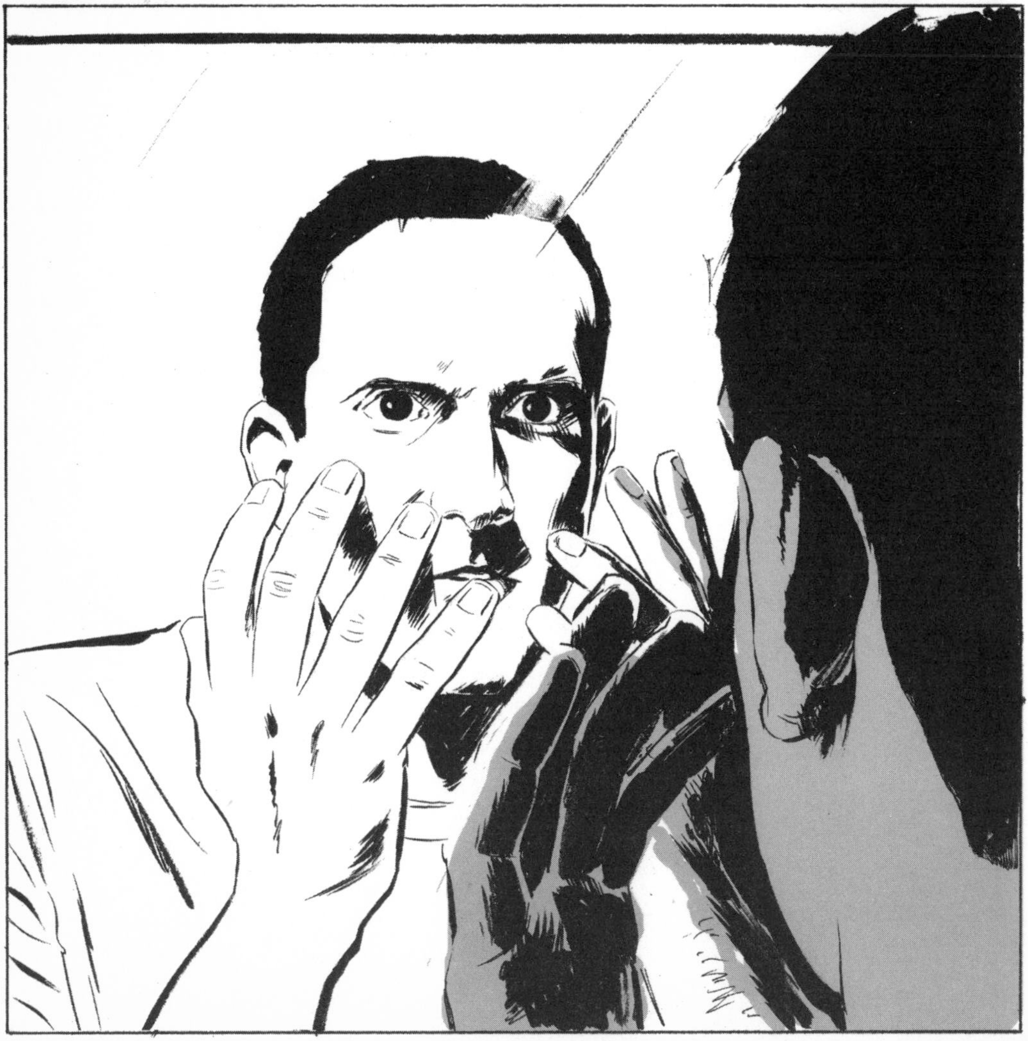

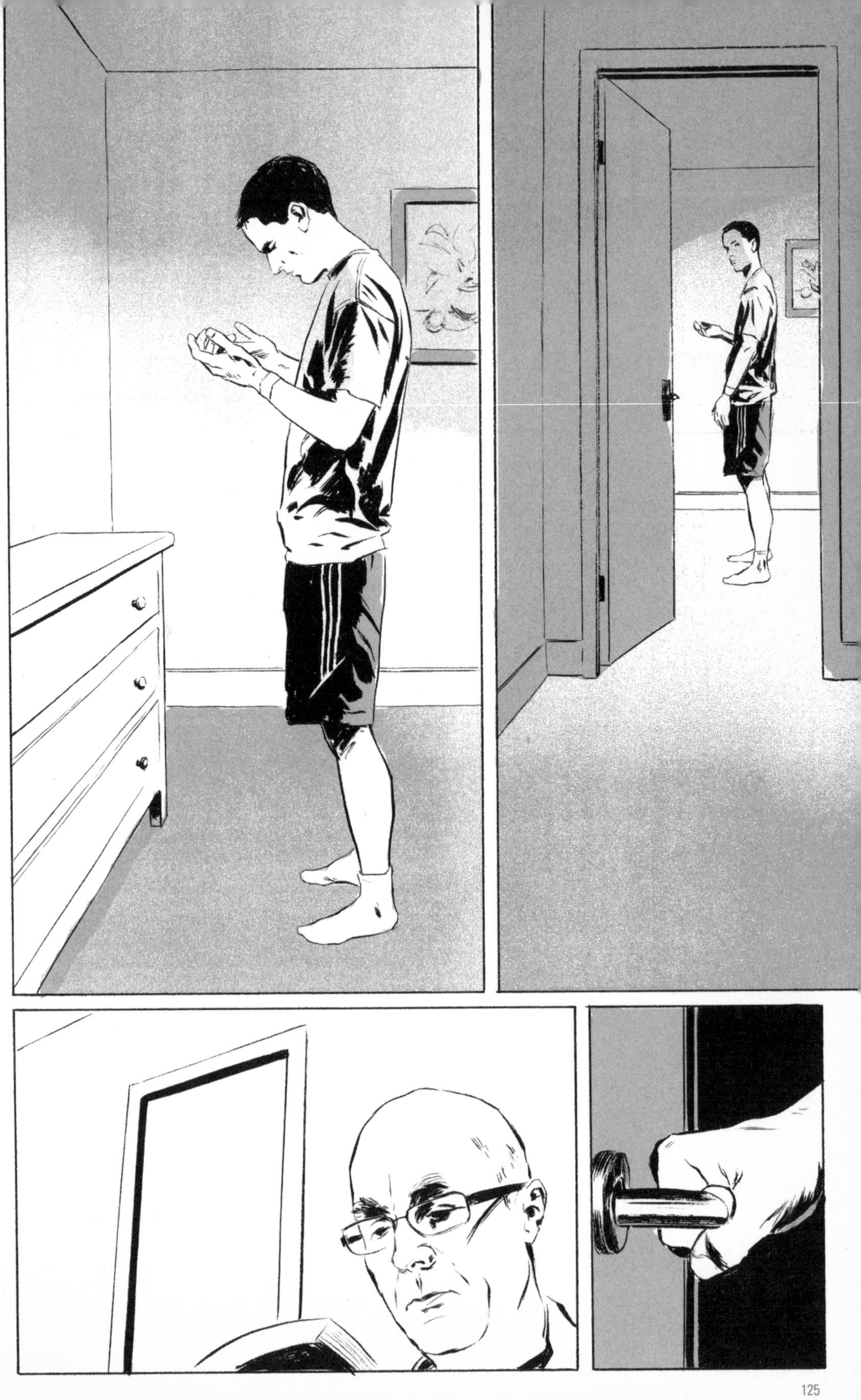

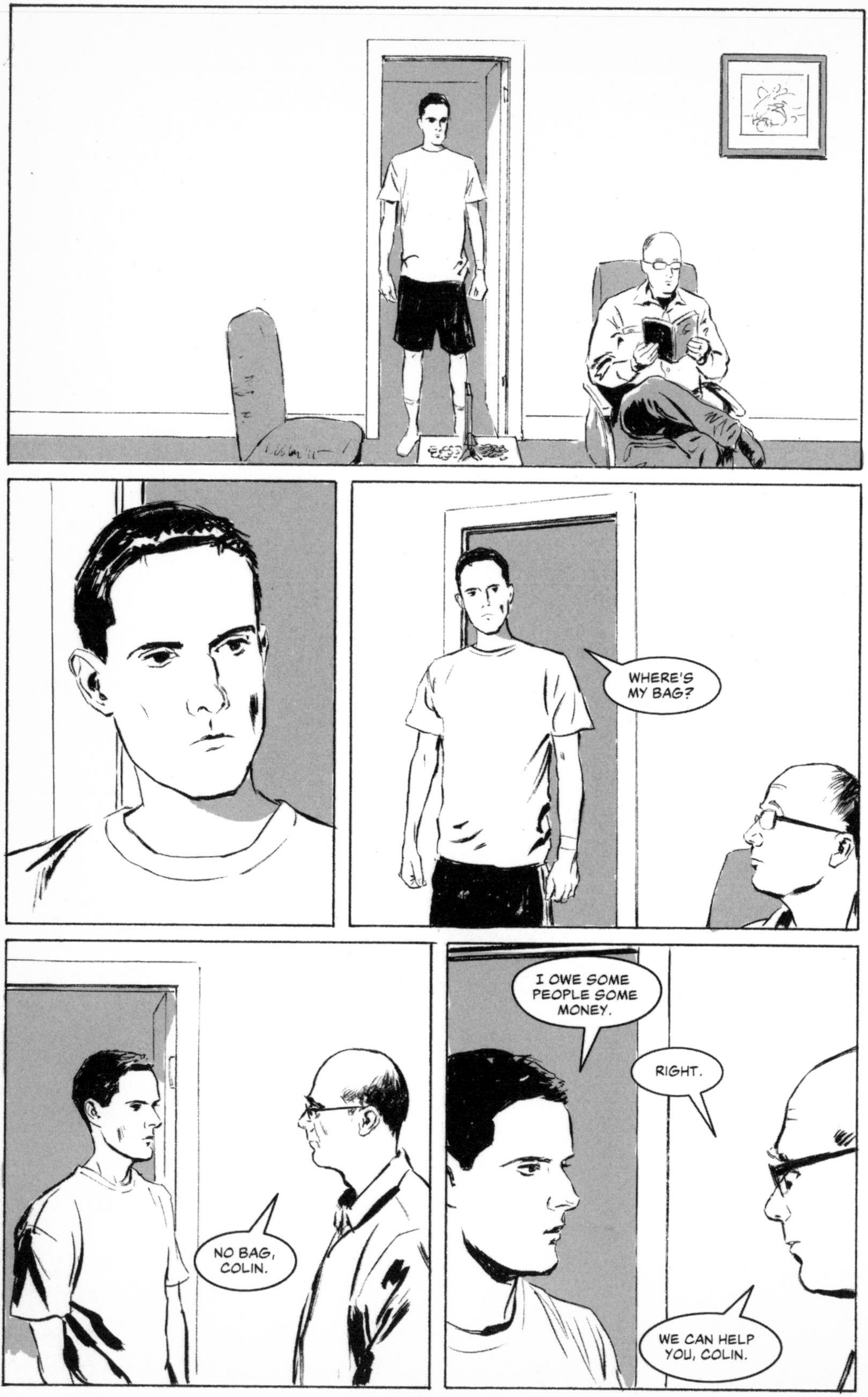
WHERE'S MY BAG?
NO BAG, COLIN.
I OWE SOME PEOPLE SOME MONEY.
RIGHT.
WE CAN HELP YOU, COLIN.

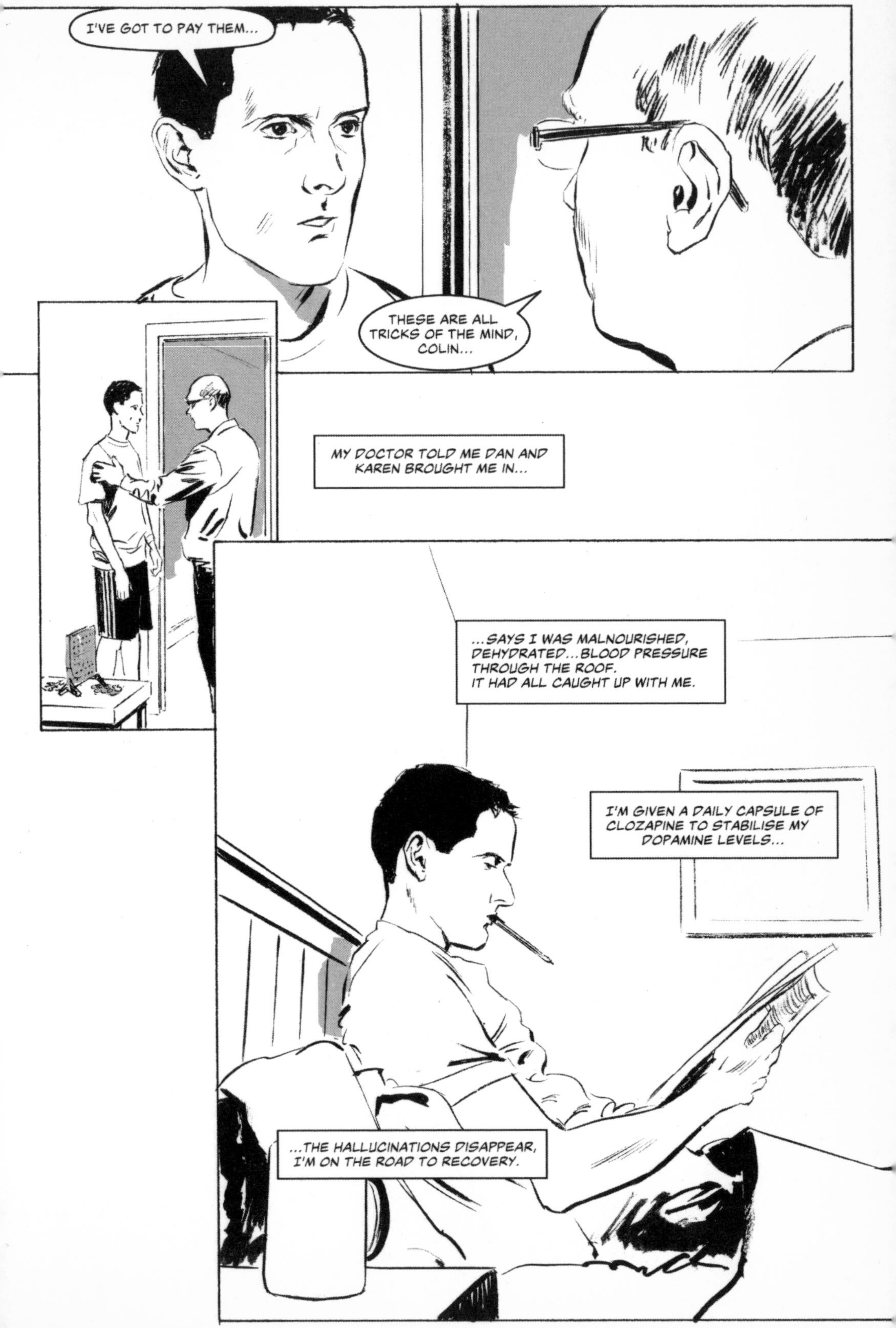
I'VE GOT TO PAY THEM...
THESE ARE ALL TRICKS OF THE MIND, COLIN...
MY DOCTOR TOLD ME DAN AND KAREN BROUGHT ME IN...
...SAYS I WAS MALNOURISHED, DEHYDRATED...BLOOD PRESSURE THROUGH THE ROOF. IT HAD ALL CAUGHT UP WITH ME.
I'M GIVEN A DAILY CAPSULE OF CLOZAPINE TO STABILISE MY DOPAMINE LEVELS...
...THE HALLUCINATIONS DISAPPEAR, I'M ON THE ROAD TO RECOVERY.

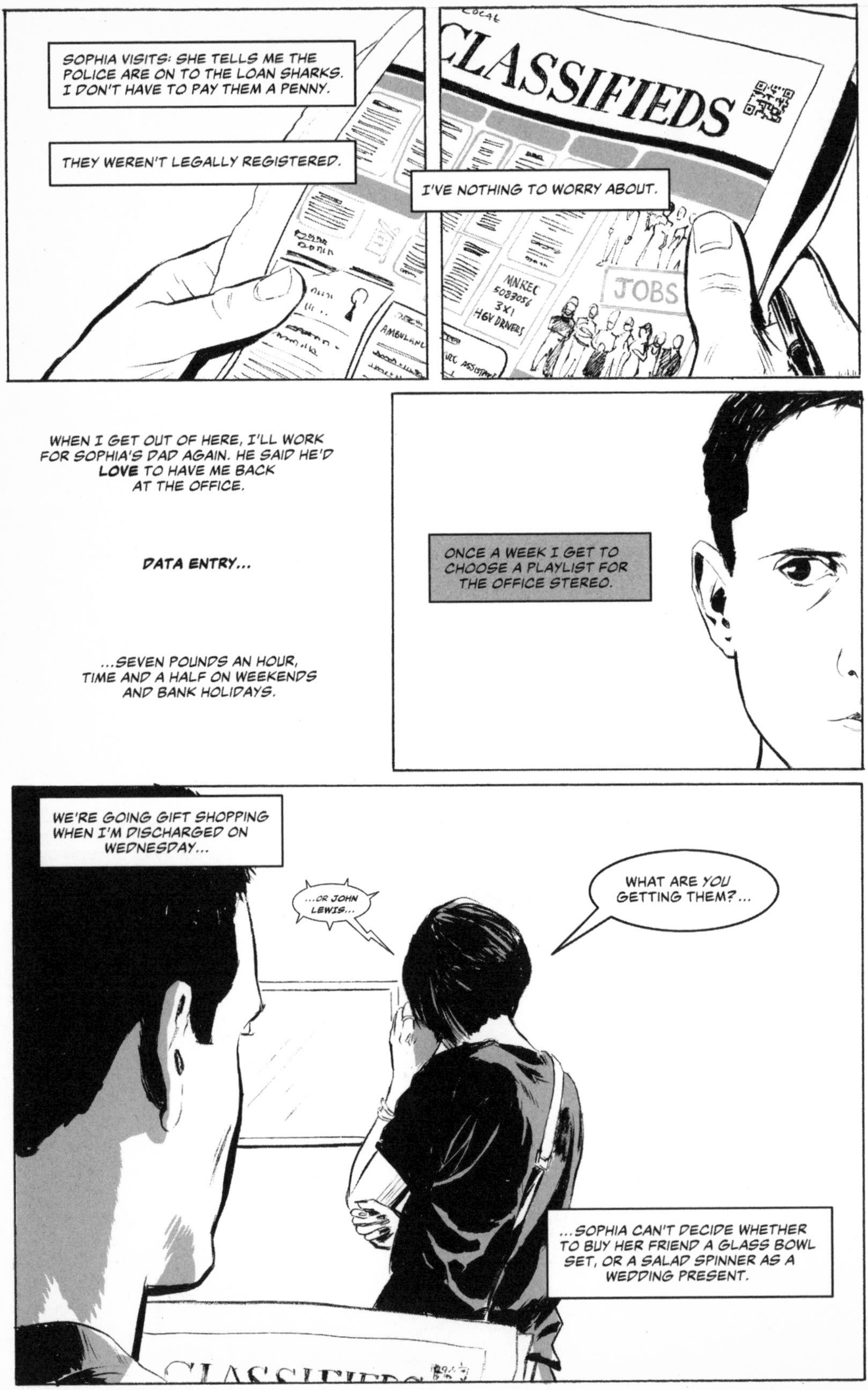
SOPHIA VISITS: SHE TELLS ME THE POLICE ARE ON TO THE LOAN SHARKS. I DON'T HAVE TO PAY THEM A PENNY.
THEY WEREN'T LEGALLY REGISTERED.
CLASSIFIEDS
I'VE NOTHING TO WORRY ABOUT.
JOBS
HGV DRIVERS
WHEN I GET OUT OF HERE, I'LL WORK FOR SOPHIA'S DAD AGAIN. HE SAID HE'D **LOVE** TO HAVE ME BACK AT THE OFFICE.
DATA ENTRY...
...SEVEN POUNDS AN HOUR, TIME AND A HALF ON WEEKENDS AND BANK HOLIDAYS.
ONCE A WEEK I GET TO CHOOSE A PLAYLIST FOR THE OFFICE STEREO.
WE'RE GOING GIFT SHOPPING WHEN I'M DISCHARGED ON WEDNESDAY...
...OR JOHN LEWIS...
WHAT ARE *YOU* GETTING THEM?...
...SOPHIA CAN'T DECIDE WHETHER TO BUY HER FRIEND A GLASS BOWL SET, OR A SALAD SPINNER AS A WEDDING PRESENT.

DOCTOR SAID IT'S GOING TO TAKE TIME... FOR ME TO ADJUST.

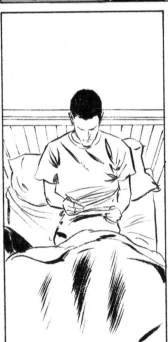

IF I WERE EVER TO GO BACK...

Do you want to earn £500+ p/w?

If you are looking for a challenge and a real business opportunity... send us some details so we can talk with you.

No experience necessary

If all you want out of life is a job, then that's what you will get... if you are looking to make something out of your life: start here!

Call: 07949 8

...IT WOULDN'T BE OUT OF CHOICE.

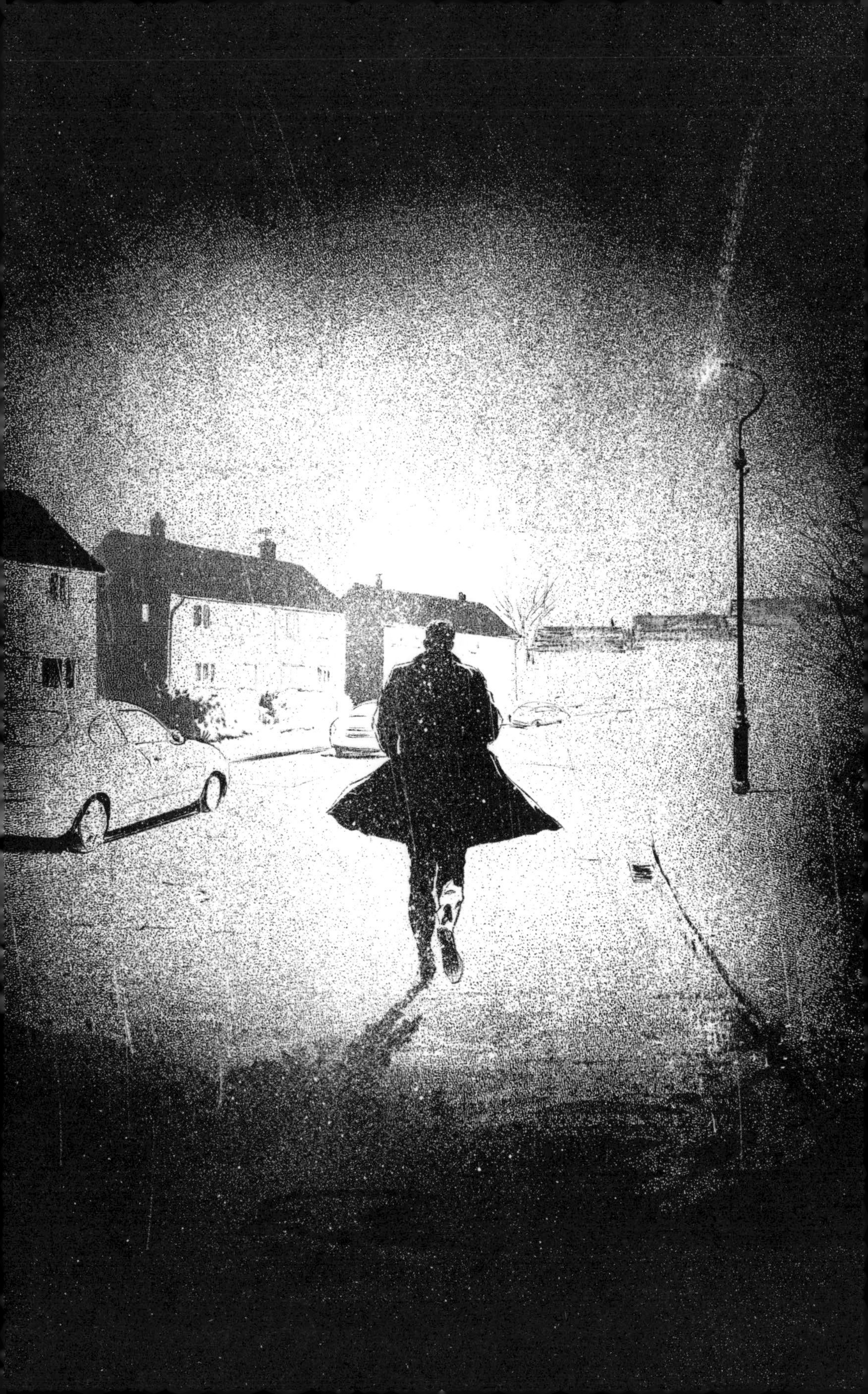

# A F T E R W O R D :

*'Are you sports minded? Do you want to earn £500+ p/w? No experience necessary, all training will be provided.'*

The fictional sales company in *The Opportunity* is based on existing sales companies, or multi-level marketing companies (MLMs), that are spread throughout the UK. They operate under the control of a much larger multi-national sales company, which supplies them with their clients, hosts annual awards and determines the promotional structure.

Many graduates will have answered a job advertisement in the local paper, like the one above. They will be asked to turn up at one of these MLM offices the next morning. They will be driven miles away to a residential location by a salesperson, who will talk incessantly about how close he or she is to achieving their financial goals. They will be asked about theirs, and told that they are achievable at the company. The job role has yet to be explained in full.

As they stroll from the car towards a row of houses, a sudden realisation kicks in for the applicant, that the job is, in fact, commission-only, door-to-door canvassing. Too far to walk home, the applicant concedes to tag along, listening and shadowing the salesperson as they go house-to-house, pitching for charity donations.

So from the very outset, a dupery has occurred; and this minor deception signals an introduction to a world rife with double-talk and secrecy, where everything is scripted, everything is a performance, and everything is interconnected.

The business is legitimate, however. Each company is independently owned and each salesperson is self-employed. It's up to the manager to conduct him or herself as they wish.

The primary objective for these MLM companies is to increase and maintain their sales staff. As there is no basic pay for the manager, all revenue is generated by the sales force. To achieve this end, each salesperson is encouraged to constantly visualise and talk about a personal or business goal. They are then persuaded into thinking that this goal can be quickly accomplished by working their way up the 'fast-track' promotional structure of the company, to become a manager, and in turn reaping the financial rewards that will enable them to attain their personal goal.

However, it takes years for a salesperson to get promoted – a lot longer than is let on, and each newly appointed manager is disappointed to learn that a large percentage of their income is withheld by the multi-national group, to contain the manager, to prod him or her on to continue climbing the promotional ladder within the company.

With this in mind, the new manager will either quit, or stay on and attempt to get promoted up to regional manager. The smartest managers will try to get their foot on the property ladder, holding back their top sellers so they can raise a mortgage deposit, whilst stringing along the lower-ranked sellers to help pay their bills: telling them that the miles of pavement pounding, the long hours, the low income and large credit card debts, are all necessary steps towards reaching their financial goals. 'You have to fail to succeed.' Some will quit, some will burn out.

The story itself grew out of my fascination with the people telling these lies. What are their true circumstances? What drives them? Do they really believe all the jargon they espouse? Why are they so ambitious? Is it purely survival, or greed? Or something in-between? Are they trapped? Externally or internally? Do they feel guilty? Are their options in life confined by their personal decisions or by the limitations they may face outside the business?

Whilst the inner workings of MLM companies serve as an important component of the plot, the book is not intended to be an exposé, nor a critique of the business. Above all, I set out to write a cause-and-effect drama instigated by the protagonist's inner flaws. Colin is extremely ambitious, driven by money and the burning desire to 'make it', to become a 'somebody': wealthy and self-reliant. He is the embodiment of sales people that live and breathe a particular strand of positive thinking preached by American (and British) entrepreneurs – a philosophy heavily adopted by MLM companies, promoting a doctrine of beliefs and motivational phrases designed to help a person persevere in the face of adversity, to accomplish their goals. These ideas can be used to keep an individual in a constant state of expectation, driving them to physical and mental exhaustion over time. (Or becoming 'toast', as the condition is termed in the industry.)

Ironically, it is Colin's pride and overconfidence that finally sow the seeds of his downfall: the very traits he has been encouraged never to compromise.

But it's not the end, not unless he wants it to be. The door is always open for a chance to turn this negative into a positive. As the message in his mind will repeatedly remind him: 'You'll never fail so long as you never quit.'

Will Volley
*October 2015*

# ACKNOWLEDGEMENTS:

First and foremost I'd like to express my deepest appreciation and gratitude toward Corinne Pearlman, for all her generosity and encouragement over the years, for having faith in *The Opportunity* from the start, and for contributing to making it an improved version of what was initially presented. I'm for ever grateful. Thank you for being you!

I would like to thank Candida Lacey for all her support, vital suggestions, and for making me feel very welcome at Myriad Editions.

Thank you to David Lloyd, for all the encouragement and advice he has generously given me over the years, and for being a source of inspiration.

Thank you to the Myriad team, Eleanor, Vicky, Holly and Emma, for all the help and guidance.

Special thanks to my mum for putting up with it all! I love you very much.

I would also like to express my gratitude toward the following people, who have all helped out in some way, both during and before the making of *The Opportunity*.

Clem, Nancy and Sam, Raphael, Rosie W., Peter, Bill and Lynne, Joe S., Nick and Renée, Pritesh and Manisha, Minh, Joe M., Olly and Francis, Danny, Matt, Jo and Julian, Robert and Rosie B., Lucy, Grandad Roy, Larry and Carrenca, J. Radvan, Ben Dickson and Sylvia.

This book is dedicated in loving memory to my father.